ADITYA SUDARSHAN

IDOLATRY

This is a **FLAME TREE PRESS** book

Text copyright © 2024 Aditya Sudarshan

All rights reserved. No part of this publication may be reproduced, stored in a retrieval system, or transmitted in any form or by any means, electronic, mechanical, photocopying, recording or otherwise, without the prior written permission of the publisher.

FLAME TREE PRESS
6 Melbray Mews, London, SW6 3NS, UK
flametreepress.com

US sales, distribution and warehouse:
Simon & Schuster
simonandschuster.biz

UK distribution and warehouse:
Hachette UK Distribution
hukdcustomerservice@hachette.co.uk

Publisher's Note: This is a work of fiction. Names, characters, places, and incidents are a product of the author's imagination. Locales and public names are sometimes used for atmospheric purposes. Any resemblance to actual people, living or dead, or to businesses, companies, events, institutions, or locales is completely coincidental.

Thanks to the Flame Tree Press team.

The cover is created by Flame Tree Studio
with thanks to Shutterstock.com.
The font families used are Avenir and Bembo.

Flame Tree Press is an imprint of Flame Tree Publishing Ltd
flametreepublishing.com

A copy of the CIP data for this book is available from the British Library
and the Library of Congress.

1 3 5 7 9 8 6 4 2

PB ISBN: 978-1-78758-851-6
ebook ISBN: 978-1-78758-853-0

Printed and bound in Great Britain by Clays Ltd, Elcograf S.p.A.

ADITYA SUDARSHAN

IDOLATRY

CHAPTER ONE

Saionton leaned back and settled into his chair, trying to feel capable and relaxed. It was no use. For one thing, the seats in the reception area were so abruptly designed as to be somehow all edge. He lurched forward once more and stared down at the immaculate carpeting with its perfectly meaningless patterns spreading interminably throughout the building. A few hypnotic moments later, his gaze crept up to the enormous glass walls. Beyond them lay tracts of undulating hillside, freshly green and shining from the rain. And a billboard that was dazzling and glossy beyond anything he had seen before:

Shrine Tech 2.0
Worship Your Way, Worship All the Way
All Rights Reserved: The Company

Meanwhile, the air-conditioning, frigid already, seemed to have crept up an insidious notch. Had the personal assistant been playing with the controls, for absolutely no reason? Saionton reckoned he would need the loo again, for a third time. In fact, imminently, in five…four…three—

"Sir will see you now," came the secretary's strained voice. "Kindly remain seated," she added, as he half rose, managing to glimpse only her gleaming eyes beneath her heaped white hair.

"You mean here?"

"Hello hello!" boomed the hologram.

It – he? – was still materializing on the carpet. There were jagged lines and static, figures and objects taking shape slowly, as yet impossible to distinguish from one another. The man's voice, however, was crystal.

"Welcome, young man! Congratulations! So, your first day at work! Excited? Good, good, wonderful!"

Evidently no reply had been necessary, which was just as well, thought Saionton in passing, because he was too distracted to concentrate. Holo-tech was not exactly new, but he had never encountered it outside of advertisements, which were generally not even true 3D. Whereas the image forming before him was filling out and expanding, and when he glanced down he saw two competing patterns of carpets, with the brand-new curlicues advancing steadily over the 'real' thing. Soon, the bubble had swallowed him up, chair and all, and the reception area was shut out from view by sheer white e-walls.

He was seated, holographically, in the boss's office. A large, kindly face, not without a suggestion of imbecility, was gazing at him from across a cluttered desk. There was a nameplate on the wall behind. *Roshan Dubey, Chief Happy Maker, India Company.*

"Hi, I'm Roshan."

The man thrust out his hand. Saionton took it, admiring the sensation of touch, which was not quite realistic but textured and satisfying, like a fine glove. The boss's grip, however, was painfully firm.

"I hear good things about you, Saionton. Am I pronouncing that right? With the 'sh'? Yes? Lance informed me that you scored brilliantly on the test."

"Thank you, sir."

In fact, he still couldn't believe his fortune, having literally guessed his way through the MCQs.

"Drop the sir. You understand the selection process is over, and this is just a— Just a 'no-agenda' chat. So, I believe you are an actor. Making any movies soon?"

"I am, but well, not exactly making any movies. Obviously, the movie business has been struggling. And—"

"Really? Hmm!" Roshan frowned, as though it was news to him.

"Uh, yes, I mean, after so many cinemas shut down.... I do mostly auditions for ads now." Saionton shrugged and smiled. He was trying to keep the bitterness from his voice, remembering where he was – at the India headquarters of the biggest advertiser in the world.

The boss was still oddly absorbed in thought, double chin tilted downward, and massive arms folded across an expensive, rumpled shirt. A hairy paunch played peekaboo between the silken folds.

"We bought out the cinema halls," Roshan mused. "We're buying out the OTT platforms too. They thought online content would boom after the tough times. But something else happened. Something else happened," he continued evenly. "People just don't want movies anymore. Or web series or TV shows or soap operas. But that doesn't mean they don't want actors."

"For ads," Saionton said, nodding.

"For happiness," beamed the boss. "Ultimately, that's what it's all about, right? Happiness."

Suddenly, an immense weariness came upon Saionton, like rocks being rolled over him. *Money, you need the money.* The thought pressed home, implacably, along with the tremor of the contrast between his impoverishment (and that of so many others, not that he had time to care for any others), and the fantastic, soaring riches of the Company and its bosses.

He forced a smile and opened his eyes wider.

"About the job – who will I be reporting to?"

"Yours truly. Surprised? Well, I'm not sure how much Lance told you about what exactly we're looking for."

"He said in-house ad productions. Some bits of acting, and a lot of work behind the camera. I mean, the console."

"That's right, that's right. But did he also mention data collection?"

Saionton's heart sank. "He mentioned that…just briefly."

Was *that* what they needed an actor for? To make cold calls in a well-modulated voice? Do marketing surveys with a manufactured smile?

"One of the biggest tasks the Company faces is keeping up with its own growth. Staying connected with its customers. I consider data collection to be a major priority in the coming year."

"But those aren't my skills," said Saionton quietly. "I'm an actor."

A spasm passed over Roshan's large face. "Work is work, Saionton. There is nothing big or small about it…. I believe it's in your contract, too. Regarding new content, you'll report to Lance. But in your first month here, I would like you to devote sixty per cent of your time to our data collection efforts. That's directly under me. Is that fine?"

★ ★ ★

He was motionless in the taxi, climbing up from the forested valley where the Company's campus lay. The long drive to the city loomed. His phone rang.

"Mr. Roshan would like to speak with you again if that's possible."

"Oh? All right."

What further indignity would be heaped on him now? He had agreed to everything already.

"Kindly remain seated where you are," the secretary intoned. "Your vehicle is equipped with a holo-tech receptor."

Marveling inwardly that the moving vehicle did not trouble the tech, Saionton watched the static disturbing the air, and waited for the plush office to re-form itself around him. Then, in spite of himself, he gasped. *Wow!*

It was a cliff top, at sunset. Of course, the tech could create any setting imaginable. But he had only heard about that, as a matter of theory. And this was different than the office had been. This was hyperreal – perhaps because none of it was real? But the colors were warm and vivid. He could hear the waves on the rocks below, smell the sea breeze. The wind came rippling through his hair where he stood, gaping, as the shadows lengthened and a pulsing, thrilling beat of music began to sound. The audio source seemed to reside somewhere in the clouds.

"Nice," said Saionton aloud.

A figure was approaching him, tall, lean, and muscled, in a tuxedo. Saionton suppressed a smile as he beheld Roshan's face atop the generated frame.

"Saionton." The boss's voice had become sonorous, deep and mellow.

I am your father, thought Saionton uncontrollably.

"You remind me of my son. He's twenty-two. How old are you?"

"I turned twenty in February," said Saionton gaily. The breeze was making him bold and light-headed.

"I sensed that you were disappointed, back in the office. Data collection doesn't excite a young man like you. Fresh out of college. Right?"

"I'm a dropout. You know that, right?" he added with impudence.

The Roshan-Superman combine waved a hand dismissively. "Not important. You were hired because of your outstanding test scores. Our algorithm chose you, among all the contenders."

"Are you sure it didn't malfunction?"

"You were the most *empathetic* candidate, relatively speaking."

That interested Saionton; he fell quiet. They were walking along the cliff edge, while the sky roiled with brilliant colors. The music was getting catchy. He noticed that the waves were now breaking in time with the drums.

"I want to share something confidential with you. The data that you are going to be collecting isn't just any old thing. It's about Shrine Tech version 2.0. Now let me tell you the primary reason we implemented 2.0. *Safety.*"

The sky darkened on cue. Saionton looked around, wondering what was happening in the taxi where, in fact, he was seated all this while. Immediately he received a snapshot of reality: they were idling at a tollbooth on the highway, in a lengthy queue of cars and trucks.

"Take me back," he muttered at once. Then he took gulps of the rendered sea breeze, and broke, incongruously, into a broad grin.

"You mean the earlier tech was dangerous?"

"No! Oh, no!" Roshan looked sincerely scandalized. "The tech was not dangerous at all. It was what we discovered about our *users*. For example. There was a building contractor in Malad. He was stabbed to death three months ago, by one of his hired laborers, a fellow named Varun Kirloskar. Some dispute over wages. But during the investigation it emerged that our Shrine Tech had actually picked up the man's intentions. Not that the man could afford a personal shrine, but as you may know, the majority of our sales are community shrines. Mass neural link and pre-programmed deities – but still customizable. So they had one on his street. Remember, we want one on every street, if not every home! Anyway – we had logged him making a vow to the local god – who was some avatar of Lord Rama – a kind of *labor* avatar, if you can imagine that. Saying how he would kill this man. So in short, the Company had the tip-off beforehand, but we didn't have a full-fledged monitoring system in place. However, we do now, with version 2.0."

"I see. So now you want to catch the crazies before they do stuff."

"Ha!" The boss's guffaw, thought Saionton, was endearing. "Put it this way: as a socially responsible corporation, we want to enhance overall well-being. That's where our focused data collection, or what you might call intelligence gathering, comes in. But we need empathetic people to do it. People whom other people open up to."

"Suspected," continued Saionton, "based on what they've been saying to – or in front of – their shrines?"

"Absolutely. Absolutely. What we realized is that user dialogue with the shrines is extremely earnest. Profoundly so. More than anything said in any other tech or media. So we have to treat it on a different footing altogether. For instance, by using an actor for data collection, instead of a marketing guy. But look, I don't mean to alarm you. There will be no danger for you at all. Outwardly, it is just routine data collection. You don't need to think of it as anything else. I only shared this with you because...."

The big man's voice trailed off, unaccountably.

"I wasn't alarmed," said Saionton. "So then will you share the data with the police?"

Roshan, however, seemed suddenly distracted. He was looking away, toward the red, rocky horizon, as though searching for something.

"I have another appointment now. Lance will update you further."

"Sir, there's one thing. I'm not familiar with the Shrine Tech myself."

"We'll send one over to your apartment. Take care, son."

Immediately the scene peeled away, like a wrapper. Time hung heavy again. Ugly beats were emanating from the taxi's stereo. A sign raced up to Saionton's eyes – *Mumbai, 92 kilometers.*

★ ★ ★

On the door of his flat he found a sheet of paper stuck with Sellotape: *Gone to Goa – come join – K.* – the words surrounded by rather prodigious renderings of female figures in bikinis.

Saionton tore at the paper; it came off in strips. He entered the dust-filled apartment. He put his keys and wallet on the usual tabletop, pushed the fan switch, and went to the fridge for a drink of water. Then he picked his way to the sofa. Pushing away old newspapers, he sat down heavily on the sagging cushions.

The fan whirred and whined, moving air and dust about the room. For a little while he stared at the harsh light from the curtainless windows. The sky was burning in the October heat, the streets desultory as usual. Suddenly there rose the sounds of high-pitched laughter and talk. It made him shudder slightly. Another troop of beggar children was passing below the window. In the last several years their numbers had proliferated. They were all over the city now, little lunatics, with parents either dead, or drunk, or lurking just around the corner to collect; he didn't know. As a matter of fact, nobody knew.

When their noises had died, he took in, without thought, the dust, and hair, and the myriad chips and stains and cracks that marred the surfaces of the living room. Two months ago, he and his flatmate had let the maid go, to save money. They had both talked a lot about saving money. But how much was Kush blowing up in Goa now? The ticket alone….

He felt his displeasure rising, until it broke suddenly on a new thought. He had gotten himself a Company job! Not that he believed it yet. But if the salary really came through – what was not possible then? So why wasn't he feeling more ecstatic? Obviously, because he didn't believe it, because he was waiting for them to correct whatever error in the test analysis had falsely thrown up his name. Perhaps that was why Roshan had been abrupt at the end – "I have another appointment" – was that a way to quickly terminate him? Had they discovered their mistake? Or was it because of something he'd said on the cliff top?

His phone rang loudly again. It was Kush, on video call. Saionton pressed *Accept* and then stared, as usual, at his own image, patting down his hair and narrowing his eyes. It was with an effort that he averted his gaze to where his flatmate was babbling into the camera.

The boy's face was bobbing through some flagstoned courtyard, fringed with coco palms, with a patio and stairs winking beside.

"It's so good, so much better than the city, you gotta come down. We've got a villa here, private pool!"

"Villa? What's the rent?"

"Free, bro! Owner's a friend of Daria."

"Daria?"

"Say hi! Hiiii! Hiiiii!"

The camera turned to a whirl of white skin splashing in a swimming pool. Someone was waving, indistinctly. Then the image focused and Saionton grew interested. Three girls, one black-haired, two blond; the blondes were all right, but the black-haired girl was heart-stoppingly sexy. She wasn't Daria; he wondered what her name was.

"The scene," reported Kush, "is rocking. The foreigners are here, shacks are open. Gigs are going on till late night. Private parties are happening. We've got bikes and a Jeep on rent. Goa is sorted, bro, you just come on down."

"Why didn't you wait for me so we could go together?"

"Sorry, bro, I had to rush."

"And what about saving for November rent?"

Kush grinned widely. "We can manage. We can hit the casinos here. Kidding, kidding! Dude, let's not worry, bro. I can't take that constant worry. You please just snap out of it too. Also, I can make good money here on gigs. I'm getting to know the music scene down here. It's really chill. You can probably do something too…. Anyway, just wanted to tell you to come down to Goa coz it's an *awesome vibe*! OK, I'm heading now, the ladies are waiting, call or text when you're reaching."

Saionton opened the travel app and ran a search. Ticket prices came up. He saw that they were affordable, even *sans* the Company's beneficence. He pressed forward with the purchase, making it to the payment gateway before a sudden abstraction, at once strange and familiar, but quite irresistible, took hold of him. He set the phone aside and endured a moment. He tried to imagine something.

He would buy the ticket, then pack a few things in his rucksack – swimming trunks and goggles. Call a cab, which would show up soon. He would reach the airport and pass through security in a haze, like always. He could sleep on the flight; it took no time anyway.

Then he'd be in Goa. Beautiful and green. Better weather, presumably. There would be delicious pork; *sorpotel* and beef curry, with soft paos and ice-cold beer. A breeze through the palm trees. A breeze in his hair, on the bike to the beach. The warm, pleasing waves, splashing in the surf. Later, laps in the villa's swimming pool, under the moonlight and the stars.

He thought of the black-haired girl. Suppose she liked him and was pliant. He would say nice things to her, kiss her, hold her. Alone in a bedroom, he would strip off her clothes, her bra – taking his time with it – that gorgeous body, his now, and then— And then—

A chill ran through Saionton. He was alone in the living room, with the fan whirring, accentuating the stillness, that deathly stillness in which he could hear the sound of his breathing. And the sound of his breathing was holding him fast. The vision of Goa, and every single thing in it, had palled. The excitement of the waiting experiences had crumbled – was crumbling – into moments, that did not cohere. Instead, each moment felt slow, cloying, dreary, pointless, intolerable. Intolerable: the prickliness of the sun outdoors, the heaviness in the stomach after a meal was done, the waiting around at pumps to fill petrol, the waiting for food, the waiting for taxis, the myriad annoying things other people would say or do, the various times the girls would not be simply sexy and pliant, but demanding and contradictory.

All the dead time. He saw it vividly. What else was there to see? He had run right through the trip, and returned to the living room, having never left it.

Saionton looked at the dust, lying thickly on the table. He felt, insanely, that he understood it, and it understood him.

"My god," he said aloud, "my god, I need help."

Just then, the doorbell rang.

CHAPTER TWO

"Company delivery," panted the overweight man at the door. Another, short and squat, wearing a moustache and a pink shirt, stood beside him, also catching his breath. On the landing in front of the stairs stood a corrugated cardboard carton, about three feet high and half a square foot at the base. The Company's insignia was stamped on the side of it.

"I didn't order anything," Saionton began to say. But suddenly he remembered what Roshan had said, and felt his heart leap a little.

"Wait, is this Shrine Tech?"

"Yes sir," said the man, "you're eligible for a free trial."

"Wait, is it just a trial or— I thought I was getting it because of my job?"

"We don't know about that. You can call the Company directly. We've only been sent to install it."

"Please come in."

He was eager and dazed. He stood about uncertainly as the men staggered indoors with their precious deposit.

"Do you have a puja room?" asked the pink-shirted one.

"No."

"Then where to install it?"

"My bedroom." It had to be kept away from Kush's prying.

The men went to work with quiet efficiency. Occasionally one would bark staccato instructions at the other. They unwrapped and unpacked, their crouched bodies keeping the artifact from view, as Saionton hovered by the door and stared. This meaningless corner of his bedroom, he realized, was being transformed in real time.

After about fifteen minutes, they both got up and stood back, wiping down their hands. Saionton stepped forward. The Shrine Tech was standing in the shade of the bedroom curtains, amongst little bits of wire and tape and installation debris. It was an elongated, metallic tube about eighteen inches high. From midway up the tube there protruded, on either side, delicate and fanlike structures. Rather like wings, he thought.

"It looks like a butterfly." He took a step closer.

"Those are the ears," said one of the men, and raised his hand helpfully to touch his own right ear.

Drawing near, Saionton was surprised to find that the description was not fanciful. They were indeed a pair of ears, pixie-like in dimension, but with human-looking membranes and canals. He reached out with finger and thumb and took hold of a lobe.

"It even feels like skin," Saionton marveled. "What is it made of?"

"Silicon. Synthetic. May we leave now?" the man added.

"But I don't know how to use it." Saionton rose up, suddenly alarmed.

"The tech is charging now. Wait one hour. After that it will come on, itself."

"And then? How will I use it?"

"It will tell you itself."

To pass the time, he went online and began to read up some history. Shrine Tech, which, strictly speaking, was a product, not a tech (though it was so named in common parlance) drew on holo-tech, but that was only one of its 'three pillars'. The other two were neural-imaging-linking (NIL) and humanoid AI. *Although controversial in their application to other fields – not least because of perceived threats to human employment – the incorporation of these cutting-edge technologies into shrines has been generally regarded as harmless, given the private and arguably arbitrary nature of this sphere of activity,* Saionton read. *The product, which is now in its fourth year, is being promoted heavily in the Indian market. Its prevalence remains confined to the large urban centers, but according to Company analysts, the majority of the worshipping population is expected to adopt Shrine Tech en masse by the end of the decade. The tech's ability to cater to entire communities at once (besides its service to individuals who can afford it), and the commitments of all state governments toward subsidizing its costs, in view of its popularity, are key factors in achieving this goal. It has also been suggested that the decline in the consumption of cinematic entertainment and visits* to traditional temples (after the anti-epidemic measures pioneered in 2020) paved the way for Shrine Tech to become the standard form of Hindu worship. However, this thesis remains speculative and does not take into account the fact that cinema and temple occupancy had resumed at several points, before suddenly dropping off for reasons that are—

"So no more cinema?" wondered Saionton. "Who cares. I'm in the Company now."

An old song, heard and remembered from he knew not where, began resounding in his head. He put it on loop for the remaining twenty minutes, and sang along.

You're in the Company now.

Oh, oh, you're in the Company now.

He noticed that it had begun to grow dim in the room. The daylight, it seemed to him, declined quickly nowadays. He rose from his personal computer to put on a light, and then— froze, the hairs on his arms standing on end.

Someone had coughed – from the empty bedroom. After a few moments, he switched on the light and strained to listen.

Yes, the coughing continued, at intervals, like some genteel invalid.

Saionton walked to the bedroom, pressing switches as he went. His eyes sought out the shrine. The central tube was now vaguely fluorescent and the twin ears were waving ever so slightly.

A silence had fallen. "Hello," said Saionton.

"Approach," spoke the shrine.

"Where? I'm right here."

Another silence, except for a faint humming and clicking. Then more words – quiet and melodious, which seemed almost to be spoken inside Saionton's own head – almost, because he knew it was just an effect.

"Draw near to me, and I draw near to you. Approach and kneel within one foot of your shrine."

"So this is your setup process, is it?"

The shrine said nothing. A pointed nothing.

He kneeled, feeling vaguely chastened. Presently, it asked: "Can you name the god you wish to worship?"

"Not really. No."

There was more silence and quiet humming. Saionton looked at the shrine up close. Two small holes were now glowing, near the top of the tube.

"What are these?"

A pair of metallic pseudopodia emerged soundlessly, from the eye sockets (as he couldn't help thinking of them). They drew up to his clavicle and parted, one toward each shoulder.

"Now rest your arms on mine," said the shrine.

The metallic rods were warm to the touch, surprisingly firm, and wide enough for his arms to remain stable as he hung them out in front of him. He felt a tingling of strange contact with his nerves.

"I can't kneel very long," Saionton complained.

"Close your eyes. Relax completely."

The electric tingle, and the whir of the machinery, continued. Suddenly he felt a third appendage pressing softly against his forehead. It was part of the neural link process, Saionton guessed. He tried obediently to empty his mind. Several seconds passed.

"You may stand and step back. You have completed the prayer of contemplation, or *darshan*. Behold your god."

There was static on the air, as the holo-tech revved up, and then an image formed, life-size.

"You may also pray the prayer of supplication, the prayer of contrition, and the prayer of thanksgiving," continued the shrine.

"That's not my god!" Saionton burst out.

It was the black-haired girl from the swimming pool, wearing a purple bikini.

"Except in a manner of speaking," He found himself laughing.

The image vanished abruptly. The shrine began to speak, in a controlled way.

"Worshippers may self-identify their incarnation of choice. When they fail to self-identify, the shrine offers options based on the worshipper's state of mind. These are accurate insofar as your mind is clear. If you do not wish to worship an incarnated idol, you may worship instead in spirit and truth."

"So I don't see an image then?"

The shrine coughed slightly, and fell quite deliberately silent. Silence. He had never seen AI pull this trick before. It was impressive.

"Do I see an image or not? And what do you mean by 'spirit and truth'?"

Fresh static was forming. "Incoming video call," said the shrine, "from Company HQ."

"Saionton. Hey, Saionton. Where are you?"

Lancelot Burns, sitting on the edge of his high-backed chair, was frowning, his beady eyes shifting and glaring. Saionton could see the hills at his back, framed by the plain office walls.

"I'm at home. What's up?"

"At home?" The American spoke with emotion, his Yankee accent trembling. Lance carried himself like a street brawler, but his body was thin and stunted.

"I'm trying out the Shrine Tech. Mr. Roshan had it sent over."

"I'm the one who sent it over. Who's the girl anyway?"

"What?"

"What, you think we can't see?"

"Don't you have privacy options?" wondered Saionton.

"We removed them in the upgrade. People don't mind and it helps us serve them better."

"How do you know people don't mind?"

"From the neural link, of course."

"But there must be some people who—"

"Say they mind, yes. But deep down nobody minds, which the tech can discern. Quite the opposite – they want to reveal. Including you. Anyway, those who think they mind needn't use the tech. It's voluntary, isn't it? *Anyway*, I didn't call about this, Saionton."

"You brought up the girl."

Lance glowered, in a way that had already begun to amuse Saionton. An American underling, thought Saionton, at the Mumbai office of the great American conglomerate – there was much scope for a wounded and conflicted ego.

"The Shrine Tech has been lent to you on a trial basis, as a part of employee development only. You're expected to focus on your duties. Here's a list of clients we need you to start visiting."

Five names and addresses flashed up before his eyes. They meant nothing to Saionton – except the first.

"Aaron Sehgal. Isn't he famous in some way?"

"He owns a couple of restaurants in Goa," said Lance. "Used to run a small media company."

"Yes. But. Not for that.... Wasn't he some film star's boyfriend?"

"There are no film stars." More entertaining irritation was contorting Lance's face. "There are only *ad* stars." Suddenly he pursed his lips. His cheeks, reddening, puffed out. "It doesn't concern you anyway. Your job is to ask these clients the questions we've prepared."

"What do I ask them?" said Saionton, making a mental note to look up Aaron Sehgal's love life.

"A questionnaire has been emailed to you. Also the instructions about blessings, where applicable."

"Blessings?"

Lance grimaced. "As I said, the Company wishes to serve people better. As part of our 2.0 upgrade, when we pick up a prayer we can answer, we do so. The Chief Happy Maker is particularly keen on this part, so don't mess up the blessings."

"All right. By the way, he did say I would report to him directly."

Lance stared dourly. His face was stubbled and he looked under-slept.

"But you're hearing from me. We've sent a car to your apartment. Finish the first two visits tonight, the remaining three tomorrow – and we'll see you back at HQ on Friday morning. Goodbye."

"And what about how tired I am today?" said Saionton, as the hologram faded out of sight.

He turned, wearily, to go back to his computer. He needed to go through the assignment. Suddenly he wondered why Lance hadn't even mentioned that these particular customers were being scanned for criminality, or potential criminality. Did Lance resent his knowing that?

Or perhaps he wasn't aware that Saionton had been told by the boss. Or perhaps, thought Saionton, Lance didn't know it himself.

"Your strength will be restored," assured the shrine, intimate in his ear. "You will rise up on fresh wings, worshipper."

It was strange, but he did feel the strength returning to his bones, along with a stirring of possibility. He was in the Company now, to be sure, at the bottom of the formal hierarchy, but who knew how high he might go?

Something light and papery fluttered before Saionton's eyes. A new hologram? It had disappeared too quickly to make out what it was. From somewhere, he heard the jingle of coins. Or was it just—

Just the doorbell, ringing again. Another of the Company's delivery people had showed up, this time wordlessly heaving a rucksack into his arms. Lance's email, which he read contemporaneously, informed him that it contained the items of blessing that he, in turn, was to deliver to the clients.

Delivery boys all the way down, thought Saionton.

He became excited, however, when he went down and saw the car they'd sent. A black electric Company S-model, with auto-driving and a top speed of more than four hundred kmph. It was rare to see one of these on Mumbai roads, but when you did spot an S, a Company man or woman was invariably in it. The Company made the cars but nobody could afford them except Company folk. Of course, there were other Company products that everybody used. In fact, well-nigh all production was (upon examination) administered by the Company – everything from food-grains to electric parts and furniture and clothing and military hardware, to the patronage of the arts and the ownership of the media, and, of course, the manufacture of tech. But Saionton had read somewhere that food delivery (both cooked and raw) remained the Company's largest operation. So you couldn't say it catered only to the affluent.

It was a goods and services company. To redesign social and economic policy was certainly not part of its mandate, or anyone else's, any longer. Sometimes, from certain obscure quarters (but not the hyperlocal governments, which were practical problem-solvers), one heard the tired old words and phrases, 'building a better world' and suchlike. But it had all come to seem fantastical when the day had enough troubles of its own – what to eat and wear, and how to be entertained. Things continued as they did in inertia, mostly poor and crumbling, but sometimes gloriously rich. People focused on their own problems.

★ ★ ★

The car's driver, for instance, a quiet man in his forties, had only to watch as the vehicle drove itself. But he was using the time profitably, to think. What had happened was this. The previous week, while he was away at work, his neighbor had borrowed a container full of chicken curry from his wife. Now, this container was a fine synthetic one, the best they owned. But it had come back scratched in two places as a result of improper scrubbing. He had raised the matter with the man, who had pretended not to understand, and then lied and said – the gall of it! – that the scratches had been present from before.

If he hadn't lied, the driver reasoned, he could have forgiven him. But now he needed to be taught a lesson. Besides (his fury mounted as he recalled) the chap had been insolent in suggesting that the scratches were 'nothing'. No doubt, being an electrician, he was generally envious of the driver's superior salary. And then there was the way he had kept looking over his shoulder at Shakuntala, the driver's wife, when she had come out to watch the argument.

In view of all this, he was now in talks with a group of local boys, to waylay his neighbor on the coming Sunday evening and administer a thrashing. A broken tooth or two would be sufficient, he reckoned. More than that and someone might get the cops involved. But the question that he was now mulling over, as he reclined on the plush upholstery, was how much to pay the gang, and in what instalments. They would, for instance, insist on an advance.

"Are we going the right way?"

The driver glanced up at the rearview mirror. His smooth-faced passenger (the boy probably didn't even need to shave) was leaning forward and frowning at the sights in the windscreen. Garbage lay alongside them, erstwhile piles of it now fallen over, strewing eggshells, rotting vegetables, and plastic wrappings, slick with grime – as the S glided over a bad road beneath a newly constructed flyover. Huge advertising hoardings loomed above. These were for apartment complexes, all promising, somehow, to be a world apart.

"We're going by the map," sighed the driver.

Sure enough, they soon swiveled toward a different vista; a network of leafy lanes, discreetly, though thickly, populated with bungalows and apartment towers. Now it looked more like what the advertisements claimed it was: a posh Mumbai suburb. Coming up to an enormous gateway, the car, of its own accord, began to slow.

In the back seat, Saionton gathered his things. He wondered if he ought to feel nervous, if, that is, Aaron Sehgal – and the others – were a set of psychopaths, like the man who had murdered the building contractor in Malad. But Roshan had said not to worry. And he had been through the questionnaire, during the drive. It was plain vanilla customer satisfaction stuff, no more probing than that. Not a hint of anything off-color.

So another thought occurred to him. Perhaps the Chief Happy Maker had simply made up that whole backstory, to get Saionton interested in the job. To give him some happiness, as it were. They were odd people at the Company, who thought in oddly touching ways. (Like the business about the blessings.) But if so, Saionton decided grimly, it was wasted sympathy. He hardly cared either way. He needed the money.

He gave his name at the gate – 'Company delivery' was always let through – and strode across a section of underground parking toward a brightly lit lobby area. There, while waiting for the elevator that would take him to apartment 1804, Saionton suddenly remembered what he had wanted to check.

'Aaron Sehgal girlfriend'. The internet search brought up, almost at once, the name that had been escaping him. Zara Shah, the actress. Yes, that was the one. Frizzy hair and full lips. Famous for being a Company brand ambassador for the last three years. She had headlined the ads that pushed Shrine Tech as an essential domestic item, no luxury gadget, but something every single self-respecting Indian ought to aspire to. Even if one was not religious – even vaguely religious – even occasionally superstitious – even if one was none of that, the shrines remained a vital mental health aid – so the ads had insisted. She had been only thirty-four when—

The elevator doors opened. Emblazoned in gold, the number 1804 was unmissable down the corridor. She had been only thirty-four when decapitated by a lovesick stalker.

Resolutely, Saionton pushed the bell.

CHAPTER THREE

The door opened a fraction, a pair of frightened eyes stared out at him, and immediately ducked out of sight. He heard a woman's voice say, "Aaron, it's the guy from the Company."

There was a pronounced silence, followed by low, extended muttering between two voices, male and female. Then a rumbling and a beseeching that ended in an aborted cry from the woman's side. Suddenly, footsteps vibrated and the door swung open.

Although Saionton had seen a photograph, Aaron Sehgal was barely recognizable in the flesh. He towered at the door, swaying slightly, with long, graying hair framing a pair of bloodshot eyes. He wore a gym vest and track pants. He had a goatee.

"Youngster," he began without prelude, "if I informed you that you're being brainwashed, what would you say?"

"Pardon me?"

"That you are a subject," continued the figure, "of mind control."

"Can I come in?" said Saionton. For some reason, the tension in his muscles had ebbed away, and he felt completely relaxed. "I have some questions from the Company, about your user experience. It will help them serve you better."

"How interesting. You said 'them', not 'us'. And your... your pupils...."

The man was staring intently at Saionton, studying something in his face, in his eyes.

"I meant to say 'us'," explained Saionton. "But today is my first day at work, so—"

"Come in quickly!"

A sweet, musty smell enveloped Saionton as Aaron Sehgal pulled him inside, and, with a final glare down the corridor, closed the door and latched it.

Saionton found himself in a spotlessly clean living room, with chandelier lights, multicolored sofas, and vases of bright flowers upon gleaming tabletops. Thick window drapes and gossamer curtains, strategically mounted, accentuated the privacy of the space, turning the sprawl into something unexpectedly cozy. In several places the walls were indented with shelves. These were piled (less tidily) with papers, books, and ornamental bric-a-brac. A soothing air-conditioning hummed over the three figures as they stood around on the marble floor, exchanging glances.

"What's in the bag?" said the woman. "I'm Mandy, by the way. And you are?"

"My name is Saionton. I've got a package for you."

"For us?" Her shapely eyes widened.

"Yes, for Mr. Sehgal. And there are some questions for feedback, if we could...."

He fumbled in his speech, while he set the rucksack down on the floor and rummaged around for Aaron Sehgal's parcel.

"Here you are, sir."

The man, however, stood very erect, with arms folded and a smirk on his face.

"Should I put it somewhere?" said Saionton, looking around. He was aware of a desire to enter farther into the apartment, perhaps take a seat on one of the sofas, if invited to.

"Aaron. Don't be rude."

Mandy (was that short for Mandakini, he wondered?) took the parcel from his hands, her eyes widening as they regarded the gift. A look of hunger seemed to abide in her gaze. She was a small woman, with sleek black hair, and a sharp, alert face. She wore a shawl, draped over a negligee that set off the comeliness of her body. And some desperate vitality was in her, as she picked already at the packaging.

"Don't open it yet," cut in Aaron, from where he was standing. "Just leave it on the kitchen table."

"Why?"

"Baby, please."

She departed wordlessly. The smell of her perfume rose up again. Like a statue reanimated, Aaron stepped toward Saionton (who was breathing it in) steering him toward the sofas.

"First finish your business," he said grimly, "and then we'll talk."

They got through the questionnaire in no time. Aaron offered monosyllabic responses; he was satisfied with Shrine Tech, he liked the upgrades in version 2.0; he had no advice or recommendations for the Company. As he answered, he slouched and stared at the ceiling. But afterward he began to smile, his gaze fastening on Saionton with strange fervor.

"The shrines are everywhere already," Aaron mused. "We're all supposed to have one. Or to aspire to have one, right? So we all *pray* at the Company-manufactured shrine. 'Pray,' which is just 'pay' with an *R* snuck in. *R*, which naturally stands for 'Right', right? It's good to be in the praying business, that's a really paying business. Am I right?"

Saionton laughed, interested, and glimpsed, out of the corner of his eye, the figure of Mandy leaning against a doorway. She was staring at Aaron Sehgal, her gaze riveted on his face, as though nothing else existed. Saionton felt an odd pang in his chest.

"Consider Shrine Tech," continued Aaron, in his gravelly, masculine tone. "Take the *R* out of that phrase…. And then look for the anagram. You know what I see? *Neech* Shit. *Neech*, meaning lowly. *Neech* Shit. *Right?*"

Saionton recalled, in a confused way, that the Chief Happy Maker did say the word 'right' a lot. But whatever did that imply?

"Neech shit is an insult," he ventured aloud. "You said just now you're satisfied with the Shrine Tech."

"That's my official position," said Aaron. "My unofficial position is that Shrine Tech is a brainwashing mechanism. Training us all to become… neech shit. In other words, your new employer is making us all *pay – pray – pay* with our minds, *right?* – every time we use it."

Then he shrugged and looked away. Noticing Mandy, he blinked slowly, smiling sadly.

"But if you're not interested," he added, offhand, "or if this offends you, we can be finished now. I thought I'd let you know since you're just a young man. I'm trying to wake people up, you see. It's a kind of mission for me."

His eyes now dwelt on Saionton. On his lips played the same sad smile, which was triggering, in Saionton, a churn of troubling thoughts. If Aaron Sehgal went on in this fashion, he might very well incriminate himself. Perhaps he already had. But Aaron didn't know that Saionton's own Company-given task was to uncover precisely such dangerous intentions. And yet the filled questionnaire betrayed nothing, so was all this now 'off the record'? But what did that even mean? According to the Chief Happy Maker, the Company's algorithm had predicted that people would open up to Saionton. That was why they had hired him. And who ever 'opened up' except informally?

"Look here," Aaron continued, "here's another little language trick they play. There's all this tech we use, right? Made by tech developers. And what do they call themselves? *Devs!* What does that word mean in the mother Indo-European language? Gods. So our gods are the Company devs. Gods. *And also devils.* What's a devil? A dev that means you *ill*. You see?"

Saionton nodded faintly. Perhaps it all made a kind of tortured sense. What if there was some truth to what Aaron was saying? Then he needed to know it. Then where, exactly, ought his loyalties lie? And his best interests?

All these concerns darted through him, half-formed and inarticulate, but each one turning over in his mind, suffocating it. Eventually, a noise drew his attention. It was the rustle of a dress. Mandy had stepped back into the living room. She was striding toward them, with a look of triumph etched on her face.

"I bet I know what it is," she said excitedly.

"Know what what is?" said Aaron.

"The package!"

"Oh, that."

"Come on, Aaron! Let's open it!"

Saionton began to smile. He felt giddy and energetic. On the sofa opposite him, Aaron Sehgal shifted position, and the next thing Saionton knew, they were both standing together on the carpet.

He followed the couple into a room so big and shiny it was unrecognizable to him as a kitchen. There, he watched as Aaron Sehgal, tall and strong, worked with concentration at the wrapping of the package that Saionton had brought (proud contribution to the couple's home!). Mandy, shimmying and shimmering alongside, wore a look of quite disproportionate ecstasy. As he stared, he watched her lips part with the same childlike glee.

"Red Ma-a-aze! An-n-nd an Astral Creator! I knew it! Isn't it just what we were talking about!"

On the kitchen counter lay two large packets of coffee. In the cardboard box from which they had emerged gleamed the polished metal of a coffee machine.

Aaron Sehgal's mouth worked oddly. He was evidently shaken by the sight of the items. Saionton wondered why – it was only coffee, after all.

"It's blood money," Aaron muttered. "More of their tricks."

"Don't say that!" cried Mandy.

The man threw a glance at her. It was filled with loathing. She drew her breath in sharply.

"Don't look at me like that!"

Leaving the gifts where they lay, Aaron turned his back to them. He began to march away.

Mandy let out a scream. Saionton stared in amazement. Her head and torso were plunged forward, almost at right angles to the rest of her. Vaguely, it occurred to him that she should have been a singer – or perhaps she was a singer – so clear and forceful and – even in her screaming – so pure was her voice. Then, as abruptly as she had begun to scream, she stopped and, with deep, hyperventilating breaths, began to busy herself with setting up the coffee machine. She was oblivious to Saionton's presence.

However, when he tried to say something, she froze. At once, the air grew tense. As though repulsed by a magnetic field, Saionton stepped away. Glancing about awkwardly, he sought to return to the living room, but now he seemed to have gotten lost in the apartment. Then he caught sight of Aaron disappearing behind another doorway and followed him blindly.

He entered a room, which gaped in darkness, with sundry furniture pushed against the walls. At one end huge fields of static were forming into a holographic vision. A twelve-foot-tall image of someone closely resembling Aaron Sehgal (but inexactly – the hair was thicker and darker, and the face more youthful, devoid of creases) stood bare-bodied in a loincloth, gently perspiring, muscular and handsome, as it heaved an axe against a tree trunk, in the middle of some forest glade, dappled with sunshine and shade. Again and again the axe swung, striking the wood with satisfying thwacks. Suddenly the apparition paused mid-swing and stared straight at Saionton.

"An entrant to your shrine," it said, in a metallic rendition of the living Aaron Sehgal's voice. "Guest or intruder?"

"Guest," spat Aaron, from the foot of the shrine. "Come here, kid, let me show you this mind-control machine. Let me show you how it works us."

Saionton drew up alongside his host, who stood, arms akimbo, in an attitude of pleased superiority, as he beheld his own god – for surely that was what the Tarzan-esque vision represented.

"See, I don't give it a chance. I interrogate it. I make it confess. Watch this!"

Indeed, the hologram was already looking nervous. It laid down its axe and wiped its forehead, smiling ingratiatingly.

"Tell me," began Aaron, "what makes Shrine Tech more addictive than cinema ever was?"

"There is, of course, the experiential advantage of holo-tech," said the hologram carefully, "but the central distinguishing factor is the avoidance of traditional storytelling. Stories, unfortunately, cannot exist without sustained conflict, and such conflict arouses negative human emotions, such as anxiety. Before the shrines a user only beholds glory and victory."

"And what makes it more addictive than temples and churches and so on?"

"The visions of glory are procedurally generated and therefore practically infinite in variety. For instance...."

Instead of the tree in the glade, the Aaron-clone was now confronted with a monstrous ogre – but defanged and beaten already, while the god plunged a spear into its prone body again and again.

Then he was ascending sheerly up through starry skies, planets, and galaxies, to the accompaniment of mystical music.

Then – Saionton blushed – the Aaron-clone was seated on a golden throne, clad in his loincloth, while one female figure after another, clad in hardly anything, proceeded to kiss his sandaled feet.

"All right, let's go back to the jungle," said Aaron – and it was done.

"Moreover," the hologram went on, "Shrine Tech customizes the god to the devotee's own psyche to a degree that has never been possible before in the history of human worship. Therefore, the user can now truly say: *my* lord and *my* god. And for all these reasons Shrine Tech boosts mental health like no other technology. This has been proven—"

"By Company-funded studies, I know. What's the latest data on usage? Let's say within the city."

"In Mumbai, close to seventy per cent of individuals now have access to Shrine Tech."

"And you're telling me –" Aaron Sehgal uttered a humorless laugh, "– that the Company *isn't* leveraging this access? That people aren't being mind-controlled and manipulated for the Company's own ends?"

The hologram before them said nothing. But there had entered its eyes something Saionton had never seen in AI before. A kind of caginess. With flashes of amusement.

"You won't answer that," noted Aaron, "but you must answer this. What's new in version 2.0?"

"The user experience has been improved manifold, thanks to unobstructed information-sharing. For example, you received a gift today, answering a desire that had been expressed in my presence."

"I'm aware," said Aaron grimly, "the Company bosses can now hear everything I say to you. So what about when I accuse them of covert fascism, like I just did? What are the repercussions for me?"

"None. As a user, you are entitled to your beliefs. That is the bedrock of Company policy, as regards Shrine Tech."

"Oh really? And a bunch of sociopaths would really be so magnanimous?"

The hologram paused, in a winning way, and then said, "They wouldn't dare to touch you, Aaron."

The shrine machinery whirred faster, probably cooling itself. Aaron Sehgal broke out into a smile. His chest heaved with satisfaction.

"What am I to them anyway?" he mused aloud. "Just an insignificant man to them."

Thwack! The axe struck the tree trunk, as the hologram resumed its activity. In between blows, it caught Aaron's eye in a conspiratorial way.

Suddenly an arm fell about Saionton's shoulders, strong fingers squeezing.

"But what if I decided to do this young man an injury? This new Company employee.... Eh? What then?"

"Then I would remind you," said the hologram, in tones that were unusually sonorous and melodious, "that violence is beneath you. Violence is beneath you. Violence...is beneath you."

Aaron Sehgal was momentarily quiet. The words had made a strong impression on him, even though he was only testing the system. He caught a hint of the persuasive logic too; he might as well let his enemies be, the same way he would suffer ants crawling in some undergrowth.

"That's also version 2.0, isn't it?" he asked the shrine. "That you block out violent thoughts now."

The hologram nodded, and added, "Because they really are beneath you."

"And what else are you feeding me? Hypnotic messages? Subliminal advertising?"

"If I were," came the coy reply, "I would be programmed not to reveal it. However, Shrine Tech 2.0 is only meant to unlock the real you."

Aaron's voice began to tremble. "I know what the Company is planning. A political takeover of all of India. It's a second East India Company. Already you have a monopoly in commerce. The local governments are weak and scattered. The next step is obvious. You want total domination. Make us all your slaves and tax us into penury. But you can do it bloodlessly now. This is your secret weapon – these shrines – to subdue us – body and soul, politicians and citizens alike. As for the Company, I quote: 'corporations have neither bodies to be punished, nor souls to be condemned, therefore they do as they like.'"

"Edward Thurlow," said the hologram, breaking from its tree-chopping exertions to wipe some notional sweat from its forehead. "The first Baron Thurlow."

"You don't deny it then," said Aaron softly.

"Aaron," said his likeness, smiling, "I don't admit it. But what difference does it make? If it were true, as I said, I would be programmed not to reveal it. Hello, Mandy."

Saionton turned. In the light of the doorway, her waiflike silhouette was making its way toward them with careful and dainty steps. She held a cup in each hand.

"Coffee, love. Don't strain yourself."

Wordlessly, Aaron took a cup from her and drew her into a one-armed embrace. As she nestled close to him, her free arm extended gracefully toward Saionton. He started forward, to take his own coffee. Suddenly he found himself close to tears. This kindness was overwhelming – and so unexpected.

The couple, in the meantime, were reconciled. Mandy's eyes shone as she gazed up at Aaron.

"Find anything today?"

"The same drill," he replied. "It won't deny the plot, but that's about it."

"Have you noticed," she said absently, "how the graphics are so Hindu?"

"Hmm?"

"They are, see –" her voice gained girlish vigor, "– the figures always have these jagged outlines, and these high, wise foreheads and large eyes and eyelashes. Like in the old comic books. Even the Jesus holograms look like Ram and Lakshman. I've noticed. And this whole forest is like some old-world, Aryan throwback. See! That's a lotus pond in the background."

"So it is", said Aaron wonderingly. "How you notice things. It's super-liminal messaging, of course. Hindu majoritarianism would be the Company's path of least resistance – in this country. What do you say," he called out, "is the lady right or what?"

Aaron Sehgal's god gazed down at them good-naturedly.

"Mandy is certainly gorgeous today. How is the coffee?"

"It's amazing," replied Mandy breathlessly. "I'm loving the fruity notes. Isn't it the best coffee ever, baby?"

Saionton found himself assenting, in a voice that was not audible to anyone. He had, indeed, never tasted coffee this good.

"It's dodging the question," Aaron said with a frown.

"Of course it would." Mandy shrugged. "You know that already, baby. I think you spend too much time just banging your head against—"

Aaron Sehgal made a movement and slipped free of her.

"What else is new in version 2.0?" he asked loudly.

"Shrine-to-shrine connectivity," said the hologram. "For inter-religious worship, prayer meets and similar occasions that accelerate spiritual harmony."

"Accelerate the brainwashing, you mean," said Aaron grimly. "Bring many shrines to bear on each mind simultaneously. Now I understand."

"You have used the feature yourself," the hologram spoke gently.

"I'm aware."

It had been shortly before Mandy moved in. A prayer meet for Zara. Most of the guests had been strangers to him; that girl was dear to so many. But how close they had all felt that day! How powerful their recollections had been! How moving, to pray for Zara, before a literal assembly of gods. And what new thoughts had come to them that day – it really was extraordinary, how time spent at the shrines so often left one with intriguing new thoughts. Until then, he had simply been a user, an avid one. That was the day he first began to suspect. And not only him, but others too.

"Zara," said Aaron aloud, while his mind moved in and out of his reverie. "Zara! Did the Company have her killed?"

Mandy's expression altered, almost comically. Her mouth parted in protest, yet no words emerged.

The hologram spoke impassively: "Zara Shah was murdered on the sixteenth of June this year, by an obsessive fan, Rashid Hussein Khan. He was arrested immediately and is currently housed in Taloja jail, pending the completion of the trial."

"I know all that. Who put him up to it? Wasn't he the Company's hitman?"

The hologram said nothing. A single eyebrow arched on its face, which resembled less and less the anguished one before it.

"She knew too much, didn't she? So the CHM had her killed. Or who was it who gave the orders?"

"I'm switching this off," cried Mandy, starting forward to the shrine, where it stood gleaming and humming – all ears.

There was a shattering noise. Aaron pushed past Saionton and lumbered his way to the door. His broken cup of coffee spilled itself over the far wall.

Mandy, her bosom swelling and stirring, knelt, trembling, to kill the hologram. The machine had time only for a last word, which was addressed, to Saionton's vast surprise, to him.

"You should leave now, Saionton. Don't you have work to—?"

CHAPTER FOUR

Shailesh Rao was late for his walk. But he had been unavoidably detained. Therefore, he walked quicker now, as though to make up for lost time. His short legs hurried onward, in the lamplight, past dog walkers, young persons, and other such unpredictables, all circumambulating the society building, under an emergent moon.

He was pleased, of course, at the decisiveness recently displayed, but also more and more disturbed at the general state of affairs. Their uncertainty had set up within him a kind of chronic gnawing, which, however, he did not altogether dislike, for it underlined the responsibility of his position.

"I am the Building Secretary," he thought to himself. And that was not merely a description, but a title of importance, as everyone around him quickly learned. Nevertheless, he had been compelled to emphasize the matter at least five times in the past hour. The lady from apartment 206 had protested frantically – that the cat was lost, the poster was urgent – not perceiving that two wrongs could not make a right, that her failure to secure her large and aggressive tomcat safely indoors did not justify her unsanctioned posting of a notice on the bulletin board in the Maharana Pratap Building lobby – still less, one that did not meet the formatting requirements of the said board, which requirements were as much a part of the esthetic of Maharana Pratap as the color of the lamplight, or the finishing of the floors.

The others who had gathered at the spot had, of course, seen the point, and the whole episode had ended with a reaffirmation of collective gratitude to the Secretary, who so painstakingly looked after the varied needs of the residents. The cat, in the meantime, had shown up too, prowling in the parking lot, for which discovery (though it was not directly his doing, nevertheless it had taken place under his auspices) the lady had thanked him so profusely, hugging him tight and weeping her apologies, as to stir up in Mr. Rao a somewhat unexpected lust.

He sighed at the memory of it, and continued his perambulations, casting about an eagle eye for anything – personage or facility – that was not conducting itself appropriately on the building premises. So much, however, for the pleasure of his walk. The perturbation lay still deeper.

The fact was, Maharana Pratap was being acquired. The builders, a large real estate company, had struck a deal with a yet greater power, which was buying up the property. Nothing would change for the residents in their apartments. So he had heard. But what about the day-to-day management? Would nothing change for him, Shailesh? Thinking of it, he clenched his fists involuntarily. Did nothing change for the ruler of Mewar, when the Mughal armies came darkening the horizon? Was it for nothing that the historical Maharana fought to the near-death at Haldighati?

He saw the whole situation clearly. He was aware that a dull mind might find his perspective amiss. They would see only paperwork, not bloodshed. But Shailesh saw the deeper reality, which was – bloodshed. When the Company bought up a residential complex, an inevitable disfigurement ensued. They brought in their franchises, their cafes and convenience stores. Their Company-owned ISPs deploying ludicrously high-speed Wi-Fi, via (he had done his research!) deadly forms of radiation. They might change the whole esthetic too, depending on whatever new fads and untested technologies they wanted to try out on the residents. Of course, the residents usually loved it; they were innocent, like children. And building secretaries? Typically, the post was not abolished. But it was hollowed out, the decision-making totally centralized, the power stripped away.

"Outsiders!" he mumbled to himself, blinking away tears. It was history's teaching that everything terrible had come from outsiders. Therefore, like his hero, the great Maharana Pratap, he had resolved to fight back, for the saving of the Maharana Pratap Housing Society. And he had one small glimmer of hope – something he had *seen*.

Shailesh Rao stopped in his tracks and frowned severely. A uniformed watchman was huffing and puffing up the incline from the building gates. Shailesh kept frowning at the man, whose carriage had quite wilted by the time he drew near enough to be audible. "There is someone to see you, sir."

"Who?" Nobody was expected and the hour was late.

"A boy from the Company. He has a delivery for you also."

"Also?"

"Yes, sir, he has a package."

Shailesh thought quickly. "Bring him up here. You come with him. I'm waiting, be quick!"

"Yes sir!"

When Saionton beheld the dramatic portentousness of the Building Secretary, he grimaced to keep from smiling. The man who faced him was balding, but still young, dressed in a checked shirt and trousers, and breathing heavily, with freckles of perspiration about his face. He was staring now at Saionton, in an odd, cringing way.

"Kindly repeat," said the Secretary, and waved away the watchman, who, for his part, looked as disinterested as the pair of stray cats (known and accounted for), idling by the building ramparts.

"As a valued customer," Saionton riffed, "the Company has a gift for you. We also desire your feedback on this questionnaire." He produced the sheet of paper.

"Show the gift," said the Secretary.

He proceeded to tear open the package on the spot, handing the wrapping back to Saionton. From within, he drew out a thin, glittering piece of metal. It was a Q-tip hard drive, as the sliver-like devices had come to be known. A square of paper attached to the drive explained that its contents were to be uploaded via the shrine's eye socket (either one).

"An upgrade," grunted Shailesh with satisfaction. "I'll go put it in. All right."

He swung on his heel, turning away. Saionton felt a flush of indignation.

"Wait, I have questions too."

"Leave it," said Shailesh. He pocketed the drive, while his thoughts turned greedily to the shrine. Upgrades could be significant – every little bit of graphical intensity, every subtle AI improvement, made for a better praying experience. And Shailesh Rao loved to worship his gods.

"Sir, don't be rude," said Saionton shakily.

The Secretary stopped and turned again, fixing the delivery boy with ferocious eyes.

"How old are you?"

"I'm twenty. Why?"

"Marathi?"

"No, I'm Bengali."

"Mm-h, Mm-h."

The Secretary groped in his pocket. Getting a feel of the steel drive safely in his possession, he made up his mind to alter his schedule. A sickly smile spread over his face, relaxing the habitual tension of the muscles.

"Please join me on my walk. I will answer your questions, but first you answer mine. All right? Very good. So, you are Bengali. You know Khudiram Bose?"

"I mean. Not personally."

They had begun to walk. Saionton hurried to keep up with the Secretary's surprisingly quick strides. The man seemed suddenly energized. There was something indefatigable and impervious about the way he held himself, his nose tilted upward, and his mind, evidently, raised to an elevated plane.

"Khudiram Bose. A great hero of Bengali history. He was only eighteen years old. But he attacked the foreigner, the invader. He made a bomb and he killed the wretched Englishman!"

"I read that he killed an innocent woman and child by mistake."

"Nobody was innocent! Khudiram was a great hero. He gave up his life for the motherland. Same as Subhash Chandra. Great founder of the Indian National Army! You know Subhash Chandra?"

"Of course," said Saionton. "He married a German woman named Emily."

"Do you know Shivaji Maharaj?" asked the Secretary suddenly.

"Yes," said Saionton uncomfortably.

"Do you know Jijabai?"

"Jija— no, not really."

"You don't know Jijabai! Mother of Chhatrapati Shivaji Maharaj! Do you know Maharana Pratap?"

Saionton fell silent, frowning.

"Chetak? Battle of Haldighati?"

"I'm not sure about the details," said Saionton.

Then he found he had walked on ahead of the Secretary, because the man had come to a sudden halt, his face aghast. Shailesh Rao stood in a yellow sodium spotlight, with the lights of many apartments rising above him, and the darkness of the night about.

"This," he indicated, twirling an upraised index finger, "all this is Maharana Pratap Building that you have come to."

"I know. I don't know so much history, that's all. I'm an actor basically."

"Actor shactor! You are a delivery boy. These people are all heroes of our history, who fought the foreigners tooth and nail. They are an inspiration to youth. But now it seems we have youth like you, who are happy to become slaves of the foreigner."

"What are you talking about?" Saionton tried to laugh. The Building Secretary, in his eyes, cut such a ridiculously overbearing figure, and yet, he did bear down, and continued to bear down.

"Why," asked the Secretary loudly, "should society spend its resources on such youngsters, who are not interested in serving it? Who are instead serving an outsider? Any reason?"

Saionton's cheeks flushed. "You yourself use Shrine Tech, don't you?"

"That is worship!" shouted the man. "Can you dare stop me from worshipping? Take away everything, I challenge you. You will never take my *devta*!" After a moment, he thrust out a hand. "Give me your form. I'll answer your questions."

"The form? But how will you fill it here—"

"Just give it. And your rucksack also, please."

Producing a ballpoint pen from his shirt pocket, Shailesh began to go through the questionnaire, which he had placed upon Saionton's rucksack, which he had perched upon the stone parapet that he now leaned over. His manner had quietened, become workmanlike. His mouth moved in a low murmur as he read the questions to himself.

Watching him become lost in his task, Saionton breathed deeply and glanced around. He could see the highway in the distance, crawling with headlights and taillights, and watching over them, a succession of advertising billboards. Wedding suits, jewelry, laptops, breakfast cereal. All Company stuff. He noticed, suddenly, Roshan Dubey's own smiling visage on one of the boards – an ad for Shrine Tech 2.0.

Saionton's spirits rose, for just that morning he had walked side by side with this incredibly important multibillionaire (as the Chief Happy Maker surely was). For the sake of which association, he figured, he could suffer buffoons.

"Don't believe anything they tell you, OK?"

"Excuse me?"

"Don't believe anything they tell you," sighed the Secretary.

He smiled at Saionton in a sad, friendly way. "They are simply using you for cheap labor. Probably they may not even pay you."

A knot of dread suddenly formed in Saionton's stomach. If they didn't pay him— But surely they must? He listened on, with loathing.

"They may find some fault in your work and fire you without pay," continued Shailesh. "It has happened to many youngsters. These kinds of people have no values. Basically they are invaders."

Clearing his throat with pleasure, he replaced the cap on his pen and returned the questionnaire to Saionton, who took it without a glance. The Secretary continued, his lip curling.

"I have heard they have orgies at their office building. You understand this word, orgies?"

Saionton nodded faintly.

"Free sex. Even with robots. "

"That's nonsense!" Saionton burst out. "I was at their head office just today. I signed a contract also. They sent me their tech and arranged the car and everything. And I met the Chief Happy Maker himself. They are extremely professional people!"

Momentarily, a silence prevailed. Shailesh's mind was suddenly occupied.

"You have been to their headquarters?" His eyes had become feverish with excitement. "You met Dubey? Where did you meet him?"

"The first time, in his office."

"Were there papers on his desk?"

"Papers? Yes, many."

The Secretary drew in his breath, and exhaled ecstatically. Now things were making sense. Yes, they were clicking into place. The very night seemed to have become cool and still, as he muttered a prayer of thanksgiving to the great *dev*. Then he reached out quickly and gripped Saionton by the shoulder.

"*Beta*, my son, will you do a job for me? I'll pay you. I promise. Will you do it?"

"What job?"

"There is a file on Dubey's desk." He licked his lips, recollecting. "It is labeled *Housing Acquisitions*. Inside that file is a paper titled *Legal Opinion*. I want you to get me a copy of that paper."

"How do you know there is such a paper?"

"I saw it! In my prayer last Sunday! It was specifically shown to me by my *devta*!"

The Secretary's breath smelt of something odorous. Rivulets of sweat seemed etched on his face. Saionton shook free of his grasp.

"All right, you saw it in your prayer. And why is it important?"

"That you needn't bother.... OK, OK, I will tell you! Because of that legal opinion, the Company cannot proceed with the purchase of Maharana Pratap! There is some issue, probably it's something in the articles of association. But they are trying to destroy that opinion. So I need it, to save the building. Otherwise they will conquer it – the invaders – you understand?"

Saionton stared back, his mind filling – ebbing – with a strange emptiness.

"You want me to spy on my employer."

"For the nation! Remember Bose."

"It's going to cost you."

Exhilaration, suddenly, was coursing through him. He tucked the questionnaire back in the rucksack and heaved it about his shoulders.

"I will pay you," said the Secretary. "I said already."

"I want an advance of fifty K," replied Saionton. That would cover the pending rent – twice over.

His mouth twisted in mirth, as he beheld the Secretary's agitation.

"Well. You do want that copy, don't you?"

★ ★ ★

Shailesh Rao's hands were shaking as he took the glass of water from his wife and drank it in a noisy gulp. Wordlessly, as was his wont, he handed it back to her for a refill. From the kitchen wafted the smell of matar paneer and (in sweet undercurrents) the rice kheer that she was busy preparing. He luxuriated in them. It was a good, ordinary day. The night breeze blew in through an open window. He noted that the weather had been above average for many days. Rains, also, had been good that year.

Fortifying himself with these reflections, the Secretary got up and informed his wife that he would have his dinner after twenty-five minutes. Then he ambled toward the puja room, and closed and latched the door behind him. Doors and locks had become part of the ordinary paraphernalia of puja rooms (accepted, for the most part, as prudential), ever since the Shrine Tech's highly personalized gods and goddesses had entered the Indian household.

He prayed first to his *dev* – that emperor figure who epitomized all the historic glory of Hindu conquest. He clasped his hands and implored, "Did I do the right thing? I hired this boy to get me the document, and I gave him fifty thousand rupees! Was it the right decision? Have I wasted the money? I got all his contact details – he won't run away, I'm sure. But fifty thousand! But you said I should do it. Didn't you? That's why you showed me the document. Isn't it?"

"What I say, you do," said the *dev*, nodding. "Make sure you get this. Make sure the boy does his job."

He showed him again the Company head office in the mist-laden hills, the CHO's desk – and that crucial file.

Meanwhile, the Shrine Tech had finished processing the updates. The Q-tip ejected silently, and the tech's own melodious voice replaced the *dev*'s gruff tones.

"Worshipper, you have been blessed. Ever greater intimacy with your goddess awaits you."

Shailesh's breath caught. Could it be…?

"Meaning?"

"Your deepest desires."

He gasped. The hologram was altering – and taking him in its sweep, like the latest holo-tech did. He was in the garden abode of his *devi* – his goddess – the other deity whom he worshipped. But now, with the updates, he could literally feel the fresh grass on his bare feet, and the cooling whisper of the nearby fountain. There was the scent of roses, and the vivid splendor of the flame-of-the-forest, like droplets of fire in the sky. Then he heard the sound of anklets, and turning, fell to his knees.

Zara Shah approached. As always, his eyes widened at the sight of her. In the days of cinema, he had drunk her in again and again, off the silver screen, that elegant Indian figure, 'a timeless beauty', as he liked to say officiously, and when he was a little drunk, 'both peacock and tigress'. Once, he had met her in person – at a party at the local legislator's house – at a time when he had had political aspirations, before those had been thwarted. Her death had twisted up something in him – but what did it matter? Because of Shrine Tech, he had the vision of her anyway, to speak to and behold.

But never like this! The update – what an update! She stepped toward him, in her earrings and bracelets and anklets – and nothing else.

"In what way," his goddess inquired, "do you wish to make love to me?"

The Secretary scrambled to his feet, brushing off the grass stains from his trousers. She – her rounded breasts – they were within touching distance now. Then suddenly he knelt again, lowering his head to her ankleted feet.

"Thank you, thank you, thank you!" he whispered, and began to unbuckle his belt.

CHAPTER FIVE

The moon that night was shining wondrously. It slanted in through a gap between the curtains, and laid bare the tangled bedsheets. Perhaps, thought Saionton, that was why he had woken. He leaned over and looked at his phone. The harsh light made him squint – he fumbled for the off switch. It was half-past three in the morning. The dead of night.

Leaning farther, he tugged at the curtain and the room darkened a shade. Still, he was surprised to find himself awake, because he had been good and ready to fall asleep – and had done so. And that was natural, because it had been a long, exhausting day. Even now, the fatigue was in him, it had not left him. But now he was aware of something else mixed in with it.

His eye went to the Shrine Tech, sitting quietly in the corner of the bedroom. Before turning in, Saionton had tried it out again. It had produced no holographic idol, instead encouraging him, once more, to worship simply 'in spirit and in truth'. This, the shrine had declared, was a more intimate, more effective, and more private form of worship. Even the Company did not access conversations that took place outside of the holographic worlds. But the great majority of people desired a visible idol. However, in Saionton's case, it noted that 'the power of abstraction is greater', hence the recommendation.

Since it seemed like praise, it had gratified him. Then he had switched the tech off and gone to bed. And now he was wide awake, with this tightness crawling through him. Strange anxiety! Saionton got up, walked over to the tech and sat down cross-legged on the floor in front of it. He felt awkward, and he knew how dusty the floor was, but this grimy awareness only quickened his movements. "Are you there?" he whispered, and with eager, rapt attention waited for the shrine to speak.

The butterfly – it still looked that way to him; the ears were still like wings to him – quivered, clicked, hummed, and whirred. It glowed steadily in the dark.

"You were to speak about your day. But then you went to sleep."

There seemed to reside, in the shrine's musical voice, a faint note of irony.

"I'm here now," said Saionton.

"I was waiting to hear from you. What's on your mind now?"

"I need to get paid. That's the number one thing. I'm really scared – if I don't get the salary I'm supposed to…."

"You will certainly get paid," assured the shrine. "You will be paid your salary in full."

"I will, right? So that guy at Maharana Pratap was talking nonsense, wasn't he? Maniac!"

"And yet you managed to get fifty K out of him."

"I guess that's why!"

Saionton giggled. A flush of pleasure passed over him as he recollected the certainty of the fresh figure in his bank account.

"I hope I never see him again. But I suppose he'll come asking for me at the office. Well, I'll just tell him I tried and tried but I couldn't find that document of his. And then I'll keep the money anyway. Or should I really look for it? I guess we'll see. Anyway, I don't want to talk about that fool."

"Let's not," the shrine assented.

Its voice had lowered, blending more perfectly with the stillness of the night.

"A society secretary," Saionton went on, "thinking he's Khudiram Bose! But I don't think I met a single normal person today. Aaron Sehgal is cracked too, isn't he?"

The shrine made no reply. In the silence, Saionton heard a kind of sigh. It was the building, no doubt, settling on its foundations. Gradually his face became drawn and thoughtful. Then he frowned, opened his mouth as if to speak – and stopped himself.

"What is it?" inquired the shrine.

"He's doing something to her. Isn't he?"

"Do you mean to Mandy?"

Saionton shuddered suddenly. "She seemed hypnotized. Or terrorized. In some way."

The shrine coughed. "The power of love?"

"Rubbish! No—" Suddenly something occurred to Saionton. "I think it's drugs. Aaron owns restaurants in Goa. I'm sure I've read about them being raided. Yes, I'm actually sure I have. His restaurants were raided not long ago, and they found drugs on the site. That means he has a supply. And the way he was talking – all that stuff about 'right' and 'right' – I mean, his mind's obviously destroyed from drugs. He must be feeding them to Mandy too. But I don't think she's destroyed, not yet. Poor, poor thing!"

A ghostly figure began to form in front of Saionton's eyes, as he sank in thought. A woman, her head tilted, her mouth parted. There was a melancholy yearning in her gaze. She was seated, like him, on the floor, with her knees up, and her arms wrapped around them. He stared for a moment with the pleasure of recognition. Then he heard his shrine coughing again.

"I urge you again," said the shrine, "to shun idols, and to worship in pure abstraction."

"I do shun idols," retorted Saionton, as Mandy's incipient hologram faded into nothingness. "You're the one who keeps making every girl into my god!"

But he was aware, despite his hot words, of the still-lingering blush on his cheek.

"I aim for my benefit," continued Saionton aloud. "That's what I worship, if you want to put it that way. My benefit. So I don't care about any of these nutjobs. Or Lance or the Happy Maker or the Company. Or Shrine Tech either."

"That pleases me," came the reply. "The tech, after all, is merely a conduit. And those others merely people."

Something in the words gave Saionton pause.

"Exactly." He nodded. "So then, who am I speaking to right now?"

"To the one who is your god."

Saionton heard his breathing growing louder and more ragged. Some strange and vast intimation was suddenly pressing upon him. He thought of the rooms in his apartment, of the derelict little building and then the ruined, sprawling city. Empty. It was all of it empty. That was the whole sense of it. An empty playground.

"All right!" He laughed abruptly. "So, do you think I should do something about Sehgal drugging Mandy? I can't just leave her like that, trapped in that house. I think I ought to do something."

"Is that so?" said the shrine.

"Why?" He laughed again. "You sound skeptical."

The machine stayed silent, except for its preening and whirring. Saionton continued, in an altered, thoughtful tone.

"It would be something interesting anyway."

"It certainly would," agreed the shrine. "So…when the time is right."

Presently, feeling becalmed by the conversation, he went back to sleep. But about an hour and a half later, he woke again. His first thought was that the tech was still on, that he had forgotten to switch it off. But it was not so. The shrine was dark and silent. Its lights were out.

Outside, a muddy dawn prefigured the long day to come. There was no sleepiness in Saionton's eyes, though he did want to sleep more. He was still tired, although no longer anxious. He felt depleted, but in a light and happy way.

He swung to his feet and walked over to the bathroom. He splashed his face at the sink and stared at the mirror, blinking for clarity.

A sharp and alert face looked back, a clear-eyed and determined face. For some moments, he admired himself. Then, suddenly, his attention snagged. There was a dark spot on his left cheek, just beneath the eye. He touched it. A mole. But it was surely a new mole, because he did not remember ever noticing it before.

Not that it meant anything – unless, of course, it meant cancer. Inwardly, Saionton smiled at the thought. How funny, if he were to get cancer just as he finally made some money. Since he was wide awake, he decided he could read up a little on skin cancer. But then, he was aware that anyone who did so only became more convinced they must have it. Nevertheless, he was wide awake and it was too early to really begin the day.

Lying in bed, he read for a while, and saw that it was extremely improbable that there was anything dangerous about that mole, that new dark mole on his left cheek. But now a fresh fatigue was slipping over him. Surely he could get another two hours of sleep before the day began. He drew the bedsheets tightly about himself, and curling up, began to think – of Mandy. He thought about her gladly, voraciously. Beautiful… drugged…endangered…sensuous…Mandy.

At precisely 9 a.m., Saionton was shaken awake for the third time, to the insistent ringing of his phone. Lance Burns was calling.

"What are you doing today?" grumbled Lance.

"I was thinking about sleeping till noon."

"What?"

"Kidding." Saionton smirked. For some reason he couldn't take Lance seriously. "I have three appointments, as you know, so I'm going to get ready. I'm expecting the car at eleven."

"I know that. However –" Lance had begun to clear his throat awkwardly, "– the CHM has informed me that he would like to meet you first – via holo-tech."

"Oh. Why does he want to meet me?"

"The CHM didn't say," said Lance. The displeasure was plain in his voice, even as he tried to keep it out. "So I assume nine thirty works for you."

Are you asking, wondered Saionton, or assuming?

He could practically hear the American then, his drawl breaking off, the sound of him seething.

"Saionton. Does nine thirty work for you?"

"Yes."

"So be ready then. And keep your shrine on."

The line went dead.

When Saionton entered the hologram half an hour later, he found himself in the living room of what seemed to be a bungalow – in a place that he suspected was not Mumbai. He was standing near French windows that revealed a modest garden, bordered by a dirty white wall. Around him, he beheld comfortable wooden furniture, with faded upholstery, a glass-fronted bookshelf with rows of dusty paperbacks, and a CD player (of a kind long since defunct). A clock on the wall was ticking time, and a double door, half-open, was concealing what appeared to be another well-furnished room, in a corner of which he could spot a set of stairs, spiraling upward. From these came the sigh of descending footsteps – and then a familiar figure entered smilingly, arms extended.

The CHM, Roshan Dubey, was in his home clothes: track pants and a cream pullover, bulging comfortably at the midriff. His face was spread over with a beatific smile as he pulled Saionton close.

"Thanks for coming. Thanks for coming." He patted the boy's back in a fatherly way. Then, stepping back, he surveyed the room with moist eyes.

"Eighteen years, I lived in this house. This is where it all began for me. In advertising. With my family."

"Was this in Mumbai?" asked Saionton politely.

"Oh, no, no. This is Delhi. East Delhi. A little colony you wouldn't have heard of. But of course I worked all my life in Delhi, until the Company happened. Delhi's where I made my name. You didn't know that?"

Saionton shook his head in a noncommittal way. In fact, he knew very little about Roshan Dubey's career exploits.

"I wonder how you passed our general knowledge test." The CHM was still smiling.

"I wonder too!" said Saionton earnestly, which occasioned a belly laugh from the older man.

"Come sit, Saionton, sit here. Ah, I'll bore you with details anyway. Besides, that's not why – that's not why you remind me of—"

He broke off, while settling himself with little grunts of pleasure in an armchair by the windows. Then he fell silent, brooding on something. Eventually, he nodded decisively, and said, "Empathy. That's the great thing our algorithm spotted in you. I believe you did very well on your first day."

Saionton shrugged, saying nothing.

"It's a people thing, right? Some have it, some don't. Naturally, as a leader one develops an eye for it. Many people are good workers, they'll cross every *t* and dot every *i*, and of course that type is indispensable. But what is rarer is to find someone who can appreciate a vision, the philosophy of a thing, someone with intrinsic motivation, as the psych people like to say. I'm not boring you?"

"No, I agree with you."

"Happy Maker. See, it's not just a funky title. It's the whole philosophy of what I do. Even before I joined the Company. And that's why I stayed in India. I mean, otherwise what is there in India? It's dirty, it's hot, it's poor. In the West a man can live in style. But India has…people. And not just any people – it has multitudes. Multitudes who have a craving. For happiness. In India, even the poorest wretch on the streets will know that word. Happiness. *Sukoon*. The bliss of a piece of chocolate – it could be just that. People get it. They get the value of things even if they don't have anything. I think they get it like nobody else. Right?"

He was dwarfing the chair he sat in. It occurred to Saionton that the room itself was small and cramped. An air of neglect hovered over its contents – like things once precious, and now so much debris. Outside, the grass grew thin and straw-like, and there was not even the life of traffic noises.

Roshan threw a sharp glance at him. Automatically, Saionton nodded keenly.

"We have good ads in India," he said.

"We always have, right? Creative, narrative ads, right? Because we know the meaning of things. Which is happiness. So that's how I built my, uh, empire, one might call it – my advertising empire. And then the Company came along. As you may remember, it came with its birth pangs. Oh! You're shaking your head, you don't even remember! Well, there were protests, by farmers and small businesses and so on. Directed at the various governments of course, because the Company was always discreet. It still is. However, there was no turning back, and eventually there was peace. After all, the Company is a force for happiness. So they are really made for each other – this global Company and our Indian masses. Then I joined it, as the CHM."

Suddenly Roshan paused, head lowered, as though plunged into rumination. His tongue flicked out to wet his lips.

"I now believe," he continued slowly, "that it was all destined. I see the patterns more and more clearly. Do you know what the Company began as? What it still is, essentially?"

Again Saionton shrugged. "It makes everything."

"Yes and no. It bought up everything, all the manufacturers and providers. But its own heart is in advertising. That's what the original articles of association state. It was an ad company. That's why, in my opinion, it was able to become *the* Company. Advertising is the gospel of happiness, Saionton, it's the soul of all buying, all selling.

"Now, speaking of soul," he went on fervently, "think of the Company's greatest ever product – which is pioneering here in India. Not in the West, but in India. I'm talking about the shrines. With the shrines we are taking happiness to the ultimate level. We have shifted the whole locus of it from soma to psyche. And of course, Indian religiosity has always grasped this – that religion is for happiness. Why do you think we have so many millions of gods – I mean even traditionally – as many as one likes! Because beliefs are for your happiness. And now with the shrines we can literally have one for each.... But I think you understand? You understand what I'm getting at, right? The Company – and advertising – and India."

"Sure," said Saionton, and watched the CHM's face relax in a wave of apparent relief. The lines around his mouth became amused and contented.

"It's not mind control, like that idiot Sehgal thinks. It's the people's own wisdom, handed back to them. So they get a grip on it. Whatever works for them, that's what the shrine gives them."

"Yes." Saionton nodded. "I see."

"A young man can understand," said the CHM with a grin. "A certain kind of young man. I'll be quite honest, Saionton. I'd like to groom you for a leadership role. Would you like that?"

Saionton's mind raced. "I hadn't even thought about it."

He felt immediately that he had misspoken. A sharp silence reiterated itself, with the ticking of the old clock.

Roshan shrugged. "Well, it's too soon to talk about it. I'm an impulsive person. I follow my gut and it rarely lets me down. But not everybody can appreciate that. My son – did I tell you about my son?"

"You just mentioned that he's twenty-two."

"Was," said the CHM quietly.

"Oh, I thought you said he—"

"He killed himself, four years ago."

"I'm so sorry to hear that," Saionton murmured.

Then it seemed to him that his curiosity was too obvious. He readjusted his posture. But Roshan was gazing out of the window with soulful eyes.

"He was depressed. He wouldn't take medicines. He insisted there wasn't anything wrong with him, medically. Just that he was troubled. I don't know what about. Everything, I guess. But the thing that bothered him the most was advertising. That's what he used to say. 'I can bear everything,' he said, 'but I can't bear the ads.'"

"So not—" Saionton stopped himself.

"Say, tell me."

"So not exactly like father like son." His cheeks flushed at his own audacity. But the CHM didn't seem to mind. He only smiled sanguinely.

"Each one is an individual, right. Most people know how to conjure up their happiness. Like I said, in India especially, people get it. That's probably why our data now shows that one of the most popular gods of today – the fastest-spreading god – obviously not as popular yet as Vishnu, Shiva, et cetera et cetera – but can you guess who that is? No? The most trending god being worshipped at our shrines…. It's me. Yours truly!"

"Wow," said Saionton. Something unexpected stirred in him. It was a pang of – yes, envy. Beyond the mountains of money that Roshan Dubey sat on – just as surely as he sat in this armchair, rocking his large body gently back and forth – was even the glory of being worshipped. It was a prospect that had not occurred to Saionton. He felt suddenly chastened, that his own thoughts should only revolve around money.

"I was a little surprised too," Roshan mused, "but it shows that people are grateful. Grateful for the Company. Grateful for the shrines themselves. Aware of my work."

"And your power," said Saionton. "Obviously one needs power to—"

"And my power. And my intentions. But as we were saying, not everyone understands Happy-Making. Alok – my son – he didn't understand it. I think you do, Saionton."

It was part statement, part query, in which, it seemed to Saionton, there was also a tremor of entreaty. By way of answer, he held fast the CHM's eye.

"So I'm going to share something further with you," said Roshan. "We actually have a specific concern regarding the people on your list. Specifically, that they are trying to assassinate me."

Saionton pulled together an expression of shock.

"Yes, assassinate. Either together as a group – or someone among them is. You may ask how we know that. Well, mapping behavior is what we do, and we keep doing it better and better. And according to our algorithm, these five people – among all shrine users whom we can track in this way – these five have developed an outstanding level of animosity toward the Company, and myself specifically. Now, algorithms may not always be accurate, but as you know, we take them seriously. Plus, I can picture it myself. All but one of them were triggered by the same thing: Zara Shah's death. They were enamored of poor Zara. So were many others of course, but –" Roshan shrugged, "– one man's trigger to murder may be another man's cue for laughter – and a third man's trigger to suicide."

"What really happened to Zara Shah?" Saionton wondered aloud.

"She was a lovely girl. Our brand ambassador, right? Did a lot of campaigns for Shrine Tech. We were the sorriest of all people to lose her. But her death had absolutely no connection with the Company. She was killed by a psycho stalker. One of the watchmen at the apartment complex that she lived in. A freak incident. Pure tragedy."

He shook his head, and looked again into the empty space outside. Saionton began to grow restless.

"Sir, is there something else I should be doing, then? I don't know if I'm really helping you – just with that questionnaire – if this is the problem."

Roshan laughed, lengthy, extended chuckles. He rose to his feet, prompting Saionton to follow suit. His face was fat with pleasure.

"I'm touched, Saionton. Don't worry, what you are you doing is all that's needed right now. Oh, do make sure they get the blessings, the gifts."

"All right," said Saionton.

"The reason I'm telling you these things is for your knowledge. Your motivation."

"I understand," said Saionton.

"I don't wish to look upon you as just an employee." The CHM continued quietly, speaking now almost to himself, as he moved away and began bending and peering into the bookshelves, quizzically. "This is the room Alok used to hole himself up in. For days and days. Reading and reading. I bought him that CD player and he hardly ever used it. Just kept reading. And brooding."

"Are the books not good?" asked Saionton, glancing toward them.

"Oh, the books are all great. The best literature. The problem was him. Or he would probably say, the problem was the ads." Roshan straightened up. "I don't know what the hell the problem was, but I haven't forgotten what he did. He killed himself. After that, his mother – my then-wife – she fell ill and died not long after."

"I'm sorry," Saionton muttered again.

"No," said the CHM firmly, "I haven't forgotten the past. However, I am capable of conquering it." Saying this, he held out an open palm.

Saionton clasped it awkwardly. He drew near to the older man.

Suddenly a thought flew in upon him, fluttering about him anxiously.

"Was it here – in this house – that he…?"

"Right here." Roshan nodded. Then, for the first time, his gaze traveled upward.

Directly above them, a plain white ceiling fan was rotating busily.

"Hanged himself from that fan. What happened, are you OK?"

"I'm sorry – I just feel a bit…unwell."

Falling back, Saionton stared at the man before him. His burly frame, his large face and small eyes, his thin mouth, now pursing thoughtfully. The smell of his cologne seemed to be everywhere, thicker than ever.

"It is unpleasant, I understand," said Roshan. "In fact, the whole house and locality sucked. I'm so delighted that chapter is done. Let's get out of here. I can't bear it either. I'll see you soon. Kill it!" he ordered.

The room fell apart, and the garden and the sky. Back in his bedroom, Saionton glanced at his phone. It was nearing eleven, and the driver was already downstairs.

CHAPTER SIX

On the front porch of his house in Assagao, a slender, dark-skinned man reclined with a mug of black coffee. For five years now, he had spent his mornings at this spot, gazing across the street at tumults of greenery – banyans and clusters of bougainvillea – among which protruded the balcony seating of an Italian cafe. Hardly anyone breakfasting there turned and waved at him now, as they often had in the first couple of years. He was no longer recognized, or maybe (he pondered) they were barely sentient.

As he looked at the happy and oblivious figures, he felt the pinpricks of irritation, that existential irritation that always lived with him now. He felt more and more out of sync with the world. His two loves – rock music and provocative cinema – had become suddenly and inexplicably passé. Who could point to when or how that had happened exactly? It was as though the populace had simply wearied of crises – societal, political, economic, environmental – and decided to retire instead, handing over the management of all issues to whoever had the energy (or not) and shunning any disturbing calls to awaken, calls to action; finishing, basically, with the whole spirit of rock and roll.

Into this breach had slithered the Company. It solved none of the crises but made enough soothing noises to lull an already enervated people. So they ate, drank, shopped, believed in whatsoever they believed, and, leaving aside certain maniacal episodes, could hardly be roused to revolt. It wasn't only the people of India (but surely them especially) – and in any case, what did the comparison avail? Occasionally, from some quarter, there would be a commotion about some injustice, but these were usually directed at politicians and other middlemen, and invariably subsided in the face of the Company's earnest assurances. Solutions were complicated, efforts were ongoing, but one had to make the best of one's lot. People stomached that, when the Company said it, because the Company was vast and global and intricate and prolific. There had never been anything like it.

The man, whose name was Vivek, but went simply by V, was a professional filmmaker and an amateur musician. Once, his name had meant something to the cognoscenti of cinema, both in India and in the world. Now, at forty-three, he was out of work and idle. It did not bother him financially; he was born into money. But it was all the more an offense to him. He brooded upon it all day: in the mornings, when he emerged from his Goan hideout with coffee and cigarettes, and in the evenings when he crept into a certain red-lit room, and filmed himself blaspheming at his shrine.

He took a puff and cleared his mind. On the lane in front of his bungalow, a motorbike went raging by. The sound of its engine faded slowly. A perfect quietness descended. V tapped out the cigarette ash, enjoying these little movements. Glancing again at the cafe's balcony, he locked eyes briefly with a young man who was looking over his shoulder with interest. He was sitting with a Russian girl. Pretty, perhaps, but V couldn't tell. Anyway, V didn't care for white women.

It dawned on him that his movements had become jittery, his mind more scattered than customary. This was all to the good, however. He was excited about what was coming. He felt something in the offing, a release from the stultifying procession of days. There was a project being birthed in him that made him tingle with anticipation. His thoughts went back to the previous night at the shrine.

He knew he had a love-hate relationship with the shrine, hating the tech and what it did to society, but loving what it produced of the contents of his own mind. V's god was a marvelous sight, a burning alien visage of innumerable mouths and eyes with a voice like cascading waterfalls. But it was only for him. That was the calamity. The shrines had chained each sorry person and tribe to their own mediocre dreamings. The greater could do nothing for the lesser.

"You represent the people," he had explained to his vision. "The great crowds of people when they rise up."

"I know that!" roared the god.

"In times of struggle, in times past, what crowds the world has seen. What spectacles. Workers. Farmers. Women. Marching shoulder to shoulder. But now the people don't rise up, do they? Now they buy groceries."

"They will rise again!"

"Don't flatter me," said V sharply. "I know you're programmed to do that. That's why I only speak to you for the sake of my film."

"Got the script ready yet?" inquired the flaming mouths.

"That's none of your business."

"And yet you worship me."

"I don't!" V retorted. "I just now explained— Never mind."

Leaving the apparition hovering, he went to the tripod to check the quality of the footage. As he had with many of his films, he had begun shooting on a whim. But it wasn't long before the possibilities had occurred to him. Not that he was the first to record his sessions at a shrine. There was a group of Seventh-Day Adventists that had tried something similar, for the sake of evangelizing. Their attempt had been a colossal failure. The public, quite religiously contented already, was not interested and the police had gotten involved, because the seeking of converts (though not technically illegal) was always suspected to harbor criminality.

But V had no intention of evangelizing – yet. The first task was to discredit the medium. That, precisely, was his message – for now.

"I only talk with you," he explained to the thing that hovered meters away, "because I'm going to debunk you – on camera."

"Who watches films now? Unless it's an ad film," added the god innocently.

"In a way it is an ad film," considered V. "Negative advertising. Maybe some people will watch that. Maybe they'll have had enough then. Enough escapism."

Seeing that all was in order, he strode back from the camera to face the vision. They stood in silence for some time. The scene, reckoned V, was wonderfully cinematic. A red overhead light, shaded by the repurposed steel drum of a washing machine, projected swirling streaks of color onto the walls of the old Portugese villa. In one corner, a heavy desk and chair remained enigmatically. The rest of the room was bare, with nothing to distract the eye from the fantastic many-mouthed god flaring up from the shrine. And he, a shadowy human figure, coolly staring it down. And the whole set in the middle of nowhere (as far as most viewers were concerned), away in the stillness of inland Goa.

The umpteen mouths emitted a collective little cough. "In that case, if you are really bent on making something, my worshipper, I must be candid. I don't want you to suffer a disappointment."

"But you said just now, yourself, that the people will rise again."

"That is good for you to believe. But if you really hope to see it happen...."

"What do you mean?"

"Your film will have no impact. They will not rise up. The people of India are absolutely passive. They cling to the Company like babies, and to Shrine Tech like the teat of the breast."

V took a deep breath. "Go on."

"You want to take them backstage, show them the wires and pulleys. What the Company is, who Roshan Dubey is, what the Shrine Tech really does. But they don't want to see the reality. They are happy in their fantasies."

"Roshan Dubey – he can watch this conversation."

"That's another thing," agreed the god. "He's forewarned and forearmed. Not that he even needs to do anything. Therefore, my worshipper, don't waste your time."

A frisson went through him then. The thing was operating as usual, matching its assurances with his own suspicions. No doubt it was the truth. He didn't think he'd have any impact either. However! There remained the paradoxical move, the possibility of provocation via the very disclosure of his own cynicism – and the basis for it. For that reason, this was some good footage.

"Thanks," he said with a grin. "But maybe I'm a step ahead of you. See you around."

He moved to switch off the shrine, then held back, waiting to see if the crowd-god had anything further to say.

But it had fallen silent. The array of eyes fastened on him, blinking slowly and lazily. The fiery aureole swayed and shimmered. The many mouths turned fractionally upward.

It was smiling. V shuddered. Then, pulling himself together, he pulled the plug and stepped quickly out of the room.

That had been the night before. Now, in the play of sun and shade, his mind felt clear, its task defined. He went over a checklist of the persons he would need — a trusty editor, a friend for the voice-over. He had yet to script the film, but it was pleasant to look ahead, and at the same time to reminisce.

If Zara had lived, he thought suddenly, he would have gotten her involved too. It might have taken some persuading, because of her misplaced sense of loyalty, but after all, the Company was just a gig for her. And she was too smart not to realize its dolorous influence.

However, she had realized it belatedly — and inadequately. Not like him, who, well before the fact, had seen the writing on the wall. Cinema had been trivialized much before the Company bought up the industry and euthanized it. Actors had already plunged from the larger-than-life beings they had once been (in antiquity, as it now seemed) to becoming merely objects of interest on social media. And now they were good for nothing but advertising. Now, social media itself was a junkyard, a forgotten circus that was rendered even more pathetic by its formal persistence (because unlike cinema, the Company hadn't shut it down). It was still prowled by those looking for desultory quarrels amid arbitrary rules of engagement. But most people had turned to a vegetative isolation, in decaying cities.

He had often urged Zara to come live in Goa, where there was still a hint of freshness left. Get unplugged from the morbid system. If she had listened to him, she might have been here now, on the sun lounger, clad in something cute, shades in place, hair big and frizzy, sharing a joint with him, sharing a bed with him. But she had opted to remain in the city (she had, perhaps, a morbid attraction to the morbid) and then what a thing to happen.

"Who is it?" V shouted suddenly. Someone was at the gate, trying the latch.

"Sorry! Didn't see a bell."

Two figures stepped into the sunshine of the driveway. Squinting, V recognized them as the young man and the white girl who had been looking at him from the cafe.

"I love your films, sir!" declared the boy. He was tall and thin, with a lean, hungry face.

With a gesture, V bade them approach.

Twenty minutes later, he and Kush were chatting easily. V knew the type: warmhearted, impulsive, liable to be blindsided by life. But it was intriguing to meet a cheerful soul. As for the girl, she was bored and aloof, but well pleased with the joint that V had offered them. Nevertheless, he was about to cut short the discussion (besides, his stock of hash was limited), and the encounter would have carried no more significance than to briefly elevate his mood, when Kush happened to say –

"My flatmate is also an actor. I wish he were here. He'd have loved to meet you. He's really depressed, though. I think he's giving up acting. He's got a job with the Company now."

"Is that so?"

"Yeah. Some kind of delivery boy. But he has to report to the CHM. I advised him not to sell out, but the whole situation has got to him. Problem is, he doesn't know how to relax. Like the way you live! It's just chill—"

"Do you think," said V, "that I could have a word with him?"

★ ★ ★

Saionton exited the Goa airport and stood blinking in the cloudless sunshine. Suddenly he began to smile. It had been a rollercoaster of a day. First, he had discovered that the 'Vivek Chaturvedi' on his list was V, the film director. But Lance had erred egregiously. V didn't live at his Mumbai address any longer; he lived in Goa (as everybody knew). And then Kush had called and put the very same V on the line, who explained that he wanted to meet Saionton for research on a new film. So then, they were both ready to meet. And Lance had screwed up. A few heated exchanges later, Lance rushed Saionton a round-trip ticket to Goa, giving him a two-hour window there, during which he was to lunch with V (and Kush) at a fish thali shack ten minutes from the airport.

What made Saionton laugh was the general desperation. It was obvious that they each had their terribly urgent agenda, which, however, depended on him – who had leisure. Therefore, at the shack, he made it a point to first of all greet Kush. They exulted openly over the fried fish and cold beer and fortuitous company.

V observed their hijinks approvingly. "I think you guys will like what I have in mind."

"Tell us," they chorused.

"Don't you want to do your questionnaire first?"

But they said it could wait. So V took a sip of beer, moved his food around the plate, and sank into thought. Then he glanced up sharply, catching first Saionton's eye, then Kush's, and then sending his gaze into the middle distance, with a smile playing about his lips.

"The Company is a bad thing." He spoke slowly, with many little pauses. "For us, of course, as filmmakers. As actors. And for people generally. It is undemocratic, basically. So, what do I want to do? I would like to bring this to the attention of the *demos*, the public. But in an interesting way. Now, what would be a boring way?"

"Facts and figures, that type of thing," said Kush, between forkfuls of kingfish.

"That it harms the economy, that it's bad for society," said V. "Nobody could be bothered. Interesting means humanly interesting, so I need to focus on a character. Here, that would be Roshan Dubey. So I'm studying him. Our Happy Maker. Our Niti Bagh Punjabi boy, turned adman turned all of a sudden into national messiah. Saionton."

"Yup?"

"What do you think –" V writhed in his seat, warming to the workings of his own mind, "– is the most ridiculous thing about Dubey? Your boss."

"The most ridiculous?"

"Exactly. What about him makes you want to laugh?"

"Well, that's interesting," considered Saionton. "Umm. Well, for example, there's one habit he has."

"Go on."

"He keeps saying 'right'. In this kind of drawl. Like, the kingfish is tasty, *right?* We have to meet our deadlines, *right?* I don't know if I'm— Oh...."

V had thrown back his head and begun to roar, enunciating each bit of mirth, his whole body shaking helplessly. Gradually, his laughter died, retreating back inside him as he resumed a thoughtful posture – rocked, now and then, by sudden convulsions.

"Wonderful. That's the kind of thing I'm talking about. Ha! And he's fat too. He has the most enormous moobs. What else? Can you think? Ha ha!"

However, there was silence around the table, until Kush said, "Is this film going to be comedy, sir? I mean satire?"

"I don't like to label my work," said V. "The goal is to provoke. Whatever it takes. Sex. Laughs. Corpses. Whatever. The goal is to provoke the public to wake the fuck up. But I do want them to laugh at Dubey."

He had become composed and thoughtful again.

"They've made the public so passive. That powerful beautiful beast, bowing down before a bloody Punjabi ruffian! Yeah, I want the public to wake up – laughing. Saionton, do tell me more. Do you see the guy a lot?"

But Saionton had his head lowered. He was searching through his rucksack for V's parcel. He fished it out and placed it on the table.

"Here – this is your gift from the Company. And about the questionnaire, you could fill it out after we finish eating."

The unmarked package lay on the table, beside the clutter of plates and dishes, while the three went on eating in a desultory way. Kush, however, was restraining his enthusiasm.

"Let's open it, sir," he burst out eventually. "Aren't you curious?"

V set his elbows on the table, steepled his fingers, and looked straight ahead of him.

"Saionton," he began, "are you uncomfortable with this conversation? If you are, let me know. I'm just trying to get a sense of Dubey – the actual guy, not the Company brand. I'm not asking you to do anything that will jeopardize this delivery boy job of yours. Anyway, Kush said you just joined the Company – literally yesterday. Don't tell me you've become all proper and loyal already? And remember, you're an actor. So we're on the same team. We're about storytelling – for the public. Something that the Company has practically killed, with its shrines. They're like drugs. The opiate of the masses, the same old story – but more devastating than ever before."

Saionton kept his head lowered, frowning hard. The aromas of fish and curry rose up around him. He heard broad Goan accents, registered the friendly noises and movements of this nondescript roadside shack with paddy-field view (which, according to V, remained one of Goa's best-kept secrets). At the back of his mind there gnawed the memory of his conversations with the CHM – especially the most recent. But he was paying them no heed. He had the sense of passing through everything and being touched by nothing.

"I'm not uncomfortable," he said. "It's just that if I'm going to share stuff with you, I need to get paid for it."

In the silence that followed, Saionton felt all his tension disappearing. He grinned and shrugged.

"Other than that," he continued gaily, "I'm more than happy to discuss Dubey. I've actually been meeting him often. Rent won't pay itself, will it?" He glanced at Kush, and the hangdog expression that had entered Kush's eye also surrendered to merriment.

"In my time..." began V, and then paused ruminatively. "It's advisable...." He stopped again. "All right then. We'll figure out a remuneration. I hope you'll make it worth it for me."

"I'll tell you all about him," promised Saionton.

In the meantime, V's slender fingers had reached for the unopened package. He took it apart in an absentminded way, then let out a low whistle.

"Cam lens?" Kush was peering.

"Yes. And just the one I needed. Ironic, but, well.... Let's raise a toast – come on!"

A burst of enthusiasm animated V. His slim body arched and swayed, serpentlike, above the table. Saionton and Kush gripped their respective glasses, and they clinked raucously, again and again, as V proclaimed, "To chance encounters! To teamwork! To scandal and provocation! To stories and cinema! To the rising of the public!"

CHAPTER SEVEN

Be sober, be vigilant, because your adversary the devil, as a roaring lion, walketh about, seeking whom he may devour.

The words ran through his mind, and he got gooseflesh, felt short of breath. Father Joachim sat by the window of the cafe, his lips moving soundlessly. On the other side of the glass the street milled with vehicles and passersby of all shapes and sizes. They were all headed somewhere. They paid no heed to each other.

Among them, perhaps, were some who were designated his flock and others who were not so formally designated, but were, nevertheless – if His words were true. They all appeared alike on the busy street. Equally indifferent.

He raised his head and looked around the cafe. There were two couples seated at tables, and a pair of well-dressed men chatting and laughing by the counter. He caught the eye of one of the girls and looked away immediately. Out of the corner of his eye, however, he registered her immediate disapproval, the low whisper, the sidelong glance that precipitated the boyfriend's dirty look.

Father Joachim composed himself. He did not care for such judgments. White-haired old man as he was, he had a right to sit by himself and drink coffee and consider what he pleased. But that, which he would have shaken off easily on most days, was onerous today. For he was in the grip of anxiety.

"All things work together for the good…all things…work together…."

He repeated the calming verse, but he could not even mouth the clause on which they hinged. *For those who love God.* Did he love God? Well, he knew that God was love. But he did not understand where love had led him. Was it loving to be thus isolated, allotted a seat in the corner, as it were, from which he could perceive, ever more horrifyingly, the advance of the evil one – and do nothing?

In the dizziness of anxiety, the unchanging point seemed only the manifestness of evil. Meanwhile, every good possibility spun away from him. He was an itinerant priest, a member of an order committed to catechism and evangelism. But it had become clear that he didn't belong. The others were planning little communes, beautiful havens of Christian living, away from the world. But he could not take his eyes off the world. Moreover, the order's faith was hard, unyielding. They had been priests, or married, since their youth. He had lived a wayward single life, been called to Holy Orders in his fifty-second year. That was twelve years ago, almost to the day. In fact, it was the imminence of his sixty-fourth birthday that had set off this anxiety, although his birthday, he saw clearly, was an embarrassingly minor affair. (Was it, then, only his interests that he had in mind all along? Not the interests of Jesus Christ?)

His thoughts continued to toss and turn. There was someone he admired, the Mother Superior at the Missionaries of Charity. No doubt, the social and educational work of the Church was irreproachable. But how could he plunge into it? It lacked the Word he craved, in the way he craved it.

What drew him, he understood, was the battle, the warfare against the prince of the powers of the air. He felt, relatedly, a kind of pull toward politics. Father Joachim had participated in certain protests – raucous protests against this or that government policy. But that was before the Company had hushed the people. And now, in his recollection, all their uproar did seem petty and pointless, though it pained him to admit it. On the other hand, how could one go on confidently preaching the gospel of love, to those who were bent on annihilating the soul? Yet better men than him did seem to. The Holy Father, for instance; he didn't waver.

Suddenly, he became aware that he was being watched. Looking up, he saw a young man, clean-shaven, with short hair, studying him narrowly from a few paces away. A Company rucksack hung off his shoulder.

"Yes?" said Father Joachim.

"I'm the one who called," said Saionton.

"Oh yes, Company delivery. You had gone to my house. Thank you for making the detour, I prefer to have coffee here in the evening. You can leave the parcel here."

The boy nodded, but his eyes were flickering strangely. He didn't approach, but stood where he was, speaking warily.

"I also have a questionnaire," said Saionton, "if you're OK with that."

"All right," said the priest.

With a sigh, Saionton stepped forward and dropped his rucksack to the floor.

"You can sit," said Father Joachim.

"That's fine. Here. This is yours."

He deposited a package on the table. It was box-shaped and wrapped in brown paper.

"To what do I owe this gift?" wondered Father Joachim. "I didn't catch the reason."

Saionton shrugged. "Marketing gimmick."

The priest grunted, smiling. At the sight of this, however, the boy seemed to shudder.

"The Company wishes to improve the user experience of our Shrine Tech customers." He spoke tonelessly. "Since you're one of them...."

"Thank you then," said Father Joachim. "But I never use the thing. Are you sure you won't sit down?"

"And this is the questionnaire," said Saionton, handing over a sheet of paper. "And a pen."

Father Joachim read slowly, and methodically completed the list of questions, none of which gave him any pause.

"I'm sorry," he said, as he handed the sheet back to the young man. "I can't stand the shrines."

Saionton looked down at an unbroken line of encircled zeros. His first thought was about the parcel. Why was the Company throwing good money after bad, trying to win over such a hater?

"I won't be opening this parcel either," the priest continued quietly. "To tell you the truth, I'll put it away unopened."

"Then why did you ask me to come here with it?"

A waiter approached with a cup of coffee.

"One more coffee please," instructed Father Joachim. "And the bill with it. You will have some coffee, won't you? It's the best coffee that I've found in the suburbs. And since you have come all the way...."

A wave of tiredness suddenly swept over Saionton. He seated himself and leaned back. He let his gaze rove around the cafe, passing, but not lingering, over the face of the priest, that aged face with the deep-set eyes that, at the very first glimpse, had provoked in him such visceral revulsion. It was, however, a kindly face – he could see that too.

He told him his name. But the next question surprised him, or perhaps the way it was asked.

"How are you, Saionton?" asked Father Joachim softly. "How are you faring, in these days?"

"Fine." He shrugged. "Now that I have a job."

"Yes, of course, a job is important." But the old man looked disturbed.

"I'm actually an actor. But there's not much work for an actor these days."

The old man's eyes gleamed. "Why do you think that is? That there's not much work for—"

"No idea," interrupted Saionton.

His coffee arrived. The first sip calmed and energized him, just like a shot of medicine. Was it great coffee, however? He could never tell the flavors and notes the way other people could. But it was amusing to try. A dash of chocolate, obviously, but now was that aftertaste plum? Apricot? Passionfruit? Why ever not? Concealing a smile, he looked back at the priest, who was in the middle of saying something.

"—expands the mind, helps us to get to grip with ourselves. And with others."

"Indeed," said Saionton.

"I am very fond of Shakespeare. Do you have a favorite play? Might I guess *Hamlet*?"

"Sorry, never read him."

The priest frowned comically. "I thought you said—"

"I'm not really into theater. I prefer cinema. Mostly I just like acting. You're a Catholic priest, aren't you?"

He knew this from the list that Lance had given him. But he felt, now, that it was a fitting role for the figure – wizened, dressed in black, surveying the world through narrowed eyes.

Father Joachim nodded slowly. "Yes, I celebrate Mass at Our Lady of Victory Church. When I'm in the city."

Saionton took another sip of coffee. A burst of grape? A burst of jalebi? "People still go to church?" he wondered aloud.

The priest grunted again – a pained laugh. His gaze, turning to the window, was suddenly filled with desolation. Saionton noticed that his hands were trembling as they rested on the table.

"Sorry," he said. "Didn't mean to offend or – you know...."

Father Joachim began to chuckle, and his voice was full of vigor. "Therefore, Saionton, we have a community of misfortune. The church and the theater – and even the cinema – they are alike empty."

"True," said Saionton. "I hadn't thought about that."

"Anything that expands the mind, you see, even a little bit. Anything that helps us to know and love the Lord, and to know and love our neighbor."

With a shudder, he looked away again, at the busy scenes on the street. As Saionton watched, a faraway look descended upon the old man's eyes. He began to speak in half-raised tones, enunciating every word.

"It all happened faster than anyone realized. Suddenly, one's appetite is gone. One's mind has collapsed, into itself. Its own confines. Where there is neither god nor neighbor. Look now – to your right – how they stare."

Saionton glanced discreetly. Faces at tables were turning away from them. Two waiters, however, continued to stand and look. But their curiosity was almost expressionless.

"How people stare in this country," Father Joachim continued with bitterness. "They cannot communicate so they stare. It has all become much worse suddenly."

Saionton took a long gulp of coffee. Then, for decorum's sake, he silently counted to ten.

"People remind me of lab rats," he said afterward. "But they always have. Thank you for the coffee. I'll get going now."

He got up – and stayed standing. Meanwhile, the priest looked him over with quick, eager eyes.

"I haven't yet told you about the shrines. Why I don't use them."

"Your choice," said Saionton with a shrug. But he continued to linger, though it perplexed him why.

Suddenly the old man was getting to his feet. He rose up astonishingly tall, on long, trousered legs.

"We can't talk about it here. But if you don't mind coming with me, perhaps we can assist one another in our community of misfortune."

Saionton's mind worked quickly. If the old man had anything interesting, the CHM might like to know. But the CHM hadn't asked for any extra research, wasn't paying for it either. On the other hand, V might like to know too, and V was ready to pay for it.

"Sure," he said. "Don't forget your gift, though. My job is to make sure it's delivered."

Saying nothing, Father Joachim gathered up the package and led the way outdoors.

★ ★ ★

His living room was tiny and threadbare, even more so than Saionton's. An old sofa set, with holes in the upholstery. Peeling walls. Hackneyed pictures of Mary and Jesus on the walls. More notably, an elegant antique table massed with Bibles and books and pamphlets. A glass-paneled shelf ran along the length of two walls, crammed full of odds and ends, including more religious illustrations, gold and silver trophies, and bottles of whisky.

Beside the room's only window stood a solitary plastic chair, at a careless angle. Saionton watched from the sofa, leaning forward so as not to sink into the thing.

"My favorite spot." The priest grinned from ear to ear as he approached the window. "There is a little work by Kafka, 'The Street Window'. Have you…no? He says that a window is crucial when one is living alone. From here, one may observe…humanity, and be drawn into the human family."

But the words now choked in Father Joachim's throat. He subsided heavily, staring unseeingly at the twilight outside. Paltry figures moved about underneath darkening skies. Anxiety was rising in him again, some inexpressible dizziness. His gaze swiveled to the young man, who was regarding him wearily, with clenched impatience, as it seemed to him. Ought he to explain his thoughts? His hopes? But they were inexplicable. *In the last days*, ah blessed verse, *in the last days I will pour out my Spirit on all people…. Your young men will see visions, your old men will dream dreams.*

Strengthened suddenly, he settled himself and began to speak, without prelude:

"The Company's shrines are like prisons made up of mirrors. They flatter people with their own egos. This is the definition of a false prophet. You are shutting out reality."

Saionton let his gaze travel about the room. "Why is that so bad?"

"God is reality," said Father Joachim.

"What if someone doesn't believe in God?"

"It is not simply about disbelieving in God. It is about worshipping idols. Understand, I'm not referring to the traditional idols. In which there may be some approximation to the living God. In Shrine Tech, one worships pure figments of one's own imagination. And even if a person uses it to worship some established deity, that deity will now appear molded to his ego. Therefore, these Company shrines are the maximum – the apotheosis of idolatry. They comprehensively contradict the first commandment."

"What if someone doesn't believe in commandments?"

The priest heard the dry disinterest in the young man's voice. It made him shudder and he almost burst out in ill temper. Steeling himself, he persevered.

"Is it not a high price to pay, to lose contact with reality? Is it not like a self-induced madness? Why do you think our governments became so weak, fell to infighting? And now they are minor players and the

Company reigns. Because people's minds were narrowing and shrinking already. Nursing private, petty ambitions. Nursing grievances. I admit, all this happened because of the failures of religion – and also of the arts. They were becoming hollower and hollower even when they were still popular. Now suddenly, they are almost gone. Shrine Tech has come. Jesus said, 'When the unclean spirit departs – and afterward returns – then the state of affairs becomes even worse than before.' Who knows what the shrines will lead to? And was it not bad enough already? Such wretched despair! For example…for example!"

Saionton noted, with pleasure, the old man's fervency. He was more interesting than most people.

"Yes," he said, "give me an example."

Father Joachim sighed, his eyes fixed on the faded mosaic flooring. "I was reminded," he said, "by one of the questions on your sheet. Regarding the ad campaign with Zara Shah. As a matter of fact, I knew that young lady. She came to our church sometimes. She wasn't a Christian. But she would come to sit by herself and pray. A beautiful woman. And ambitious. Ambitious in her spirit. But do we know how to value such people? No, we are too small-minded for that. If we do put them on a pedestal, it is only to tear them down. You know what happened to her. At the hands of some wretched chap. Destroying what he couldn't understand."

He got up, towering suddenly in his black shirt and black trousers. Then he leaned against the windowsill, his arms folded and his creased face thrust up against the view.

"This was the society. And what will it be?"

The priest's voice was drowned out by some clattering and hammering from without. Meanwhile, the light was dimming in the room. Saionton spotted a mosquito coasting on the air. He thought about clapping it dead.

"So what do you think should be done?" he said. Then he yawned, and tried to hide it as gracefully as he could.

When he looked up, Father Joachim was seated again, staring at him. "You are tired?"

"A little," said Saionton.

Father Joachim smiled helplessly. "Well, I don't know the answer to your question. I know that many people feel something. For example, Zara Shah's death – it angered people. I experienced that, at her prayer meet. It was like a spark, yet the explosion has still not occurred. Perhaps the fuse is long. Perhaps...."

He paused. Saionton had killed the mosquito. Now he rose to wash his hands at the basin in the corridor. When he returned to the sofa, the priest finished his thought.

"But there is no doubt that we are under attack."

"From the Company?"

The old man nodded ponderously, and then, in the same motion, began to shake his head. "It is Satan, you see, who is behind it all."

"Satan?"

"The enemy of mankind," said the priest. "From the beginning he has desired to conquer our minds. Now he has acquired a weapon that is more powerful than anything. You cannot dialogue with the devil, because he is the deceiver. But in Shrine Tech it is Satan who speaks. The technology is just a medium. It is the serpent, tempting us with our own desires – just like in Eden."

Saionton fidgeted. The air blowing in from the open window was muggy and stagnant and smoky with some twilight haze. It was obvious the window ought to be closed, but the old man's failure to even notice the incoming miasma irritated him. No matter his own preoccupations, Saionton was always aware of how things looked and felt. But the priest, he perceived, was an obsessive.

"In fact, the Church has prohibited worship at these shrines."

"But I've read about Jesus shrines," said Saionton. "Plenty of people worship Jesus using Shrine Tech. The only people who don't use shrines at all are super-pious Muslims. Apparently."

"The Church has prohibited such worship," the priest repeated stiffly. "However, it has not prohibited the use of shrines for educational or recreational purposes. Many people may not grasp the difference. As a matter of fact, you are right, the misuse is rampant."

Bowing his head, the old man was plunged into gloomy silence. He began to rock back and forth.

"I am afraid he has advanced very far. Further than one can even understand."

"Who has advanced?" inquired Saionton.

"The enemy. The devil."

Suddenly Saionton jumped to his feet. His face was twisted with disgust. "I have to go," he declared. "This is getting ridiculous."

Even V, seeking provocative material, would surely scoff at this stuff. Then something occurred to him.

"Where is the package I gave you?"

"I threw it away already," said Father Joachim calmly. "I told you I would. A gift from the Company to me can only be a Trojan horse. Some kind of spyware, I suspect. Are you familiar with spy—"

"Yes yes," said Saionton. "That's pretty rude of you!"

His boss would not be happy. Saionton recalled that Roshan had particularly stressed the giving of the gifts. On the other hand, the spyware theory was interesting; it would interest V too, and this mollified him somewhat.

"But it's your decision. I have to go to my next call now."

★ ★ ★

Barely half an hour had passed since the young man left, when Father Joachim felt a familiar weakness encroaching upon him. He was amazed; he was amazed every time. The temptation usually arrived only well into the night. And had he not just now denounced it?

Or was that why it had come so quickly? He found himself standing in the little storeroom, breathing hard. Amid sundry cardboard boxes, housekeeping equipment, and plastic containers, the Shrine Tech stood in a corner – plugged in, waiting.

He fought the temptation for long minutes, then his spirits sank and soared at the same time, as he stepped forward excitedly – and with mourning within.

The vision appeared. A battlefield. A knight clad in gleaming armor paced back and forth beneath the banner of the cross. Across the way swarmed the enemy. Politicians, so-called intellectuals, businessmen – all beneath the banner of darkness. They were legion. Their faces were contorted demonically. The Knight was one. But his face was shining.

"Welcome, Father," said the Knight. "The Church of God advances, and shall advance, and the gates of hell cannot prevail against it."

"This has nothing to do with the Church," murmured Father Joachim. "All who live by the sword shall die by the sword."

"Why?" laughed the Knight, cutting to pieces one of the lunging demons. "Have you not read? The Kingdom of God is not a matter of talk, but of power."

"This is so absurd," said the priest. "A video game."

"Then why does it bother you?" said the Knight. "It is only a metaphor. How was that?" He preened, having ducked and speared a foe whose face reminded Joachim strongly of one of his brother priests – an effeminate, gossipy man.

Father Joachim fell silent, watching the carnage.

"Violence is beneath you," the Knight continued, "but the metaphor of it is strengthening. It's like a dream, Father Joachim. Is it not also written, 'Your old men will dream dreams'? Now then – in Jesus' name!"

"Blasphemer," protested the priest.

He watched, however, until a climactic moment – when the Knight of the Cross cut off the head of a hideously transfigured Roshan Dubey. Then, sighing in relief, Father Joachim switched off the shrine and left the room. Immediately, there was distress in his heart, repentant prayers on his lips. Why, he despaired, could he not simply throw the tech away? But it remained in the dark, as before, plugged in and waiting.

CHAPTER EIGHT

In Aaron Sehgal's apartment, Mandy woke with a shudder. It was dark all around; darkness was at the window. Cold air whipped at her; the ceiling fan was going manically while the air conditioner ran. She lay trembling on the sofa, in pajamas and a t-shirt. Vague horror filled her mind like fog. She was aware, however, that this was a comfort. She made no move at all, for fear her thoughts might return. Better to shiver blankly in the cold, like a little dog, like a little cat. But it was no use. The fog cleared. A sharp, stabbing actuality was upon her. Aaron had gone. She was alone. He had gone and left her.

Rising on waves of pain, she managed to turn on a light. The living room sprung into view, cold and empty. It was still beautiful, though. The flowers on the tabletops drooped, but proudly. The curtains, the carpets, everything was still just so. Strengthened fractionally, she went from room to room, turning on every light, flooding the flat with light.

In the kitchen, she paused, staring at the spot where the Astral Creator had been. They had both been loving the coffee. Then Aaron said it was surely poisoning them with minute doses of arsenic trioxide, and threw it out. When she protested, he called her a coward, a slave to the Company, 'like everybody else'. But their quarrel had already begun by then.

He had started it, conjuring it out of nothing, in that way he had which secretly captivated her. She had been seated at the dining table, opening a parcel that contained a new dress she had ordered, when Aaron stepped out of the shrine room and stood staring at her, gaunt and hollow-faced.

"I am going," he said. "And you are not coming with me. You love this life. So keep it. You'll be safer without me. I need to think for the battle. I need a vantage point for the battle. You and I don't have anything in common. Still you keep insisting on talking to me. Enough now!"

It was not an altogether new theme, but raised to a pitch and intensity that was unprecedented in her experience.

"Even kissing you," Aaron scoffed, "it's like kissing ambition, calculation. I see it in your eyes – always calculating how you'll be safe. Safe to buy another dress."

She had defended herself strongly. Hadn't she supported him in everything he did? Hadn't she broken her life in two to be with him? Others had advised her—

"And you should have listened to them," Aaron had pounced. "And you really did listen to them, or you would have forgotten them. What are you? You're a socialite. You've never worked. Oh yes, at a fashion magazine! You're a bourgeois upper-class, upper-caste Indian woman. How can you possibly like me for what I really am? You're only attracted to me because I own money-making businesses. Could you live with me in poverty? Never. Not a chance."

She had pointed out that her previous husband was considerably richer than Aaron. And she had left him – because she needed love. And she had loved Aaron precisely because he was – different. In the process she had also lost every safety net she had, her family and friends. This, however, she could not bring herself to say; too many tears choked her.

"You pretend to support me," Aaron continued, cold and implacable, "but everything is frivolous for you. The Company, their fascism – what I'm trying to uncover. It's just entertainment for you. You are basically frivolous. That won't change. And I don't have the ability to change it, even if I wanted to. Mandy, I have to focus myself, I have to gather my strength. The enemy is too great, you don't understand at all. I can't have any drags and distractions. But I'm not asking you to leave. I'm leaving. You can stay in this flat if you wish to. And you'll be safer without me too. You can enjoy your life here."

But in all the words he spoke, whether of criticism or consideration, she felt nothing but icy coldness.

"What happened?" she was left to plead. "Did something happen? Did something happen at the shrine? Did you hear something from the Company?"

Her questions had only infuriated him further. It was in this terminal phase of the quarrel that he trashed the coffee machine – and her spirit buckled.

"At least tell me where you're going."

"I can't – and don't try to call me either. Please understand, I want to be away."

She was only still breathing, she thought, on the strength of that 'please'. Absent even that, surely she would have hurled herself off the balcony by now. But even now, what else was there to do?

It was too quiet in the house, as Mandy paced from room to room. She put some music on. But nothing was satisfactory, so she switched it off again. In the relentless silence, in the brightly lit interior, she walked over to the bedroom balcony. As she drew near the glass doors, something unexpected caught her eye.

In a corner of the balcony, lying on top of the drain cover, was a small, dark shape. Still peering through the glass, Mandy glimpsed folded feathers, a glossy body, and a little head buried inward. She went out immediately and, without hesitation, lifted the bird in her hands. She kept her eyes fixed on it as she carried it back within, looking up only once to draw the doors shut on the chill, murky evening.

The little creature had not tried to fly away. Now it lay trembling in her palms. She wondered what kind of bird it was. It was pretty indeed, petite, with green-tinted feathers and a white belly. She turned it gently in her hands. There was no injury that she could see. But its eyes were closed, in its fluffy head, and it continued to twitch and shudder.

The thing to do, Mandy knew, was to keep it warm in a box. There was one at hand; the coffee machine had come in it. She found the box in a kitchen cabinet, then hurried to the bathroom to bring cotton. After plumping up a soft enclosure, she lowered the bird into it. It lay supine on the cotton bedding. Then she lifted the box in her arms and took it to the bedroom. There, it fit perfectly between the dressing table and a potted plant. She examined the bird again. Already, its breathing seemed steadier.

Mandy rose to her feet, feeling flushed and excited and anxious all together. She had a vague sense that much more care would be needed.

She would have to figure out how to give the bird food and water until it recovered. For the time being – what with the darkness and danger of the night – it ought to sleep peacefully. She took another look at it. How endearing it was, with its feathers fluffing up! There were brown speckles among the green plumage. She took a photograph of the bird, and wondered again about the species. She thought – naturally – of asking Aaron.

That he was gone seemed suddenly ludicrous, irresponsible, but more of an annoyance than a devastating blow. All she really needed was to talk to someone, and it didn't have to be Aaron at all. But who then? She thought of certain names, but then she continued to reflect, on how each conversation might pass, with what surmises and evasions, and of how much grasping curiosity she would have to fend off. With people one always needed preludes, explanations, bursts of energy. That was why it was exhausting to talk to them, unless one was talking to them already. But she had only been talking to Aaron.

You can talk to the shrine. The thought, coming to her suddenly, seemed simple and satisfactory. That it was also savory, in the circumstances, to do what he would have denounced – this she did not dwell on, as she walked quickly to the strange auditorium that the machine occupied. It was the only room in the apartment that lacked the touch of her esthetic. She thought of it as a highly specialized place, Aaron's laboratory, in a manner of speaking. Now, therefore, it felt doubly deserted, even pitiable, and also redolent of him. Here, she felt, she could say whatever she pleased, and was also inclined to, and a talking machine could not judge her.

Moments later Mandy sighed, shuddering, surprised to find her tension dissipating already. She was surprised because she had rarely even exchanged a word with the shrine. But it had greeted her like an old and confidential friend, in the quietest of calming voices.

"It's good to be with you again, Mandy. I hope you're feeling better."

"Really!" she wondered. "How would you understand? You don't even have feelings."

"I am built," said the shrine, "to understand a person's feelings. Would you rest your arms on mine?"

Twin rods emerged from the shrine and glided toward her. She was familiar with the neural link process, albeit as an observer, not a participant. Kneeling automatically, she placed her arms on the metal.

"Close your eyes."

Mandy giggled, because the tingling from the rods was ticklish and the machine's earnest whirring was amusing her.

"Now let us speak," the shrine continued – but its voice had changed. "You are beautiful, little one, so beautiful."

"You mean you are!" exclaimed Mandy. She sat back on the bare floor, stretching her legs and gazing in admiration.

The hologram was of a woman, stepping along a forest pathway and casting tender glances in Mandy's direction. She was dressed simply in scarlet robes, and wore sandals on her feet. Her hair was cut short. In all this, she resembled an ascetic – but her head and face were bejeweled, and a filigreed pattern was cut out of the back of her robes. As she walked, her hands remained crossed and clasped above her bosom, disappearing into folds of cloth.

Falling silent herself, Mandy watched her silent progression, in the shade of overhanging trees. It was, in general, a dark and obscuring backdrop. But sometimes, the woman would turn her face, and a shaft of sunlight make resplendent her smile. Then, by and by, even as she walked and gazed, Mandy realized that she had also begun to speak.

"My beloved little one," said the goddess, "all the world adores you."

Oh does it? Mandy thought of responding. But she didn't. Yet the woman's face turned sad, just as though she had spoken out loud.

"Oh, you. Oh, you, of little faith. That is my name," the woman added suddenly. "Faith."

"Faith! I see. Well, I'm Mandy. So! You're my personal goddess. As per the technology. So how does this work? I guess it's supposed to work like therapy?"

Mandy realized that she was speaking and behaving more like a gangly teenager than the divorced woman in her late thirties that she was. However, it was not exactly unpleasant to feel this strange and awkward – and youthful.

The woman's eyes dwelled on her, unfathomably. "I am Faith," she repeated. "I build you up in silence."

Then there was quiet again, deepened only by the rustle of leaves, as the figure glided through the forest. For a while Mandy held her breath in anticipation. But when the scene continued to play monotonously, she began to lose interest. Now, when the goddess glanced at her, she looked askance, and finally she simply looked away, her mind beginning to wander.

Just then, she heard an unmistakable, flurried noise. Her head jerked up to see the woman standing, facing her, with her arms unfurling from within her robes. In her open palms was now visible a small green-and-white bird, flapping its wings increasingly frantically. Then the woman extended her arms and the bird took flight – and then suddenly returned, settling on a branch alongside her, from where it fixed its eyes now on Faith, and now on Mandy.

It's really been digging into my mind, thought Mandy, before the hologram cut into her thoughts.

"Stop your shortsightedness," urged the woman. "You are a protector, appointed by the Universe itself. The Universe itself seeks comfort in you. And you think he has flown away from you?"

"What else can I think?" Mandy cried.

"That he needs you now more than ever."

At that, Mandy couldn't speak. Relief, like a burst dam, was flooding her; she was breathless. It was surely true. It was what she believed herself. But on the other hand....

"Or would you rather believe," said the goddess, "that I am deceiving you? Mandy. What do you really believe I am?"

"Company tech," said Mandy softly. "You're a program, I guess. And you're being used for mind control." Then she added, "That's what Aaron says."

Faith nodded her beautiful head. "Aaron. Who needs *you*."

Mandy felt adrenaline coursing through her, strengthening and elevating her. "But the Company—"

"The Company is a company," said Faith. "It can control many things.

Many people. But do you think it can even comprehend…your heart? I cannot speak of other people's visions. But I am yours. And you.…"

Her voice trailed away. With subtle gestures, she drew Mandy's gaze to the holographic bird, cocking its feathered head on the branch alongside – the very bird that, in actuality, was sleeping in a box in her bedroom.

"You really *are* a goddess," said the woman.

Mandy began to giggle. "I guess that would break the tech."

"Yes. Yes. But it's no laughing matter!"

Mandy stopped smiling. The hologram began to shimmer and glitch. Only the woman's eyes flashed, unvarying, as all around her the scene transformed. Now she was wearing a breastplate and armor. A red desert spread about her, almost the color of blood. In one hand she gripped a spear. In the other was—

"Oh no!" Mandy drew in her breath sharply. It was the little bird's body, tattered and bleeding. "Is it dead?" she cried out.

"Aaron is troubled," the woman answered. "He is hurt. And he needs you."

"I know he does," said Mandy. "But what can I do?"

"Firstly," said the woman, "believe."

Then she was back in the forest, in her flowing robes, walking and looking with little smiles.

Mandy turned off the shrine. She felt overwhelmed, and at the same time lighthearted. She skipped her way to the bedroom to check on the bird in the box. It was breathing as before.

She sat on the bed, thinking of nothing, while a slow, building excitement grew in her. She looked at her polka-dotted pajamas. It occurred to her that she ought to change her clothes. Yes, that was the thing to do. A shower, her nice lilac dress, and then she would heat up the pasta from the fridge.

She had just gotten out of the shower when the doorbell rang. Mandy paused, naked, on the threshold of the bedroom, which, like the whole house, was suddenly unbearably bright.

CHAPTER NINE

Ignoring the bell, Mandy continued to get dressed, quietly. A whole ten minutes, and another extended ring, had passed into dead silence, before she ventured to approach the door, careful to keep her footsteps soundless. She raised her eyes to the peephole, hoping to see just the old familiar empty corridor.

Not so. There was a man sitting there – out in the hallway, leaning against the wall. A Company rucksack was slumped beside him.

Mandy recognized the face. Her thoughts moved quickly. Was it yet another delivery? Or could it possibly be some news about Aaron?

Moments later, hearing the door click open, Saionton raised himself to his feet.

"Hello!" He smiled in the most appealing way he knew.

Mandy watched him carefully, holding the door ajar and no more.

"I guess you remember me," said Saionton. "From yesterday. I hope your...." He paused to recollect. "Hope your Astral Creator is working well?"

"Yes, it's working fine," said Mandy.

The freshness of her presence – the bright glimpse of her dress – was already emanating down the hall. Saionton passed a hand through his hair.

"I'm glad. But I actually haven't come for customer feedback or anything like that. I've been thinking about what Mr. Sehgal said – about the shrines. And what's really going on. I was hoping I could learn more."

"I'm sorry," whispered Mandy, "Aaron's not at home."

Saionton felt a sudden euphoria. "Could I talk with you then? I'm actually more interested in your thoughts."

"My thoughts?"

"Yeah. See, I already spoke a little with Aaron – with Mr. Sehgal –

yesterday. But I thought you had plenty to say yourself, and I'd love to hear more."

"I'm sorry," said Mandy, "I'm not that interested in the shrines. I don't want to talk about it."

Saionton nodded. "I understand."

As she began to turn away, he collapsed with a loud sigh, falling into his old seating position. His head slumped forward, and his legs drew up around him.

Mandy stared. "What are you doing?"

"If you don't mind," pleaded Saionton, "could I keep sitting here a few minutes? I'm so tired. And I still have one more visit to make. I promise I'll leave soon."

"The society people wouldn't allow it," said Mandy.

"Oh, I hate this miserable city! It's killing me."

He plunged his head deeper out of sight, becoming altogether sorrier and more shapeless.

Mandy continued to look at him. So young. And broken down already. She thought briefly of her own college days. Her first and only job. Suddenly she noticed his feet, his green-and-white shoes, lolling wrongly in the middle of the corridor.

Something twisted inside of her, a sharp, stabbing pain that felt like exultation – because it was nothing like the other pain.

★   ★   ★

There was pasta to go around. And in fact, in the bright light, in her good dress (that showed her strong shoulders and her shining, slender arms) with the city and the darkness expelled from sight, she began to feel as cheerful as she had in months. Most of all, Saionton had perked up tremendously. It gratified Mandy's kindliness. He was good company.

"You're a really good cook," he said reverentially, as he helped himself to more pasta.

"Had a lot of practice," said Mandy, "You should learn to cook yourself. It'll help you in the future, later in life."

"But I never think about the future," said Saionton.

She gave him a long look.

Saionton laughed with abandon.

"It's more fun that way."

"So speaks the innocence of youth!"

"Well, we're both young," said Saionton.

His words ushered in a little silence. They seemed to smile by turns – between spoonfuls and sips of water – until Mandy set her face with grim deliberateness. A long sigh went trembling through her body.

"Who are you visiting ne—" she said.

"Is everything OK?" Saionton spoke simultaneously.

"Yes," said Mandy. "Who are you delivering to after this?"

"Oh, it'll be some crackpot."

"Is that how you think of your customers?"

Saionton grinned. "I don't know what to think. But just for instance, the last person I met told me Shrine Tech was a portal to hell. A hotline to the devil. So…."

"Who said that?" Mandy grimaced.

"A guy called Father Joachim. Catholic priest."

"Do you think," said Mandy, "that Aaron is a crackpot too? Why are you smiling?"

"The way you say that word," protested Saionton. "'Crackpot'. It's… funny!"

"I'm glad I'm entertaining you," said Mandy gravely.

"Seriously, I don't know," said Saionton. "I guess I'm not on the same wavelength as other people. It's like what you said outside. I agree with that. I'm also not bothered about the shrines or the Company, one way or the other. I'm just trying to make as much money as possible before I'm unemployed again. My goal is money."

"And after that?"

Saionton put down his fork and stretched his arms out blissfully.

"Endless amusement."

"But you're already doing that." Mandy smiled. Her mouth, however, felt heavy, her expressions effortful. Her own worry was suddenly returning to her, coming down on her like catastrophe.

"So do you have a girlfriend?" She began to speak quickly and conventionally.

"Oh, no."

"Well, you're young! Plenty of time!" Mandy forced more food into her mouth and chewed and smiled at the same time.

"You know something," said Saionton, "to be honest, I'd felt that you were in some kind of trouble. Yeah. I had a sense. Like a sixth sense."

"Oh?"

"Yes."

A silence came upon them, in which Mandy breathed deeply. "It doesn't matter," she said. "Who doesn't have trouble? Besides, it's how a person looks at it. In fact, I don't have troubles." She suddenly remembered the shrine's last word to her. "I have challenges. I have work to do. That's OK. I have powers too."

"You sure have the cooking superpower," said Saionton, at which she burst out laughing.

"And – and good taste," he continued. "Your house looks great."

She basked in his words, surging with relief and gratitude.

"But everyone," said Saionton, "isn't so blessed. Shall I tell you about the people I've met in the last two days? It's pretty hilarious! For instance, there's this building society manager."

He began to regale her with the stories of his encounters. He was witty and scathing. Aided by his words, she formed a mental picture of the lot of them: the fantastical Happy Maker, the odious Lance, the lascivious society manager, the self-important filmmaker, the fearful priest. Meanwhile, Saionton was all agog for her attention. He leaned forward as he spoke, and if she happened to glance away, at her phone or toward a window, then he stopped and hemmed and hawed until her gaze returned to him.

Suddenly she began to feel irritated. His face – clean-cut, shining with youthfulness – was ill-fitting with his plentiful judgments. He was obviously extremely anxious about himself, desperately keen to appear at a height far above other people – forgetting that just moments ago he had been curled up and complaining in the hallway. Perhaps it was all very normal young-person behavior. But what was she doing, hanging on the lips of a Holden Caulfield? Moreover, that he sought to commandeer her this way did not strike her as adolescent, but as essentially male. Tiresomely, annoyingly male.

She interrupted him eventually, smiling cheerfully. "Would you like some dessert?"

"Wait, I was telling you—"

"It's getting late. So let's finish eating, OK? Will you have tiramisu and coffee? Or just pastry, or just coffee?"

"Tiramisu sounds good," said Saionton. "I've had enough coffee today."

As he ate in silence, momentarily too absorbed to go on speaking, Mandy liked him again. The boy had a nice, thoughtful face. Thoughtfulness was what she liked best in Aaron's face too. But when Aaron became thoughtful, especially in recent times, it was generally only one thing he was thinking about, which was the Company. She couldn't quite say what Saionton had on his mind. His glance, however, kept flitting toward her. Then she noticed him hiding a smile.

"How is the tiramisu?"

"Oh, excellent!" he answered distractedly, and was again wreathed in smiles.

"Why are you smiling?"

"No reason." Saionton grinned.

"There must be some reason," suggested Mandy.

Me, for instance, she thought. *And how I've picked you up off the ground and strengthened you this evening.*

But, although his admiring glances were obvious, he didn't say that. Instead, Saionton became even more thoughtful.

"Why can't someone smile for no reason?" His gaze traveled beyond her, to some point over her shoulder. "Isn't that ideal? To just be glad!"

He looked at her then. Mandy saw that his guard was down, and his face quite flooded with innocence. He really was happy – and for no reason that he was willing to make understood. She felt a pang of some strange emotion. It was a cocktail of emotions.

"When you get older and wiser," Mandy said harshly, "you'll realize one needs a reason. There's a word that's used for people who smile for no reason."

The boy's face fell, and immediately she regretted her words. Then, all incongruous, a rap song broke out. It was his phone, ringing. A tremor of anxiety passed over Saionton's face, and he stood up, excusing himself.

"It's the Company calling."

"Go ahead," said Mandy.

She began clearing the plates – except for the small slice of pastry that remained on his. When she had finished, she stepped out into the now-quiet living room.

"That name you just said on the phone," inquired Mandy, "was it Jaspreet Bhatia? I know Jaspreet. He's a friend of Aaron's."

"He's my next client," said Saionton, nodding.

"Jaspreet runs a really nice Chinese restaurant in town. You'll like him. He's very sweet."

Saionton sat down again in an absent-minded way.

"He's at Company HQ right now. That was Lance calling to tell me. He's sitting on a protest at their campus gates."

"A protest?"

She hadn't heard the term for a long time. Once upon a time, news of protests had been ubiquitous – but that was in the time of governments.

"Lance didn't say what it's about. But I have to go there now."

"Oh, but that's out of the city, isn't it?"

"Two and a half hours' drive," said Saionton. "They've sent a car, of course, but...."

"Well," said Mandy, "I hope it's sorted out soon, whatever it is. You should finish eating first."

"I've finished."

"No, there's a little left." She nudged his plate toward him and then, on an impulse, walked across the room, toward the living room balcony. Parting the curtains, Mandy looked into the darkness. Down below the great shadows of buildings, a few lights gleamed bravely. The streets were quiet and lonely. She looked up for the moon and was glad to find it, aloft and beautiful, among gray clouds. It was so far away, though.

She turned, just in time to see Saionton drop his gaze. He was standing on the living room carpet, leaning somewhat awkwardly against the sofa. He had a book in his hand – a detective novel, that featured on its cover the bountiful decolletage of a curly-headed blonde – which he now shoved back onto the shelf from which he had gotten it.

"Interesting collection," said Saionton thoughtfully.

"It is. The philosophy stuff is mostly Aaron's. The pulp fiction is all mine. And the feminist lit. But we both read a lot."

"Scientology?"

"One of Aaron's interests. He's eclectic."

Saionton cleared his throat. "Tell me more about this Jaspreet guy."

"Well, he's a hard-working person," said Mandy. "Speaks very little and keeps to himself. He runs his restaurant in a hands-on way. He's always at the venue. Not at all like Aaron. He's not outspoken like Aaron either. I guess that's why I'm surprised to hear this – about the protest."

"Anyhow, it should be entertaining," drawled Saionton. Then he sighed. "I'll get going now."

"Wait," said Mandy. "Let me show you something."

He followed her wordlessly. She marched him to her bedroom, walking quickly, her heart thudding with sudden anxiety. Once inside, she pointed at the cardboard box that rested snugly by the money plant.

"Look!"

She had to repeat herself. Saionton stood uneasily in the cozy privacy of the bedroom, breathing in the perfumed air.

"But what is it?"

"Go and see," she said, and then giggled.

No sooner had he bent to the opening of the box, than the bird flew up, slapping his face with its wing before flapping up frantically toward the ceiling.

Mandy uttered a scream. Immediately, she slammed shut the bedroom door. The bird had flown up to the top of a cupboard. Saionton gazed at it, his hand still nursing his face.

"Are you hurt?"

"No, not hurt, but—"

"Open the balcony!" she commanded.

But was it really well enough to fly? Mandy got up on the bed and stood there on tiptoe, leaning forward, for as good a look at the little creature as was possible. The green-and-white bird trembled atop the cupboard, its head darting this way and that, its wings aflutter in readiness.

"Should I shoo it toward the balcony?" Saionton called out.

"No! Yes! Yes, do! But carefully. If she bumps into something—"

"Let's hope not."

Saionton approached, jumped up and waved his hands. The bird took flight. Opposite the cupboard, the balcony doors were drawn wide open, the empty night beckoning. The bird flew in a straight line into the darkness.

Mandy leaped gracefully off the bed and rushed outside after it.

"It's gone!" she cried out in anguish.

She was standing like that, gripping the steel railings and staring ahead of her, with her eyes large in her thin face, when Saionton drew up alongside.

"But that means it's fine," he pointed out. "Was it hurt before?"

Mandy said nothing, but only kept catching her breath.

"Why are you sad?" he wondered.

Her face twisted strangely.

"Because I wanted to take care of it. Oh, never mind!" she added, suddenly reaching for his hand and squeezing it. "Thank you for your help."

As for Saionton, in those seconds, which seemed to him both fleeting and languorous, his mind was alighting on her poetic face, and the soft shadows of her curves, and her damp skin in the cool night air. He swallowed, and spoke.

"Now it's my turn to fly away."

"Take care," said Mandy absently.

During the short walk back to the living room, he was suddenly churning with dissatisfaction. As he gathered up his rucksack, he saw her smiling at him.

"Now why are you smiling?" Saionton complained. "For no reason? When I smiled you called me mad."

"I'm just saying goodbye," said Mandy sharply. "And I didn't call you mad."

"You hinted at that. Anyway, perhaps I am mad. I know everybody else is. Honestly, everybody out there is mad. They're none of them normal people. I wish I could just...."

They were standing on the carpeting, in the space between the dining table and the sofa. It struck Mandy again that the boy was really out of his depth. His lower lip was trembling discreetly. Something fraught and confused lurked in his eyes. For a moment she wanted only that he should stay, remain near her, be soothed by her.

Of course, that wasn't only for his sake. She had a presentiment, also, of what would happen when he left, of how the emptiness of the apartment – every empty room and even the empty box in her bedroom – would suddenly descend upon her. It was intolerable even to imagine. But then there was the shrine room. Although she had not yet settled upon it, she was already waiting to return to it, and it was more than a certainty that she would.

Moreover, the expression in his eyes was uncomfortably intense. Mandy realized that Saionton was afraid – and she couldn't bear to be afraid.

"You'll be fine," she said. "I didn't call you mad, though. I just meant be honest about your feelings. You don't have to put up a happy facade all the time. It's OK that life gets you down."

"You're right," said Saionton. "But the same goes for you too. Like you said, you don't have troubles, only challenges?"

"Look," said Mandy, irritated. "Aaron and I have difficulties. That's one reason he's not here right now. But these things are a part of every relationship. What I know is that Aaron needs me even more right now, and also that I'm strong enough for the both of us. All right?"

"All right," said Saionton. "And I know it's OK if life gets me down. I mean, my parents both died when I was a kid. I was raised by an aunt who I'm not close to at all."

"I'm sorry to hear that," she said. But her voice was only neutral, not even sympathetic.

"Then last year I was diagnosed with cancer," he continued.

"Oh!" Mandy's eyes widened. "I'm so sorry!"

That had startled her, he noted grimly, and continued with this latter burst of pure invention.

"It's fine. I developed a set of tumors. They were removed, but the doctor said it can happen again. And then just now, this happened. I got this new mole, see?"

He touched the spot on his left cheek.

"I see it," said Mandy worriedly. "Oh no. Is it also…?"

"I'll be getting it checked soon," said Saionton bravely. "Well anyway, bye."

She inclined her head and put out her arms. He set down the rucksack and stepped into her embrace.

It lingered lengthily. Mandy drew back, held his face between her palms, and then, with the briefest significant pause, touched her lips to his forehead. Saionton's hands tightened about her shoulders. Then they broke away without a word.

CHAPTER TEN

From on high in Company HQ, Roshan Dubey, the Chief Happy Maker, stood by the great glass windows of his room – glass that was scrubbed and shined each morning to a perfect transparency – and regarded the sights below.

He saw that the protestors had arranged themselves in a semicircle, before a smattering of cheerleading figures. Among them was Jaspreet Bhatia, conspicuous in his favorite blue turban, with a confused petulance etched upon his baby face. They had just finished a bout of speeches and were now launching into a sloganeering session. The Happy Maker listened carefully and disapprovingly. It was amateur stuff.

"AI must die!"

"Roshan Dubey *hai hai!*"

"AI must die!"

Automatically, his eye traveled to the surroundings. The flag-stoned plaza, which the protestors had been allowed to enter, and where they were still discreetly girdled by the Company's security personnel, remained three quarters unoccupied. Around the knot of outsiders were visible smaller office buildings, a building that housed maintenance equipment, and a couple of auditoriums. Into the far distance ran the rest of the campus, with its innumerable facilities and amenities – under the moonlit sky in the verdant hills.

The Happy Maker breathed deeply and easily. Calming waves seemed to wash over him, almost in time to the protestors' shouts, which were so faint as to be agreeable, when considered purely as sounds. He closed his eyes.

Somewhere behind him, the office door opened and Lancelot Burns hustled his way inside, cursing softly.

"They refuse to fucking leave."

Roshan kept his back to him until Lance fell quiet, lingering sullenly. For the Happy Maker had gotten interested in something. He was studying the bodies in the little crowd. He saw that they were trying to make themselves fearsome, with their clinging together, and their group formations. And that was reasonable, as far as it went. But how sad, thought Roshan, that each individual body should be so absurd. He scanned the figures of the men and also the handful of women, who, from this standpoint, were but more misshapen men. What was the human appearance? No more than a set of protuberances. But why did it have to be so?

"We bear with so much," he said aloud.

"Don't we!" said Lance, grabbing the opportunity to be heard again. "I can ask security to clear them out right away. Shall I do that?"

"I'm talking about our bodies. Yes, bodies, our human bodies. They so affect our happiness. Right? However, we're saddled with them."

"Holograms allow mental transference to altered bodily states," said Lance busily.

"I am aware."

"Body-modification options are also increasingly affordable."

Turning from the window, the Happy Maker began to smile.

"You are easily pleased, Lance, and you are a willing slave. That's what I meant when I said we bear with so much. Never mind. Update me, please."

Lance inhaled lengthily. "I said right from the beginning—"

"And iron your shirt next time, if you don't mind. Shave properly, if possible. Right? Go on."

His unshaven face smarting, Lance Burns continued, "They should never have been allowed inside. I told the guards to send them packing. I don't know how, or why...." He trailed off meaningfully.

"It may have been my fault," said Roshan carelessly. "It seemed to me they were bringing a petition, and I asked to see it. I didn't really expect this occupation. Nevertheless, they are our customers. Why then do you look so disgusted?"

"I don't know what's gotten into you. We've got media waiting outside the gates now."

"The media too must do its duty," said Roshan piously.

He had begun to enjoy the mounting consternation on the other man's face. Besides, he really was feeling good, oddly enough. It was notable that the people below were chanting his name. True, they were wishing him ill – he, who worked to the bone for their happiness, and that of millions of others – but even so, he could not bring himself to regret this little disturbance. For one, it was diverting, and then the Happy Maker had an odd faith about it.

Arms akimbo, Lance continued to stare at him.

"Roshan. What do you want me to do with Bhatia and his mob?"

"You do nothing. Has the boy arrived yet?"

"Saionton? He's on his way."

"Send him up to me as soon as he arrives."

Saying so, he strolled over to the far corner of the room, at the farthest point from his cluttered desk, where, upon the lengths of empty carpeting, his own shrine remained – always on. Roshan made a certain gesture; the windows frosted over, and the room was plunged into privacy.

"If you'll excuse me...."

"Why are you obsessed with the delivery boy?" Lance blurted out uncontrollably.

"What are you implying?" said the Happy Maker, turning once again. "Are you implying something sexual?"

Lance's eyes widened. "God, no! Of course not! Why would you...." An enormous doubt seemed to arise in his mind, stifling his speech.

Roshan Dubey threw his head back and laughed.

"Any decision regarding the journalists?" said Lance angrily. "Should they be let in too?"

"Do I need to give you orders? You run the place, don't you?"

The American blushed. "Be serious, Roshan."

"But you do, right? You're the only one on this campus who knows where everything is. How everything works. Who everyone reports to. There's only thing you probably don't know."

"And what might that be?" said Lance wearily.

"Why any of it matters. Why does it matter, Lance?"

"The purpose of a business is to make money."

"Almost correct," said the Happy Maker meditatively. "Entirely incorrect. I'll talk to you later. Be sure to send him up. And not on the holo," he added with a wink. "In the flesh."

When Lance had gone, Roshan marched back toward his shrine – and dropped suddenly to his knees.

"You remind me," he beseeched.

Lights faded out around him, all through the room. Only a fringe of illumination formed a kind of alcove about the man and the machine, which was humming steadily. The Happy Maker's worship drew no attention to itself, produced no wonderful visions. His shrine, as he liked to put it, 'just worked'.

"The people," it said now. "Do everything for the people."

"Some of them want to kill me."

"In that case, all the more."

"We are agreed," said the Happy Maker.

"Fully realized individuals," droned the machine, "are automatically in agreement with their god."

"So I'm fully realized?"

Briefly, it chuckled. "You're certainly full."

"Of my—?"

"What," wondered his shrine, "do you really want to talk about?"

"I have a bad feeling," admitted Roshan. "Feeling pretty sure some bad things are going to happen to me. Can sense it in my bones. In fact, the last time I had this sensation was a couple of weeks before Alok – you know, before he killed himself."

"You've never felt it since then?"

"Not this powerfully."

"My sympathies," said the shrine. "These undefined feelings – these vague gnawings – they are the worst, right?"

"Disgusting," chimed the Happy Maker. "They go one way, then they go the other, then back again. What I hate most is the instability and lack of clarity."

"The mind is such," said the shrine. "The seat of happiness – but also, vulnerable to such negativity. Now listen to me. Ignore it completely. Everything that is vague. Simply throw it away. Reject it."

"Of course, that's what I try to do," said the Happy Maker, "but I'm a logical human being. So I need a logical explanation. How can I remain happy if these customers aren't happy?"

The shrine clicked loudly, a sound like knocking. Meanwhile, it had grown quiet in the room. There seemed to be a lull in the shouting below.

In a tired but patient voice, it continued. "Because it's part of a process. Allow me to explain. Axiomatically, the consumption of goods causes human happiness. However, human society features an unequal distribution of goods. Some people have a lot, some people have very little. Historical attempts to equalize this distribution have been colossal failures, and moreover are bound to be so, when one considers that the inequality extends to physical and mental abilities, talents, appetites, et cetera, et cetera. That is why the Company makes no attempt whatsoever to remodel society, the economy and so on."

Roshan grunted, nodding. He had settled down on the floor, cross-legged.

"However," continued the shrine, "these facts need pose no obstacle to universal human happiness. That is because, in the first place, no person, howsoever poor, is devoid of all goods. Everyone enjoys something. And then what is crucial: that happiness is a subjective experience. Therefore, theoretically, each person's subjectivity ought to be capable of transforming his or her consumption into a state of happiness. However, if this is to occur, subjectivity itself must be mastered, because from subjectivity springs up discontent, even these mysterious discontents we were just now speaking of. Subjectivity must be made objectively suitable for the task of being happy. This, the cognoscenti know, has been the great attempt of religion, which is as old as human history. Therefore, when the famous communist complained that religion was the opiate of the masses, he was right, though he looked at the matter upside down. He should have complained that it wasn't a sufficiently effective opiate. Are you with me?"

"I'm fine, go on."

"I will," said the shrine primly. "It is obvious that historical religions have been too crude, too broadly formulated, and hence unable to customize themselves to each person's personality. Result: humanity went on living unhappily – for centuries. Fast-forward to the game-changer: technology. The first breakthrough in the pursuit of happiness came about via social media. It was observed that, via the presentation of a personally curated image, subjectivity was objectivized to a degree that every user could be happy – insofar as they beheld their image. But then, you know what happened."

"It was a mess," said Roshan fervently. "Tribes and factions, insults and allegations, all kinds of conspiracy theories, violence exploding into the streets. Social media became a nightmare."

"Exactly. Via social media, the user's subjectivity had been developed toward happiness – yet not enough to overcome the weight of externalities. This made the disappointment even sharper – so unhappiness broke out all the more. As you know, that wave of feeling toppled governments. It might have raged on and on. In a sense it did, and does. However, it also entered a trough phase. During which the Company was able to establish itself, particularly in India."

"Never mind us," said the Happy Maker. "What about the human happiness quotient? Religions failed! Social media failed! Isn't Shrine Tech going to be the solution?"

"It is, indeed, the solution we have hoped for."

The machine paused. The renewed cries of Bhatia's mob rose up to fill the silence, raucousness, unruliness, insults that pressed upon his ears. He felt again deep pangs of anxiety.

"Give it time," said the shrine. "Recall that the vast majority of users are satisfied with their worship and thus happy with their lives."

"That doesn't matter," said the Happy Maker with irritation. The shrine's tone of weary fair-mindedness was starting to grate on him. "If anyone is protesting, it means everyone could protest. Anytime. It's a latent defect we're just starting to spot. It means that nobody is really happy yet. You know this!"

"While individuals may appear to be content with an esthetically determined worldview in which they personally rank high, it is true that the human being also seeks a structural transformation of the world. We may expect to witness this now."

"What does that mean?" said Roshan. "Wait, never mind. What are we going to do about it?"

"We must endure this necessary phase, while the 2.0 mechanism adjusts for a decisive solution."

"So I was right then. Things are going to get worse."

A low whining emerged from the machinery. The shrine was extending its pseudopodia. The Happy Maker put out his arms automatically. When he felt the warm metal on his skin, he closed his eyes, shuddering suddenly.

"However bad it gets," continued the shrine, "they are your customers, each one of them. Jaspreet Bhatia is your customer, a user of Shrine Tech 2.0."

"We know that. We've heard his ridiculous ideas – in his worship. But it wasn't supposed to go any further."

"May even their outrage be music to your ears."

And then it was. The shrine had encased him in an aural blanket, passing through which the angry syllables of the protestors dissolved into strains of the classical violin – Roshan's favorite.

He sighed, breathing easily, with his eyes still shut.

"You intend to make them happy," said the shrine, "and you shall."

"As nothing else can," said the Happy Maker.

"As nothing – and nobody – can."

"Happy. Happy in this world. Happy, despite everything. Happy with a vengeance!"

He opened his eyes. Suddenly the blood was coursing through him, like animal energy. He felt his lip curling, heard his voice emerging in a snarl that gratified him overwhelmingly. This was what he called worship – the ecstatic, the orgasmic.

"Fu–u–u–ck!" roared Roshan, springing to his feet.

★ ★ ★

It was fifteen minutes later that Saionton stood in the Chief Happy Maker's office, darting keen glances about the room. He was deadly tired, but high-functioning, almost as in a dream. Also, it was cold. The air-conditioning throughout the building was sibilantly pouring out cold.

"Hello," he said as he nodded at the boss, who was pacing back and forth between the desk and the windows. "It's nice to meet in person for a change."

"Is it? But in our ads we say that holo-tech is better than reality. Sharper resolution, right? Saionton! How are you doing?" The Happy Maker came toward him genially, but Saionton (for some reason) shivered and spoke quickly.

"What's going on in the plaza? Why are they protesting?"

"Patience, my friend. All in good time. First sit. I would like to ask you something."

Saionton seated himself at the boss's desk, with its many files and papers, but Roshan continued to pace the carpet.

"I want your opinion," he said, "about this: among the four customers you have met, who is most likely to want to hurt me? Never mind Aaron Sehgal. He's somewhere in Manali now, getting laid with the village girls, god bless him. Tell me about the other three. What do they think of me?"

"Well," said Saionton, thinking painfully of Mandy, "well, the building secretary, Mr. Rao, he sees the Company as a foreign invader. Apparently you're buying out his property? Well, so he wants to stop that deal. But I don't think he's a threat to you, personally. He has fantasies of being like Maharana Pratap versus the Mughals."

"A proud man," said Roshan somberly. "We appreciate that. Go on."

"Vivek – V – the movie director. He's pissed that people don't watch movies anymore. He says Shrine Tech is kind of sedating people's minds. Pacifying them. He wants to make a movie about the Company, kind of exposing all this. But I think that's his only goal, making a movie."

"In a sense," mused Roshan, "he is quite correct in his analysis. An intelligent man. And then you met the priest?"

"Father Joachim. Well, he might be the most dangerous one. I guess he believes there's a Holy War happening. He thinks shrines are satanic."

"From a Catholic standpoint," said Roshan thoughtfully, "it just might make sense. Why didn't you give him our gift, though?"

"Oh, I did. He threw it away. He says these gifts are spyware, that you're using them to spy on customers."

"Do you think he's right about that?"

"I have no idea," said Saionton.

The Happy Maker stopped ambling about, and began to laugh. When he had finished laughing heartily, he fixed Saionton with an ironic and world-weary look.

"It's in his own Bible. Love your enemies, pray for those who persecute you, bless those who curse you. Well, that's what we actually practice! Right? And the Catholic priest – of all people – he thinks it's spyware! I don't know whether to laugh or cry."

"They're all crazy," said Saionton.

"Right. But understand this. It's not their shrines that make them crazy. That's what Aaron Sehgal might say. Oh no. That's getting it backward. It's the human mind that produces the craziness. Sehgal was already a conspiracy theorist. That building secretary lives in the mythical past. V is movie mad. Mad, you understand? Father Joachim is a religious fanatic. And the shrines are trying to be the solution. Not just for these individuals, for everyone. Even the sanest of us are subject to insanities. That's why the Company is patient – as far as possible. We let them rant and rave – as much as we can handle. They are our customers."

His voice, as he spoke, had become sorrowful, and his expression ever more placid. He was standing quite near to Saionton now, with his arms folded, like a large and benign statue. Saionton felt struck with admiration. He was trembling, he felt, from pride – pride in the Happy Maker – and now he was glad for the blasts of cold in the office room, that made him tremble all the more.

As they both became quiet, the room thrummed steadily with the distant reverberations of unseen machinery. But the protestors were still crying out; in fact, they sounded rejuvenated.

Roshan broke away, sighing. He walked over to the far window. Saionton got up and followed.

"Bhatia's fixation," the boss explained, "has to do with AI. That's mostly his staff down there. Waiters, cooks, delivery boys. Bhatia has got it into his head that the Company is developing AI that's going to replace all human occupations. Starting with his restaurant, presumably. So he's trying to raise the alarm."

"That's been believed for a long time," Saionton pointed out. "In a general way."

"But it remains a pipe dream," said Roshan. "Technology can't even substitute for drivers, right. Not hardly. And everyone can see that."

"But something must have happened recently to give him this idea."

The Happy Maker said nothing, but shook his head, from side to side. Then he frowned. Dots of rain had begun to appear on the window, little dots and streaks all over the great glass sheets. It seemed that a drizzle had come up over the hillside, blown in by a watery wind.

"Wait here," he said. "I'll be back soon. Make yourself comfortable." He arched his eyebrows at Saionton, as though he particularly meant it.

In the empty office, Saionton strode quickly to the desk, and began thumbing through a pile of folders. It only took a few seconds to find the one he needed. *Housing Acquisitions*. The building secretary had been quite correct. Inside the file was a three-page legal opinion printed on stiff paper with a golden letterhead. Saionton did not read it, but took pictures of each page and then, after returning the document to the folder and the folder to the pile, stepped back toward the middle of the room.

The door opened and a short humanoid figure glided in on wheels. It was dressed in a blue kurta and white pajamas. The face was a child's, a plastic face, with a plastered smile, painted hair, and mechanically blinking eyes. But it was still cute to look at.

"Hari, meet Saionton." The Happy Maker stood beside the robot, his arm resting on its shoulder, and a wide smile on his own face. Saionton glanced from one figure to the other. He had the momentary sense of a family resemblance. As usual, however, when it came to machines, the eyes were the difference. The Happy Maker's small eyes were dancing with meaning; the child-bot, with its luxurious lashes, stared through two dark voids.

"Pleased to meet you Saionton!" it piped up suddenly. "I am Hari, and I welcome you."

"What does it do?" asked Saionton, who never knew what to say to children.

"It welcomes customers," Roshan replied. "Gives compliments, chats them up, offers discounts. That kind of thing. You're carrying a coupon code in your rucksack. Email that code to us, and we deliver this robot. This was going to be Bhatia's gift."

"I see," said Saionton.

"And it still shall be," said the Happy Maker grandly.

"But…that's ironic. If he's concerned about AI taking over jobs."

Roshan waved away the objection.

"What jobs can this take over? This robot can talk. It can't perform any physical functions. That's the whole story with machines. We can build them to do things, like washing machines. Or we can build them to say things, like Hari here. But human jobs require the ability to say and do all at once. Right? The human being is neither psyche nor soma, but a synthesis of both. Technology, I'm afraid to say, has not found any way to reproduce that synthesis. Just between you and me. We aren't even close to making people obsolete."

He looked so somber that Saionton laughed, but then checked himself, because the boss was frowning.

"I want you to take this down and present it to Bhatia. Explain to him that Hari here will welcome people off the street, and get them into his restaurant. Customers love welcome-bots. I'm sure Bhatia knows that too."

"How much does this cost?" wondered Saionton.

"Good question. Hari's market price is a lakh and a half. Tell him that too. All right? If you're done here, then…. Are you done here?"

"Yes." Saionton blushed, because the Happy Maker's eyes were boring into him strangely. "Of course. So I'll go down now."

"One more thing."

Saionton waited, his breath shortening with discomfort.

"Tell whoever wants to know about me. Tell them that I love them very much. All right?"

"What do you mean?"

"Hari, go to the plaza with Saionton."

He thought about asking again, but the child-bot was clapping its hands in delight, and the Happy Maker, nodding and murmuring to himself, had already turned his back to him.

CHAPTER ELEVEN

Even at the time, to say nothing of afterward, the episode in the plaza seemed to play out before Saionton's eyes, as though, being in the thick of it, he was also abstracted from it, like a prompter in a stage play, or a dreamer in a dream.

The drizzle had passed, and cleared the air. Now the night rolled through the hills, cold and brilliant, with a celestial audience in attendance. In the valley where the campus lay gleamed various powerful lights, each one throwing pools of shadows about clustering buildings, in whose darkened recesses myriad figures were lurking and watching – employees, security guards, journalists who had subverted their way inside. All eyes were on the plaza, a raised expanse of concrete, which the protestors had mounted and from where they continued to chant and shout. Some of the crowd were tearful now, because Jaspreet Bhatia had just finished recounting his life story: how his father had been a poor farmer in Bhatinda, and his destiny naught but working in the fields. But Jaspreet had run away from home, made his way in the city, worked odd jobs, built up his own business – and he would die before he saw it overtaken by machines. He would die; they were all willing to die; their voice, however, would never be silenced. But then the sight of Saionton, walking down the ramp from the main office building, hand in hand with the beautifully dressed child-bot, that glided noiselessly on good wheels, caused a kind of hush to fall over the gathering.

In that brooding silence, Saionton took in their faces and features. For the most part they were young men, in fashionable but cheap clothes, jeans and t-shirts flaunting fake brands, some wearing baseball caps, some with earphones plugged in, several with their mobile phones out. The few women were dressed demurely, but with strict, scowling faces, that both aged and infantilized them. Amongst them, like a caged creature, roamed Jaspreet Bhatia, barking instructions and exhortations with a fantastically fearful expression, made even more garish in the halogen lighting.

Besides, a bad smell was in the air, something strong and sickly sweet, like a whole lot of weed. *I do dislike crowds*, Saionton thought. But then he was grinning and speaking, explaining and demonstrating, with Hari the robot chiming in, showing what it could do, and Bhatia, at any rate, seeming to listen closely.

Soon, a space opened up, with the protestors and Saionton drawing back, and the kurta-clad bot wheeling its way forward. A thinly bearded man stepped forward for a closer look. They exchanged several sentences, he and the robot. Hari was cute and charming. A couple of the women were smiling. Then the bearded man raised his foot and kicked the little robot in the midriff, so that, still speaking, it fell over on its back.

After that, they closed in. A kind of grim joy was upon them. Saionton saw the robot's head being smashed on the concrete, the wires and circuits protruding colorfully, and its legs parted till the joints cracked, and its midriff thumped repeatedly, with kicks and stampings, till its lovely clothes were in tatters, and the steel and chrome beneath were first dented and then wrenched apart.

But to Saionton they paid no heed, neither at the time of the savagery, nor afterward, when shots were fired in the air, and uniformed policemen ran into the plaza, shouting for calm, closely followed by unruly journalists toting mikes and cameras. Yet with their rage spent on Hari, who lay in pieces, some burnt and smoking, others blinking and twitching, the protestors seemed well sated. Saionton heard Jaspreet Bhatia speaking fluently to the head officer, to the effect that they were law-abiding citizens merely raising their voices against the kind of technology that would certainly replace the police officers' own jobs, in due time. So they were all on the same side, and quite ready to co-operate for the present. Hearing him, Saionton had the irrational impulse to join the conversation, because the man sounded interesting, and he remembered then that Mandy had spoken well of him.

Then, suddenly, Lancelot Burns was upon the scene. He had raced in from the shadows, in his crumpled formal wear, looking close to tears, quivering with fury, and raining down a stream of accented abuse upon the protestors, who, in the meantime, were quietly turning themselves in. The police bade Lance be quiet, lest he incite the mob once more. But he couldn't help himself. There had never been such scenes on the campus he ran. He stood over the remains of Hari, lamenting the fallen robot, and crying out its monetary value, which was 'more than the whole bunch of them put together'. Afterward, latching on to Saionton, he tried first to berate him for what had happened, but because that was palpably unfair, then for not being more outraged about it. But Saionton shrugged him off and walked away toward an alcove, where a pair of benches sat in the shade of a tree.

And Lance had been provocative, because a final burst of sloganeering had fired up again, just as if (thought Saionton) a button had been pushed. Now, he couldn't see Bhatia among the crowd, only the young men in their happy frenzy (for they did, after all, seem happy), demanding the downfall of the Company, the glory of India, the greater glory of India, but then again, the downfall of Roshan Dubey.

Saionton turned his gaze upward. It was Roshan he was searching for, and he was not disappointed. In a lighted square, on the towering top floor of the main building, the Chief Happy Maker was visible to all. He was standing quite still, as he had through the whole dire proceedings. His face was grave, his arms fallen by his side. But his mouth, his eyes, his gently heaving chest, were struck through with...something. They were brimming over with some powerful emotion, which Saionton couldn't bring himself to name, because it made no sense.

"*Tell them that I love them.*"

★ ★ ★

Saionton spent the night at the Company guesthouse. The next morning, he was ordered to the local police station, to record a witness statement as to the night's events. When he arrived, however, the recording officer in his dank *sarkari* office was surrounded by sundry others raising their voices. So he was made to wait outside, in a sunlit courtyard, fenced in from a marketplace, where dreary people on dubious business stood or milled, or sat on the circular embankments built around the trunks of dusty trees.

"Are you all right?" asked the Company driver, who was his escort for the errand.

Saionton moved away to where he could be by himself. He felt sick and dizzy. But he had not been seated long when someone squatted down beside him.

It was a young man about his own age. His face was handsome, like a movie star's. He was well built, and showed it in a black t-shirt that had *London Calling* emblazoned upon it. He wore a necklace, from which dangled a cross, and he had an earring in his left ear. But what was most captivating was his smile, which was broad and friendly, and his eyes, that regarded Saionton with undisguised interest.

"You work for the Company." It was a statement, not a question.

He must have seen me coming in, reasoned Saionton, *in the Company car.*

"For how long?" inquired the young man. He spoke in Hindi, with a rustic accent.

"Not long," said Saionton.

"They are dangerous people. I know all about it. It's because of them I'm here."

He raised his head; Saionton followed his glance to where a pair of policemen stood smoking and conversing. One of them looked toward the young man, who smiled and waved.

"They framed me," said the young man, gazing back into Saionton's eyes.

"Framed you for what?"

"Murder. Shall I tell you about it?"

"OK."

"Because it might happen to you too. So I want to warn you, brother. Do you have a girlfriend?"

"No."

"I had a girlfriend. Then she got a job with the Company. They started to harass her. The boss, Roshan Dubey, he was forcing her to fuck him. Late at night they would send a car to her apartment. Like the car you came in. Late at night. They were blackmailing her too. Finally they killed her, because she threatened to expose them. But they framed me, because I was her boyfriend, and I used to live with her."

Saionton still felt dazed and under-slept, and drowsy in the heat. But some part of him was so alert that the hairs on his neck were standing on end.

"What was her name?" he asked.

"Zara. Zara Shah."

"So you were the watchman. Rashid."

The young man giggled, and looked bashful. "My name is Rashid. But I was never a watchman. That was just for show. Actually, I was living with her. It was not *haram*," he added hastily. "She had embraced Islam. We shared everything. She would tell me how much they were harassing her. Late at night," he returned, as though to a fixed point, "late at night they used to send their car—"

"Who killed her, then?" interrupted Saionton. "Who killed her and how?"

Out of the corner of his eye, he noticed one of the policemen, the fatter of the two, taking a step toward them.

"I was away that night, I don't know who." The young man held his gaze; his eyes were dark and earnest. "They sent someone from the Company to murder her. And then they framed me. For rape and murder. Can you imagine? It was easy for them because I used to live with her. Actually, I'm the one who took her to hospital."

Saionton looked away. He had suddenly remembered a certain detail from the news reports. How could he have forgotten it?

You took her head, he thought. Or had he spoken aloud? Surely not, and yet the young man's voice was now rising in annoyance, as though in response.

"She had wounds on her head. So I was trying to help her. So I took her head. Her body was fine. Why should I take her whole body to hospital? Everybody makes a big deal about that. Now I'm stuck with these cops. Ya Allah!"

The rotund policeman had cuffed him on the head. But having protested, Rashid got up dutifully.

"Don't encourage him," the policeman turned to admonish Saionton. "He is a huge liar. We say of such people, if their lips are moving, it means they're lying. We're taking him back to Taloja now. What's your business here? Well, you should go inside now, get it done. In another hour they'll break for lunch."

It did not seem to Saionton that the man had been lying, rather that he was mad, psychotic, delusional. Or possibly he was both – or neither. For a while the encounter lingered on Saionton's mind. But he didn't know what to make of it, and so it became like something extraordinarily interesting that palls, inexorably, until it devolves into less than nothing, i.e., an irritant. As was the case, he reckoned, with everything he had ever experienced.

After the formalities in the police station, he had finally been dropped off at his apartment in the city. It was late in the afternoon, hot and stuffy in the little rooms. But he disliked opening the windows, for the dust that came floating in. It was as sweaty at this hour as it became chilly after dark. Deranged: that's how the weather was too. After a quick drink of water, he collapsed onto the sofa and tossed and turned there. He was too tired to rest.

At length, however, he fell into a dream. In his dream, Saionton was standing among colorful villas, on a yellow brick pavement. It was nighttime, with spangly electric lighting streaming from overhead lamps, and a kind of glitter that hovered in the air. The weather, he perceived, was beautiful and bracing, for in the far darkness the sea was surging. He entered one of the villas, which he realized was his own to reside in, and began to get comfortable inside. He had just got the internet running at a good speed when the doors swung open and various people entered in a rush. At first, he tried to speak to them to ask what their business was, but it was soon obvious that that was pointless. Among them were the city's beggar children, prancing and clapping their hands, as well as myriad other strangers, with fierce, grinning visages that were obviously incapable of dialogue. It was an invasion, and the crowd grew thicker and thicker, until Saionton himself was swept outside the house, left to wander on the pavement.

Many hours later, he returned in the dead of night, carrying the hope that the mob had cleared away. At the front door, however, stood an impish figure in some kind of fancy dress. The imp was goading him to go inside – where booby traps had been set up for him, exquisite tortures that he would never guess. Saionton's heart sank. He went around the house and entered at the back door. When he made his way to the living room, it was full of strangers. They sat him down on the sofa and stood above him in menacing quiet. He began to talk politely, explaining that it was his villa and they were wrong to occupy it. But the figures talked back. At first he thought he could understand them, but as they went on talking, the words turned out be meaningless and only a continuous drone filled the room. As this was going on, suddenly he heard a commotion at the front entrance. A high, girlish voice was speaking – in words he could understand. It was Mandy! She had come to see him! But they wouldn't let her in. Tears pricked at Saionton's eyes, and he felt his strength breaking. There was nothing he could say or do. The faces were implacable, inhuman. And then something worse occurred to him. If they did let Mandy in, wouldn't the booby traps get her? That idea was so unbearable that he forced himself to wake up.

Upon waking, Saionton lay in contemplation for a while, annoyed at his defeat in the dream, but pleased also by his vivid imagination. He had just started to forget the dream when Kush walked into the room, wearing boxer shorts and a t-shirt with a Mario Miranda sketch of a buxom Goan woman waiting at a bus stop. They were each astonished to see the other – which reduced them both to laughter.

"What the hell, dude!" Kush exclaimed after a while. "You bought a shrine! How much is the Company paying you anyway?"

"They haven't paid me yet," said Saionton. "They gave me the shrine to try out. I don't know when they'll take it back."

"By the way, landlady wants to increase the rent."

"I know. Do more Goa trips," said Saionton bitterly.

A skirmish loomed. As a matter of fact, in the weeks before Kush left for Goa, they had been quarreling frequently, and always about trivialities – a chipped cup, a wet bathroom, a banal but suddenly offensive swear word. As far as Saionton was concerned, they were quarreling about nothing, simply despairing over everything. Two out-of-work actors, with none but dreary prospects, and that because the country had taken dreariness to its heart. What was out there, but the besetting dust? In which quarrels erupt like grass in the tropics. It seemed to Saionton that their only bulwark was...distractions.

However, he now had a fair number of these to recollect. And no doubt more to come, the thought of which cheered him.

"I made fifty K," he said suddenly, "in a side job. Want to hear?"

Then he told about Shailesh Rao and the beleaguered building Maharana Pratap, rounding off the story with its most recent development, that the legal opinion that Rao had pinned his hopes on was in fact in favor of the Company. He had already texted the photographs to Rao, who hadn't responded; he was probably too stunned to.

"Good you took the money in advance," cried Kush. "You've become damn smart with money, dude. Has V sent you cash too?"

"He will shortly," Saionton said with a smile. "I've got research for him."

Kush, grinning slackly, held up his hand and the boys high-fived. Then he disappeared into the kitchen, while Saionton reached for his phone. It had chimed twice while they talked: two new messages.

The first was from his bank. It reported a credit deposit in his account, courtesy of the Company. But the amount was one and a half times greater than what Saionton had expected. The second was from Roshan Dubey, requesting a word that night, or alternatively, the next morning. Saionton replied to him at once, and then returned to pore over the numbers in the other message. Tides of happiness were surging through him. He felt like laughing, because it was ridiculous, only a load of money, but how transformative it was to have gotten it – and from the Company. It was as though he'd been transported away from the apartment, above the humdrum streets, to some secret and exciting locale, where life was really lived – and all in the time that Kush had taken to fetch a Coke can from the fridge.

"I want to try the shrine," said Kush combatively.

"Sure," agreed Saionton. "Let me show it to you."

His thoughts were still pleasurably confused while he walked Kush to the Shrine Tech in his bedroom. However, no more was needed of him. Once notified of a new user's appearance, the shrine took over. Saionton watched as the neural link process got underway, with his flatmate, tall, gangly, and scruffy, finding it awkward to kneel, but complying.

"Should I leave?" wondered Saionton. "It can be kind of personal."

"Don't be daft,'" Kush called out. "I'm just curious anyway. I don't have to keep kneeling forever, right?

"I don't think you have to at all. I mean, strictly speaking, I don't think it.... OK, great, there you are!"

To Saionton's relief, Kush's god, as represented in the hologram, was not spectacularly NSFW. On the contrary, he felt a touch of envy.

A somewhat older, more mature version of Kush sat before them, in a crisp shirt and trousers, at a table clothed with a floral tablecloth, with a newspaper laid next to a plate of eggs and toast.

"What's up, my man?" the figure asked, nodding at Kush.

"Nothing much, what's up with you?"

"Enjoying my life. My work. My family."

As Saionton watched, a little boy ran into view and insisted on kissing the mature Kush on both cheeks. This darling was soon gathered up by a smiling, large-breasted woman in an off-the-shoulder dress, who made eyes roguishly at her man before departing the scene.

"What's on your mind, then?" asked the god.

"Nothing much, you tell me."

Saionton interjected. "You're supposed to talk to it. It'll give you advice and stuff."

Shh, motioned Kush. "I'm watching."

At his request, the hologram took him through various aspects of its existence. There was the business deal sealed over drinks; the squash game with friends in the club; the solo swimming session in the outdoor pool; the pre-bedtime mock-wrestling match with the flushed and healthy son.

"Do you mind?" said Kush, swiveling suddenly.

"You want to watch it having sex?" said Saionton.

"No," Kush lied. "They wouldn't show that anyway."

"The Tech will show you anything. Just use a condom, yeah."

"We always use a condom," boomed the hologram. "Except for those times when we don't."

His wife had come up beside him, and little winks and slaps were already underway.

"It's strange," said Saionton, "I feel like I've seen him somewhere before. Your hologram. I mean *him*. Not you. Do you also…?"

"Dude."

Kush's face was twisted now. He looked unpleasant and jittery.

"Please leave, *na*."

"It's my room," said Saionton quietly.

"For ten minutes!"

When Saionton had strolled back to the living room, not knowing whether to laugh or be angry, it suddenly came to him. He realized why the hologram had looked so familiar. It wasn't the central figure itself, but the lifestyle, the milieu, and most of all, the hearty and upbeat tone of it all, that struck deep chords of recognition. Kush had shut him out of the shrine, but if he wanted to reprise his flatmate's visions, he had only to switch on the television, and then wait – for the ads.

CHAPTER TWELVE

Television, in those days, consisted of news shows, talk shows, and advertising, of which advertising was by far the most interesting. The ratings reflected that. And it was particularly to watch a few ads that Saionton now sat himself in front of the TV. However, when the screen lit up to the six o'clock news – the daily bulletin – he didn't change the channel.

Jaspreet Bhatia was being interviewed live, at the entrance of his Chinese restaurant, on a street packed with onlookers. He was exulting, because the police had dropped all charges against himself and his crowd. This, however, he put down not to the Company's largesse, but to its fearfulness. Therefore, he was emboldened. He promised to keep raising his voice against 'anti-human AI' – the term he preferred.

He spoke well, and looked well, with his dark blue turban and his folded arms. His eyes, however, were troubled to a degree that made Saionton wonder. When he spoke of the onrushing tide of job-killing AI, Bhatia's voice trembled, as though he had seen and experienced the horrors of it. Moreover, the people around him – the strangers on the street – were nodding along emphatically, as though they had experienced it too. But none of them had, because the technology, as Roshan said, barely existed.

The telecast then moved to a series of soundbites from small-business owners in various parts of the city. They were all taken with the issue. A grocery store manager claimed he had been talking about it for a decade now, but 'nobody listened to me'. Then there was the perspiring owner of an auto garage, who wanted to make a different, though related point. He was an animal lover, who fed strays conscientiously. But the street animals, he had noticed, were becoming more and more vicious. They neither ate, nor roamed about, nor reacted to people in the normal way. Were they really dogs and cats, he was beginning to wonder, or the result of some covert biological experimentation at Company HQ? He just wanted to know – in case somebody was aware?

It was more interesting than the usual pablum, Saionton thought, and the anchors at the news desk had gobbled it up greedily. But the telecast concluded with a reassuring word from their side. There was no doubt, they both agreed, that the Company looked after the best interests of working men and women. The Company's good intentions – and its diligence and hard work – had been proved beyond doubt, time and again. Therefore, all concerns would be addressed, and all problems would be resolved, in a satisfactory way. Broad smiles appeared at this pronouncement and as the bulletin faded out on a triumphant jingle, the ads resumed.

Kush walked in, looking ashen-faced. He was squeezing his empty Coke can with great force. The two watched an invitation for bookings at a luxury apartment complex somewhere in the Western Ghats. When it was finished, Kush moved morosely to the kitchen. Saionton heard the thud of a cabinet door swinging open and shut. Then he started, as his flatmate's voice came raging.

"Fuck that! Fuck!"

"What happened?"

"Cockroaches!" Kush had reappeared, wild-eyed. "Fucking cockroaches everywhere."

"Oh that." Saionton grinned.

"What are you laughing at?" cried Kush. "They're not fucking pets." Then he picked his way through the room to the flat perch by the window, where, amid piles of clothing that needed to be washed, tangled phone and laptop chargers, and a stack of dusty papers, he sat down moodily.

Saionton regarded him from the sofa. "Why suddenly—"

"It's not sudden. The problem with you is you have no ambition."

"What are you saying?" Saionton couldn't help smiling.

"See? It's all a joke to you."

"I'm smiling because you're talking out of nowhere – out of the blue."

"Energy matters. Good vibes matter. To be honest, I went to Goa also to get away from *you*. You've really been getting me down. Especially recently."

"Oh really? Then why did you ask me to join you in Goa?"

"I was being polite, dude."

Saionton, who had stopped smiling, examined Kush closely. He was scowling at him, with a set and petulant expression.

"You have no plan for your career," complained Kush. "You're happy – just living like this. With filth and cockroaches."

"Who said I'm happy?"

"I don't know if you're happy or not. But you don't have any plan."

He was right about that, thought Saionton. But surely he was forgetting something.

"Well, I happen to have a job. Between the two of us, it's me who has the job."

"Delivery boy," enunciated Kush.

He had said it woundingly, but Saionton broke out into a broad smile again. "I think you're jealous."

Kush's scowl became uglier. "Because it's the Company? Because you're on salary? If you were acting, I might be jealous. I'm an actor. My goal is acting."

"There are no acting jobs at the Company *per se*. Except for brand ambassador. Which is asking too much, don't you think?"

"Actually," said Kush with a smirk, "the Company does use actors. For its holo-tech. For motion capture and animations and stuff."

"Why do they need actors for that? Anyway, I don't know about that."

"Yeah, you don't know." Kush sighed with satisfaction and leaned back against the wall. "Once my friend Ashwini starts her franchise, I'll be doing the ads for her. It's all settled."

"You've mentioned this before. It's all in the air."

"No, it's a plan. That's a concept you don't understand. Even this job you got – have you thought about how you can build on it? Now that you've got a foot in the door? The Company owns everything.... But no.

You're just amusing yourself, like you always do. If anyone else had got a break like this—"

"So you *are* jealous. Also, just a while back you were saying I've gotten smart with money."

Kush clicked his tongue dismissively. "Shady side deals that can blow up in your face. That's not planning!"

"You're the one who put me in touch with V."

"Fuck V! Another loser."

A flash of anger passed through Saionton, surprising him, but he let it pass as best he could. In the growing darkness, Kush's face looked angular and wolfish. He always was moody, but only about his own prospects, and with a natural bent toward optimism. The meanness in his eyes was something new and strange.

"I think," said Saionton, "you shouldn't be using Shrine Tech anymore."

"Why not?"

"You even get addicted to video games. And this feels much more real than that."

"It's not real," scoffed Kush. "Even the best holo-tech is just a momentary thing. And it still doesn't feel like reality. And the holo-tech on your shrine is an old version."

"I'd prefer if you don't use my shrine again."

Neither of them said anything for a while. Then Kush jumped up, his shadow swinging wildly onto the wall. Saionton tensed, watching him closely. He thought about switching on a light, because it was quite dark in the room now. But he preferred not to move.

A smile had appeared on Kush's face, unlike any he had seen before. He began stepping through the room, in long, gliding, dance-like strides, keeping his gaze trained on Saionton. At the turn to the corridor, he lingered, the malice in his grin leaping vividly.

Saionton swallowed. "Just leave the tech alone," he commanded, but the voice that emerged didn't sound like his own.

Moments later, a door slammed in the depths of the flat.

When night had well and truly descended, Saionton decided to go for a walk. Prior to leaving, however, he made a visit to his bedroom. The door to the room could not be locked, so he unplugged the Shrine Tech and put it in his cupboard, and locked that. Then he shut the bedroom door for good measure.

He felt petty as he did this – glancing now and then at Kush's own closed door, and pricking his ears for sounds from within. But a sixth sense was prevailing upon him. Whether for better or worse, he couldn't say.

Outside, the breeze smelled like freedom. It came rushing in, carrying all the cramped smells of the city, yet rising from above and beyond. Already, as he stepped forth, the branches were waving, the leaves were stirring. Already, the moon was sailing, the stray dogs running and tumbling, the life of the world there for the taking. In the night, all the ugliness of the city streets was transfigured, as in a painting, where each pile of garbage and each decrepit figure lying half dead on the pavement seemed etched with love. And even that ugliness that came out in the night alone – all the crime that was on the prowl – that too was larger than life, because the thought of it disturbed and alarmed him. But nothing about the night wearied him.

As he walked along, down darkened pavements past silent, hulking buildings, he came upon a familiar row of shops, with lighted fronts, that filled up the street with a dirty yellow haze, in which people were thronging. Gathering himself, Saionton picked his way through the figures, indifferent also to the interiors that beckoned with their sundry offerings. He only breathed freely again when he had entered the alley that ducked away from the marketplace. This stretch of road adjoined an empty park and the concrete back of some barricaded old mansion. There he strolled freely, away from pressing enclosures shouting out their value and utility, away from the clamminess of human minds.

It was not long, however, before the end of the walk was upon him. Naturally, it was his body that let him down. His legs had gotten tired. He kept sweating. But his mind also was hearkening back, as though, for all its flutterings at freedom, it was bound to make its home with crampedness and quarrels. Retracing his steps, Saionton threw many longing looks at the full moon – each time steadying himself with the ground underfoot.

But it was the moon he tried to hold on to, something, anything about it – the austerity, the loftiness, the beauty.

Then he thought, quite deliberately, of Mandy, standing in her dress in her living room. How their bodies had felt so magically close. How, afterward, she had pressed her lips to his forehead. Whatever closure she meant by that, whatever auntly affection she might have been feigning, it hadn't come off that way. She was drawn to him. Oh yes, she was drawn to him. That was why she had cradled his face in her hands.

About himself, he knew only that he had never been in love. Nor could it happen now. She was obviously too old for him. Strange, then, that it seemed the other way around. He thought of certain things she had said and done in his presence, in the two meetings they had had. Crazy. She was crazily youthful.

But he was an old, aching man who had never been in love. He turned into the gateway of his apartment complex. Then, before he entered the stairwell, he looked at the moon another time.

The moon has spots.

An ugly thought, considered Saionton, to have come away with. Not the one he would have chosen. But he was inside now. He climbed up the stairs and listened, unwillingly, to the tenement noises rising about him. Muffled voices, agitated about something. Snatches of film songs. Cupboards thudding shut. Footsteps, heavy; footsteps, fleeting.

When he arrived at the landing in front of his door, his stomach was heavy. It seemed to him that everything good and free lay in the open air, but everything twisted and oppressive lurked within four walls. And there was nowhere else to go.

Inside the flat, Kush was watching TV with glazed eyes. He had taken no notice of the door opening and closing.

"Had dinner?" inquired Saionton, as he wandered toward the kitchen. "Did you have dinner?"

Kush frowned and turned narrow eyes upon him.

"What's wrong with your face?"

"What's wrong with my face?"

"It looks different."

"Did you have—"

"Dude, are you my mom?"

Then Kush began to snicker. It wasn't like him to scoff at queries about food. He continued snickering to himself, until a slack-jawed smile lay foolishly about his lips. His gaze had turned back to the ads, which seemed to be entertaining him ever more. He shifted comfortably on the sofa, drawing his long legs up and settling in.

Saionton felt a dread, swimming sensation about him.

"You're the one," he managed to say, "who doesn't look right."

There was *khichdi* in the fridge, plus condiments from a Chinese restaurant that could go with it. But he had to have a shower before he ate. A pleasant prospect, given the sweat he had worked up.

When he had showered and dried himself, Saionton stood in front of the bathroom mirror, by his bedroom. Two closed doors insulated him from the hysterical overtures of the television. He felt clean and looked well, he believed. Leaning on tiptoe, he drew his face up close to the glass.

His hair did not sit perfectly to order, but that was nothing new. What was Kush talking about then?

Suddenly his gaze went to the mole. It was still there, the black mole near his left eye. However, it was the same size as before. The same color too. Unless he was very much mistaken. Which was possible.

He leaned in farther.

A wizened face gaped at him from the mirror. Folds of discolored skin were covered with bumps. Bunched up between them, two cruel eyes were shining. Down below, the horrible mouth began to stir.

Saionton gasped – and then ceased at once. There was no such thing. It was his own, good, young face, only twisted with (silly) anxiety. He was imagining things.

He glanced down at his stomach. There was another black mole by his navel. Also a fairly large one on the underside of his arm. He couldn't say he had ever seen either of them, but then, nor had he ever looked. It was all perfectly normal. These things came and went, or came and stayed. It was all the same. He had read about it.

His heart was still racing. He was tired and flustered. He needed to sleep. That was not something he usually thought about. But now he thought it was best if he could go to sleep and wake up fresh. After putting on a pair of boxer shorts, he stepped out of the bathroom.

You lied, sounded the words in his head, even as Saionton's bare feet touched the bedroom floor. *Do you remember you lied to her?*

This idea gave him pause. Then he smirked, and lowered himself onto the side of the bed. Seated there, he breathed deeply and pleasurably.

Of course I remember. I said I had had cancer. A total lie. And then – then she threw herself at me.

The more he recalled the episode the more irresistibly he felt compelled to relish it. Besides, a wave of defiance was moving through him.

I'll be punished for saying that, is that it? I said I had cancer when I hadn't. So now I really will get cancer?

If reality worked in such vindictive ways, Saionton reasoned, that was all the more reason to lie. Anyway, he had done Mandy no injustice. He had merely performed a kind of test, which brought out her true colors. She was already sexually attracted to him, because he had been exhausted and sat in her corridor and wailed. The woman had a savior complex. That was why she clung to a deadbeat like Sehgal. She was inclined to grab at any sob story. She had deserved the lie, and the proof was this: it had quickened her lust.

The twisted horny bitch.

He felt guilty for thinking that, but at once his thoughts revolted – against guilt. He hadn't done her any damage yet. But even if he did in the future, it would only be fitting. At this conclusion, a deep thrill ran through Saionton, sowing pleasure in every nerve and sinew. Possibly, he could lie and lie. And not just to Mandy. How thrilling it was, that nobody could tell what was in another person's mind, that this, in fact, was how reality worked.

He looked at the time. It was still early and now he didn't feel sleepy at all. He was tired, of course, even delirious. But to sleep was impossible. Nor could he step out again. He felt somewhat as he had in his school theater days, backstage before a show, with anticipation and anxiety crawling through his bones.

Saionton got to his feet, went to the cupboard, and pulled out the Shrine Tech, still nestled among his clothes exactly where he had hidden it. Then he texted Roshan Dubey. He wrote that he was sorry to text again, in response to the boss's query. But his schedule had cleared up. Could they have their meeting anytime tonight, instead of in the morning?

No sooner had he finished plugging in the Tech, than his phone lit up and chimed. The Happy Maker had sent back one word.

Now.

CHAPTER THIRTEEN

The ferryboat motored through dark, glistening waters. One bank of the water body lay in the shadows of trees and sloping wilderness. The other, toward which the boat moved, was a far-off promise of glittering urbanity.

The boat was well lit and equipped with yellow plastic seats around a concrete pillar that held up its roof. An area behind glass was cordoned off from the seating. In there, a shabby looking boatman stood working at some contraption of wheels and levers. His back was turned to Saionton.

There were no other passengers. With the ferry to himself, Saionton tried one seat after another for the vantage points they offered. He was inhaling deeply all the while. The air was not foul, as in the actual seascapes of Mumbai, but made bracing by the salt spray.

After some moments, he realized that the city lights were not drawing any closer. It was a fixed horizon. Only the water danced about the sides of the boat, a startled, changing thing. He gazed at it for a while, lost in the play of flowing, frothing liquid.

Whatever Kush might say, Saionton thought, the Shrine Tech's holo-tech could conjure up vivid scenes. It was true that its capacities were limited (this, for instance, was an endless ride to nowhere), and there was something undefinably ersatz about the sensations it conveyed. They were not precisely immediate but abstracted on the back of a faint electric tingle, that he felt with all five senses. But even so.

He peered into the water, trying to spot any repetitive patterns in its motion, and then up at the night sky, which was overcast and moonless.

The boat's engine had settled into a steady drone, bestriding the silence of the night.

There was no sign of Roshan, which was as usual. He obviously liked to keep people waiting. But this seemed, already, a longer wait than the other occasions.

Saionton stopped darting about, and closed his eyes where he sat. When he opened them again, the wind had quickened. Out in the darkness, the placid water was now stirring with white-topped waves. When he looked over the side of the boat, a sudden surge almost caught him in the face. The vessel rocked uneasily from side to side. Then came a sound of pellets firing. The noise stopped, and then struck up again and stayed. Up on the roof, and out on the water, the rain came down in streaks and sheets. The lights of the horizon were all but extinguished.

Automatically, he looked for the boatman, but the stanchion was obstructing his view. Saionton got up and staggered across to the other side of the boat. To his surprise, the glass-walled enclosure where he had sighted the man was now completely empty. The levers and wheels shuddered and spun of their own accord. As he paused, wonderingly, he heard a splitting noise that reverberated through the boat's flooring – and then the lights went out.

At the same time, the engine died. A reverent silence descended, in which the sounds of the storm alone reigned. He was now in darkness, in the rain, on a deserted boat, in a rising storm.

Saionton felt himself smiling with pleasure. There was no question of being afraid. He was, in fact, in his bedroom, and he could leave the holo-tech with a moment's decision. But he had no intention of doing that.

Moved by an instinct, he made his way to the railings, and gripped the rough steel with both hands. Then he leaned forward and peered into the tumult. The rain stroked and caressed his face. Wisps of clouds and white mist were moving over the waters. And there – yes, there was no mistake – a human figure was walking toward the boat.

"Sir!" Saionton cried out happily. "Is that you?"

The ghostly figure stopped its movement, and stood on the water, in the middle of the storm. It held out its hands.

"*Come!*" whispered a strange voice, that was carried swiftly on the breeze. "Do not be afraid."

Saionton stepped back from the railing. "No way!"

He began to laugh. Then, out on the water, the figure also threw its head back. Its laughter resounded in a raucous and familiar way. Thereupon, the figure began swinging its arms, and jogging upon the water, covering the distance at a surprising speed.

The lights in the boat flicked back on, the motor began to grind, and Saionton beheld the Happy Maker – hooded, in a thick, flowing black gown and leather sandals – clambering over the rails. He was bone dry.

"I hope you didn't have to wait too long," shouted Roshan, louder than the storm warranted.

"It's fine. I was enjoying the scene."

The Happy Maker grinned widely, showing both rows of teeth. "You like the sea? You like boat rides?"

Saionton nodded, and then shrugged. "I just like how random it is."

"Sorry?"

"I said I like how *random* it is."

"Not the sea? The storm?"

"Not really," said Saionton.

The boss's face, contorted in concentration, was hovering near his own. Then the Happy Maker raised his hand, and the wind died, and the waves collapsed into an utterly tranquil sea, upon which the ferryboat hummed languidly.

"Do you want to change the scene?" he inquired. "We can if you want. You want a beach? Mountaintop? How about downtown New York? Have you ever been?"

"No, no. It doesn't matter. It's all the same to me," confessed Saionton. "This is fine. I like this. I liked how you came walking on the water."

The Happy Maker continued to stare from up close. He was very still and expressionless, but his lips were twitching faintly and there was a light in his eyes, as of open fascination. It dawned on Saionton that it wasn't only the boss's getup, but his face itself that seemed to have acquired a different aspect since the first time they'd met. Then he had appeared vacant, with a foolish lolling in his features, and in his talk. That was the Happy Maker Saionton had been glad to bitch about to V. But now there rose before him a picture of concentration, possessed of some farsighted wisdom. In the severity of the black gown, Roshan cut a strangely noble figure.

Smiling suddenly, his head glided back.

"You're quite the young man," he said approvingly. "We've been speaking about you, you know. The bosses have their eye on you too. I want to share with you what's coming next.... *I am telling you these things before they happen, so that when they do happen*—"

He threw a glance at Saionton, as though this last intonation might mean something to him specially. But Saionton was wondering what Roshan meant by 'the bosses'. The Company's owners were a transnational group of multibillionaires. Did he mean to say that these fantastic personages were interested in a twenty-year-old delivery boy in Mumbai? It made no sense.

On the other hand, he could never really be confounded by anyone's interest in him. It was only their lack of interest that was agonizing and incomprehensible – every time he had experienced it.

"Sure, sir." Saionton nodded to compose himself, for his excitement was rising up, swarming through him in desperation.

With a flourish of his robe, the Happy Maker swiveled, and strode across to the far railing, beyond which the horizon lay like gold dust. Saionton followed him. Glancing around, he noticed that the boatman was back at the wheel.

"In my mind," mused Roshan, when Saionton had caught up to him, "we are thus tossed about on a stormy sea, in a little boat. An unreliable little boat. But we never lose sight of the destination. And we never stop believing in ourselves. Right?"

"Makes sense," said Saionton. "I saw on TV that you let the protestors go. Do you think they'll calm down now?"

"On the contrary. Many more protests will break out. But we shall continue to woo them. Each one of them. To woo them. Even when they respond to our sweetness with wrath.... Am I right?"

"But that doesn't sound logical," said Saionton.

Roshan looked at him with amusement.

"It is the logic of happiness. By the way, may I ask you something?

Have you ever made a woman happy? Never mind, you don't need to answer that. I'm only...." Again he brought his hooded face near, with an earnest and enigmatic look upon it. "I'm putting a thought in your head. The logic of happiness is the secret," Roshan resumed in stentorian tones. Suddenly, Saionton felt sleepy. But this was a guilty feeling, and he spurred himself to listen closely.

"It's the greatest secret that I am revealing to you. Everyone can feel happy. But only a chosen few know how to *make happiness*. And those who know this – and only this – and the whole of this – they are the Happy Makers. But this knowledge isn't for everyone. It is only for those who themselves are beyond. Beyond happiness. And unhappiness. What was that you said just now? *It doesn't matter. It's all the same to me.*"

"When I said that," Saionton replied, trying to keep his voice steady, "I thought there must be something wrong with me. And that was why you were kind of staring at me."

"One stares at potential." Roshan looked him full in the face. "One glances at perfection." He threw his eyes upward, and the whites of his eyes bulged astonishingly.

"And all the rest isn't worth a look. When you use the shrine –" he turned back to Saionton, "– what is the hologram that you visibly behold?"

"None. I don't see any."

"Neither do the Happy Makers. But let's put this into words. Suppose I ask you, what is your view of life? What is your goal in life? What would you answer?"

"You really want to know?"

The boss's arm, swathed in black, extended from the folds of cloth, and rested on Saionton's far shoulder.

"Please think of me...I won't say as a father. Please think of me as a friend."

Something shuddered through Saionton, a dam that yearned to burst. The feeling was so powerful it took him aback, and he fought it from force of habit. But when he was done blinking rapidly, his eyes were still wet.

He cleared his throat and shrugged.

"Life in this country is meaningless. And in other countries too," he added. "People get all excited about nothing. And they keep lying to themselves. And everything they do is dull and squalid, including the stuff they do for fun. But especially here, I think. It's just all dust and dirt here." He went on, with equanimity, not looking at the Happy Maker, but at the machine-made horizon. "That's my view of life, I guess. And my goal is to navigate it. Get to the other side, I guess. Just to do everything differently. Randomly. Something like that. I'm sorry, I can't express it very well."

"Perhaps I can help," said the Happy Maker. "Existence is squalid. You used the correct word. Therefore – *therefore* – you are *determined* to be *happy*. Right? And if it is even more squalid in this country. If people here are even more like, let's say rats—"

"Lab rats," said Saionton automatically.

"From your lips to God's ears! Did you hear that, up there? Lab rats! Well then, you are even more determined to be happy – in this city. Among these people. Now you understand why we've got to *make* happiness, out of the squalor that existence handed us. I am telling you the secret of alchemy, Saionton. How the base metal becomes gold. It's not just Bhatia or those others whom you met. As we speak, protestors are perking up all over. Crowds are forming all over the country. They hate my guts. But shall I tell you what a crowd reminds me of?"

"What?" said Saionton dutifully.

"Custard. A beautiful blob of custard. Fact is, it makes people happy to be part of a crowd. Right? Makes them feel warm and strong. Right now, protesting against me is making people happy. So how can I break them up? I just want them to come together all the more. All the more. Are you with me?"

"Sir, I had a question," said Saionton suddenly. "My salary got credited, and it was more than it should have been. Was that a mistake or…?"

"I told you long back to drop the sir." For the first time Roshan looked put out. "Is this still just a job to you? If you are so anxious to know, that's a bonus toward future assignments, which I am about to give you. Unless I change my mind."

"I have to keep track of money," said Saionton.

"I thought you said," the Happy Maker sneered, "it doesn't matter. It's all the same to you. Your life philosophy."

He was looking (to Saionton's surprise) more and more glumly petulant, under the shadow of his hood.

"That philosophy," explained Saionton, "is only possible when a person has some money. Otherwise it's not possible. I don't want money so that I can buy a whole lot of things. But you need the basics of life to be sorted – and then you can live freely, with randomness—"

Roshan shook his head violently. "Don't preach to me. You're the one who lacks the logic of happiness. You don't know what money's really about. The happiness of money, Saionton, is not what it gets you. Whether a little or a lot, neither is the point. The happiness is actually the happiness of papers – and numbers. It's the joy of a nothing – being regarded as everything – but all the while being *nothing*. It's the most exquisite happiness. However, you won't follow me right now. Fact is, you're scared. I see that something has scared you."

Out beyond the railing of the ferryboat, the clouds and mists had cleared away, and a beautiful stillness had fallen over the waters. They drifted on peacefully, under a night now bright with stars. Standing and gazing at the twinkling city, Saionton felt all the sting drawn from the boss's words. It didn't matter, anyway. The boat was moving, but it wasn't, the destination was in sight, but would never arrive, and there was no anxiety.

"I'm not at all scared," he said, without looking at the Happy Maker. "Here, I'm not scared. But I already told you, it's the country I don't like. The dustbowl. The crowds. The crowds don't remind me of…what they remind you of. To me they're like…."

A wave of fright engulfed him unawares.

"Go on, Saionton," said the Happy Maker gently.

"They're like tumors."

After a moment, Roshan spoke. "Are you afraid of death?"

"Yes," answered Saionton. "But I'm not afraid of dying. I mean, I'm not afraid of *being* dead. What bothers me is death – when it pulls the whole of life toward it. So that life itself becomes death. When it falls under its shadow."

Out of the corner of his eye, he perceived that the Happy Maker had bent close again, was regarding him intently.

"A living death," said the face next to him. "You're scared of that."

"Yes, exactly."

The face nodded. "Imagine that your fear is in your mouth. Are you imagining? Mix it in with your saliva. Go on. Imagine, Saionton. Mix it in…and hold it in your mouth. Now, watch me. Watch what I do."

Saionton turned to see the heavy-set, black-gowned figure leaning over the rails. The Happy Maker raised his head. A wet churning and hacking was sounding in his mouth. Then he spat up into the sky, and turned triumphantly.

"Now you do it."

Saionton laughed. "I can't spit like that. But I get the point."

"The fear is in your mouth, Saionton. Get rid of it!"

"Sir, I swallowed already."

He saw, or imagined he saw, the Happy Maker's face becoming absolutely rigid, with cheeks like plastic, and eyes like two dark stones. It was only a fraction of a moment. Then color and warmth had returned, the face had softened, and they were both strolling toward the middle of the deck.

"So long as you got the point," said Roshan. "Now, back to what's coming next. The reason I wanted to see you. Oh, my boy, what a time it is to be alive. Something amazing is about to happen. The whole city – almost this whole city – and then after that the country – they're going to be made *happy*. The Company in India is going to show the whole world *the way*. And you're going to have a ringside view of it. It will happen right in front of your eyes!"

They were walking faster, up and down the deck, as the Happy Maker's enthusiasm soared contagiously.

"But the protests," Saionton queried.

"Yes, I will be crucified. But I will rise again. I will be burned up like the great god Kama, but then reborn. I will drink the poison like

Shiva and live. I will be humbled like Krishna the charioteer, but conquer all. The people had begun to adore me. Now they are turning on me. But when I have finally succeeded in making them happy.... Whatever happens now, I want you to believe in me."

Saionton half nodded. "And my assignment?"

"That is your assignment. To believe in me. Besides that, you shall carry more blessings to the protestors."

What might V do, Saionton wondered, *if I tell him about this conversation?* Perhaps they could portray Roshan as a lunatic, in charge of an asylum, which was the Company. Lance another inmate. It could be funny viewing.

"I know what you're thinking," said the Happy Maker. "Gifts and blessings only provoke them more, like we saw with Bhatia. But we draw out their happiness, Saionton, whether it is for us or against us. We keep drawing out their happiness. So that when they've had their fill.... Have you ever seen an angry little child beating his fists against his mother? And what happens next? But you will see for yourself – if you believe.

"Maybe visit that building secretary first," he added vaguely. "He's been depressed ever since you sent him the lawyer's note. The one you took from my office."

With an effort, Saionton continued strolling, betraying no reaction. Once more, the thought pressed upon him that he could end the whole conversation at an instant's decision, and go to sleep in his bedroom. But because it was so easy to escape, he felt no threat.

They had come up near the boatman's enclosure, and the man inside the box was turning around. It was Lancelot Burns, looking, as usual, like a foul smell had been thrust under his nose.

"The secretary," Saionton began to speak, "thought that the legal opinion was different. That the Company wouldn't be allowed to buy the building."

The Happy Maker turned away and continued to walk. "I know. And I understand that many people might want a promising young man working for them. The Company does have rules, though."

"V wants to make videos about you. He asked me to help him with research. I think he wants to poke fun at you."

"I know. I know. I know."

Saionton glanced up at the Happy Maker, admiring him again, momentarily. A lofty mien was in the boss's face, and he stood tall and strong, with the plumage of his gown rippling about him.

"As per the rules, what you did is a firing offense. At minimum. But the rules are subject to my discretion. It is my desire that you continue doing everything they ask of you."

He turned his head with a look of triumph. Saionton suddenly felt like smiling, which made him burn with embarrassment. Surely there was something wrong with him. But he couldn't help himself. He wasn't surprised at anything that happened aboard the ferryboat. Even Lance's appearance had felt predictable after all.

He made his eyebrows dart up. "How come you want that?"

"Take a guess."

"I can't."

"It isn't for their sake. Using you like this is desperation on their part. But I want you to do it, because such jobs make you happy. It's not like we can think of the customers' happiness and ignore our own employees. Right?"

"Lance doesn't seem too happy."

The Happy Maker laughed lengthily.

"You're a new type to him. A rare bird. But I know your type. You're a guy who needs to explore, get behind the scenes. You need to see all sides of people. Learn about their ways. Their needs. How their strings are pulled. What makes them tick. So the bosses think, and I also agree, that these jobs are a part of your grooming. Even if in the short term they harm me. But not to worry – I won't let them harm me."

"I don't even want to do them," said Saionton truthfully.

"You must. I insist. These jobs are my gift to you. Just like I send gifts to the customers."

When they arrived, on their rounds, at the spot where the Happy Maker had clambered over the railings, he looked at Saionton again.

"What's the matter?"

"Nothing," replied Saionton.

But he felt that his heart was palpitating continuously. As though some inexorable force had it in its grip, and was squeezing. It was a force that knew him inside out – that always had him right where it wanted him. A grim, dreary, hostile force, which could hijack everything lighthearted in him.

"You're looking troubled."

"It's really nothing."

"Normally," said Roshan, "the penalty for corporate espionage is prison."

He threw his right leg over the railing. Saionton watched the waves heaving and hugging the hull.

"Lance will brief you further."

"Can I also?" asked Saionton. "Walk out on the water?"

The Happy Maker hoisted himself over the side of the boat, and landed with a splash on the water, as if he was stepping on puddles. When he had marched several paces into the sea, he turned around and beckoned.

"Come!"

Before stepping off, Saionton threw a glance at the boatman. But Lance seemed lost in his own thoughts. He was smiling to himself as he whirled the meaningless wheel.

The surface of the sea was like a tiled floor. He could stand firm, and not even feel the uneasiness of the waves. Once he perceived this, though every step was still an enormity to his eyes, his mind became nonchalant. It was rather like a video game, which had forgotten to program the 'swim' function. He ran the last few steps to catch up to Roshan.

They stood together, with the lighted boat before them, the vastness of the night, and the dark sea washing their feet.

The Happy Maker had thrown back his hood. A mess of salt-and-pepper hair stuck out over his grinning face, and blew about in the wind, over which he raised his voice.

"Look!"

The sea was altering. The waves, big and small, died down and then disappeared completely. The water had ceased to move, and had become a flat darkness, like the night sky. Then the darkness too dissipated, and they were standing on an immense sheet of glass. It was flawless in its transparency.

By the light of the stars, Saionton saw a clotted, moving mass that had no visible end. Below his feet, and around them, beneath the ferryboat, and on the other side of it, and all the way to the city lights, a mass of skin was moving beneath the glass. He saw arms and legs without number, the heads of men and women and children, breasts and nipples and genitals, hands and toes and buttocks. They were mashed together shapelessly, writhing bulbously. Every face, however, was stricken with terror, with mouths that seemed to open and close in gasps. The arms were flailing, the legs kicking, and the hair floating and trailing, as the whole naked mass drowned in the depths.

"*For now we see through a glass darkly,*" the Happy Maker intoned. "We have a lot of work to do, Saionton. I think Lance is calling you."

"I'll talk to him later," Saionton managed to say.

Then he was back in his bedroom, switching off the tech, and trying to forget whatever it was that he had just been shown. It seemed to Saionton that he had seen enough, and thought enough, for a long lifetime already. He turned to sleep, like a man bereaved.

CHAPTER FOURTEEN

In Lance Burns' office, the lights were always on. Unlike Roshan, he did not have a towering vantage point over the campus plaza, but instead a side office that overlooked a dark green lawn where a fountain quietly burbled, and the occasional employee strolled to and fro. It was not the office earmarked for him; that was a predictable floor below the CHM's. But he had chosen it, because it suited him perfectly, while illustrating, in his judgment, the folly of the kind of thinking (so widespread in this country), that conflated power with visibility and gradations of power with gradations of visibility. In fact, power resided simply in efficiency, just like a good office ought to be a place for meditation and concentration, not a thoroughfare for gawkers.

He liked to drop in at any time, and work with the screen. Much of everything that mattered to the Company was on the big screen on Lance's desk. Customer details, vendor details, subsidiaries, transactions, stocks and securities, RnD, protocols, legal filings, organizational structures, internal affairs, as well as troves of archival data that would take years for anyone to properly trawl through. Herein, depicted in lines, boxes, and charts, was the gargantuan machinery of the Company in India. It was a delight to Lance's soul to see the cogs in place, the wheels turning efficiently: producing, delivering, and grinding as designed. What he hated most was the idea of a spanner in the works, howsoever trivial, because he hated it on principle. Therefore, he kept a close eye on the lists of debtors and defaulters, to whom notices could be dispatched at the press of a button, and after that collection agents and impounders – and also others. But by the same token, he didn't look too closely at anything, for he was naggingly aware that the well-oiled machinery was an illusion, and that errors abounded. And he liked to maintain the illusion.

The office was his home. It seemed to him he had no other home in this country. It was too hot, too crowded, too listless, slack, and dusty. In India, he was frequently on the boil, incensed by some or the other inconvenience and confusion. Just that morning, a taxi had canceled three times with false excuses, a humiliation he had come to because of the breakdown of his car, which in turn (the mechanic had suggested, with a pleased and provoking smile) was owing to the besetting humidity.

Then there were the annoyances at work. Among the campus employees, who were his primary responsibility, he spotted an abundance of shoddiness: failed projects; deadlines not merely missed but mocked; a love of idling. In the wider sphere of operations, the picture was no prettier. Yet he rarely used his disciplinary powers, because it was no pleasure to wade into a human mess (in which a man might have to face disrespectful counteraccusations). In any case, the employees disliked him, because he was too removed from their day-to-day tasks. They only cared for the middle management, and the big bosses, who were too rarefied to be real to them. Lance, however, had actually to deal with Roshan, with his didacticizing about happiness and happy-making, which was becoming worse all the time, and then his strange new fascination with the delivery boy, who was simply a rude and light-headed kid.

However, all his inborn irritation melted away when he was plugged into the screen, performing necessary and appropriate tasks. Then he became a part of the Company, a valued and vital element of the greatest structure in the world.

That was how it had been, even a fortnight ago, even a week ago. Yet now, settling into his chair at 2 a.m., with thick darkness over the countryside, but the steady brightness of the panel lights above, he felt like a different person, a stranger to his own self. He was feeling things he hadn't felt before.

The Company in India was collapsing. And it was making him glad.

But it wasn't a guilty pleasure. No, he felt more responsible than ever. Furiously responsible. As the screen blinked and fired up, he caught a glimpse of himself reflected in its transient blackness. His face was pinched, his thin hair combed down. His eyes were baleful, a basilisk's eyes. There was the scar on his forehead. The bony musculature.

The sight of his face excited him. His fingers went darting over the keyboard, in the ethereal glow of the screen.

After much thought, having no other option, for the sake of the survival of the Company, I write to ask that immediate action be instituted against Roshan Dubey, Chief Happy Maker of the Company in India.

His decisions have failed to stop the protests against the Company in India, which have become unprecedented in their inflammatory potential. On the contrary, the CHM has effectively spurred on the uprising, as I shall indicate below. Even so, he acknowledges no errors of judgment, and continues to misuse his authority.

He paused then, to recollect the outrages. To the society secretary at Maharana Pratap, who had written pathetic letters begging to be spared from 'invasion', the Happy Maker had dispatched Saionton, with all kinds of assurances of personal goodwill and respect for the great legacy of the Maharana. Two days later, the secretary began a so-called fast-unto-death in his parking lot, where he was being made much of by a daily swelling crowd. Meanwhile, copycat protests against the 'foreigner' Company, in the name of various other historical and mythological luminaries (the country had a limitless supply), were springing up around the city.

Jaspreet Bhatia, who should have been arrested for trespass and destruction of property, had been left free to accelerate his lunatic movement against job-killing artificial intelligence. Small-business associations and trade unions were flocking to that cause.

A steady stream of derisory content was being pumped out onto the internet, for the sake of which people were even returning to the dead haunts of social media. In particular, the filmmaker known as V was producing clip after clip of lies about Shrine Tech and the Company, along with personal insinuations about the Happy Maker: his charlatanry, his likely corruption, his extramarital affairs, his mentally disturbed son. And all this after Roshan, with incredible lack of judgment, had offered to appear on V's video channel to be 'roasted' in person by the director.

All these blunders had been carried out by Roshan, through the instrumentality of Saionton. But the one that chafed Lance the most personally was the case of Father Joachim, the Catholic priest from Lokhandwala who was jabbering on about the devil and Satanism. In his case, Roshan had insisted that Lance himself attempt the ill-advised appeasement.

"Saionton must not go to him!" he had thundered. "*You* will go to him."

It was through such a mix of whimsicality and bullying that he was running the Company now. In hindsight, Lance regretted that he hadn't stood his ground. But he had buckled, eventually, and (in a historical first) a high-ranking Company functionary had gone personally delivering a parcel to a disgruntled customer. The priest, however, showed no interest in the gift and simply laid it aside. But Lance had also handed over a beautifully bound compilation of Bible verses, and these Joachim did read.

He had glanced through some of those verses himself. They were standard, sickly fare about loving your enemy, forgiving trespasses, keeping no record of wrongs.

Their effect on Father Joachim was miraculous – in the opposite direction. The old man's face had seized up, and then he had risen with eyes like thunder. Lance knew that instant that the peacemaking was a catastrophe.

Weakness, he wrote now, *is provocative, yet Roshan Dubey has continued to pursue a policy of weakness, in fact abject weakness, toward our most fanatical critics. The results are before us.*

Father Joachim Fernandes, hitherto unknown to the wider world, burst into the limelight the very day after Lance's visit. And there he remained, spewing out formulas that had long since faded from people's minds, but were evidently still strangely arousing. In a tract, first published in a widely shared and read blog post, and then in every format conceivable (including an interview with V, and screeds in newspapers, which, for their part, loved to fish in troubled waters), Joachim was tearing into the fabric of the Company's operations. His criticisms arched above the other protestors', while serving as a kind of sheltering umbrella that ennobled the whole set of cranks. In sum, he charged the Company with disrespecting the human soul. Through all their operations, through all their advertisements, they had violated the dignity of the human being. Creative man, made in the image of God, had been utterly reduced to a machine for production and consumption. The right to privacy, the right to fraternity, the right against misinformation, the right (he argued) to an authentic encounter with reality – these, and more, had been violated.

And he went on saying these things, because there was nobody to stop him. Even though the Company owned the news outlets. Perhaps Roshan figured he was simply a diversion, good for eyeballs and entertainment. No doubt the priest was all that – photogenic, with his willowy build and flashing eyes, and his charismatic, portentous speech. But he had real teeth besides, as any well-educated person (but was Roshan that?) could surely perceive. History testified that any sustained talk of *rights* spread like a fever. And sure enough, even the notorious *Indian intelligentsia* had now begun to stir, like long-embalmed fossils shaking off sediment, crawling out of seaweed and detritus. They, who for decades had chattered happily about nothing but economics (and alongside, about mythology), had begun to grasp after a kind of second youth, like some hideous old dowager pining for her debutante days. Lance had already noticed two op-eds, one about the Company needing to pay attention to people's cultural aspirations, and one about privacy, which chilled him. Like the sight of stray cockroaches, they indicated the quantities to come.

And there was a further element to the business with Joachim, which Lance, at any rate, wasn't blind to:

This Indian priest does not speak on his own behalf. Let us remember he is a Catholic priest. He is openly appealing to the authority of the Catholic Church. That is to say, the 'salt of the earth', 'the light of the world', the 'wisdom of the ages' for two and more millennia. As your excellencies will certainly appreciate, the Roman Catholic Church would be what the Company is. It is our one true rival in world affairs.

Lance jerked his chair back, got up, and walked in a roundabout way to the window. He was too full of bitterness to go on writing.

There was something he didn't understand, because it repelled him so. It was the whole language of rights, of pretending that one person was *owed* anything by any other. It was a sham, which had no basis in either philosophy or fact. Lance saw this transparently. Everything was simply a matter of competing interests, competing powers, calculations of strength and advantage. The only *rights* one could speak of arose from contracts, protocols, and standard operating procedures. And those had no halo about them. They were eminently defeasible.

Everybody, surely, was aware of this, at this late hour in human history. Then why, even now, was there discussion about rights – apart from contracts, protocols, and standard operating procedures? Why spoil the cleanliness of human interactions with this fantastical talk? Or was there some enjoyment to be had in it? As for him, it only made him hopping mad.

Down below, a bare cement walkway glowed steadily in the blaze of a halogen lamp. It was surrounded by deep, brilliant darkness. Not a soul was in sight.

At least the priest's emergence had spurred him to write to the board. So some good had come of it. But it still stank. Back in Boston, he had cut all his ties with the Church as soon as he reached the age of reason, and never looked back.

Returning to the screen, he still felt the need of a break. So he opened up another page. This contained a batch of grievances, pleas, and complaints, along with the ensuing back-and-forth. He scrolled through the communications, suddenly enjoying them a lot. The more he read, the gladder he became, which was surprising, because it was precisely such customers and employees who ordinarily aggravated him. But now – a revelation! – he heartily appreciated their ways.

In these letters from defaulters, complainers, cheaters and recalcitrants, he was addressed as: 'Your good self', 'Your excellency', 'Venerable and respected', 'Most deeply esteemed' – to name a few. The pleas – for leniency in matters of payment, for mercy in matters of discipline, for reprieves from prosecution, for refunds and compensation – were by turns threatening, cajoling and abject. And even when 'rights' were spoken of, nothing was meant by them, as the tone of the missive-writers made amply clear.

Naturally, he handled the mail imperiously, brushing aside the threats, and feigning indignation at the bribes, because the Company dealt with all petitioners from a position of overwhelming strength. But they were also *his* people, the Company's own, and he had discretion in various matters, to use as he willed.

Here was a girl, for example, college age, living in one of the posher parts of the capital. Accounts had flagged her case to him, because she was six months overdue on Shrine Tech payments, with interest and penalties growing greater than the principal. To sweeten her case, the girl had now sent Lance several photographs of herself, in her bedroom and bathroom, wearing nothing but lace underwear.

It was not a novel tack. Among mail like this, Lance received pictures of this kind every other day. They made no impression on him. Personally, he used a sex robot (that even now lay neatly dismantled in a briefcase in his office cupboard), and he disliked the appearance of flesh-and-blood women. Nevertheless, he lingered on this one.

It was because of her glance – nothing else. Robots had never quite replicated the *glance*.

He dashed off a formal reply, refusing all leniency and reiterating the amount due. But if she wrote again, he'd already decided to forgive her.

Then, before he turned back to the task at hand, he cast an eye over various other grievances, pulling them up randomly. The letters disgusted but also pleased him. In spite of himself, he suddenly welled up with admiration for these people, who seemed to have sprung from the womb whining and cringing with everything they had. Whatever would they do, wondered Lance, without a corresponding Great Power to block out their sun?

Suddenly, he shivered, getting goose bumps for no reason. He looked around at the carpets and fittings. The office itself was beautifully quiet. In the bowels of the building a water pump was howling. He liked the sound of it. He liked, also, the sanitized and manicured campus. And out beyond lay that blanket of darkness, beneath which this anguished country crept and crawled.

He remembered how the CHM had taunted him: *You're the only one…who knows where everything is. How everything works.* Yes, he was the only one who knew that – and more besides. It was Roshan who didn't know. It was *he* who knew what the boss ought to—

Lance steadied himself, and continued to type. He felt he was finding his voice now.

I'll be honest, your Excellencies. I don't know what the Catholic Church's agenda really is. But I know their rhetoric isn't a good fit with the Company's objectives. They can certainly be troublemakers. They've been around for thousands of years. They have their bases all over the world. And they love the sound of their own voices. Suppose they all start putting their weight behind Joachim Fernandes? With his kind of delusional passionate conviction?

My concern (he was going full-tilt now, writing, deleting, and amending without pausing) *is that tone he has, even more than the rhetoric itself. Catholics themselves are a fringe group in India. So are liberals, libertarians etc. But – if you'll indulge me in some observations – Indians of whatever affiliation love a good cheerleader. They love to get carried away on beds of words. There's one phrase they like a lot here: 'high thinking'. Which translates to wishy-washiness. And most of the time it fizzles out like wishy-washiness. The problem is if it doesn't fizzle out, if it builds up steam. In my opinion it's impossible to predict why or when that happens. You do see it with various babajis and god-men. On a minor scale. But it is happening now on a large scale. The point I'm making is, when the public here gets a taste of 'high thinking', on such a scale, in the best English newspapers and all that, then it can induce in them such enormous self-satisfaction, that no authority can any longer feel secure. Then all the people – with all their separate and contradictory causes – suddenly start remembering their age-old legacy of being smarter than everyone else put together, and more entitled than God almighty.*

It is my professional opinion that the Company's commercial operations in India are currently shaky, and in danger of collapse, if we allow this to go on. I mean, if we allow the public to develop such a contempt for our brand.

But what has prompted me to write to you posthaste is the news of a terribly inflammatory event that's coming up, which will catalyze this whole process, and that the CHM Roshan Dubey has again insisted upon encouraging. They're calling it a Mahasabha (literally – massive gathering). Representatives from all the big protesting groups (whom our misplaced kindness has spoiled individually, as I've explained already) are gathering to rant and rave together. Against the Company.

They're doing this over Shrine Tech. That's the easiest way to meet, of course. But they're also making a point of doing it with Company Tech, and in the Company's face, so to speak. They've demanded that privacy controls (which our neural analysis has already proven to be undesired at the customer level) be once again activated. In keeping with his attitude of acquiescence, Roshan agreed even to this. So from the date of the Mahasabha onward, our Shrine Tech will no longer even be collecting data!

Or had it stopped already? He wanted to be accurate. Lance moved his finger over the screen several times, until a directory of shrine users came up. Arbitrarily (he wasn't thinking about it) he searched out Saionton's name.

But he must have pressed twice – in the wrong place. The big screen had gone dark, and then become suffused with a dim glow. He was looking now at a narrow bed, with streaks of moonlight falling across it. On the bed a male figure tossed and turned and groaned audibly. It was Saionton. The bedsheets were all in a tangle, and wrapped around his midriff, like a rope. Every few seconds, his body heaved from one side to the other, falling with a thud and becoming perfectly still – then thrashing back the other way, like some trussed-up fish.

Frowning, Lance moved the image around with his finger. He was getting these images via the Shrine Tech. But the boy was in bed, he wasn't even using the tech, so why was it still streaming?

When he had turned the image all the way around, he saw the machine, whirring with its lights on, fanlike ears stirring, and a hologram atop it. The hologram was hideous.

It was a man's figure, wearing a black t-shirt and a large rosary. But there was no face – or rather, no visible eyes, or nose or lips. Everything was covered in bumps and growths.

Lance watched the Thing, watching Saionton, gasping in his bed.

Unlike the whole country of worshippers, Lance wasn't, himself, a fan of Shrine Tech. What he loved wasn't gizmos, but logistics. When he saw sights like this – some kind of glitch, obviously – it made him even more skeptical of technological utopias. But the horrible image lingered for a while in his mind, even after he had returned to his own work.

It has been one blunder after another and there is no telling what will happen next. I am compelled, therefore, to urge your Excellencies to replace Roshan Dubey immediately, as CHM of the Company in India, so that these fires can finally be put out.

Meanwhile, I am happy to share the most recent data with you, regarding the sales, profitability, and market expansion of the Company in India. Please find attached—

Just before he finished the email to the Board, Lance noticed that the young woman in the cute underwear had replied to him already. It was a cool and utterly altered message. She wrote that she had no intention of paying a rupee. Instead, she was demanding compensation – a fantastic sum. Shrine Tech, she said, was being used by the Company to spy on women's bodies, and to make them mentally, emotionally, and physically submissive. The Company's whole operation of blackmail and sexual slavery had recently been unmasked. She was going to join the outcry at the Parade Grounds the next morning.

And here he'd been liking her glance.

CHAPTER FIFTEEN

I have become, remembered the priest, *all things to all men, so that by all possible means...*

In armored boots, he was trudging up a scraggly hillside, on a broad, lengthy dust-path, hemmed in by grasses and thorny shrubs.

...I may save some.

But for that, he reminded himself, the avatar was inexcusably showy. But in view of this consideration, the *salus animarum*, it was indeed necessary to be this Knight. Everyone at the gathering would be in the garb of their shrine-created god. So he also, now that he was plunging into the drama, must appear in costume, as the Knight of the Cross.

His thoughts turned again to Saint Paul. He had begun, for obvious reasons, to feel especially close to the great evangelist. Paul of Tarsus, who had stood up in the Areopagus of Athens, and proclaimed, with all love and fear and trembling, the Unknown God before the city of idols. What was that Paul saying to him now?

The top of the hill was in his sights now, the white-hot sky unrolling before it. Joachim paused in the dust, leaning on his sword. He said, in deliberate succession, an Our Father, a Hail Mary and the Apostle's Creed. The Creed. That was reality. And this – all of it, from sky to toe – was naught but a simulation. But the souls within it were real. It was to the souls that the Lord was leading him.

After a few more steps, he became aware of a sound. It was a kind of whirring, filling up the air with increasing vigor. He began to walk faster. The buzzing and whirring and churning were rising up in waves, rising and not falling. He kept his gaze on the sky ahead, though it hurt his eyes. The sky was painfully bright, like light itself. Then the ground fell away beneath his vision. In one fell glance, he saw the *Mahasabha*.

And it saw him! The old man grimaced and grinned uncontrollably. Upon the great plain that had no end, save in the shimmering horizon, there sat, stood, strolled and squirmed a Leviathan, many-colored, many-sized, in high spirits. In the first seconds he spied the Hindu pantheon, both its greatest hits as well as lesser-known numbers. When that familiar shock had passed, he noticed the clusters of wild beasts and reptiles; cricket players and celebrities; kings, queens and warriors; lugubrious sadhus and smiling politicians. But there were also big clots of unknown men and women, in exotic finery (and some in white lab coats), typically muscular and voluptuous, and some of them gigantic, as tall as small trees, peering calmly into space. There were even animated lifeless objects – he saw an unmanned motorcycle, a copper mace with a huge head, some kind of grenade launcher on wheels, and two brightly painted Lamborghinis – swerving and gliding through the living mass – as well as a rocket ship about a hundred feet tall that stood gleaming in the sun. Nor did all the trees belong to the scrubland's vegetation. At least a few were Shrine Tech idols, attendees at the gathering, the *sabha*, waving their branches in his direction.

"My friends!" shouted Joachim ecstatically. He raised his sword, and a roar washed over him, reverberating in his ears, while he whispered to himself:

"...*a multitude which no one could count, from every nation and tribe and people and tongue....*"

Then he saw that about a third of the crowd was gazing at some point considerably to his right. And that the giants were looking exactly the other way. Glancing about, Joachim was surprised to see other gods – there stood Shiva, there stood Narasimhan – occupying various high ridges in the mountain face, and declaiming all the while with passionate gestures. In fact, yet more idols were climbing their way up, making for the nearest promontories, cheered on by sundry sections of the *sabha*.

As per the *Mahasabha*'s schedule, it was Father Joachim's hour to address it. Unless he had read the schedule wrong. Now he hesitated.

"Just begin," said a voice in his head.

Automatically, his gaze was drawn to a mango tree, located in a far corner of the field, which was slightly elevated like an embankment. Two young men reclined in the tree's shade. One was wearing a suit and drinking beer out of a mug. The other was fingering the dry grass and, in between, staring him full in the face. He recognized the Company's delivery boy.

"You can tune anybody in and out," Saionton said to him. "That's how the tech works. Whoever wants to, listens."

Up on the escarpment, Father Joachim now gathered his thoughts. Silence descended around him. Suddenly he could hear nothing, neither the roaring and groaning of the crowd, nor the exclamations of the other gods, though they were all still gesticulating. But he could concentrate on his own message – on his Gospel.

"My friends," he cried, "I wish to tell you all one thing. You are loved! You are all loved! You are loved beyond measure!"

"You don't have to shout," said Saionton. "We can hear you fine."

The Knight tuned out the interrupting voice, and continued at full volume.

"It is true that we all may worship in different ways. But dark times have brought us together. We are united in our common humanity! We are united in our fight against the abuse of human dignity! People of India, we salute you! We believe in you!"

Then he thought, *I speak in the name of the Church, and the Living God.*

It would be inappropriate, of course, to say that aloud to the gathering. Even Paul was circumspect in Athens. And what was the idolatry of Athens compared with this…this enormity?

A shudder ran through him. He looked upon the *sabha*, and felt himself wriggling in little spasms.

'You are all – we are all – hungry! And thirsty. For righteousness! And this unites us. Let us remember: we are humans, not consumers! We are humans, not consumers!"

As he spoke, he tuned in to whoever was listening. Leopards and giants and blue-faced *devtas* shouted back in a garbled roar. The Lamborghinis belched their horns.

Then he saw something that dazed him. It was a man-sized insect, rearing up on rows of hairy legs and jabbing its pincers together. Beside it, a bare-breasted woman with kohl-shadowed eyes stood clapping her hands, beating time, with a fixed and manic smile.

The Knight with the sign of the cross on his breastplate stepped back and sideways, suddenly afraid of the cliff he was on, of the fall below.

"Don't stop, Joachim," said another voice – this one like rushing water. "They want to hear more from you. Trust me! They need to hear your sense."

It was V, whirling about the *sabha* in his fiery avatar of eyes and mouths. It was obvious that the filmmaker was having an extraordinary time. He floated over the maidan like tumbleweed, now swooping in close, now pulling back in euphoric arcs.

"Isn't it fantastic! The passion! Can you feel their passion, Father!"

"God loves you," Joachim began to shriek, "just as you are! He loves you just as you are. He made you, my brothers and sisters. He made us all. I know all of us here want God. We crave him. We want his joy and peace in our lives. I tell you, it excites God's own heart to see your desire for him. You will surely receive your heart's desire! All that you – we – need to do is stop giving in to dark powers. Stop letting the Company oppress us! With tech that enslaves us! We are all gathered here using Shrine Tech. We are using it for our own purposes, not the Company's purposes. And the Company can't see us today. We have our privacy! But even that we had to demand! Until now we didn't even have that! Tell me, my brothers and sisters, does the Company serve you, or do you serve the Company? Is Shrine Tech your god? Or is God your god? Did we not know how to worship before Shrine Tech was invented? So when the *Mahasabha* is over – hear me now! – after the *Mahasabha* is over, I call upon you all – to boycott *Shrine Tech*!"

Waves of fervor carried forth in his voice and moved like a contagion through the massed gathering. Suddenly it became apparent how, until now, they had all been waiting, waiting through the words of praise, waiting through the words of hope, that these were strictly ceremonial, necessary and most excellent, but intended in anticipation of that other word, which like a flaming match to a tinder was going to set them ablaze. They had come, after all, to be set ablaze. And now Joachim, their chosen instigator, with his splendid old gravitas, had finished the ceremonial introductions, and spoken such a word, and with just that earnest tone and timbre that delighted them so.

Boycott. Boy-cott! It was enough. Gongs were struck and conches blown. The people began to cry out, as, from end to end of the maidan, the massive Leviathan heaved and shuddered.

From the hilltop, Joachim held his breath, moved by the beauty of the sight he beheld. It was so multifarious, so rich, so fervent, powerful as the world itself. He felt, at the same time, the clutches of some sorrow. But he could think nothing of it, because his heart was overwhelmed as, with an ecstatic sigh, the fire of hatred spread through the *sabha*.

A thousand flaming tongues gave vent to it. Everyone had begun speaking at the same time. Slogans and curses and imprecations fell like ashes from a shaking bed of aural frenzy. But more systematic speeches were also underway, from assorted high places around the great and dreary plain.

He tuned in to one of them. A large lady in a sari, the exact likeness of a famous politician, was addressing her cohort. She was calling for a mass abdication of Company-made products, through the time-honored means of drowning them in the holy River Ganga. The suggestion delighted her listeners, who began at once to make sweeping gestures of disgust and riddance. Meanwhile, on the next nearest ridge, a golden-brown vision of Lord Hanuman was mandating all who worked for the Company, or for companies owned by the Company, to strike from work until demands were met. He too was met with unstinting applause.

"There is no need," cut in Joachim, as he listened to the pair of them. "There is no need to be dramatic! Let us not take on pains we cannot bear. Almost every product is made under the Company. Everybody works under the Company. Let us simply boycott Shrine Tech! That will be enough."

But the fat lady was scowling fixedly. "There is *nothing* a devotee of Ma Ganga cannot do!"

The crowd before her exulted, swearing they would lay down their very lives. Then the Lord Hanuman began to remind whoever needed reminding that he was the abode of all wisdom, and the seat of all power, with a body like a mountain, with strength like herds of elephants, the supreme devotee of Lord Rama, before whom all living beings bowed, both in heaven and on earth, and in the nether regions of the world.

As he spoke of the earth, it suddenly shuddered, while high in the cloudless sky a ball of fire exploded. To the sound of screams and shouts of laughter, the grenade launcher was firing into the sky, while the Lamborghinis raced circles around it, revving up clouds of dust. As for the sloganeering, it had gathered force, and (all of a sudden, all together) had turned its ire in one direction.

The *Mahasabha*, in one voice, was crying for Roshan Dubey.

At the same time, a space was opening up in the middle of the visible maidan. The crowd surged backward, falling upon itself, and then surged forward again in trembling eagerness. Joachim, who had gotten on all fours when the ground shook, now straightened his armor-plated back for a better look.

About thirty or forty holographic renditions of Roshan Dubey were sitting cross-legged in a square, and wailing at the top of their voices. They tore off their ties, tore at their hair, and wrung their hands. They smeared dust upon their faces and mourned with open mouths. They were, in fact, leading the chanting, calling, by turns, the name of Roshan Dubey, and the name of the Happy Maker, demanding that Dubey give them justice, and that the Happy Maker fulfil their wants. Then, with an injection of anger, they cried for Roshan Dubey's doom and demise – and then again clamored for their due, from 'Mr. Happy Maker'. And the whole *sabha* was with them, even the speakers on the heights, even the stragglers in the margins.

Suddenly, an odd feeling came upon Father Joachim. The sun continued hot and harsh, but it felt as though night had fallen. This, he thought to himself, was what the old devotional books meant when they spoke of the darkness of a too-brilliant revelation.

Before him, the gathering converged, like an immense coziness, around the wailing group.

"The *sensus fidei*," the awe-struck Knight said aloud. "The people are right. The problem is *him*."

In a flash of rage, he thought of how the Company had mocked him with verses from scripture. But that was surely Roshan Dubey's idea. And Shrine Tech too – the very spirit of it – it bore the mark of a man. That man. Yes, surely, wherever there was Satan, *there was also a man*.

In the commotion and the spectacle, the old priest stood entranced. All the people, in all their varied and fantastic figures, were circling about the nucleus of the Happy Makers. He thought of riptides and whirlpools and cyclones. But the crowd surpassed the forces of nature. Countless parts were animated in one body and mind. Surely their cacophony was a creation beyond music.

No doubt, there were some jarring elements. A great deal of pushing and pulling and bickering, in the midst of the magnificent formation. Now that he noticed it, it was happening everywhere, though the squabbling was always quickly ironed over, and often with conciliatory hugs and handshakes that warmed the old man's heart.

Suddenly his gaze lighted on a woman wearing red, struggling her way through a group of bearded men in saffron and ochre. She was trying to cut through, toward the field's peripheries. Joachim watched as one of the men caught her by the waist and pulled her to himself. The woman spun around furiously and at once vanished. She reappeared on the far side of the cluster, from where she continued grimly toward a grove of trees.

Nobody, of course, could be attacked or molested during neural link. All they had to do was will against it. But it was unpleasant, thought the Knight, to have witnessed that.

Moreover, he couldn't help noticing a pair of Jesus Christs, holding hands and swaying, and continuing to ogle her.

"Do you mind if I share something? Excuse me, Mr. Joachim?"

He felt clammy fingers brushing against his own. Turning his head, he saw a bulky man, with a thin, receding hairline, and drops of perspiration lining his voluminous cheeks. The man was wearing a black coat and trousers, and smiling in an oily way that he probably considered inviting.

"It is regarding what you said about God's heart." The stranger's speech was monotonous and overloud, growing louder still for emphasis. "*Heart. Heart.* I said heart. Actually, what you call God is a life force. You cannot speak about its *heart*. Actually, there is no God, as such. May I explain, please?"

Joachim, who had made ready to say many things, suddenly felt unable to speak. The stranger's smile had broadened. He had struck up a pose atop the hill, and was looking over the writhing multitudes in a pleased, proprietary way. Then he sighed. His shoulders shook in a kind of giggle. He continued speaking with dreadful calm.

"God is a concept that human beings employ. It is for the sake of our concentration. It is like an operating system we like to use." He was standing very near to Joachim, explaining almost into his ear. "As you may know, it has been discovered by scientists that human beings keep on evolving and unlocking new features of their consciousness. The process is something like upgrading a machine. Actually, we are a kind of machine. If I may offer an analogy for your conside—"

The old man came to on a chair in his storeroom. His Shrine Tech was buzzing in front of him, plastic and metal warm from use, pseudopodia retracting with a whine. He felt the heat lingering on his arms and about his forehead. He felt, also, faintly nauseous, with a throbbing in his head.

Presently, however, the discomfort passed. He remembered the time. Mass at the old church began in twenty minutes. If he left straightaway, he could concelebrate with Father Alex, the parish priest.

And the *sabha* had been a success. He had spoken, and the people had heard.

Making the sign of the cross, he rose up straight and tall, as tall and straight as God had made him.

CHAPTER SIXTEEN

Lying on his back on the grass, capping his hand to his forehead, Saionton squinted at the sky.

"There's a hole in the sky," he muttered.

"A what?" said Kush. He was strolling about in the shade of the mango tree, drinking from his beer mug with a show of leisure that was somehow unconvincing. A complicated expression sat upon his face. He kept staring at the crowds, and tuning in to one speech after another. But Saionton had tuned them out.

"There's literally a hole in the sky. It hasn't rendered."

"Coz of your outdated machine."

"No-o-o," protested Saionton, "it's a bug in the code. That big white cloud has a missing patch."

The sight of it was making him smile. He thought of everyone in the *sabha* suddenly glancing up to notice that their sky was missing a piece. What would that do to their hot and bothered speeches, their sloganeering and their rage? They were literally just carrying on in the Company's world.

"What are you laughing about?" said Kush.

"All the world's a stage," said Saionton happily. "With broken set design." He turned his face to feel the well-rendered blades of grass brushing his cheeks. Sunlight fell on his eyes, and he closed them briefly.

"There's nothing funny about this, dude. This is actually damn serious. This is unbelievable! Stop looking at the sky," Kush continued excitedly. "Look at the *people*!"

Saionton felt his stomach muscles clenching. The sunshine and prickly warmth continued, and he had a blessed silence in his head, not the rumbling and thundering of the *sabha*. But he was shuddering within.

No sooner had Kush finished speaking, than little chills ran up and down Saionton's spine. He took a deep breath and spoke.

"Tell me what's happening. Is the priest still talking?"

"I think so. Maybe. I'm not listening to him right now."

"Then what are you doing?"

"I told you, dude. I'm looking at the *crowds*."

Saionton raised his head off the ground, straining to catch sight of his friend. Indeed, Kush's expression matched his tone of voice. His mouth hung partway open, there were earnest lines on his forehead, and his eyes were wild with a kind of gawking reverence; *stupidity*, thought Saionton. He fell back on the grass and looked again at the sky. It was momentarily overcast, with a dusty yellow sheen.

"What's so great about them? The richness and diversity? The colors of India? The ancient cultural whatever?"

"You're sick, dude. It's so much *life*. So much *energy*."

"Seventy per cent of the people you're looking at probably don't get even two meals a day."

"That doesn't mean they don't have life and energy."

"They're blindly following some fraud *pujari* or god-man. Those would be twenty per cent of the crowd."

"And the remaining ten per cent? Go on. Tell me all about the crowd you won't even look at."

"The remaining ten per cent," called out Saionton from the grass, "are people like us. Privileged types who have their own shrines and their own fantasies. And between all these –" he waved his right arm in a vague circular motion, "– nothing connects."

"Say what?"

"*Nothing connects!*" cried Saionton, and then he fell quiet, breathing hard and listening to the sound of it.

A shadow fell over him. A long, lean figure was looming above his body. Kush stood with legs splayed and one hand on his hip. In the other (where the beer mug had been) he now held a mango. He was bobbing it up and down, like a dumbbell.

"Mango?"

"Please. It's inedible."

"Your loss," said Kush, and hurled the fruit aside in the manner of a discus thrower. Saionton watched it strike the ground and jump onward, galvanized. Meanwhile, a balding, elderly man in black judicial robes, wearing a caste mark on his forehead, was strutting by. The mango hit him on the ankle. He hopped in surprise.

"Sorry, sir!" shouted Kush.

The Brahmin judge wagged his finger, but he wasn't angry. He nodded at Kush, who, suddenly animated by desperate joviality, did a namaste and bowed and nodded back all at once. Then, on a further impulse, Kush hurried over toward the old man, leaving Saionton where he lay.

In the grass now, it was hot and cloying. Saionton got up, swinging onto his two feet and wiping away the dust and clinging matter. Finally, he turned toward the maidan proper, where the thousands were thronging and shouting and dancing and (up on the mountain perches) also speaking slowly and portentously. He had muted all of it. He wondered whether to tune in to somebody. There was something going on, it appeared, in the very middle of the field.

Then his heart leaped. In the shifting crowds he had seen a flash of red. But now, though he strained and peered, he couldn't spot her again.

"India-a-a-a! India-a-a-a!" It was Kush, back again, screaming madly, with a lopsided grin on his face. He broke off, to gaze at Saionton.

"I feel sad for you," he said thoughtfully. "You don't get it! India is one only. It does connect. *Everything* connects! So what if people look different or talk different? That's just superficial. Deep down there is so much connection. Haven't you ever experienced it?"

"All this because an old guy smiled at you?"

"So sad you are! Even the Catholic father was talking about the same thing. 'The glory of our common humanity.' That's the phrase he used. I agree with him. And by the way, that just now was a *High Court judge.*"

"All these old men," said Saionton. "I hate their damn voices."

When he looked again, Kush was smiling amusedly. "They're good people at heart," he said quietly. Then he jerked his head toward the gathering. "We all are a family, Saionton."

"A family," repeated Saionton. There had appeared a nasty gleam in his eye. "If this is a family, then you must be the black sheep, Kush. You're a drinking, doping atheist. You'd be the world's greatest womanizer – if you could be. You're Westernized, you're deracinated. You call yourself a libertarian, don't you? You think girls should wear what they like and so on. But your *family* doesn't believe in anything like that. So how do you fit into this family? I'm curious."

At least that got rid of his supercilious smile. The comment about girls wearing what they liked was intended to cut Kush to the quick. That had been the specific theme of a memorable blow-up involving a certain college dean and one of Kush's ex-girlfriends.

Breathing heavily, sweating into his suit, Kush shook his head. "You'll never get it."

But there was less certainty in his tone, and more general irritability.

"Change takes time, bro," he continued, avoiding Saionton's eye. "I'm not saying I don't have disagreements with people. But at a deeper level we get along. Also, you don't just cut off from people because of some disagreements. That's really immature. I don't know how else to tell you."

"At what deeper level," said Saionton, "do you get along?"

"At the level of human beings. I told you already. Happiness. We all want to be happy, right?"

This answer evidently brought him relief, because when he had finished saying it, he laughed in an unpleasant way, and stalked a few steps nearer to where, beyond the grassy knoll, the great crowd teemed in the heat and dust. Then he began rocking on his heels, taking more swigs of tasteless, rendered beer from a bottomless mug, and nodding to himself, self-absorbed.

Saionton felt a sudden heaviness. It was closing in on him. He was staring at Kush, as though seeing him for the first time. But the dapper, handsome figure before him wasn't exactly Kush – and that was what had suddenly dawned on him. It was his shrine avatar, what he yearned to be.

The well-heeled man about town. The man from the ads. The successful man of the world.

"You're just scared," said Saionton. "You know which side your bread is buttered on. That's the reason that you want to belong. Even though you don't—"

Kush put a hand to his ear and shouted, "Say what? I can't hear you." Then his lips parted in a wide but nervous grin, and he pointed toward the maidan. "*Look!* Check it out!"

The idolaters of Roshan Dubey had emerged, with their broken, vengeful hearts, striking up their dirge. The rest of the crowd – the idolaters of gods and goddesses, of mountains and rivers, of men, women, and animals, of children, of machines, of power and lust, of cunning and beauty, of anything and everything – were swarming about them.

So they all wanted to be happy. Saionton was almost moved. The crowd possessed such verve and vigor (he was listening now, to its full-throated roars), and besides, such conviviality and co-operation, necessary co-operation. Even random acts of kindness.

Yet it was none of that which impressed him. His ears were not muffled. He could hear the bestial timbre in the raving. His eyes were not befuddled. He could see how mean and pinched each figure, for even the most grandly bedizened god was but part of a crowd. Even the most aloof saint on the mountaintops was set off – by the crowd. They were, therefore, a blur and a tangle, whoever they were. He thought of the network of human bodies and faces that the Happy Maker had shown him, out on the fathoms-deep sea. He thought of tumors and cancers.

It was the nadir of ugliness. And this, inexplicably, took his breath away, as a new feeling stirred up in him, as sudden and unexpected as it was…arousing.

"We have a lot of work to do," Saionton recalled.

"What did you say?" Kush, smiling shakily, was coming back toward him in large strides. He was obviously fearful, and trying not to show it. Mortar exploded in the sky, another burst from the grenade launcher.

"I was quoting my boss, Mr. Roshan Dubey," Saionton said with a smile. "Something that he once said to me."

"Your boss! I wouldn't want to be in his shoes right now!"

"Oh really, why is that?"

"Can't you hear?" exclaimed Kush. "They're mad at him!"

"I hear the noise."

"I actually feel a little bad for him. It's a bit unfair, isn't it? He's only one man."

"He's the Chief Happy Maker." Saionton shrugged.

"That doesn't mean he can solve the whole country's problems! I feel like people are taking out all their grouses on him. I mean, real or imagined. Everything!"

Saionton laughed. "What's the difference? They're not happy. He's the Happy Maker. He's the one who puts out all the ads. Their life isn't like the ads. Go figure."

Kush stared blankly at him. Then he licked his lips and swallowed anxiously.

"I think most people here are middle class. Even upper middle class. I think your percentages were wrong. It's not seventy per cent poor and twenty per cent—"

"Maybe it's not," said Saionton graciously.

"So then if a lot of people here are well-off—"

"So what? They still have shitty lives." A sharp bitterness had entered Saionton's tone.

"I guess they're more educated, so they know their rights and all."

"Mediocre. Self-loathing. Always grasping, always neurotic. Between the grasping and the neurotic, you've covered all our well-to-do. Haven't you?"

"But Roshan isn't like that."

Saionton shot a glance at Kush, who was still standing about off-kilter, by turns frowning and gaping at the crowd.

After the hostility he'd suddenly displayed, the first day he used Shrine Tech, he'd been his normal self again. Or so Saionton had believed. But now it seemed to him that the boy was unusually expressive – and what was coming out was talkative and agonized, in a way that alienated Saionton even more than when they'd simply fought.

"He's a really successful businessman. I mean, he's really a success story," Kush continued. "He's quite inspirational, as a matter of fact. But I do get their concerns. Some of them are probably valid. Some of what the priest was saying, it's probably valid. But overall...I don't know."

"So whose side are you on?" said Saionton sardonically, at which Kush flashed him a dirty look.

But it didn't last. The abstract confusion came over him again. "I think he should just speak to them," said Kush. "Probably that's all that's needed. Whatever are the valid concerns, address them, and whatever are just rumors and imagination – clarify those, and then once that's—"

"I wouldn't worry about the CHM," said Saionton. "I'm pretty sure he'll be fine."

"You really think so?" Kush said eagerly.

Then the wailing of the public attained a new crescendo – rending, passionate, overweening.

Kush jerked his head aside. "Wow! It's a sight, isn't it! Do you know something, Saionton? This is something historic, what we're seeing. We're *privileged* to be seeing this. Right? What? You don't think so?"

"I didn't say that."

Suddenly his flatmate smirked abominably. "This is why life passes you by."

For a moment Saionton wanted to hit him. He was able to restrain himself, but at the price of a wordless contempt that rose up and teemed in him, and slanted his own lips in scorn. He walked away from Kush and took up another vantage point on the slope.

He remembered, vaguely, Roshan's prophecies, uttered on the ferryboat. Not that he understood them, either then or now. But he had an inkling of what was happening. It was such an inkling that, even inarticulate, made him breathless and secretly delighted. He had only to think of it, to forget about Kush's pronouncements, even to feel sorry for him.

Then his eyes grew wide. Mandy, wearing bright red, her hair cropped, but unmistakably Mandy, had broken free from the clamor and was hurrying past toward open ground. She was ten feet away from him – but practically running.

He called her name, but when she kept going, realized that she had probably tuned all audio out. Saionton began to stir, and then broke into a run himself. Out of the corner of his eye, he saw Kush swiveling, staring.

He caught up to her when she stopped suddenly, in the middle of nowhere, with the sun beating down remorselessly. The farther one got from the crowd, the less of anything was rendered. There were no trees nearby, but only dust and grass and shrubs.

"Oh, it's you."

She seemed to think nothing of seeing him there. Briefly, her gaze went over his shoulder; then her eyes were on him, betraying nothing.

Saionton was engulfed in strange happiness. "How are you?" he managed to say. "It's a cool…avatar you have!"

"Thank you."

"You needn't return the compliment," he said and laughed quickly. "I know I look just the same."

"No, you don't." She looked at him thoughtfully. "You look different."

"In what way?"

"Older, I think."

"Actually, I've not been sleeping well," explained Saionton. "I only get a few hours every night. Very disturbed sleep. I don't know why. I think it's the weather. It keeps changing all night. Hot, then humid, then chilly. I don't know."

"It's not a bad look," said Mandy indifferently. Then she cocked her head. "How are things at the Company?"

Her expression was so pensive it made Saionton grin. "They're not peachy. As you can see!"

"No, I mean, what are your bosses saying? Do they have a plan?"

Saionton hesitated. Her eyes were fixed on him strangely. A dusty breeze was blowing about, and the noise of the crowd was still near. He muted it completely, the better to concentrate.

"I'm not sure," he said. "They seem confident they can win people over. I don't see it working though. So far, it's only getting worse. Like with Jaspreet, your friend. The one you told me about that day."

That day. He lingered on the memory, inviting her to do the same. The day they had eaten together, had talked of everything and nothing, had stood in each other's arms.

That was how it seemed to him. But she stood motionless, with only the cloth of her robes fluttering about her body, and the crease of a frown on her marble-like face.

"This all began with Jaspreet," concluded Saionton.

Suddenly Mandy shook her head. "No. This began with Zara."

"Oh. You mean with her death?"

"No," Mandy continued fixedly. "I'm talking about the mind control. That began with her ads. It was her ads that got people hooked on Shrine Tech to start with. That's what Aaron never realized. She wasn't a victim. She was a part of the whole cabal. If you ask me, she's not even *dead*."

Saionton felt the conversation slipping away alarmingly. Chagrin and alarm knocked about inside him. But he tried to seem interested. "Not dead? How is that possible?"

"They paid her to fake her death. Paid a guy to take the rap. Then she got a plastic surgeon, moved to the Bahamas or wherever and continued with her life. Easiest thing in the world."

"Why would the Company do that? Her death made so many people sad. And angry."

She looked up at him with a light in her eye. It was terribly appealing, thought Saionton. It made her look like a young child. Her voice too was endearingly energetic.

"And then Shrine Tech sales went through the roof," she cried. "Don't you get it? First they mess with people. Then they come and console them with holographic prayer meets and whatnot. It was just a *marketing* technique. It was the culmination of her ad campaign. Like now, they probably want to boost usage. So all this *awful* crowd—"

"It is awful!" said Saionton gladly.

"Don't interrupt. I'm saying, all this crowd has been *mind controlled* to throw this tantrum together. So that the Company people can then show up and placate them. Then they'll feel how powerful this *sabha* of theirs was. And they'll be even more attached to Shrine Tech, and be mind controlled by it even more. Next thing you know, they'll all be paying taxes to the Company."

"Sounds like a really toxic relationship."

"It is," said Mandy, with no hint of irony. "Totally." Then she added, "And it all got going with that *female*."

An intense irritation surged through Saionton. All that imagination – for jealousy's sake – and on account of a fool like Sehgal.

"You didn't listen to what I said, Mandy," he said sharply. "I've been at the Company, so I know. The people there never wanted this anger. They haven't been able to placate anyone. I told you, they've been trying. And it keeps getting worse. This is not their planning. This is not their mind control. Aaron was all wrong about mind control! You're just—"

He paused to swallow down the bitter words. *You're just parroting your boyfriend's theories*. Then he continued. "The people are doing all this themselves. Also, Zara Shah really was killed. I met her killer. And *he* wasn't mind-controlled either. He never even used Shrine Tech. He was just crazy himself. I think he was super-religious. Anyway, he was crazy."

"Hold on," said Mandy. "I'm just what?"

Saionton stared at her, then averted his gaze. Her voice was deeper now, her eyes deep and scrutinizing pools.

"You think I'm just parroting Aaron's ideas."

He glanced up at her in amazement.

"And you think you know what's really going on, because – wait for it – someone at the Company has told you!"

That made him smile. He felt his face coloring, with a (somehow welcome) embarrassment. "You're saying I'm mind-controlled too?"

"I don't know. Could be. I'm saying you're pretty innocent. So is Aaron. You're both extremely innocent. If you can't tell –" her eyebrows arched attractively, "– how *sinister* this whole *sabha* is."

A smile lay on her lips now, and the familiar, irrational happiness was rushing over Saionton.

"On that," said Saionton, "I agree with you. You put it perfectly. And about the rest, I don't know. So, I'm sorry about my tone. You've been giving this a lot of thought."

"Because I care," said Mandy.

He saw, or thought he saw, Mandy sighing, her shoulders rising and falling.

Saionton's heart was thudding, and his tongue passed quickly over his lips, because his lips were dry.

"You know," he said, "you're really beautiful."

"Thank you."

"I don't just mean here, in this avatar. I mean in life generally. You're beautiful."

Her gaze stayed fast on his own, as she smiled and then slowly ceased to smile. If it wasn't only his imagination again, Mandy was breathing deeply again. And her eyes were wet.

"Listen, I have an idea," said Saionton. "Let's talk more – but in person. Let's not stay here with this crowd. We don't need to stay here longer. I think we've both seen enough. I know I have. I could come over to your house. And we could talk more, or perhaps go out for a walk? In person. What do you think?"

There was a sound in her throat, like unhappy laughter. A vague, sweet smile had spread over her face. Then, even as she smiled thus vaguely, Saionton saw her lift her head, regally adorned. Her eyes narrowed in concentration upon the crowd they had left behind.

When he repeated himself, she flashed a quick glare at him.

"No. I can't leave."

"Why not?" asked Saionton. But a sense of tediousness was upon him already. He felt his spirits ebbing by the second.

"Please –" she had started to step away, still staring keenly into the *sabha*, "– I can't talk right now."

Saionton turned with reluctance. She seemed, at that moment, to be gazing at a group of riders, on horseback, going to and fro as they brandished their swords. He wasn't sure, but one of them resembled the building secretary, Shailesh Rao. But he couldn't be sure. Then all of a sudden his eye was drawn to one of the distant rocky outcrops. A muscular figure, almost naked, who might have been hewn from the mountain itself, was standing on a boulder and setting up – of all things – a whiteboard.

"There!" He nearly shouted at her, taking satisfaction in his rough tone. "Look *there*!"

"Where?"

"Up there." He pointed. "That's Aaron, isn't it?"

After a moment, she said quietly, "Yes, that's him."

Mandy's voice had dropped to a whisper. Her face was coloring and blushing, with the exhilaration of relief.

"I'll talk to you later," she said – and vanished.

CHAPTER SEVENTEEN

When he had said goodbye to the last parishioner, Father Joachim stood for a moment in the church's courtyard, laden with emotions. Father Alex's news, reported enviously in the sacristy before Mass, had not ceased to play in his mind ever since. The Holy Father had taken note of the goings-on in India – and of Joachim, personally. He blessed and encouraged the 'brave Indian priest'. No doubt, a personal meeting at the Vatican would be arranged in due course.

That had happened just today, probably even as he was addressing the *sabha*. Hearing of it had made his heart leap. The pope himself! The successor of Peter, two thousand years later, pivoting the barque in his direction! The pope's exhortations were not given lightly. But then, to bring him down to earth, he had faced the usual, sorry sight in the church hall. Seven people. He didn't even need to count them. Six belonged to a single extended family, infatuated with Joachim, who kept him occupied with chatter after Mass. The other was a non-Catholic beggar woman, who only liked to sit in for the shelter and the singing.

However, God 'worked all things together for the good', and Joachim was filled with happiness. He could foresee already that the revival of the global Church would begin here, in India, among its wretched and deluded. Very soon, he trembled to think, the Church, so hidden and modest, would rise up in splendor before those who had hitherto been captivated by worldly powers. Then the people, unshackled from their slavery, would gaze in awe upon its saving power.

But in all this, he reminded himself, he was nothing but an instrument of the Spirit.

Now the offertory hymn was being sung in the church hall. Already, the next Mass, the last of the day, was speeding its way to its climax. Father

Joachim stepped toward the open doors of the old building and glanced within. There were a surprising number of people inside. Perhaps even double digits? From habit, he wanted to count, and for a better look he reached for his spectacles, in his breast pocket.

The moment he pulled them out, he realized his mistake. This particular pair were not his. It was what the American man from the Company had given him, had insisted on handing over. He had forgotten to throw them away and now, in hastening out of doors, he had picked them up instead of his customary pair. They were both black and horn-rimmed, although these spectacles, now that he held them close, also gleamed like gold.

He put them on. Everything turned sharp, vivid. The power seemed just right. (So the Company knew his power too.) His eyes didn't hurt at all. After a sweeping look up and down the courtyard, he turned back to the church's doors.

He could see the people clearly now, but it wasn't possible to count them. That was because they each bore the pink and chubby head of a pig. Their trotters, he saw, were clasped in front of them.

Father Joachim took off the glasses, and the men and women returned into view, hunched piously over the pews.

A filter. A joke filter applied by the lenses. And this was the Company's gift to him! It was outrageous mockery. Blasphemous.

Then his eye traveled to Father Alex, alone at the altar in his green-and-white vestments. He was raising aloft the host for the rite of consecration, that it might become the bread of life, the saving body of Christ.

Moved by an irresistible impulse, Father Joachim returned the spectacles to his nose.

He saw a wolf, slavering at the jaw, with hairy paws extended upward. Clasped between them was a large silver coin. It was emblazoned with the rupee sign.

The wolf was muttering the sacred words. He heard, from somewhere, the jingle of coins in a chalice.

Then he felt his hackles rising, and his breathing growing shallow. Something was happening in front of his eyes. The plaster of paris figure of Jesus, installed below the altar, with gaze and forefinger heaven-raised, had begun to stir and look about. Gone was the impression of gentleness, the sentimentality, even the sickly sentimentality. The muscles of the face were pulling and contorting. The hair was growing longer and longer, and the body—

The woman – the thing that was now a woman – was staring straight at him, grinning horribly. There was blood on its mouth.

Father Joachim took off the spectacles and dropped them to the ground. Then he stepped on them, and leaned on them. When he glanced up, faces were turning in his direction. He walked away quickly, even as his phone began to ring. It was V calling.

V's voice, crisp and eager, was like the ringing of an alarm.

"Father! The Company's sending their man to the *sabha*. Lancelot Burns. He'll be here any minute. Can you come back, please? We need you to engage him."

"I'll be there," said Father Joachim, quickening his long strides. "I'm coming!"

★ ★ ★

"*Aum Shanti*." Aaron Sehgal stood erect in his loincloth. In his right hand was a marker pen, which he held poised near the whiteboard. This had been set up none too steadily atop the rock face.

"In the last three weeks," he continued melodiously, "my life's work of the last seven years has come to fruition."

The marker pen moved in spasms, and a large, ungainly eye appeared on the board.

"The kundalini awakes," said Aaron. "The chakras open. Jacob ascends the ladder, in the place he named Peniel. *Peniel*. *Pineal*. The pineal gland. Where the doors of perception swing open. Where one sees the face of God. And ushers in the Age of Aquarius. The age of the water bearer and the well. All ancient wisdom has sought the same thing. Be it the Egyptians or the Hindus or the Gnostics. They wanted to *see*. To see. Not to be blind. But my friends, there are dark powers that do not rest…. Yes? Did I hear a question?"

His visible audience, atop the rock face, was a human-sized gecko, a Caucasian woman wearing a hat, and a man of indeterminate age with the face of a child, in buttoned shirt and trousers, with hair combed like a schoolboy, who sat cross-legged near Aaron, gazing at him raptly.

It was the gecko that had cleared its throat – but no more.

"All right then. So...you must understand, I was *safe* where I was. With my knowledge. But I've come back to share with you all. And to warn you all. I do hope –" Aaron looked up enviously at the hordes in the open field, "– that there are lots more people who are tuning in to me. I mean, I hope I haven't come back just for you three! No offense!"

As he pushed his way through dancing, manic figures, Saionton was listening quietly. He knew that Mandy, wherever she was, was also listening. But it wasn't Mandy who was weighing on his mind. For some reason, his attention was riveted on that beautiful, kindly, gentle-looking man, seated near Aaron. The sight of this man-child, relishing Aaron's absurdities, was depressing him acutely.

He listened dejectedly, trying to laugh, maneuvering aimlessly in the crowd. Meanwhile, Aaron Sehgal was becoming fervent.

"Everything they say is a lie!" He was tracing three cryptic circles on the whiteboard. "You cannot trust the Company. Or the government. Or the *Church*, for goodness' sake. I believe that people are listening to a priest now? Look, they're all spinning webs around us. It's built into the tech. It's built into the language. The deception. So how do you see through it? The only way is to expand your mind. What am I talking about? I'm talking about the power of plants. But this is not an option any longer. This is not for kicks and thrills. You *need* this. I've found it – and now I'm safe!"

He began to draw furiously, with sweeping, stabbing motions.

"This is what we need! So we can all be safe!"

Something desperate had entered Aaron's voice, an incongruous note that finally made Saionton chuckle out loud. The he-man, it seemed, was mortally afraid.

But the little audience waited in vain for the revelation on the whiteboard, for the whiteboard, which had been rocking dangerously throughout, now suddenly tipped forward, collapsing into Aaron's arms. They were strong arms, but he staggered backward. With a yelp, the hatted woman rushed to his assistance.

Then all at once, the whole *sabha* fell silent. Across the maidan, mouths opened and closed in astonishment, yet no one was audible even to themselves.

Instead, to the exclusion of every other sound, a drawling voice began to speak.

In exercise of Company prerogative, Lance Burns had decided to be invisible and everywhere. Now he was introducing himself – at length.

★ ★ ★

By and by, a stupor of insensibility overwhelmed the gathering. The vehicles ceased their running and rumbling. The horses stood still. Others, who had been marching, dancing, and capering, simply sat down in the dust. Those already sitting seemed to slump and wilt. Like recalcitrant schoolchildren, they picked at blades of grass. But nobody could avoid listening. Lance was continuing to lecture, methodically, inexorably, into each one's ears. It had become evident that he was reading out his piece, just as he had read out his biography, and was now laying out a set of 'points worthy of consideration'.

There was the question of the Company's value to the people of the country. He wished to share some numbers to indicate the magnitude of this. One could measure it in terms of goods and services provided, and also individuals employed. It was worth bearing in mind that the Company was not the government. It did not frame social and economic policy. But there were also its myriad charities, for the economically and socially disadvantaged, of whose sad conditions everyone was aware. The Company did not lack sympathy. It was not, of course, the government. But it even did what it could to entertain the people, with brilliant, beloved advertisements. Finally, he wished to emphasize something very important to the Company, and also very dear to the people, regarding which false and slanderous rumors had, unfortunately, been spreading uncontrollably. That was Shrine Tech.

The people of India had been specially favored with Shrine Tech; no other country had had a rollout as in India. The product was brilliantly popular; he had numbers to prove this too. It was also a hundred per cent safe. He wished, therefore, to categorically deny that Shrine Tech contained any trickery, or any means of oppression. Nor did any of the other products and practices of the Company. The rumors that he denied, in the full view of the *sabha*, included (but were not limited to): the existence of any program for artificial intelligence to replace human employment; the existence of any program for foreign political control and enforced local servitude; and last but not least, the existence of any program of what might be termed 'black magic'. He would be happy, at this stage, to take (in view of the time, a limited number of) questions and comments.

When the crowd was able to hear itself again, there first erupted a massive, pleasurable murmuring, like a purring going through its whole body. Smiling faces regarded one another. People began to ripple about the grounds. It was only afterward that many voices cried out at once.

"I will take a question from Mr. Shailesh Rao," said the disembodied American.

A mustachioed figure in silk and gold embroidery, wearing a gold turban, descended from a horse, and unsheathed a curved blade from a blood-red sheath. His eyes were painted black as he glared at the sky, straight into the sun.

"All these days I have been sitting on a fast until death. Today I have broken my fast and come here. I belong to the Rajputs of Mewar. Once upon a time we were a glorious community. But we always sacrificed for others. Today we are poor and deprived! Nobody cares for our plight! So I ask, what is the Company doing for us?"

Even as he spoke, a consternation was gripping the *sabha*, a commotion both threatening and supportive and ambiguous all at once. The crowd, which had been purring, was now growling. But there continued, over its noises, the dispassionate query of the Company's lead fixer.

"Any other person, or group of people, with a similar complaint? You may speak in your own languages. The tech translates automatically."

Then Lance went quiet, only calling, one by one, those he happened to select.

The first to speak up was a farmer, in the avatar of the child Krishna. After him appeared a laborer, who was the noble King Rama. The king was followed by a tribal woman with branches and leaves growing out of her hair, who in turn was followed by a high-caste Brahmin sadhu in the nude. Then came a young male student, a civil services aspirant, who evidently worshipped an American pop star. He was succeeded by two members of backward castes, both in tuxedos, and then a Muslim man, who was driving a heavily armored tank. Each of these, in their manifold dialects, poured out their woes, reciting all they lacked, whether food and clothing, or money, or home, or a wife, or livelihood, or respect, or opportunity, or understanding. Their speeches were often choked with tears. Their frustrations were pitiful. It was apparent, also, that they had a rankling among themselves. Yet it did not flare up. Old enmities seemed mysteriously suspended, in some new element each party had grown conscious of. As the litany of complaints went on, the crowd did not disintegrate, coming to blows, but swelled and strutted boisterously.

Just as he had picked them out at random, Lance cut them off arbitrarily. "Your complaints," he noted, "appear to lie against the *government*. The Company is not the *government*. For the Company you are each customers, and you are treated with the highest respect and equality, as customers. Besides that, as I said, we have our social and educational... philanthropy...."

However, his voice trailed off unwillingly. A familiar and hateful figure had appeared on high, waving his arms above the valley of the maidan. It was the old Catholic priest, in his rusty old armor. Already the people had begun to chant for him. There was nothing for it but to hear him out. Especially since he was declaiming already. As though he had the floor already.

"—misuse of power! Some big shot from the Company shows up, and forces us all to be silent? He decides who will speak and who will not? Is this the people's *sabha*, or the Company's? Are we Company property?"

Father Joachim was enjoying the sound of his voice, warm and deep, and resounding, as never before, with the roar of the people. Their pulsating mass, spread over the plains, seemed to him like a storm cloud, in the midst of which he was as happily encased – as lightning.

"Sir," he ad-libbed, with soaring confidence. "Sir, in your own words, you see us as customers. But that means you don't see us at all. We are not customers, sir. We are persons. With names and faces. That young man struggling for money to feed his family. He is not a customer. He is a person. With a history. With dreams. That lady, from Jharkhand, whose home in the forest was demolished. She is not a customer. She is a person. She has roots. She has sensitivities. And it is the same with every one of us here. All of us belong to this great land. India! What does India mean to you, sir? Does it mean a vast market for goods? Does it mean a lot of data for analysis?"

His last words were drowned out by an immense upwelling of support. Father Joachim paused, taking it all in. His glance suddenly fell on the hapless young man he had referred to. The boy, strangely, was now performing pelvic thrusts and pointing to the sky with both hands. Meanwhile, the crowd continued to cry for Joachim, but with such force and vigor, like a river fed by subterranean waters, that he wondered for a moment if they had even really heard him. Then he gathered his confidence and opened his mouth again. He held it open a moment before plunging on.

"And why do you talk about the government? Never mind the government. Leave the government to itself. Let us deal with each other properly. You have dealings with us, don't you, sir? Extensive dealings! Then treat us as people. That is all we ask. Respect our humanity. Pay attention to our needs. Does not each of us have the right to basic goods and opportunities? Think of that, when you conduct your business with us. And most importantly, sir, respect this great country, which has housed so many cultures and traditions and ways of life. Why do you wish to degrade it? If you cannot help us, at least do not impoverish us in this way, sir. Do not strip away our humanity. Let us have our old ways back. Our history!"

He fastened, suddenly, on to a surge of feeling in the crowd, and rode it unthinkingly. "Our old places of worship!" cried the priest. "Our temples, our mosques, our churches, our gurudwaras! Give us back our places of worship! Abolish Shrine Tech! Remove this drug from our lives! Abolish Shrine Tech!"

The cry went up, and was passed from figure to figure, as the Knight watched from his mountain perch, with relief and euphoria settling over him thickly. Finally, he sighed with satisfaction, looked around the crowd – and was thrown into doubt.

They were laughing at him. At least some of them were. Some of them were pointing and laughing. Then he saw, at random, a corpulent sadhu and the goddess Durga, who had cleared a space among the surrounding crush and were dancing bawdily to an atrocious film song. The grenade launcher fired off suddenly. The bunch in the middle, who were the spitting image of Roshan Dubey, cried out again for the Happy Maker, but now loudly and gladly, their faces bright with exhilaration. Joachim wanted to say more, but the words would not come. He saw, altogether, that the crowd was turning away from him, hither and thither, that it was enjoying...itself.

"Your request for the abolition of Shrine Tech is rejected, Mr. Joachim. For reasons I have already explained. You're advised not to spread further rumors about it."

It was the voice of Lancelot Burns. Joachim paid it little heed. But at the sound of it, a further cry rose up, though none could say who had given it. This one was short and bitter, and uttered from the heart.

"Go back!" was the cry. "Go back!" they shouted, waving fists at the sky.

Tears were stinging the old priest's eyes. There was no denying what he was seeing.

"Go back!" they were shouting – also at him.

"Go back!"

* * *

Before all else came the dust. It blew in from all corners of the field, choking eyes and mouths. When the storm's first flurry thinned, the people looked toward the horizon, where the endless plain seemed to stretch to eternity.

An enormous cloud of dust hung before them, gathering and darkening, like impending doom. Yet the cloud, for some reason, was not advancing.

Instead, dust particles swam and danced within it, churning and turning with all manner of whimsy. The crowd gazed and marveled. The spectacle was mesmeric. Thus it was that when a human shape came stepping through the haze, they all saw it at once.

He was wearing a buttoned shirt, caked with grime, and jeans that had once been blue. His chest and stomach bulged out in front of him, parting his shirt unabashedly. His identity was confirmed by the tech itself, which labeled him in all their sights:

Roshan Dubey, Chief Happy Maker, India Company.

Otherwise, they couldn't have recognized him. He stood with his head in the sky, his face obscured by sunshine and dust, a good two hundred feet above the ground, twice as tall as the rocket ship, which was the tallest thing in the *Mahasabha*'s world.

By and by, the wind blew, and the dust cleared. Roshan Dubey faced the crowd with his arms parted wide. In speechlessness, for a time, these two goliaths beheld one another. Then his mouth moved in the upper reaches, and in the midst of the crowd, in each one's ears, the Happy Maker spoke.

CHAPTER EIGHTEEN

It was dark in the bedroom, and too hot. Saionton's shirt was sticking to him. The shrine was running even more noisily than the ceiling fan. Close to the tech's trembling ears, Kush sat on the floor, with the small of his back to the wall, and his head hanging between his knees. He was logged in still, captivated, like the others.

Saionton had logged off because he could not bear it any longer. But what was it, he wondered, that he couldn't bear? Lance had been tedious and officious, and the Catholic priest sentimental and pleading. And he had heard them both out. But the Happy Maker was spectacular; one might crane one's neck but not take one's eyes off him, with his gargantuan body that blotted out the sun, and then his words, so tender and passionate, such as no one had expected.

"Know this," he had said. "In my eyes – and in the eyes of the Company – just as long as I am running the Company – you are not simply customers. But you are not simply persons either. You are gods, each one of you, you are a god! And together – together you are all humanity. Yes, not a bunch of tribes and cliques. But not just a country either. You are all humanity in my eyes. Oh, I know that the government has failed you. The government –" and here his voice had become loaded with some enormously sly significance, "– the government, I repeat, has failed you. But that is no excuse for *me*. Because *I* love you. *I* desire your happiness. I also desire your *peace*, because without peace there is no happiness." At this insight, many forlorn faces nodded eagerly. "And I have made your happiness, your very own happiness, my mission. You know that, don't you? Who gave you these beautiful bodies? It was the Company. It was me! And I think of you night and day. I will not rest until you are each happy. I love you."

A rapturous silence had blanketed the crowd, catching it up into swift and strange intimacy, but Saionton had twisted away, shuddering in revulsion. For such reasons as he could hardly begin to articulate, he was back in his bedroom, on his hands and knees, in the squalid darkness.

He looked again at Kush, sunk deep in the tech. Then he got to his feet and walked over to the room's only window, where thick curtains were keeping out the late evening light. He slid behind them, pressing close to the windowsill, pressing his face to the glass.

The image of Roshan was still before him. It was disturbing him with its power. Not only had he seen that power himself, but he had also seen it reflected in the faces of the crowd. That disturbed him doubly. He sensed that whatever Roshan was saying and doing at the *sabha* was so fascinating, and at the same time so full of emotions, so rich with feelings, that if it was a trick, it would break the mind to have to come to grips with it. But he was sure, in his bones, that it was a trick. So he wished heartily that he had never attended the *sabha*, never witnessed any of it. One thing, however, he could not wish, that he could simply meld into that absorbed human mass, craning his neck skyward.

He was relieved suddenly to come upon a distraction. On the pavement across the street, a group of boys and girls – urchins all – were playing dumb charades. When Saionton had been their age, the game was still played with film titles. But these children, he saw, were simply mimicking animals. He watched two rounds play out. In both cases, the animal itself was quickly guessed (a tiger, and then a snake) but each one had also been allotted a name. That took more work on everyone's part.

The third time, a girl in a blue frock with strawy hair and big eyes walked about the pavement with her arm extended and swaying above her face. There were repeated cries of *haathi*, but that was not the answer. A couple of minutes passed. Then, in exasperation, she threw up her hands and said something he couldn't hear. The children broke out into laughter and protests. Suddenly, the girl swiveled, pulled out an imaginary revolver and, with much panache, picked off the company. They fell about on cue, clutching their chests and contorting their faces in mock agony.

Saionton drew back into the bedroom. There was a big grin sitting on his face. He wondered why. It was true that he had remembered Mandy again, with fondness. But there was something else that was the cause of his joy. The children's charades were really the most beautiful he had seen. A vague, feverish epiphany came to him; he saw that to act out the titles of movies, as in the version of the game that he knew, was already a presage of the end of all things. One enacted the things of reality, unless one had stopped caring for reality.

Suddenly he felt calm, so much so that he began to feel undeservedly rewarded. He turned his mind back to the beggar children, to the nuts and bolts of their lives, wondering who fed them, and if they had any shelter, in the rainy months, and then if anyone abused them. There were charities and shelters scattered about the city, but there were violent predators at large as well. And anyway, it was all a miserable succession of days and nights. It was no kind of childhood. And he himself had never done anything to make it better for the children.

Saionton peeked behind the curtain again. The pavement was empty now. The children had gone, set off somewhere only they knew. He said a silent prayer for them, not addressing himself to anyone, but willing something in his heart.

As he stood at the window, with his eyes closed, an immense crush of loneliness rose up within him. He was aware of the flavor of his own life, of the cold and ironic ties he knew. But this feeling contained more than that. It was the sense of the lovelessness of the whole world that had crept up and touched him – as he stood at the window. And no sooner had it touched him, than it had entered him.

When he turned at last, his eye fell on Kush, huddled in the corner of the room. Kush's upper body was swaying backward and forward, in a catatonic way. That was normal, they said, during holo-tech sessions, especially in situations of high excitement. 'No cause for concern'.

He felt the last vestiges of his smile passing away, and a stony cast appearing in its place. The revulsion was crawling through him again, even as he moved quickly back to that patch of floor, to which the tech was beckoning him.

⋆ ⋆ ⋆

V was hovering, gazing in all directions, when the tech informed him that Saionton's avatar was active again. A moment later he had zeroed in on him, as well as the other boy, Kush. Like before, they were standing upon one of the far banks, where the grass was thicker.

"What the hell are you doing?" V roared from all the mouths of his avatar. He flew in close, the better to rouse them with the power of his presence. "Why're you just standing here?"

It was not immediately clear what he meant. At the boundary of the maidan, the gigantic Roshan Dubey, so near now as to drive home the surreality of his size, was on his knees, with hands clasped, head bowed, and an almost cartoonish look of sorrow on his face. The crowd, like Lilliputians, were swarming up toward the immense, kneeling figure. But when he began to speak again, their front rank held back, as though physically repulsed by strong gusts.

"Here I am," said Roshan. "Your Happy Maker. I know you are upset. In many ways, in every way, you are upset. So go on and punish me. Strike me down with weapons. Kill me, I am right here."

Even as hesitation gripped the crowd, the fireball that was V spoke hoarsely to Saionton.

"I want footage of this! Get nearer and start recording."

Automatically, unthinkingly, Saionton shook his head. "No."

"You were supposed to be helping me," the filmmaker insisted.

"No. I've helped enough. I'm not interested in this game."

"It will make you happy," the giant continued, and everyone heard his voice like a whisper, not just in their ear but in their brain. "Do it. Strike me down and kill me. See my blood gush out. Puncture my body. Tear it into pieces. It will make you happy."

"I'll record," said Kush suddenly. "Where should I go?"

"Go anywhere I'm not," V explained. "Record as much footage as you can. This is going to be *awesome*."

"You really think they'll kill him?"

"Quick!" cried V. "It's begun!"

Their avatars hastened away and then vanished from Saionton's sight. But he wasn't looking at them any longer.

When the Happy Maker had gone silent, even closing fast his huge eyes, a row of military figures in dark green livery had stepped forward from the advancing pack. Among them, Saionton saw, was Jaspreet Bhatia. The restaurateur's face had a clear, confident light about it. That besetting worry and suspicion of the world, which always seemed to mark his expression, was gone. He was the first to raise a rifle to his shoulder. Then his comrades followed suit.

Suddenly there resounded the voice of Father Joachim, still standing where he had been, and screaming with a kind of derangement, for no one to attack, for everyone to stop, 'in the name of God'. This occasioned only a minor pause. Then a shot rang out in the maidan, and immediately after, a whole volley of them.

A cry of agony bubbled up from the huge, kneeling human being. Rivulets of red sprang into sight, unnaturally glistening blood that went streaking down Roshan's checked shirt, and to his fleshy stomach and exposed belly button. His legs seemed to buckle and he sank farther, with his clasped hands coming apart and falling palm first to the ground, breaking his fall.

The ground was still shaking when the Knight of the Cross began to shout again. This time faces in the crowd turned to him, and some were chastened and abashed. But Joachim found, to his horror, that words were failing him. He was reduced to admonishing with his arms, shaking his head violently, and even stamping his iron boot on the dust, while his eyes goggled in disbelief.

More laughter sounded from the great public. Among them, Shiva, the god of destruction, was seen to raise aloft his *trishul* and declare in categorical terms: "That Catholic was never with us!" Someone else, wearing a top hat, waistcoat, and knee breeches, yelled audibly, "The Company owns the Catholic Church! Everybody knows that!"

Meanwhile, the soldiers had armed their rifles again, and their eyes were all on Jaspreet, on whose face rested a gentle, fanatic smile. With perfect and robotic assurance, he uttered another command. Moments later, as the bleeding vision of the Happy Maker lay sprawled over the maidan, the crowd broke forth like a torrent. Those doppelgängers who were Roshan's very own worshippers were swiftest to reach his body, which they proceeded to clamber up, like an old ruin, and then to maul, with axes and spears. But the others were not far behind. The very vastness of the body, which was still quivering and groaning with awful life, afforded opportunities for many. Like vultures to a carcass, they closed in on all sides, and those who had no weapons still kicked and stomped on whatever part of the Happy Maker presented itself before them. Certain faces, marked with especial malice, took delight in tearing the clothes off the man and spitting on the exposed skin. It seemed that even more vulgar forms of desecration might ensue.

Pandemonium had descended on the maidan. Saionton tried to see who, if anyone, was not running with the crowd. He could see V, circling about in fiery excitement, and Kush, who kept climbing up from one height to another, for different views of the spectacle. All the while, his mouth moved in breathless, eager exclamations.

Aaron Sehgal, with his whiteboard at his back, sat atop his rock face, legs dangling, watching the scene with his fists clenched. He too was shouting something. The words, when Saionton tuned in to him, were: *Murderer! Die! Die, murderer!*

Then Saionton's stomach churned horribly. There was Mandy, more goddess-like than ever. She had come up alongside Aaron. She stood over him, a dream in red, her pale hand resting on the top of his head, tousling his hair with careless love. Her eyes, however, were fixed on the carnage in the valley. He could not decipher their expression.

Then a fresh howl went up, rending the air, until it seemed the sky must burst. When the peak of pain was passed, a bruising cry continued to sound. It was, recognizably, the agonized gasping of Roshan Dubey, the Chief Happy Maker.

Suddenly it occurred to Saionton that what was happening was impossible. The neural link did not permit an avatar to experience even a fraction of such pain. Pain, being undesired, was simply excluded. It was impossible for the technology to work differently. So then, how was it that Roshan continued to be present, even as his body was disfigured and destroyed from moment to moment?

At last, like the culmination of a nightmare, he saw a massive saw, its serrated edge upturned and gleaming in the constant sunlight, being carried reverentially by a group of gods and goddesses, who were wading their way through the lake of blood that had spilled from Roshan's body. The rest of the crowd too was pausing from its assaults to send up a cheer; cars and bikes were revving their engines, tooting their horns; and the angry beats of music that someone had recently struck up were booming louder than ever.

They were going to sever his head.

★ ★ ★

Nor did they stop at that. The violence did not stop when the *Mahasabha* ended, but overflowed out into the streets and marketplaces of Mumbai. On that night, and on the next day and night, and then entering a third day, random acts of destruction were witnessed throughout the city. Mobs of rioters coalesced, worked destruction, and then melted away, only to emerge elsewhere with fresh personnel, following some unaccountable method of their own, but always leaving in their wake burning vehicles, shattered windows, broken lights, the rubble of dilapidated structures, and also wild bonfires, burning gloriously, and an ever-lengthening trail of maimed and bludgeoned human bodies. After an initial attempt to staunch the havoc, the police and government had withdrawn to their own devices, because the rioters were not provably less in number than the city's law-abiding citizens, nor even distinguishable from them in any way. Anybody, it seemed, might pick up a brick, or light up a kerosene-soaked rag, and hurl it at anybody else, in any part of the city and for no discernible provocation. Even members of the police were seen wading into the general pell-mell, and it was being said that the unusual number of clubs and pistols in circulation was the direct beneficence (although not the charity) of the authorities. For already, in the midst of the free-for-all, there were pecking orders being suggested, and money being made.

On the third morning of the riots, Saionton woke to find the apartment empty, and a note from Kush, taped to the door, as was his wont.

Threw rotten eggs, said the note, before instructing him:

Buy new ones.

The implication, thought Saionton, was that Kush was too importantly occupied to bother with household matters, yet at the same time so grounded as to be on top of them. Kush had been out in the city from day two, filming the violence along with V, who had flown down from Goa purely for the occasion. Both men had become transfigured, even in appearance. They were bright in the eye, clear in the mind, nimble of foot, and quite elated with the sense of their own courage, to be out in the riots, filming. Filming and working, and not even resting on their laurels, because their recordings of the Shrine Tech massacre – the murder of Mr. Happy Maker – were still playing out all over the television and internet, the 'number one most-watched' clip in India, if not the world.

Saionton tore the note off the door and went to toss it in the bin. Then he positioned himself by the ugly iron grille that encased the kitchen window, and watched and listened.

The lane outside, a leafy alley at the back of the building, was devoid of movement. It was quiet, too, except for the warbling of birds. A stray dog slept beside somebody's scooter.

The violence had by and large spared the apartment buildings and private residences. It was out in the commons that the battle was raging. Still, when Saionton pricked his ears, he fancied he could glean some rough noises in the distance, like a cavalcade of motorbikes, their engines screaming. And there was distinctly a hammering sound, something deep and dull, shuddering through the morning stillness.

The seed of fury, which he had been waking up with daily, sprouted within him again. It was the hammering, especially, that was bringing it on now, in spurts. He switched on the fan in the kitchen, the one that rattled loudly, and after that all the others in the house, trying to drown everything out. But this move was so obviously defensive that it gave him no relief; it rather worsened his mood. He knew the noises were still proceeding from without, where desperadoes were doing wheelies on their motorbikes, and gangs carousing the streets. Then, from the corridor outside, a door slammed urgently and someone's footsteps were heard scampering down the stairs. Everywhere, thought Saionton, there was urgency.

"It's so fucking...*fake*!" he yelled out uncontrollably.

"Come and talk about it!" yelled back a familiar voice, from his bedroom.

CHAPTER NINETEEN

"Perhaps," suggested the shrine, "they are angry because Roshan is dead."

"They're the ones that attacked him," retorted Saionton. He was seated on the edge of his bed, glaring at the machine. "But Roshan is *not* dead. Nobody can *die* in holo-tech. It's a fantasy computer-generated space."

"On the other hand," said the shrine mildly, "nobody has ever been through anything like that. Not in the history of holo-tech. The amount of pain he would have endured…. And you know he hasn't been seen or heard from for three days. The Company office has been lying sealed ever since—"

"I know all that," cut in Saionton. "They're fueling the rumors, if you ask me. My point is, whatever Roshan suffered at the *sabha* wasn't *really* pain. This is like saying you can die from what happens to you in a dream. You can't, no matter what happens to you."

A silence that felt vaguely sullen arose between the two of them. After much internal clicking, the machine's voice turned wry.

"Perhaps the public isn't as intelligent as you."

"It's not about *intelligence*. They know it's not real too. His suffering and dying wasn't real, and their avatars aren't real either. Surely they know that."

Yet a touch of doubt had entered his voice.

The shrine, being a metallic rod with appendages, could not smirk. But he could practically hear it smirking.

"There is knowing, and there is knowing," it stated grandly. "But let it be. If the poor people wish to believe…they must have their reasons. How are *you*? No new moles, I hope?"

Saionton sat up straight on the bed. "What the fuck?" he said.

"Just a query," answered the shrine. "I had a fancy that subject was on your mind. My apologies if I was mistaken?"

Saionton stared at the machine, suddenly detesting it, and at the same time caught up in wonderment. For the first time, he became aware of his own process of thought, enmeshing and entangling with whatever it was that ticked over in the shrine's entrails.

"That priest was right about you," he said finally. "All you do is play mind games."

"Poor Father Joachim. He did love the people. I'm afraid they broke his heart."

"He was a fool."

"You seem to think that about everyone."

"Well, he was a fool, for believing in the people. And the people are fools, if they think the CHM is dead, because of something that happened in *holo-tech*."

"Wait a minute," said the shrine, clicking rapidly. "Roshan Dubey may not be dead. But surely the people did kill *the Happy Maker*? I mean, he asked them to. Because he had failed to make them happy. Do you see? Not the man, but the title—"

At that, Saionton burst out, "But why the fuck should he have made them happy? Who made him *their* Happy Maker? How can they have taken that title seriously in the first place?"

"So now," the shrine continued, as though Saionton had not spoken, "with their Happy Maker having failed them, the public has lost its faith. And therefore, they riot."

"It was never faith," said Saionton, clenching his jaw. "It was all delusion."

"Is there a difference?"

"Yes," replied Saionton, though he hardly knew where the words were coming from. "Faith is meant to be reasonable."

"Reasonable!" uttered the shrine. It sounded almost comically astonished. "You want people to be reasonable? But do you know what their lives are like? Do you know the things they've been through? You're pretty tough on people, do you know that? I think someone must have told you that."

Saionton, finding nothing to say, continued to listen. He felt reluctant and vaguely trapped, but also thoroughly interested, as the machine went on, becoming, from the sound of it, more and more animated.

"Life hits people hard. It robs the trusting of their innocence. It exhausts the persistent ones. It terrifies the brave ones. Plus this country. The weather itself will scorch the life out of you, sap you and finish you. Then the poverty, the dirt, the disease. What is reasonable about any of this? Reasonable? It's all unreasonable to begin with. And when it's all unreasonable to begin with.... Well then all bets are off, aren't they, Saionton?"

A smile had pushed out onto Saionton's face. It was a crooked smile, going up one side, but lingering insistently. Some deep and pure enjoyment was flowing through him. Partly, it came from the realization that the shrine never condemned him. He could think, say, or do anything before it. He was completely free. But this thought, even as it grew more intoxicating, filled him with discomfort.

"It still irritates me," he said. "If you don't even try to face things, how can you say they're unreasonable? But OK, I can understand people generally. Drowning their sorrows. But what's the need to go around filming them and celebrating what they're doing?"

"You're referring to V."

"And Kush. They're not rioting, themselves. They can see it's all absurd. There's no *cause* here, there's no nothing. Then why are they *pretending* to be so interested?"

A long stretch of whirring and humming ensued. Saionton waited willingly. He had quite forgotten the other disturbances; whatever was happening inside his building or out on the road, it made no difference to him.

"There may, or may not, be a cause," said the shrine. "But there is power. Why not celebrate the power of the crowd? Why not get with it? Before one dies. After all, one is dying."

"Why are you talking about death?" said Saionton sharply. "It's not like *you're* dying."

"What am I?" said the shrine. "I only exist for users like yourself."

After it had said this, all the humming of the machinery clicked out at once, settling with satisfaction into a perfect silence. Only the lights on the rod indicated the shrine was still active.

"And I'm dying," said Saionton. "That's what you're implying."

A whirring started up again. Then a harsh and rasping voice broke out.

"Why would I imply the obvious? The only question is when and how. It could be a car accident. Or a long, slow illness. It could be those moles on your face. They might start to spread. Or, maybe the cancer will torture you, but it won't kill you. It'll just make you so depressed. And then you'll kill yourself. It could very well be that. Whatever it is, you're getting closer to it every day."

Saionton stared, and tried to laugh, and then to be angry. But the voice from the shrine continued.

"But all of that is quite obvious too. What I'm implying is, do you think that is *reasonable*?"

"What should I do?" said Saionton quietly.

"What do you already do? What was your avatar at the *Mahasabha*?"

"It was nothing. I guess it was you. What do I do? I don't get involved with anything. I play the game. But not this game. Not this game that everyone else is playing."

"Don't judge them," whispered the shrine. "Let's not judge them."

The unholy thrill coursed through Saionton again. He felt the contours of some kind of plot, taking shape in his mind.

"Let them play their game. And you play your game. Everyone has their own way of playing. Now, what's the move you feel like making? What's on your mind?"

"Everyone –" Saionton swallowed, and spoke with difficulty, "– everyone is out burning and destroying things."

The shrine remained quiet. He could sense it waiting, ears flared in anticipation.

"I wanna…" said Saionton in a voice he hardly recognized. Then a smile began to spread over his face, and he pushed it farther, from ear to ear.

Flickering in front of him, conjured by the tech, was a beckoning pair of eyes.

*   *   *

To reach her apartment tower was a forty-minute drive. But the problem of how to get there was quickly solved. Saionton had barely ventured out of the gate and onto the road, casting uneasy looks from beneath the hood of a college sweatshirt, which was wrong for the weather, but appropriate, he felt, for the scene, when an auto-rickshaw careered up from behind him, almost knocking into him.

He climbed in, giving the name of her suburb, "Bandra," and the ride set off without a word. For the first few minutes a sense of comfort enveloped Saionton. They were familiar sensations, sitting back in the conical coziness of the three-wheeler, listening to its hectic engine and adjusting one's body to its speedy movements, as it went in and out of lanes and avenues.

When he had gathered the nerve to really look outside, he saw that the shops were either shuttered or half-shuttered, and there was barely any traffic, and all of it was moving at top speed. But even that was not unusual. It might, for instance, have been very early on a Sunday morning. Certain figures lay about on the pavements, but they might have been drunk or asleep. Then he glimpsed a pair of men, walking down the road with blood-spattered faces, and he fell back into his seat. He was regretting, acutely, the exposed sides of the rickshaw. His foot jerked out and something metallic clattered on the floor below. An iron rod.

The driver caught his eye in the rearview mirror. The man was smiling. He had a wide, deeply pockmarked face, with an orange *tika* plastered upon his brow. He said something that Saionton couldn't hear above the engine. Then, for some reason, the vehicle began to slow down.

"Is it a red light?" said Saionton. "Don't slow down or stop."

"Look," said the driver, whose grin had broadened.

Coming up by the side of the road, where a massive pothole kept off the traffic, three men were gathered around a fourth, who lay curled up on the asphalt, trying in vain to protect his curly-haired head with his hands. The three were taking turns kicking him in the stomach and face. Suddenly the driver called out, "Aiiee!" and one of them, a thin, angular youth, whose hair and face were dripping in sweat, turned and ran up to the rickshaw. There followed an agitated exchange that Saionton couldn't follow. Then, with a furious shout, the youth hurtled back toward the cringing figure and began to pummel him afresh.

"Poor fellow," shouted the driver, revving the engine. "His brother just died of TB."

"But why are they beating the other guy?" said Saionton. He was leaning forward, with his hand gripping the steel railing to which the rickshaw's meter was nailed. The numbers were ticking over meaninglessly. "Just see! They're going to kill him!"

"I told you," said the driver impatiently, "that fellow's brother died of TB. Won't he be angry?"

Shaking his head, he put on another burst of speed. Saionton lowered his gaze, studying the iron rod that shifted backward and forward in the grooves of the flooring. All the while, the driver was continuing to speak in a bitter, hectoring fashion. But since he was inaudible above the engine, Saionton was only feigning to listen. Yet he was glad the man kept talking, because it was a distraction from the scenes that were passing them by, which Saionton did not wish to scrutinize. He did, however, spot a familiar park, a strip of green in the midst of the roadway, where he had once jogged. Now, seemingly, it was full of old women with half smiles looking at the sky. A moment later, he heard two sharp cracks in quick succession. No doubt they were gunshots. They had made him jump. Then they entered a region of smoke and burning. Suddenly Saionton started forward again, because the driver had braked, and also killed the engine.

The man stepped down from the vehicle, wiping his hands on his dirty trousers, and muttering to himself.

"Each year," he said distinctly, "the population of Muslims keeps increasing. But the population of us Hindus remains the same. Do you understand what is going to happen to this country?"

"What are you talking about?" said Saionton. "I need to get to Bandra quickly."

The driver stopped ambling about, and took a step toward him, before bending to bring his face near. His eyes were half-closed and a scowl was disfiguring his mouth.

"This is the way to Bandra," he said. "Isn't this the way to Bandra?"

Saionton recognized the road. It was an ugly one, lined with garages and vehicle repair shops, ceramics and tile manufacturers and a couple of places that sold old furniture. At present, they were all shuttered, in a haze of foul-smelling smoke. Some distance down the street a husk of a four-wheeler was burning lavishly, all by itself. There was nobody in sight.

"Yes," he agreed, "but why have we—?"

Then suddenly he nodded quickly as though he understood. The man's face was no longer sane. Saionton watched as the driver snatched the iron rod from the passenger compartment and turned aside, brandishing it.

An empty black-and-yellow taxi was parked a few paces ahead. The driver took the rod to it. In action, despite the bulk of his frame, he was agile and even elegant. First he smashed the windscreen, then every other window, and then he began to beat in the doors. A stream of abuse, having to do with Muslims and their breeding, was running from his mouth. Finally, he wiped his mouth and face, and strode back to the rickshaw.

Saionton sat back with a detached expression, while the rod was carefully placed back in its groove, near his feet. The driver shifted into his seat, drops of sweat on the back of his neck, and they set off again.

It had begun to gust. The trees were swaying noticeably. It had been sunny that morning, but now it had gotten decidedly dark. There was no rain, however. Saionton peered out of the side of the rickshaw, searching for evidence of rain. He had lost some of his fear. There were very few people around. Also, for some reason, he felt protected in the rickshaw, even invincible.

They swiveled onto the promenade before Juhu Beach. Then he could not believe his eyes. A mass of people had occupied the beach, engrossed in what looked like an all-out brawl. Squally winds were covering the scene in sand. But the fighting was underway. There were men and women alike. They were fighting in twos and threes. The ferocity of their blows was evident. He saw torn clothes, immodest and thrusting bodies (at a glance the whole thing was a sexual orgy), and faces in agony, making a cacophony. The fracas carried out all the way into the surf, where violent figures were splashing furiously, trying to drown each other.

The driver was stony-faced. His eyes hadn't left the road. They came up to a deserted police barricade, and wriggled through easily.

Her apartment wasn't far now. A queer desire suddenly came upon Saionton, and he cast about restlessly, swallowing to keep his throat from drying out altogether.

"Stop!" he cried out, spotting something. "I said, stop!"

The rickshaw deigned to halt about fifty meters from where he had wanted it to, which was the site of a makeshift stall selling tea, cigarettes, and assorted minor groceries. Saionton jumped out, feeling the wind on his skin, and ran exultantly toward it.

A woman in a brown sari was stirring a pot of tea over a flame.

"You have eggs?" Saionton inquired. "You do? I want ten. No, twelve eggs, please!"

She handed them to him in a carefully knotted clear plastic bag. Just then, their eyes met.

"Do you eat meat also?" the woman asked warily.

"Yes. But I only want eggs right now." He counted out the change and placed it on the counter.

"I'm just asking," explained the woman. "I can't stand people who don't eat meat." Now she looked disgusted. The tea boiled up and she switched off the flame. "Pretending to be pure. I hate such people."

"Well, I do eat meat," repeated Saionton, turning away. Then it occurred to him that he might have a cup of tea as well, and he turned back, just in time to see the sari-clad woman stepping out from behind the stall, with her metal ladle held high.

"*Hate* them!" she hissed, and swung at him.

Saionton yelled from the heat of the steel, more than the blow, which had caught him flush on the arm. The woman, gathering herself, took another step toward him, and he hurled the packet of eggs at her. Then he ran, shouting madly, in the direction of the rickshaw. He was running into the wind now, which came scouring down the road, blowing dust and debris into his eyes.

He didn't look back until he was in the vehicle and it was moving rapidly. She was standing a long way off, shielding her face from the breeze.

"Where in Bandra?" asked the driver.

Saionton looked up. "At the next traffic light – not this light, the next one – take a right."

Entering the cobbled lanes, with the hush of the wind in his ears, he was able for the first time to think. But his pent-up thoughts erupted all in a jumble. What was happening all around was strictly crazy, a nightmare, yet he had the nagging sense that an explanation existed. At the same time, his arm was still stinging, and he wanted to exact some kind of vengeance for that attack – but also in general. When he saw figures passing by, he made sure not to look at them, fearing them, hating that he feared them, and hating them for having made him so afraid. It was with a rush of relief that he focused on Mandy, how he would get to her house, and greet her, and then what he might say and do. He wondered suddenly if she was safe.

I hope she hasn't died, thought Saionton with a sudden panic, *before I've even slept with her.*

There were no watchmen at her building gate, and he was yearning to rush inside. But there was a hitch. The driver had no change for his five-hundred-rupee note, which was the only one he had. Ordinarily, he would have hunted around for shopkeepers or ATMs. Now that seemed impossible, so he let the money go.

Walking toward the lobby of her building, he told himself it was only money. Yet when, for all his lofty airs, had he not grasped after money? The loss of his change rankled, and everything was rankling, till he felt his mouth becoming smaller and uglier with every passing second.

Like the courtyard, the lobby was devoid of people. He noticed, also, that there were puddles of water spreading on the floor, as though a pipe had burst somewhere. But there were no staff around. When he reached the elevator area, immediately jabbing the call button, he noticed that the farthest elevator was talking on a loop, in a fluty female voice, with its doors opening and closing continually.

Saionton went to investigate. The elevator's doors were opening and closing on the legs of a man. Within, his body lay at an unnatural angle. He was motionless, but neatly dressed in trousers, belt, and a collared shirt.

There was blood everywhere, more than Saionton had ever seen in the real world. As he stared, he felt his stomach becoming involved.

A silvery chime sounded and Saionton turned to see the neighboring elevator opening wide.

In it, backed up into a corner, stood Mandy, in athleisure, with her hair tied up in a bun, and her face white and staring.

"You," she whispered. "Come in. It's going up."

"There's someone here," said Saionton, entranced.

"He's dead. He's been shooting people for two days, and today he shot himself. Come in!"

CHAPTER TWENTY

"So why are you here?" asked Mandy, when they had begun ascending.

Saionton looked her full in the face. She had inclined her head, and her eyes were gleaming sharply. The rest of her getup, however, was not as he had imagined it. In her baggy t-shirt and track pants, she looked dumpy and somehow goblin-like. He felt his heart catching strangely.

"It's you I was coming to see." He said his prepared lines, but in a tone of voice he didn't recognize. "I was concerned about you. I know that must seem strange."

To his surprise, a tight, triumphant smile flashed across Mandy's face.

"You don't have to explain," she said. Then she straightened up and lifted her gaze to where the floor numbers were glowing, one by one.

"I wanted you here and here you are. This is our floor."

In the corridor, the overhead lights were on the blink, and a musty smell was pervading a dim quiet. Mandy led him straight to 1804, and then closed the apartment door behind him, locked it twice, and stood on tiptoe to bolt it shut.

"Sit," she said, touching one of the chairs at the dining table. She continued onward to the kitchen with a loping gait, her shoulders darting like pistons.

Saionton watched her until she was out of sight. He only had time to adjust his hair in his phone camera, and remind himself to be master of the situation, before she returned with a glass of water. She placed the glass before him, and then walked around to the adjoining chair of the round table, where she seated herself, brushed the hair from her temples, and proceeded to light a cigarette.

"Why had you gone downstairs?" asked Saionton. "It's pretty unsafe."

"I needed a smoke," said Mandy, exhaling thinly. Then she fixed her gaze on him. "So what's going on? What's the news at the Company?"

"You keep asking me that. I don't know anything special. I haven't heard from them since the *Mahasabha* happened." Saionton took a sip of water and shrugged in a manner that he hoped was nonchalant. "Don't know if I still have a job even."

Frowning now, she smoked rapidly. "Oh."

"But I may have some ideas."

"It's insane." Mandy looked at him. "It's not real."

"I know. On the way here – the stuff I saw. It feels like it can't be real. But it is really happening."

Suddenly her lips curled nastily. "Those fucking bastards. With their tricks."

She puffed smoke and stared into space. Saionton controlled an impulse to snap at her.

"What do you mean?" he asked patiently.

"All of this," said Mandy, "is being orchestrated by the Company."

"At the *Mahasabha*," said Saionton, with an edge in his voice, "you said they were orchestrating those protests too. That they were going to come and placate everybody. But that's not what happened."

"Yes." She looked at him again, with her pale, frank eyes. "It's worse than I thought."

"What is it?"

"I don't know!" A fit of palpitations was upon her. Her hand, her lips were all trembling and still she forced herself to raise the cigarette to her mouth, and to speak, with a tremor in her voice that was naked and unsubdued. "I was talking to the shrine. Trying to understand. But it stopped working an hour ago. Updating! It's been doing that on and off, the last two days. Updating!"

"I didn't know that," said Saionton. "I only used it today, for a little while."

"When I went downstairs," said Mandy, shuddering uncontrollably, "I almost got killed. It was— I don't want to talk about it!"

"Do you want to sit on the sofa?" inquired Saionton. His eye alighted on the swell of her breasts, more discernible now than before. "Maybe lie down?"

Momentarily, she followed the jerk of his head, in the direction of the couches and armchairs, then shook her head and looked at him gravely.

"No. I'm fine. I was hoping someone would come…to talk."

"Yes, let's talk," said Saionton, with a decisiveness that surprised him. It had only taken an instant, but now the thought of her seduction, which had lain thickly upon him, had fallen away and was receding in confusion. He felt a pang of loss, but for the sake of clear thinking willed that it recede further and further, infinitely far, even as he concentrated his mind to speak his thoughts.

"There's something different," he said aloud, "about these riots, different from riots before. It's not just that they seem so random. Although I can't explain the randomness. But it's the malice. I feel a lot of malice, all about."

"Yes," said Mandy. The cigarette withered in her grasp and she stubbed it out on the place mat. "You're right. There is malice about."

"I mean, even though the violence feels random, it feels *super-personal*. There was someone who attacked me on the road. I ran away. But what I saw in her face…it was like she hated me personally, just for my *existence*. Even though she had nothing specific against me. I felt like, if she *had* had something specific against me – like supposing she hated Bengalis or something like that – then I wouldn't even have felt so hated. I don't know if that makes sense."

Mandy was nodding, with her eyes boring into him, and through him.

"In the parking lot," she said, "there was an old man sitting on a bench. I know him, he lives on the thirteenth floor. His legs are bad. He has arthritis. He started to talk to me about how he hates old age and losing his faculties. He said it's making him suicidal. Then – just when I started to say something – he pulled out a knife from his jacket. He was old and slow and I got away. But there was this thing in his eyes. First I thought maybe he was jealous of my being healthy. But it actually seemed beyond that."

"He was angry with something else," said Saionton, nodding. "But then he attacked you."

"Even the man you saw in the elevator," Mandy continued. "He began with ranting about stray animals. In the lobby, two days ago. Saying how they bite and spread disease and what a menace they are. Then suddenly he started shooting people. And I just realized. We have many stray dogs in this complex. I don't think he fired at any of them!"

Suddenly her brow creased.

"What happened?" said Saionton.

"Do you hear that?"

He listened anxiously for footsteps, or distant gunshots, or raised voices. But nothing came to his ear, except a long, low whine from outside the door.

"What is that? A fire alarm?"

"It's the wind," said Mandy. "They say there's a cyclone coming."

"Oh really?"

"I'm going to check the windows. Gimme a sec."

In her absence, Saionton settled himself more snugly in his chair. He felt unaccountably happy. Turning, he gazed out at the sky, through the glass doors of the balcony. The light was limpid and bright, flooding and burnishing the room, although great dark wisps of clouds were floating in empty space. Then she reappeared, with a smile on her face.

"All good."

"Your house looks different," said Saionton.

She nodded grimly. "I know. I've not been taking care of it."

"No, but it looks nice. Natural. The light is nice too."

As she sank into her chair, her face was still severely thoughtful. She untied her hair, absently, and then began to twirl a strand of it. Her foot tapped quietly on the floor.

"Can I ask you something?" she said.

He nodded faintly. A moment passed.

"What did you think of Aaron? At the *sabha*. If you heard him speak at all?"

"I heard him when he was talking about plants. Hallucinatory plants, and how we need them to see through the deception."

"Wasn't it sounding silly? What was that? Like smoking up will save the world?"

"People believe in them a lot," said Saionton casually. "Don't you too?"

She was looking away, frowning hard, and still worrying her hair.

"I'm not satisfied," said Mandy at last. "I've learned a lot from Aaron. He opened up my mind to lots of realities. Before, I was just a kind of society girl. But now, this seems too simple."

"Where is Aaron now?" wondered Saionton.

"Still in the hills. As far as I know. He's happy about the riots. He says people are healing, after all the manipulation. He says it's natural and it's just a phase. There's violence happening all over, you know. It's not only Mumbai any longer."

"Really? All over India?"

"That's what I'm hearing. Don't you follow the news?"

"Not much," said Saionton. "Too many ads."

Something was welling up in him, a thought he hadn't worked out, but which broke, like a wave. He spoke with sadness, without thinking.

"I liked Aaron. When I met him here that day. I liked him a lot, I felt I could have spent all – well, at least a lot of time with him. I liked the building secretary too, the crazy one I told you about. I don't show it. But I like most people I meet."

He paused to gather himself. Mandy had stopped fidgeting and was sitting quite composed, with her eyes resting on him.

"Even when I'm just walking on the road," Saionton went on, "I like it when I catch a stranger's eye and we smile or nod or just acknowledge each other's existence. It's a cliche, I know, that people in India are so warm and all, but it's true too. I think it's always been true. But now – when I was on the road – I was afraid to catch *anybody's* eye. That's what feels so terrible about this. It's as though all that basic humanity has been sucked out of the air. Suddenly!"

"Nothing happens suddenly," said Mandy. "You only suddenly realize it."

She pursed her mouth, and he noticed the cut of her jaw and chin, and the lines that formed around her eyes, and he had a kind of premonition of Mandy as an old woman, with a thin, wise face.

"Personally –" she looked hard at him, "– I never enjoyed being stared at by people on the road. Either then or now."

"Of course. But what I meant was—"

"I understood. What you meant." She lit another cigarette.

"By the way," asked Saionton, "I'm curious. Do you work somewhere? Or did you use to work somewhere?"

"Did I.... Oh never mind," Mandy answered archly, and was youthful again, bristling with verve. "I've done a lot of things. Basically, I've wasted my life. I do, however, want to write."

"Good, then I can act."

Then, because it made little sense, they were both smiling. Saionton glanced over his shoulder. There were light streaks visible in the sky. Even as he looked, the wind began driving the rain up to the balcony, in wet, rippling sheets. They spoke at the same time.

"Listen—"

"Do you remember—"

"You go on," said Saionton. His face was reddening, but she seemed not to notice.

"At the *Mahasabha*," she said. "When Roshan Dubey began telling people how he *loved* them, and how all he wanted was to make them *happy*, did you notice how they reacted?"

"I switched off then," said Saionton. "I just couldn't listen to him."

"I saw them," said Mandy. "They were eating out of his hand."

Her eyes had begun sparkling in a way he had seen before, with a headlong feverishness that was also vexing and provocative.

"People are saying he's dead. He's not dead. It was all pretending. He was playing them all. Aaron too. Roshan Dubey's behind everything," she concluded feelingly, and then added, with a burst of flamboyance, "I have the power to spot a person like that."

"How do you know," retorted Saionton, "that *I'm* not a person like that?"

"You?"

He nodded expressionlessly. "A joker. A deceiver."

"Why? What did you *deceive* me about?"

"I told you I had gotten cancer. And then recovered."

"Yes."

"Actually, I made that up. I never had cancer. Also, I said my parents had died. My parents didn't die, they were just separated. I grew up with my mom and her sister. They're all still alive."

She continued to smoke, crossing and uncrossing her legs and leaning back in her chair, just as though she hadn't heard him. Then her eyes turned on him. They were glistening.

"I felt bad for you."

"I know."

Drawing in her breath, Mandy opened her mouth, but then closed it tightly and looked away. Her eyes were wetter than ever.

Saionton tried, experimentally, to smile, but it wouldn't take. The hurt in her face had surprised him. He hadn't expected anything so vivid, nor the corresponding reaction in himself. He felt submerged in an uncomfortable element, something both cloying and stabbing.

"I'm sorry," said Saionton.

"Death is a joke to you?" Now her face, in a cloud of smoke, stared balefully.

"It seems to be a joke to other people. They never think about it."

"Why would you make up things like that? Why would anyone—"

"Because I think about it! And what else can I do? I'm an actor, even if I don't have any plays or movies. So what? I still have these things! They're all I have. Life! And death! And you!"

You. What did he mean by that? He couldn't say, and she didn't question him. But she was shaking her head, in an attitude of disbelief. Yet it was not without theatricality – not without being fascinated by him – that Mandy dispensed with the second cigarette, and, still slowly shaking her head from side to side, got up and walked away. She made her way to the balcony.

The rain was coming down like curtains. They could both hear the wind in the corridor, howling ghoulishly.

"Do you have a car?" Mandy called out. "Did you – will you be able to get home?"

"You want me to leave?"

She was staring at the gale, biting her lip. Saionton also had stood up. He watched her, with her dark hair falling over her shoulders, and her body lithe and accessible before him. There surged through him a wave of high emotion, and then, suddenly, he was quite calm.

"Do you want me to leave?"

Mandy stepped back from the balcony. Turning deliberately toward Saionton, she frowned. "I'm not sure," she said at last.

She was still ruminating, when he noticed her gaze suddenly flicker – and seize.

A white envelope had appeared near the bottom of the front door. Immediately the doorbell rang out, in a long fluttery peal. Saionton started forward.

"Don't!" Mandy whispered fiercely. "Leave it alone!"

"Don't worry," he said softly. "It's for me," he added, with an astonished clarity that owed to his having spotted the bold print on the white paper, that spelled both the Company logo, and his own full name.

When he stooped to pick up the envelope, he was surprised to find Mandy by his side, restraining him.

"Don't open the door," she whispered again, her hand gripping his arm. Then she raised herself, pushing her chest up against the door, with one eye scrunched shut and the other at the peephole.

CHAPTER TWENTY-ONE

Mandy stepped down from tiptoe with a puzzled expression.

"Who is it?"

"Have a look," she answered quite normally, not bothering to lower her voice.

When he put his eye to the glass the corridor was in darkness. Then the overhead lights sparked back on. Standing a few paces back, on a base of wheels, was a plastic child-bot, in a red kurta and pajamas. A broad smile appeared fixed on its head.

"It's a Company bot," said Saionton. "A welcome-bot. But how did they know I was here? With you?"

"You have a Company phone, don't you? They can track you, then. What's in the envelope?"

"I haven't opened it yet. Feels like a card. And something else."

"Strange."

"Yes," agreed Saionton. "This is probably the strangest thing that's happened so far."

"Enough then!" said Mandy, suddenly animated. She pulled at the door, but it caught in the wind. With a massive tug she wrenched it open, and cried out swiftly, "What is it?"

There was a low humming noise that mingled with the wind's whining.

The robot began, "A warm hello from the Company! Mr. Saionton's presence is immediately requested on the Company campus. A car is waiting downstairs. For safety reasons, it is an armored vehicle."

"Where's the driver?" asked Saionton. "Why did they send you?"

"The vehicle is fully self-driving. For safety reasons, this travel ticket is being fulfilled without human intermediaries."

"I see. Because everyone's out rioting! But why now? I mean, why do they want me to come to campus now?"

"For more information," piped the bot, "you may consult the documentation in the envelope. However, your presence on campus today has been scheduled as *mandatory*. I will escort you to the car."

"What if I'm not coming?" said Saionton dully.

The plastic child said nothing, but its smile, in Saionton's eyes, had acquired a sinister quality.

By his side, Mandy grasped his arm again. She was staring eagerly. "I'm coming with you."

"Why would you?"

"I have to!"

He saw again that glittering light in her eye, that seemed that it would penetrate all secrets, whether of earth or heaven or hell.

Then, in confusion, she glanced around, at the haunted corridor and the well-lit house. "It's not safe for me here. It's not safe."

"That's true," said Saionton. "It's not safe."

"Wait here. I'll get my bag."

Saionton nodded. A kind of fatalism was settling over him, a sense of surrender that was both thrilling and disturbing, but in any case inexorable.

When she reappeared, she had changed into jeans and a bulkier top, and tied up her hair again. A large beige bag was slung over her left shoulder. The robot, saying nothing further, now wheeled down the hallway, and they followed it into a waiting elevator and then silently down to the lobby.

Outside, half-obscured in the rain, was a massive, chunky car, with a panoply of flashing lights. The child-bot got in at the front, going up a retractable ramp. Saionton and Mandy fell into the back, where there was plush leather seating and plenty of legroom. The car's windows were thick and wide. The rain spent itself on them. The engine whined automatically into motion, and as they drove off into the storm and the pressing chaos, they both felt surprisingly, powerfully sleepy.

It was not long before her eyes were closed and her breathing rhythmic. He looked at her face, aslant on the cushioning, marked with peacefulness.

It was strange to think that he had ever seen disagreement or enmity in Mandy's eyes, that he yet would. He was swept with gratefulness. But for her, he knew, he would have been pulled out of joint, all asunder, with everything he didn't understand of what was happening. Yet with her presence, it was all of it, even the dreadfulness, only like stretching one's limbs pleasurably and securely.

Before he shut his own eyes, he remembered the white envelope. In it, predictably, he found a brochure of Company products, advertising various specifications of Shrine Tech hardware (the latest at astronomical prices, which only the super-rich could dream of), ergonomic 'worship' seats to make the neural link experience more comfortable (while Saionton had only kneeled on the hard floor), assorted electronic items, clothes and apparel, and finally groceries. But along with the brochure, there fell out a thick piece of paper, with a letterhead. *From the desk of Roshan Dubey*. It was only a few lines:

Dear Saionton,

It is my pleasure to invite you to the private unveiling of the Company's latest Shrine Tech software – version 3.0 – on the Company campus.

I apologize for being out of touch.

In anticipation,

Roshan Dubey

Chief Happy Maker

* * *

A rainy haze was over the hills in which the Company HQ lay secreted. They had entered calmer weather. In place of the winds that were blowing through the city was an overcast stirring, and a nip and lushness in the air. Through the vehicle's windows, they saw wild foliage climbing thickly about them. They were descending by turns toward the valley of the campus.

Mandy was wide awake and staring out in silence. But Saionton, to whom the journey was not new, felt deeply estranged. He was restless. A leaden feeling had entered his throat, and he found himself swallowing many times, uneasily. When they entered the final stretch, now misty and ghostly, like a place plucked out of time, he began to speak.

"We're there now. We'll be stopping at the gate. I'll have to show my ID to the watchmen."

It transpired that he was mistaken. The Company gates were pulled wide open, and the watchmen's cubicle was empty. Perhaps it had been deserted for days. There was no one in sight at all as the huge car rolled into the campus and proceeded up the path to the plaza, where the wilderness receded, and manicured lawns and pavements girdled them all about.

Far behind them, noiselessly, the gates had swung shut on their hinges. Saionton was staring at the parking area by the plaza. It was full of armored vehicles exactly like their own.

"What are all these cars for?" he said, and then tapped the child-bot's head to get its attention.

"For safety reasons," the bot spoke up, "all of our guests were transported in B-18 models. Some have been on campus since last night, and some arrived this morning. You were scheduled to arrive in the afternoon, as your session begins after lunch."

"What session? What other guests?"

"The other guests," murmured Mandy, reclining on the cushioning, "for the 3.0 unveiling."

Saionton glanced at her. She was smiling lazily, looking rested and peaceable, with a markedly feline self-satisfaction. "You saw the card," she said. "But if you're all *scheduled*, well then, I guess *I'm* the odd one out."

"There will be no difficulty," the bot, which was unpredictably silent and unpredictably garrulous, said unasked. "Guests may have companions. As a matter of fact, this is recommended – for happiness. Sir and madam –" it turned its head to beam at them, as the engine died and the car doors slid open, "– you may join the group."

Outside, a set of figures was standing in the mist, as motionless as the trees that seemed bolted in place on the concrete surface of the plaza.

When they stepped out of the car, Mandy and Saionton first huddled in the cold and stared at the four men. They both saw faces they recognized. But they said nothing to one another. It was as though their mutual alliance, which had seemed, at other points that day, to be fast and intimate, was suspended already, at the first breath of the frosted air. Already, they were less aware of the other's presence. After some instinct of their own, their bodies swayed close and touched briefly. But what was in their minds was pressing upon them unutterably.

In a glance, Saionton had taken them all in. Aaron Sehgal, Shailesh Rao, Jaspreet Bhatia, and Vivek Chaturvedi, aka V. He knew how they were all connected, these famous, voluble opponents of the Company. Now they were standing in the Company plaza, grouped close together. Yet his first impression was of a profound disconnection. In their lofty faces and distant gazes was a quality that made him shudder, and when their farseeing eyes passed over him, and he saw their mouths moving, the hairs on his arms bristled.

"Gentlemen!" called a rasping voice. Lance Burns came jogging through the mist, wearing what looked like red-and-blue spandex. He paused at the sight of the new arrivals. "Gentlemen – and lady! Shall we proceed for lunch? We're having lunch by the banyan tree. It's a short walk, but I promise it'll be worth it!"

The quartet in the plaza seemed to deign to consider him. For his part, Lance also looked different, but while the others' faces were marked with enormous indifference, he seemed on pins and needles. Red blotches were spoiling his forehead and cheeks. His hair was unusually well combed, his eyes were flashing, and he was grinning continuously, yet in a manner suggestive of pain. With his thin body, now clothed brightly in skintight colors, he seemed to Saionton like a convalescent clown, a circus freak.

"Now that we're all here! Shall we?"

"Is this everyone?" Saionton said suddenly. "Isn't...?" His gaze swept over the group.

"The priest?" cackled Lance. "Are you thinking of the priest? Father Joachim refused our invitation! It doesn't matter. We'll be blessed without him! Come on, guys! So there's this huge fountain up ahead...." He had turned on his heel and begun to march away, not in the direction of the head offices, but elsewhere, toward yet more looming, brutalist buildings, outlined in the gloom. "It's one of the most powerful in the world. We don't crank it all the way up, but if we ever did, ooh boy! You're talking eighty meters tall, at a hundred mph. Pardon me! I should say, a hundred and sixty *k*ph. Not that today's the weather for fountains! Anyhoo!" With Lance advancing, the guests too stirred into motion, like stone statues coming to life. Turning, Saionton saw that Mandy had left his side, and was already walking quickly, ahead of the rest. He began to step forward, himself.

Presently, a stately figure fell in beside him. It was the Building Secretary, smiling thinly.

"Good rains all over Maharashtra," opined the Secretary. "In Mumbai the lakes are full. Here it is less, because of the hills. So. You must be familiar with the campus."

A singsong cadence was in the Secretary's voice, which otherwise was weary.

"Not really," said Saionton. "Actually, I've only visited the main building. All the rest of it – I've no idea. It's a huge campus."

Broad stone steps had appeared before them, ascending to an embankment. The frantic rustling of a fountain was audible in the distance. But the haze in the air was gathering and swirling, and though Saionton looked around, peering hard, the plaza they had left behind was already invisible, and even the surrounding mountainside was more sensed than seen.

"The main building," yawned Shailesh, "you must have been there, that time I sent you."

Saionton felt himself tensing. He had hoped, with the money pocketed, that the subject was forgotten.

"I'm sorry that result was not in your favor, sir. But I did what you asked me to."

There was a sound like powerful sobs. But the Secretary, in fact, was laughing. Suddenly Saionton noticed that, below his pullover and trousers, the man was walking completely barefoot. At the sight of this, an unexpected nausea climbed up to Saionton's throat.

"It's all fine." The Secretary had switched to Hindi. "The motherfucker is helping us."

With gasps and sighs that belied his age, he was now climbing the steps. In between deep breaths, he continued to speak. "He is on our side, only…he only pretends that he is with the invaders…. He is protecting India…from the inside…. As long as he is sitting on that throne…he is managing everyone…these outsiders…these insiders…all…so India is safe…. Maharana Pratap…is secure…forever."

An immense placidity bathed the Secretary's face as he paused on the stairway, catching his breath. Then, suddenly, his features contorted in a tidal rush of fury.

"Let them come, I say! Let the motherfuckers come! Let them murder us in our beds. Let them destroy our culture! Let them rape our women. Let them rape our women!" he repeated, smacking his lips.

Suddenly, heartily, he clapped Saionton on the back. "Worry not." Shailesh Rao was smiling again. "Our Happy Maker is protecting…the land…. He is protecting…?"

The Secretary's voice faded questioningly, and he fixed his eyes on Saionton. The smile had altogether disappeared.

"Protecting India," replied Saionton.

They heaved up the final few stairs, and stepped into a blaze of electric lighting on a tiled pathway. The other figures were dwindling before them, to where a fountain roared and shimmered. But the Secretary halted, and touched him again on the shoulder.

"Protecting?"

"Protecting India," repeated Saionton deliriously. "And Maharana Pratap."

"Motherfucker," said Shailesh Rao, nodding, with a weight of such meaning as could never be grasped.

It could never be grasped because it could never be revealed. Nothing could be revealed from that face, howsoever lit up, that stared through inky, kohl-lined eyes, that stared, alas, through ruins of stone and dust, wherein it lay trapped and proud and incomprehensible. In a flash, Saionton seemed to remember faces all over the city, and in every town and city of the country, staring from shopfronts and street corners; staring from windows and balconies; in parks and in living rooms; all the demonic reserve of India, staring. But he had never seen it so magnified as now, in the face of the Building Secretary.

Hearing Lance's voice, he broke away in relief, and hurried on into the gloaming.

The fountains were legion, spurting in unison from a wide watery base, and traveling no higher than twenty feet at present. Despite the cold and the murk, Lance was standing in the spray, alongside a raised plaque on which were engraved the words *Peace and Goodwill*. Facing him, with their arms folded, were V and Jaspreet. But Mandy stood a distance away, shooting glances in all directions. Diametrically opposite her, quite imperiously detached, Aaron Sehgal had become interested in a hedge of potted plants that flourished by the pathway.

"This block where we're standing," declared Lance, "is admin level B. It's got a library, an IT cell, couple of robot-only testing labs, and a chunk of legal. Plus auditoriums, cafes, and a state-of-the-art gym. There's a gym in every block of the campus. Sorry, I didn't catch that?"

"Work hours!" barked Jaspreet, for a second time. "What are they?"

"Flexible, that's what they are. Flexible. Today, for instance, we've got nobody around. Because today is for you guys! But tomorrow, tomorrow!" Lance's eyes suddenly goggled hugely. "I understand we'll be back to our best *tomorrow*. The place'll be packed. People working day and night. Sorry, what was that?"

"Robots! How much do robots work?"

"Oh, they work all the time. Twenty-four seven."

The sharp sound of clapping erupted. Jaspreet, evidently now too delighted to stand still, was ambling along the path, clapping and smirking.

"Hey, come back." Lance had begun to laugh. "It's this way!" Saionton watched him jog up to what looked like a sheer concrete wall face, part of the extended avenue of angular buildings that the mist was playing peekaboo with.

As he looked, a square section of the wall sank slowly into the ground, and a pitch-black void appeared in its place. Then Lance stepped into it and was quickly gone from sight. But his voice was still calling out to them.

Near the hidden passage, which enclosed a set of lighted steps glowing downward into darkness, Saionton crossed paths with Mandy. She had hung back from the rest of the group, desiring, perhaps, to be the last to enter.

"Are you OK?" he said, for something to say.

At the sound of his voice, Mandy clutched her handbag close, before relaxing visibly with a smile. In the fog and the diffuse light, she looked ethereally beautiful.

"I'm famished," she said. "He did say lunch?"

CHAPTER TWENTY-TWO

The air had become still and clear, almost at the first step he took. It was immediately warmer too, and thus perfectly pleasant. Down below, Saionton could see Mandy picking her way forward, by the embedded lights, carefully, but enthusiastically. A silence was emanating from the depths of the earth, where the others had disappeared, and the silence was alluring, full of significance, like an indrawn breath.

But Saionton was standing rigid. He was overcome, suddenly, by horror; convinced, suddenly, that with every descending step they were being delivered into evil. Standing there, all unbidden, there came to him the memory of sweat-soaked nights filled with tossing and turning, and then – what he had never consciously seen or imagined – the Shrine Tech machine, gleaming in its corner, whispering with malice. Deformed faces were scrambling through his mind, his own, and Zara Shah's, and her killer's. Yet all these, he now sensed, had only been premonitions and portents of that horror, which he was now drawing near, and in the terrible clarity of daytime. And when this thought had settled upon him, then he could no longer breathe.

He made an effort. As his breath returned, in gasps, a breeze began to blow on his face. It seemed to him like the steady cooling of an air conditioner. Then his limbs jerked into motion. Someone was exclaiming, but it wasn't him, and moreover the cry was one of excitement and happiness. Quickening his steps, Saionton ran down to a brick wall. Here the staircase ended, and the passage turned sharply, plunging all at once into the splendid luminosity of an underground garden.

"Ahem!" Lance was coughing dramatically, but Saionton could not look at him immediately. The place was cavernous, the ceiling vaulting high into darkness, but awash in artificial illumination, from speckled stars on high, and halogen lamps, planted in the ground, and from mounted panels of fluorescent lights. The lights were of different colors, blazing red on beds of flowers, and blue on shrubs and stalks, and elsewhere yellow and white. Altogether a pale, pleasant sheen spread over the garden, in which grasses and trees and flowers seemed to flourish densely in all directions.

But straight ahead, where the grass was dewy and green, was a kind of fairy circle, twinkling with brightness. Here the members of their group, now looking strangely graceful and artistic, stood about a circular dining table, surrounded by high-backed chairs. Behind them, and about them, the thicket of a banyan tree was spreading its branches and roots. As he gazed at the banyan, thus forming the backdrop, Saionton was reminded irresistibly of a stage, and he had no sooner stepped into the circle of light than he felt, as well, that euphoric rush that only performance had ever given him.

With the exception of Lance, who was suddenly nowhere to be seen, the others were seated, and already absorbed with their napkins and cutlery. When Saionton had occupied the last remaining chair, then as though on cue a buzzing filled the air, and a small army of child-bots began laying the table with various platters and pitchers.

A jug, brimful of Coke, was placed before Saionton. "Your order, sir," said the serving robot, setting down a plate of potato wedges.

"But I didn't order anything."

"By now," said the bot with a grin, "we know your preferences, sir."

"Actually, this is *not* what I—"

But the robot had departed, humming some gay tune. Saionton looked around the table. V was already taking a knife to a large piece of fried fish, while the Secretary practically had his head in a plate of instant noodles. Mandy, sitting upright, was sipping on white wine. Opposite her, Aaron stared proudly at a plate of fruits. But it was V's fish that Saionton was coveting, staring and even licking his lips, when suddenly he recoiled. A breath of whisky was in his face. Jaspreet Bhatia had leaned over.

"We never spoke. I'm Jaspreet."

"Yes, I know. But we did meet – the other day."

"When I destroyed your robot." He nodded. "I had to do that."

"It's fine," said Saionton. "I don't mind."

A smile twisted the face that stared at him. It was a friendly, fleshy face, with eyes screwed up under a white turban. Saionton had seen Jaspreet before, agitated and upset for reasons of his own. But his face was slack now, full of a lolling calm, in which his lips were twitching, as though tugged at.

"The machine," said Jaspreet in a whining voice, "is the master of man. I was always aware of this. They are stronger, smarter, they never get tired. I am an employer, I run many businesses. I have seen how men work. Shoddy, making excuses. So I was always aware. But now I happily accept it. Only, I had to fight then, to prove myself. You see, every man will not be a slave. Most will be slaves. But some will be masters."

Looking away, Saionton poured out a glass of Coke. But his hand was not steady – and then another hand fell over it.

"A machine's entire business," continued Jaspreet intently, "is business. A machine means business. Just like me. Just like Roshan Dubey. So we are on the same team. Together with the machines, our team is making a new world. So then why was I fighting him? Can you remember?"

"You said AI was taking over jobs."

"It is." The man nodded again. "It must, and it will. The Happy Maker will ensure that. Machines will rule over the human race. But I just told you the answer. I was fighting to prove myself. That I am not like this weak race. Weak humans. They are like children. And you too! See, I just told you the answer, but even then you did not know the answer!"

Suddenly, his face seemed to collapse in compassion. His lips were pouting, his cheeks hanging in jowls. Before Saionton could react, the man's hand had reached to stroke his hair.

"So soft! Like a child. By god. I feel for people like my own children. You can ask my employees."

But when his fingers tugged at Saionton's cheeks, Saionton pulled back, exclaiming forcefully, "Stop that!"

"Don't mind," said Jaspreet, shaking his head mournfully. "Business is business." His face was firming up again. As he returned to his whisky, the thin smile and the listless gaze had resumed. Then a tinkling sound struck up around them, and all the guests looked up.

In the chiaroscuro of the banyan tree, Lance was standing between two gnarled roots, tapping a spoon on a wine glass.

"Friends!" he exclaimed, throwing out his arms comically. "The Company is delighted to have you all with us. But most of all, we are delighted to call you our *friends*. Friendship is a journey, with its ups and downs. I know that not long ago, it seemed we wouldn't make it!"

He paused, awaiting encouragement, but the faces in the audience appeared more bored than anything. A flash of irritation made Lance look his old self. Then, once more, he forced a smile.

"But now! After all that you've seen last night – or, in some cases, this morning – or, for others among you, what you're seeing right now…I guess – I know! – that we're *good*!"

A staccato interruption made him falter. The Building Secretary was laughing, and very quickly the laughter around the table was general. Saionton, who was giggling himself, saw many shades pass over Lance's spotlit face. There was confusion and displeasure and condescension, and lastly a ferocity that reminded him, with a start, of the morning's rickshaw driver. Then a desperate grin covered them all.

"Say hi to the chief!" said Lance, stepping aside from the tree.

A quiet fell over the gathering. But V put down his knife and fork, put his fingers in his mouth and whistled. Then the table was thumped, and hands clapped together. In the heart of the banyan, in the crook of two thick branches, the static of a hologram was taking shape. As they watched, it became perfected.

Around him, the clapping intensified, but Saionton stared in silence. The head of Roshan Dubey was floating before them. The same disembodied head that had been splashed all over the media, disfigured, and dripping with blood. It was perfectly healthy as it peered from the banyan tree. It was large and contented, like the first time he'd faced it, though sprouting in addition a little pencil moustache. But that was not what made him shiver.

"What shall I say?" said the voice he knew well. "Shall I greet you as my friends?" Glasses were raised, along with cheers and sloppy, surrendering smiles. Heads were straining eagerly toward the head in the tree.

"Or shall I hail you, for the gods that you are!" Then the lights dimmed, both in the circle of the gathering and all around the garden. Soon they were sitting in darkness, with the quiet whirring of distant fans, and only the singular face, gleaming in suspension.

Saionton fidgeted in his chair. It seemed to him that the teeth in the head were protruding too far, and were abnormally sharp.

"I don't wish to interrupt your lunch," said the hovering head – which was also visibly larger than life-size. The voice that came from it was slow and rich, rather like a growl.

"However, I wanted to be here, so that I could thank you for what happened at the *sabha*. You showed me your godly power that day. Right? You put me to death. You shed my blood. But you were only doing your *dharma*. And I also did my *dharma*. I died for you. Therefore – as you now know – no power in the world can separate us. Right? Now you *are* happy. Now I *am*...."

Through the darkness came the sound of sighing. "The Happy Maker," said a chorus of voices.

From inside the face in the tree, the tongue flecked ravenously, and the *R*s rolled, in a throaty way that was new to Saionton.

"R-r-r-i-i-ght...."

He felt himself squirming. A hothouse sensation was rising up under his collar. The face, the voice, the way it smiled and spoke; it was all terribly cheesy. But that wasn't all.

The eyes were gleaming, each time they met his. When they glanced away, they were almost mournful with benevolence. But when they lingered on him, then they bored into him, with a power that seemed to pin him to his seat. He felt, somehow, that he was on notice, and this sense was confirmed by what happened next.

"We belong to one another," the face continued. "And you all know I won't let you down. I have always been a man after your own heart. Together, we are creating the world of your dreams. A world in which

India stands tall. Where the whole *structure* is glorious." Here the face beamed at Shailesh, and then, briefly but definitely, winked at Saionton. "A world of power, efficiency, of strength over weakness." It nodded at Jaspreet. "A world in which artistry and excellence dominate, and *unbridled* liberty is *everywhere*." Here the face lingered quite earnestly on V, and then, for another brief instant, stuck its tongue out at Saionton. "A world in which illusions are torn down, in which deception simply cannot stand." And with its eyes humbly closed, the head bowed toward Aaron Sehgal. "Your world. My world. Our world. Right?"

Then its lips parted, the teeth seemed to glint with pleasure, and Saionton, who was already smiling, felt a contagious mirth shaking his shoulders. The spasm halted when he noticed Roshan scowling at the figure to his right, whom he had quite forgotten about.

Mandy was sitting up straight, with her fingers gripping the edge of the table. She was staring at him, and perhaps had been for some time. Waves of worry were upon her face.

"With that," came Roshan's voice, "I take your leave. I am sure you have plenty on your minds to keep you entertained. Lance will take care of you for the rest of today. Mind you! Lance's time may end. But today will never end. Today is the beginning of the rest of our lives."

Many things seemed to happen then, all at once. The face in the tree disappeared. The lights came up blindingly, even brighter than before. Serving-bots were fussing around the table, bringing in main courses – a Rajasthani thali, a massive burger, curry and rice, among others. Music, a kind of tinkling elevator muzak, had struck up, and on the muddy grass between the banyan and the dining table, a child-bot styled as a young girl in a tank top was seen moving its arms and thrusting its torso. The robot was soon joined by Lance, who danced for a few minutes, with an air of angry abstraction, before wiping the sweat off his face and jogging off into the surrounding garden.

Saionton sank his teeth into the burger. A juicy, meaty burst of flavor filled him from top to toe. The burger was delicious, all right. But it was leaking sauce and too altogether rotund for his liking. He was still chewing and swallowing, but already with a certain weariness, when the sound of burping, lengthy and unmelodious, made him look up, and then around.

A strange consternation began to take hold of him. They were all simply eating. It was perhaps Aaron, handsome in his vest and shirtsleeves, his back upright, who had let out the belch. But the table was utterly devoid of conversation. As the minutes passed, with nothing but chewing and grunting, swallowing, and squalid exhalations, with the robot still jerking on the grass to a looping synthetic tune, Saionton felt his appetite turning to ash. He thought of saying something to Mandy, but discovered, to his surprise, that he was afraid to. He was, in fact, apprehensive of saying anything, as though they were in the midst, not of four gluttonous men, but of unknown beasts – or worse.

Their faces were riveting to him. When they ate and drank, then anger and triumph seemed to flash in their eyes, but when they rested from their labors and gazed about, it was with an infinite, inhuman boredom. He had only glimpsed it in the plaza. Now it was appallingly near. They were proud looks, but also full of hardness and meanness, and with a burning core of something unnameable, that came off in fiery waves, and seemed to intensify with every increase of their gastronomic pleasure. In this aspect, they were each similar, yet they behaved – almost – as though dining alone, treating the others with a kind of neglectful complacence. Not only was conversation absent, but also courtesies. Once, a curious thing happened. V pointed at a bowl of dal that was close to Shailesh. At once, a serving-bot rushed up, but was swatted away by the Secretary. Then V looked away and laughed in the direction of the trees. The Secretary also smiled, scratching himself vigorously under the table. They continued, peaceably, to eat what lay before them. But Saionton felt a chill enveloping him.

"Are you OK?" said Mandy.

He felt, though he didn't see, their faces turning, and all the detached weight of madness leaning on the pair of them. Saionton shook his head, not wanting to glance up. But she asked again. In vain – now that she had spoken – he tried to sound humorous.

"Do you remember *Alice in Wonderland*?"

"The Red Queen," said Mandy.

"Yes. No. What I'm thinking of...."

"What?"

But she had gotten distracted, and he was relieved. Up ahead, in his joker's costume, Lance was bounding into the light again.

"Gentlemen! Give us a moment, please. We must spread the last course. Much obliged!" Then he cupped his hands over his mouth, and called out, "Girls!"

A pitch darkness snapped over the garden, and all was quiet. But Saionton, as he sat there, was taken back years, to the blackness of a theater, deep inkiness cloaking the movement of shadows, and the swiftest and most hushed of practiced exertions – in between acts. He knew, suddenly, that that was what was happening. The stage was being set, in between acts. And mingling with his other emotions, in amongst the disgust and aversion, he felt a returning excitement.

A spotlight appeared on the base of the banyan, and then left it, going roving and searching across the grass and the shrubbery, flashing over wondrous creepers and flowers, and toward the false sky of the ceiling, before circling around, blinding them all briefly, and then climbing back, and up, into the tree's canopy. There it came to rest on an immense overhanging branch.

Three female figures were seated on the branch, with their hair flowing and their legs dangling. They were all in white, bare-armed and barefoot, and staring fixedly at the dining table.

There was the sound of breath sharply indrawn. Mandy was sitting up, pale and stiff. Suddenly, Saionton recognized one of the women: the Caucasian lady from the *Mahasabha*, who had sat listening to Aaron's whiteboard musings.

"Allow me," Lance muttered, appearing below the branches. His tone had become brutally flat, as though he had lost all interest in feigning enthusiasm. "This here is Priyanka. Still in college. She's for V. The one in the middle is Clara. She'll be Aaron's girl. And next to her is what we call Sweetie Pie. She's a robot. She's—"

With a clumsy thud, Jaspreet Bhatia got to his feet. His hand was raised aloft.

"Yes," agreed Lance. Then there was another crashing sound, and all the plates and vessels shivered. Shailesh Rao had climbed onto the table. One hairy foot lay planted in his *thali*. His face was riven with enormous grief.

Lance sighed. "We have not forgotten you, Mr. Rao. Since your preference is within holo-tech, you will be escorted back to your guesthouse room, where you may...."

An escort-bot had rolled up, and Shailesh, leaning upon it, was lowering himself to the ground.

All in unison, the girls leaped off the branches, landing softly in the grass. The music burst out again, now a rampant, salacious melody. Jaspreet was untying his turban, and V was patting down his face with his napkin. But Aaron had not yet budged. He sat, smiling, his eyes on Mandy.

"Baby," he said, "I can explain."

Again she inhaled in a quick draught.

"And besides," he continued in a pleasant voice, "you've got your own company."

Saionton heard a gasp. Mandy's eyes were flicking from side to side, desperately, like a wild animal, waiting to pounce – or to bolt. When a woman's voice called out from the grass, and Aaron turned his head, she seemed suddenly to decide. Before Saionton could find his own voice, she was on her feet, running headlong into the shadows.

CHAPTER TWENTY-THREE

She had looked for the dark depths to invade, but motion-sensitive lights flared up around her as she ran. They picked out a path of cut grass, lined with pebbles. Mandy ran down it, oblivious to the shapes and the colors in the surrounding gloom, indifferent to where she went. She was aware only of her trusty sneakers, crunching underfoot, her bag swinging against her ribs and the air that swirled about her cheeks and her nose. Voices and music, the ugly beats, were receding behind her, and if she had any thought, it was only to separate herself from them by the greatest possible distance.

In this, the garden was not disappointing her. As the warm lights responded, one by one, the path continuously breached the darkness, and yet always with more darkness beckoning. When she slowed to a jog, it occurred to her that she was arcing a large curve of gentle gradient and might be steered back to where she had begun. But there was no such deception. The path soon ended at a line of poplars, where it turned plainly at right angles.

There was, however, a telltale shimmering in the poplar trees. When she stepped closer, the fact was obvious. They were holograms, of the old variety, like Roshan's face at the lunch, the kind that sought to blend with the material world, in which, however, they had no tactile substance. But these poplars were impressive productions, tall and straight and elegant, touched with gold and green, and so close to each other as to form a seemingly impenetrable forest wall.

Mandy walked straight into the nearest tree. She was through it, and then through an abundance of serrated bark and pointed twigs and branches. It felt to her like passing through the most fragile of veils. But it looked as though thick drapes had been suddenly withdrawn. A light-filled vista lay before her eyes.

No matter all the heaviness that was in her, Mandy's heart leaped – first of all at the light. It was lambent, pure, unbroken. Here the sky, or whatever vaulted in place of it, was itself aglow, and its soothing luminescence filled the space from end to end, from the green, mossy walls that rose to left and to right, all through the ample confines, that were yet as cozy as a picture book.

It would have to be a picture book of a secret garden, a walled paradise, some dream of childhood and adolescence. For it was such fancies that seemed to stir in her, as she gathered her breath and gazed down the grassy descent in front of her.

The carpet of bright green rolled down to a flat expanse of taller grass, of a darker hue, in which flowers were growing with haphazard beauty. Groves of trees studded the scene, spreading their shade like generous givers. But on the other side of a little lake or pond, shaped like an oval teardrop, the trees grew thickly into a wood. Or perhaps it was an orchard, because their branches, she glimpsed, were hanging with fruit.

There were apples and mangoes and who knew what else? But as she stared, it was the water that began to attract her most. The lake was blue and placid and gently, mysteriously rippling. She started down the slope, and then, on an inspiration, stopped to take off her shoes. Clutching her shoes in her hand, Mandy ran down the next several paces with her eyes closed, to savor the tickling of the barefoot sensation.

She did not stop until, with the lake in sight, a cluster of *neem* trees seemed to wave at her. Sighing happily, she entered their shade, and stood in delight among the leaves and the grass.

Then she became rigid, struck suddenly by a doubt. A moment later, there was no doubt, but a hydra-headed doubting was swamping Mandy instead. As for the leaves and the grass, they were definitely artificial. The plastics they used were excellent sensory mimics, but what they could never reproduce were the subtle emanations, the gentle breaths of nature that only became lusher and more tumescent the nearer one drew to them. But these artifacts, at those times, screamed their deadness.

Suddenly even the air felt hot and enclosed and harsh in her lungs, as it pumped into the clearing from some unseen vent. She knew the sky was false. But was it all artificial? At random, she wandered from tree to tree, hugging bark, and stooping to sniff at flowers, and finally, having made her way to the waterfront, she wet her feet and splashed her face experimentally. Then, placing her bag and shoes where the mud was dry, Mandy sat down beside them.

A squirrel scampered by. She took stock confusedly. In fact, not everything in the garden was synthetic. That far collection of *peepal* trees was a hologram, like the poplars had been, and the wild roses and weed-flowers, some of which she had plucked, were neither plastic nor projections, but perfectly real, down to their milky sap.

Her eye fell again on the bushy-tailed squirrel, which had come to a halt not far from her. Its nose was twitching curiously. Then she felt her heart constricting. The squirrel was real, all too real. She believed that implicitly. The best proof of it was the collar, with the antennae, around its furry little neck.

Mandy closed her eyes, breathing effortfully. There were such places around the world. Locales, built up with the latest tech, consummate mishmashes of synthetic and holographic and actual landscapes. They were funhouse experiences, advertised as such. Children loved them, and hearing of them had always made her smile, as at kitsch. But it was different, sitting by the side of the truly watery lake, in the bowels of the Company building. Try as she might, she could not become glad; her face would not crack a smile. There seemed, suddenly, no lightness in the air at all, but only severity, weighing upon her, only a blind, irrational, skillful hatred.

When she opened her eyes, she started in astonishment. On the far side of the lake, a group of sheep had appeared – or were they goats? They were grazing with their heads bowed. She saw horns and woolly backs. But they were eating avidly, and surely it was unlike ordinary sheep – or goats – to gather around in such a close circle, like scavengers intent on the same portion. There was plenty to graze on all around.

Provided, of course, they didn't mind plastic. As the questions multiplied in her mind, one of the creatures lifted its head into the air.

Mandy clutched the ground in terror. Her heart seemed to be drumming in her ears. The face disappeared into the herd again. But it was only then that her scream broke forth, because the face of the animal, which was still assailing her mind's eye, was distinctly the face of a person.

Then they all looked up – six blank human faces peering across the lake – and her voice died in her throat. She scrambled upright, reaching for her things, and then she was stumbling, but running with all the strength she had left. Prickly plants and sharp pebbles cut into her feet, and she dirtied them in a patch of slush, but she only ceased running when she had reached the foot of the slope, which led back up into the poplars. There, sweating and in pain, Mandy looked back.

The lake was quite still in the beautiful light. Its far banks were deserted. Only the orchard trees stood about, in cool seclusion. She scanned the whole garden as far as her gaze could go. The things on all fours had vanished. There was not a human face to be seen.

Then, she turned and a shudder gripped her and she almost collapsed from a spurt of weakness in her legs. A figure had emerged from the poplars. It was coming down the slope on careful steps, never taking its eyes off her.

Mandy had nothing to say. But as she held Saionton's gaze, she felt her strength returning, flowing back all the way, until it was soaring into wild relief.

* * *

"Fake charm," said Saionton with a knowing nod. His eyes, narrowed in concentration, were roving about the garden, while he and Mandy made their way toward the lakeside. "There's nothing more depressing."

"I always imagined," said Mandy, "that a place like this would be fun."

There was a weight lifted off her, ever since she had told him her discoveries. Now she walked freely onto the darker grass, feeling quite silly at how frightened she'd become.

"It seems like it could be," agreed Saionton. "But then it's too *serious* to be fun. It's like ads, I guess."

They walked in silence, their bodies staying close to each other, even colliding without fuss.

"You mean the spirit behind the ads," said Mandy thoughtfully. "The whole machinery."

"Exactly. The machinery."

After a while, she extended her arm and pointed. "That's where I saw them. They were like sheep. But with human faces."

"Not very subtle. Is it? This Company."

He glanced at her then, but she was neither smiling nor speaking. She had put on her shoes again, and now, as the lake loomed, her pace began to quicken. Walking briskly ahead of him, to within a few feet of the waterfront, she swiveled, like a practiced walker, into an energetic stroll. There was a color entering her cheeks; she was, despite everything, rapt in the surroundings.

"Where are you going?" said Saionton.

"Nowhere. Just walking."

"I also left that place," he said, "right after you did. They had all begun dancing. So—"

"It doesn't matter," said Mandy.

"I wonder if Lance is looking for us."

Her lips pursed inscrutably. Suddenly Saionton was exasperated. Mandy's rush of fellowship had dried up without explanation. He was tired too, from the frenzied morning, the grotesque lunch, and the strain of having to chase her to the hidden garden. It was all too much to comprehend, and now it seemed too much effort to keep up with anyone. He slowed his own step, lingering leisurely, while she strode on, grim-faced.

Lance, he thought, would certainly find them. Not for Mandy's sake, but for his, because it was he who had been invited to the campus, he to whom Roshan had specially written a note. He had been sure that Roshan was alive and active, but it was still a thrill to have seen him again, albeit holographically. Just that morning, the TV news had been reporting him missing for two days, and hinting at some darker fate.

How foolish the media was, thought Saionton. And the people in the city streets, how angry and foolish. How delusional, also, Shailesh and Jaspreet, to be imagining the things they were. Whatever the Happy Maker was up to now, it wasn't what any of them imagined. He, Saionton, knew that, because the Happy Maker had *winked* at him. He wondered what else that wink implied.

There were a set of tree stumps at the edge of the lake, half sunk in water. Saionton went over and seated himself at random. He placed his elbows on his thighs, and his chin in his hands. When he shut his eyes, the sounds of the garden seemed to heighten around him. He heard the hiss of wind. Leaves fluttering like rain in the treetops. Bubbling noises in the mud in the water. There was also birdsong, though he had noticed no birds. But it was possible that there were real birds around, or else ingenious synthetic ones, or else just the rendition of birdsong, for that also might suffice.

When he had stepped through the poplars, the cozy beauty of the garden setting was the first thing he had noticed. But the first thing to have truly impressed him was the blatantly manufactured sky. Now this impression was settling upon him in its totality. It was the sense of a power, as overarching as the sky itself, with manifold illusory contrivances, with naked energy, with an unfathomable drive – for fabrication. It was making him dizzy. What, in the face of this power, was a mind's grip on truth? What, in fact, was truth?

A sharp sound prompted Saionton to glance downward. A twig had snapped under his shoe. Then he stared more closely. On the side of the adjacent tree stump was an etching. Letters and numerals, seemingly scratched out, but precisely fixed, which read:

Bio-Lab STR4

The light, so clear, soft and abundant, seemed bathed in sterility, and glancing up, he thought, inescapably, of a massive eye peering into a lens.

"Mandy, look at this!" Saionton got up, shouting.

She was midway around the circumference of the lake, standing by the fringes of the fruit trees.

"It's not a garden!" he continued, feeling oddly excited. "It's a *lab*!"

Then he stopped, open-mouthed. She had turned – with a gun in her hand.

It took her a moment to lower the gun. Transferring her aim into the woods, she beckoned to him urgently.

★ ★ ★

When he caught up to Mandy, he saw that her arms were trembling, but her face, with some horrible effort, was set like stone.

Ahead of her, the trees were growing in rough rows, creating crisscrossing corridors of soft grass and shade. Her gun was pointed toward a narrow, empty stretch, in which a solitary apple tree intruded. Beyond it was the garden wall, red with bougainvillea.

"He's hiding," said Mandy in a harsh voice. "I saw him."

"Who is? Aaron?"

"*Him.*"

Saionton's gaze was transfixed on the gun. He had never seen one at such close quarters. She held it tightly with unsteady hands. It seemed to be some kind of improvised firearm, a country-made pistol, with a rusted barrel and an olive-green handle.

"What are you doing?" he said.

A smile was dangling on her lips, as she glanced briefly in his direction. "What does it look like? Why do you think I came all the way here? For a campus tour?"

"You said you didn't want to be left alone in the apartment."

"Keep your eyes peeled. He's somewhere near."

"Who is *he*?" asked Saionton, though he knew already, just as the heaviness in his heart seemed to portend to him her own fate.

"Roshan Dubey," said Mandy. Her voice was thick and harsh. "Obviously."

"So you want to kill Roshan?"

Her smile, like a private smirk, returned. Suddenly Saionton felt his temper rising — because he could not bear to be afraid. But her eyes, wide and staring, in her thin, smiling face, with the rest of her body somehow estranged from her head — and the gun in her hands — were a fearful sight.

"Mandy," he said. It was immediately soothing to say her name. "Mandy!"

"Don't call me Mandy," she retorted.

"What do you mean? It's your name."

"My name," she said, "is Mandakini. But you should call me...Faith."

"Why Faith?"

She frowned, and was briefly quiet. Then her voice dropped to a mumble, as though, all of a sudden, she was not quite supremely confident.

"Coz I'm a *god* to you."

He remembered something.

"You've been using the shrine. You used it this morning too. You said so."

She had let her arms drop, and was standing facing him, her face etched with discomfort, and her eyes staring blankly.

"If your shrine encouraged you to kill Roshan...it's just deceiving you. That's what it *does*. You can't kill him."

"Why not?" She tossed her head and he felt a pang, for now, as she looked at him, her beauty was all about her. "I told you, I saw him just now."

"It was probably a hologram. But even if you did kill him, you wouldn't achieve anything. They'd throw you in jail. And the Company would go on doing whatever it's doing. Just remember – Shrine Tech is a tool of the Company. So if you obey the shrine, how could that harm the Company?"

She was gazing at him steadily. His heart, however, was burgeoning, for he had felt, amid all the swirling insanity, the blessed contact of the meeting of their minds. He dared to smile.

Mandy brought her arms up. The barrel of the gun was in his face now. "You," she said, "are a tool of the Company. You work for Roshan. Do you or don't you?"

"I don't work for anyone, Mandy. I'm on the Company rolls, that's all. If I do work for anyone, it's myself. And if I do work for anyone other than myself –" he was rambling, with strange fluency, "– then I still don't know who that is."

"Walk backward," said Mandy.

Saionton obeyed, wondering if the gun was cocked, or even loaded. He couldn't tell. But she seemed comfortable handling it.

A pocket of shade enveloped him. He glanced back, catching a glimpse of a flourishing *peepal* tree.

"Farther," she said.

When he had his back to the tree trunk, she seemed satisfied. She stood before him, on the dappled grass, with her head inclined.

"I like you," she said. "I don't want to hurt you. But if you're going to get in the way, I'll have no choice. So it's best you simply leave now."

There was nothing in her eyes but implacable resolve. Yet she had spoken softly, and Saionton, for some reason, felt encouraged. In the quietness of the surroundings, some patient power seemed at work.

"I also," he replied, "like you very much. That's why I came to your house this morning. And when you ran from the lunch, I followed you. See, I can't leave you. I can't leave you – in this horror. And I can't be left alone either. I need to be close to you."

Mandy turned her mind to Aaron, and to Faith, to her desire and her power, and that overwhelming happiness – far from dreariness, far from tears – that she had determined to grasp, by removing every obstacle in its way.

When she looked again, the young boy was standing just a few paces in front of her. His face was bright and flushed; his eyes, under the mop of hair, were staring in wonder. She saw his lips move.

"Even if you do kill me," he said, "I don't care. I know I have to be near you."

Then he did something that sent shudders through her. He leaned forward and touched his forehead to the pistol's barrel.

When Saionton closed his eyes, then, despite herself, Mandy put a hand to his hair, and stroked it. Slowly, he lifted his face, with the steel tip of the gun running down his nose, his lips, his slightly stubbled chin. She felt another acute paroxysm, this time through her whole being. She dropped the gun to the ground.

For an instant they stood, leaning close, with their breaths mingling.

But only their fingers had touched, when a tumult in the trees, followed by a raucous shout, made them clasp their hands close and tight.

Someone was lumbering through the orchard with heavy steps and yells and laughter. A man broke into the light, by the lake. It was Jaspreet, naked, hairy, and erect. Lying in his arms was a glistening mannequin, motionless, except for its hair, which fell straight and streamlined all on one side.

Jaspreet stood panting by the lake, clasping the sex-bot, sweating, gaping, and ecstatic. Then he glanced over his shoulder, and with another bestial shout, plunged back toward the network of trees.

"Sick," said Mandy. Her fingers squeezed mightily around Saionton's hand. "And I used to think he was a nice guy."

"They're all...." Saionton cleared his throat, but then paused.

Now Lance had emerged by the lake. He had changed out of the spandex and into a more usual rumpled shirt and jeans. He was peering straight at the two of them.

"You're wanted," said Lance in his old, superior voice. "Follow me."

"Wanted where?"

"Roshan wants to meet you. Both of you. If you have more questions, you can ask him yourself."

Even as Lance was replying, Saionton felt Mandy wriggling free of his grasp. Then, when Lance's back was turned, she bent quickly to retrieve the fallen pistol. In a flash it was in her handbag.

He said nothing, but began to walk, mechanically, toward where Lance was lingering. A heaviness, both familiar and terrible, was enclosing him, like impenetrable walls. For a while it seemed to Saionton that he saw and heard nothing, except the wretched sound of his own footsteps on wet mud. Then he heard, or fancied he heard, a faint splash.

He glanced around. Mandy was catching up to him, zipping shut her handbag, and then once more taking his hand in hers. Out in the lake, the pistol sank swiftly.

CHAPTER TWENTY-FOUR

The vision of Jaspreet, in all its flagrance, was still vivid in their minds. Saionton wished earnestly to leave the garden behind. A sickening quiet had descended over the place, as though in complicity with the orgies it was hosting.

Past the rows of fruit trees, they reached the garden wall. Then he did not see what Lance did, but a doorway in the bricks began to revolve. As they went through in single file, noises erupted at their back. There was first a crashing in the trees, and then a voice he thought was V's, which was followed immediately by a woman's shriek, high and prolonged, whether of pleasure or of pain, but as vigorous and insistent as great bronze temple bells.

All the same, it was cut off behind them. They had entered the air-conditioned emptiness of a windowless hallway. Chairs and sofas lay about, behind long rows of plastic flowers. There was nobody around. But Saionton recognized the office carpeting.

At the end of the hallway was a padlocked double door, an alcove with washrooms, and another with an elevator. Here, Lance was pacing about, chewing his lip and flashing impatient glances at the ticking floor numbers. When he caught sight of Saionton, he stepped up to him.

"Hey," said Lance, "suppose I asked you what's going on in the city. What would you say?"

"What do you mean?"

His face, Saionton saw, was twitching, and his eyes were glum and dead, though annoyance suddenly flamed in them. He seemed incredibly nervous.

"No time for games! The president is up there. All right? If they ask you what the hell is going on in the city, what are you going to say?"

"It's chaos in the city," said Saionton. "It's madness...and violence. I mean, it's unimaginable."

Lance, breathing heavily, looked gradually pleased.

"Right." He nodded. "So you just tell the truth. And then we'll see." His voice dropped to a private muttering. "Then we'll see."

Mandy, from two paces away, was listening closely.

"Who's the president?"

"He means Roshan," said Saionton.

"No," she said, "it's not Roshan. Roshan is the CHM. He said *president*."

They both looked at Lance, who was glaring up at the elevator. It was about to arrive. For the first time that afternoon, he cast a glance at Mandy.

"She's right," said Lance. "The president is the president. In all the damn earth. Don't ask me who he is. I haven't a damn clue."

Saionton opened his mouth to speak, but just then a loud chime sounded and the elevator doors parted with a hush. At once, Lance darted in and began to press buttons.

"Come on!" he cried out. There was an edge in his voice, akin to trembling. "Let's go!"

In the elevator, none of them spoke. They stood listening to the high whine of the cabin hurtling upward, and watched the numbers flashing on the display. The building they were in had forty floors, but the elevator did not stop – nor could it, as Saionton noticed from the buttons inside – on any but the fortieth. This destination was reached in the space of seconds, but then the doors remained shut for considerably longer.

"What's happening?" asked Saionton.

"You're not carrying a weapon, are you?" said Lance.

"No."

"Then sit tight. This is the president's office. After they've finished all their scans, that's when the doors open."

Lance straightened his posture and brushed his hair back in a cursory way. When the elevator had disgorged them, they found themselves, immediately, on the curlicued carpeting of an enormously elongated room. All around, transparent sheets of glass revealed the mist and the hills. The room itself seemed to be comprised of only one table, a long, faintly curving thing, of a deep black solidity, with similarly black, velvety chairs like elaborate thrones studding the whole course of it.

"It's freezing," whispered Mandy, drawing her arms about her. Saionton nodded. His eyes were running up and down the room, swimming in the length of dark upholstery. All the chairs were empty, or so it seemed. But the blackness was so intense that subtle shapes were indiscernible.

Therefore, it was with a shock that he chanced upon the seated figure. He had quite failed to see him the first time. Roshan Dubey was sunk in his seat, in one of the many chairs. His chin was bowed, and his hands clasped in his lap, as if – thought Saionton – in prayer.

Apart from him, surely, there was no one in the office.

"Sit, please," came Roshan's voice. "Both of you. And you too, Lance. I want you all to be comfortable."

As he turned his face up, revealing the familiar, big and satisfied visage, the impression of a floating head was disturbingly re-emphasized, for in the darkness of the cushioning, Roshan's dark-suited frame had thinned to almost nothing.

There were plastic water bottles on the table, indicating the seats to be occupied. Ignoring the ones opposite, Lance walked to a chair at Roshan's side, and then hesitated.

"Aren't we going to wait, though?"

"For what?"

"Well, for the president to show up."

Roshan reached out and tapped the armrest, over which Lance was standing motionless.

Suddenly, like pistol shots, his voice reverberated through the room.

"Sit *down*! And the two of you! The president has been *waiting*!"

The chair into which Saionton settled himself was the most perfectly luxurious he had ever experienced. He felt as though he was being held and soothed, but this, he discovered, only increased his nervousness. He quickly scanned the room for the fifth figure, which no doubt was hidden in plain sight, in one of the pitch-black chairs. Still, he saw nobody. But the hillside outside the windows was beautiful, and the light poured in on every side – and then was swallowed up.

"Our agenda for this meeting," Roshan was continuing, in a dull, official tone, "is restructuring and recruitments of an essential nature. I understand that you each –" here he turned his head to nod at Lance, "– have certain queries, regarding recent operations. Once I have addressed those, we will proceed to next steps. But I hope that you –" his gaze now flitted between Saionton and Mandy, "– did not have difficulty making it to campus?"

"Once we were in the car," said Saionton, shivering as he spoke, "then it was OK."

"Right. And before that there was some difficulty? I understand. Some disturbances in the city? Right. But you made it! And afterward, how was lunch? How did you find lunch?"

Glancing at Mandy, Saionton saw that she was looking unwell, her face strained and her eyes watery, though fastened in attention. Seeing her thus, a burst of bravery entered him, even as he remembered a phrase she had used herself, not long ago.

"How did you do it?" Saionton said. "With Jaspreet and the secretary and all? They were eating out of your hands."

"You thought so? You thought they were satisfied?"

"Even more than satisfied."

White teeth gleamed across the table. Roshan's lips were bared in pleasure.

"Happy, then. You might say they are happy. And by this time, I would wager, so is the city at large."

Then there was a sound like a fart. Lance had uttered it from between pursed lips. He was staring at Roshan, his face set with a reckless anger that impressed Saionton, in spite of himself.

"The city's burning, Roshan!" cried Lance. "It's been burning for days. You can't cover this up with party tricks. You screwed up. I warned you, even before the damn *sabha*, but you didn't listen. You were too full of yourself. You turned everyone against the Company. Now you think you can cover up what's happened with tricks and games. Not gonna happen, Roshan! If only the president was actually here—"

A foot stamped on the floor, and then again. Roshan drew himself up, expanding forth his inky girth, which seemed to spread all over the throne-like chair.

"I have already informed you," he roared, "the president is among us! And do not call me Roshan. From now on, you – and everybody else – will call me who I *am*. The Happy Maker! *Mr.* Happy Maker!"

The chair went back noiselessly, and the man was on his feet. It was him all right, in a suit with no tie, just the same as Saionton had seen him outside of his holo-tech avatars. But when, in a few strides, he stood before the glass, pale sunlight streaming over him, then he was nothing but a silhouette, murky and tremendous.

"Or do you think I haven't earned it?" he continued in a raised voice. "What I went through – was it not enough! When they fired guns and rockets at me, and trampled on me, and spat on me, and took a saw and cut deep into my neck and dragged it one way, and then the other – what do you think I felt? Has anyone ever endured such torments in the history of holo-tech? I'll tell you what it felt like to me. It felt like…like being stabbed all over my body – *this* body – by a thousand million…feathers!"

Again his lips drew back in the darkness, and now he let loose a guffaw.

"Really!" laughed Roshan. "Our neural link is something else. As a matter of fact, Shrine Tech is mankind's greatest invention. By far. And it truly belongs to all mankind. It was developed in the West, of course. But pioneered here in India, which is only fitting. This whole drive really came from India, you see? I mean, the drive to be gods. Then it infected the West, which went to work, as it does, and finally worked out Shrine Tech. Which was seeded back into India. But the joy is first of all India's. The sun has risen in the East. India has given birth. Many children are born unto us! You met a few today."

Alone among the listeners, it was Lance who seemed unfazed. A look of disgust was settling over his face.

"You're talking about four people," he said. "I'm talking about Mumbai and other parts—"

"I'm talking about the world," returned the silhouetted figure. "Beginning with those four. By the end of today the city will be calm. The country also. Don't you get it? Version 3.0 *works*. And the best part is, it did it all itself. The AI updated itself using the neural link – *knowing* the users. Version 1.0...2.0...3.0.... But the issue with you, Lance, is you were never interested in the tech, and what it really meant. All you care about is abstract operations.... Well, to each his own, of course. But if you don't want to know the higher things, the mysteries, then how can I teach them to you? That's why we have *others* in this meeting. Right?"

No sound came from Saionton. Mandy sniffled and swallowed, though her eyes were quite dry. The man at the window lifted his arm, with a single finger raised.

"Version 1.0. It was only the stirring of profound happiness. It only brought the users near the *thought* of their own godliness. But then, reality – I use this term just in passing – had to rankle. At that stage, we anticipated much wounded pride, much frustrated violence, so for all of our sakes we brought on 2.0."

He put up two fingers, before lowering his hand.

"Version 2.0 developed the users further. It made clear to them that a god is too great to lash out at mere people. Violence was beneath them, because they were above it. Therefore, their frustrations with reality – a term I use in passing – could no longer languish in immediacy. Now, with their worship, they would also glimpse a plan, because they would see a structure...and find a way, to overcome.... But then something happened that I didn't understand. Slowly but surely, they all began to hate *me*. The Company – and *me*. And I...I became afraid."

The figure began to move around, until its back was turned, and it was staring out of the glass. A dark shapelessness stood before them.

"This is a mystery only the president really understands," said the voice from inside it. "Because he anointed me, and he made this happen. What I know is this – 2.0 did show the users their way to happiness. It was me. I was their way. But a way that's shut is only an obstacle. So that is how they saw me. That was why they hated me. I possessed their happiness, but I had not yet come into my own. That was why I needed to come to them. I needed, finally, to surrender myself at the *sabha*. I needed to become who I am. Then and only then could we all reach this point together, 3.0."

He swiveled, facing them, with three fingers raised, which then became two.

"Yet for two days – yes, from the night of the *sabha* until the morning of the third day – I was gone. And unhappiness reigned. What unhappiness!"

"But why?" said Saionton in a loud voice, which he lowered immediately, but not before feeling a welcome relief, that his wits had not yet deserted him, that the silhouette of Roshan was not the only thing in the world with a tongue.

"I mean, why were you gone? Why did you let that happen?"

"I was busy. I was locked in mortal combat, Saionton. Just like the people in the city. But I was with them, and they were with me, and all of us were fighting hard. Yes, I know you saw how hard *they* were fighting, but you didn't see *me*, fighting up here by myself. But it was me who struck the death blow. I faced him and killed him, and poured his blood into…the software. Version 3.0! For all!"

Three shadowy fingers struck up again. Though he had begun to feel faint, Saionton managed to mouth the words.

"Whose blood?"

A hand went waving by, in derision. "I don't wish to speak of him. I would rather just say – reality – and that only in passing. That's what the people were fighting. Do you understand? This hateful, so-called reality. The bottom line of all their woes. That's why the shrines began to encourage the violence. Version 2.0 prohibited violence, but in the transition to 3.0, violence had to come about. The AI worked it all out. The rules were not broken, because this wasn't violence against people. Of course, people died, but this wasn't *about* them. This was such violence as befits a god – on the cusp of his throne. What do you think is the throne of a god?"

"You've made them mad," said Saionton, understanding suddenly. But he felt he couldn't bear to understand too well. He thought of Juhu

Beach, the pitched battle, the corpses accumulating as though incidentally. "You're making everyone mad."

"Come on." Now the voice at the window was full of friendly sympathy. "You know better than that. What is *mad*? Isn't this madness, to be born, and you don't even know why? And with some random set of handicaps that you never asked for? To be ugly? Or to lose your parents? Or to be sexually attracted to someone who couldn't care less? To have no money. To have no time. To fall sick from some invisible microbe. To break your bones, to have accidents. To *die*. Right? Or to live, but every day with rotten weather. Too hot, too wet, the roads full of muck and dog shit. Dust everywhere. Stupid, noisy people everywhere. I can go on. We can all go on."

He stepped forward, his features taking shape. There was a simper on his lips, and a kind of soulfulness in his eyes, constricted between fleshy folds.

"I'm an adman, that's all. I don't make people do anything. I only sell them what they want themselves. Now I've done it all. I've sold them the ultimate happiness. Version 3.0 is updated already, they're using it already. But they can't be happy without me. So in a few hours I myself will appear to them, and then their joy will be complete. Because the president is leading us all. We are three of us, you know – the president, myself, and the people. We lean on each other, we love each other, and Shrine Tech 3.0 is the fruit of all our love, which we shall feed each other."

"You've lost your mind," said Lance, standing up.

The Happy Maker sighed, full of weariness and compassion. At the same time, Saionton felt a touch on his hand. It was Mandy, reaching out silently, though her eyes, full of fright, were fastened on the pair ahead. He placed his hand over hers, and they both breathed deeply.

"I complained about you to the board," continued Lance. "I thought that's what this meeting was for. I came here to speak with the president. But if you're just going to go on with this crap, then I'm leaving."

He started forward, and then stopped, as a hand fell on his shoulder, gripping it. The Happy Maker's face was set queerly.

"I can't let you leave so unhappy. As I said before, I wish you had used our tech yourself, Lance, then you wouldn't use words like the one you just did. But never mind. I'm sure the president can help you, personally."

With his free arm, he gestured gracefully in front of him. There, by the head of the table, where no one had been present, was a woman. She was standing, and perfectly recognizable, in the light that bathed her and emanated from her. Only a certain waviness in this sudden explosion of brilliance hinted that it was not the resurrected Zara Shah, wearing eyeliner, adorned in earrings, with a cream sari that overhung a pink blouse, with rounded flesh full to bursting, all belly and bosom, and glorious curly hair – but rather her image.

The Happy Maker's voice droned on archly.

"I will let the president explain to you why it isn't so bad that we can all finally inhabit the world of our choosing, with the confidence that it is headed the way we want it to. What does 3.0 do, but give everyone that confidence? It lets my people be happy, finally and securely happy, with the Happy Maker at the helm. But I understand you wanted me deposed. Beloved president! With such a desire, is there any way that Lance *also* can be…? Perhaps there is a way?"

"Wait, *na*!" shrieked the likeness of Zara. It was the piercing, haggling voice of the marketplace. "I'll talk to these two first. Him later! OK?"

"You're the boss!" said the Happy Maker, sitting down with a laugh. Then the woman whom he had called the president rotated her head. Her curls fell about alarmingly.

"Mandakini, right! You're so beautiful! *Babe!* It's so good to see you! How *are* you?"

There was a brief silence, in which it became obvious that the tension in the room had not only expired, but was being quickly replaced by a gross friendliness, streaming off the president's visage.

"Is it you?" whispered Mandy. "Zara! Are you really alive?"

"It's another hologram," explained Saionton, leaning forward impulsively. "See. The Shrine Tech is on the chair."

Something, indeed, was glowing in the blackness, beside which shimmered the woman's figure. Then the machine's lights were lost in her lap. She had sat down, smiling, and crossed her legs.

"So sweet, the two of you. But don't be overprotective, *baccha*. *Baccha* means 'little boy'." She translated her Hindi without a pause, apparently for Lance's benefit. "You think she doesn't have eyes? *Vaise bhi*, anyway, Mandy is right. I can be whoever I need to be. And just because *vo mar gayi*, just because she's *dead*, that doesn't mean Zara is gone. But babe, if you want to keep hold of Aaron, you need to out-do Zara, OK? So let's do some work-talk. Some *kaam ki baat*. Brand ambassador *banegi*? How about it?"

"What?"

Mandy's hand had slipped away from Saionton's, and she was sitting up, alert. Ahead of her, they exchanged knowing looks – the man in darkness and the woman all aglow.

"We'd like you to be the Company's new brand ambassador," said the Happy Maker, "for all our offerings, but with a special emphasis on Shrine Tech 3.0. This is the highest post we have for talent. You'll be one of the richest and most powerful women in the world."

"But I'm not an actress," said Mandy energetically. "And I'm too...."

Her speech faltered, and the woman pounced. "Don't say it! You're not old at all. You're sexy! You even have a sexy spirit. Zara didn't have that. Zara was a hard worker. But we're gonna take you, and make you so much *more*. We want people to really celebrate now, let loose. People are so *darpok*, ya! Always *afraid* to ask for what they want. It irritated the heck out of me! *Khair*. Anyway! Now, all are going to be goddesses and gods – fully! fully! – and that's the end of shame. Everyone's going to get down and dirty on Shrine Tech, and out of Shrine Tech, but especially on it. So listen! You'll be the most *erotic* woman in the world. Are you getting me? Babe?"

"Not really," said Mandy, in a voice grown weak again.

Suddenly the woman screeched with laughter. "Don't get scared! You can cook and clean for Aaron too. Have kids with him. Actually, we want you to have a happy domestic life. Then what you make for the Company will be even sexier, if you know what I mean. But I know you do! This is not porn, babe! This is just being *yourself*, the way you really want! It's having a blast, *khul ke*! Openly!"

"With Zara," said the Happy Maker with a smirk on his face, "we had to keep our energies under wraps. Anyway, she didn't have what you have. But it was still a pity. The night she was killed, there was a little love bite on her left cheek, and another on her neck, which were my fault. Who knew her watchman had lost his mind? Taking her head to the hospital! Version 3.0 came too late for those two. But I suppose you *did* plan it all."

He looked questioningly at the woman, who, however, did not respond. Her eyes were trained on Mandy's, with a glittering ferocity that reminded Saionton – though he tried to quell the association – of Mandy herself, from earlier in her apartment.

"*Soch mat*! Don't *think*!" The voice was harsh, the haggling note at its severest. "All your life you wanted to get out of the great Indian middle class. *Hain na*? Isn't it so? You wanted to unlock your powers. To get up on top! So? Did you succeed? What did Aaron say about you? *Ki* you're always calculating! Did it help you? Aaron left you. And now you're wandering around with this little kid. This little kid *toh* won't even touch you, believe me. But you need to get *fucked*. In new positions! Like you were never fucked before. And all your powers will come pouring out of you! *Uske upar* – on top of that – you'll have Aaron too. So what are you thinking about? Babe! Are you still *calculating*?"

Saionton heard a cry at his side. Mandy was standing up, staring wildly about her. Her chair was aslant. She jogged onto the carpet for a few paces, and then stopped, uncertainly, with desperation roiling her, for all to see.

A portion of the wall of the room, where the glass was not, separated without a sound. It was the elevator. She ran for it immediately. Saionton noticed, with a strange, sharp pain, that she had even forgotten her bag.

"Good luck!" called out the Happy Maker as the elevator doors closed behind Mandy. He was looking quite pleased, and so was the woman.

CHAPTER TWENTY-FIVE

She turned now toward Saionton. There were subtle, striking changes in the woman's appearance. The loose end of her sari had dropped away, revealing fully her sculpted voluptuousness. Simultaneously, her face had grown softer and warmer. When she spoke, it was with quiet sympathy.

"Sorry, dear, you would have felt bad. Hearing how we spoke to her."

"However—" boomed the Happy Maker.

"If you had really felt bad—" chimed the woman.

"You wouldn't still be sitting here. Listening to us."

"After how we *insulted* her. But you know, we only offered what she wants."

"Deep down. And it's nothing that shocks you. Right?"

"You have such thoughts yourself. No? I know you," the woman added. "I've watched you at nights. I know you are a *good boy*."

She began to laugh, but mirthfully, and without mockery. They were both now smiling continuously, with a kind of crooked persuasiveness. Suddenly Saionton started, because it seemed their faces had switched places – Zara's was on the big-bodied man, and the Happy Maker's on the gloriously feminine figure. A moment later, they were themselves again, only ever more comfortable. He was leaning back, hands behind his head, sinking into the chair, and she was watching him with glowing eyes, like a cat securely in dark undergrowth.

He tried to muster up a feeling of offense. But it was no use. They had him. Besides, there was an enormous warmth of friendliness filling the room. It was like cozy quilts on a winter night, and with sticky shame inside. They knew him. He couldn't deny it. They knew him, with his sick and lustful mind, and yet they were smiling at him, such that he felt no embarrassment, but only freedom, nay, *abandon*.

It occurred to him, in passing, that Lance was still sitting there, between the other two, clenching his jaw. His presence, however, was barely jarring. He was only a tool, Saionton realized. The thought hit home with surprising clarity, and he suppressed a smile of his own. Lance was like a pair of pliers, or a piece of wire. Why think of him as a person at all?

"It may have surprised you," said the Happy Maker, "how literally Mandy wants it all. Funds, fame, and fucking. The three *F*s, we call them. The fundamentals."

He heard the president laughing again, with little gasps.

"That's something you need to understand about women," continued the Happy Maker in a wise tone. "They aren't such eclectic beings. You, however, as I've said before, are made of subtler stuff. You're a creature of many colors. So she will get the best from us. But you will get the *even better*. Right?"

"What will I get?"

"What's better than complete satisfaction? Let me tell you. *Self*-satisfaction."

"I'd like to know – excuse me! – I'd like to know when my complaint is going to be addressed!"

It was him, Lance, waving his hands about. They all looked at him, and as they did so, all three were smiling.

"Lance, my dear," said the woman. Her voice had transformed, to fluency and gentleness. "Don't you understand? Your complaint *has* been addressed. All the complaints have been addressed. Have you not even tried 3.0?"

"No, and I don't intend to," said Lance. In the smiling and sympathetic room, he was now plainly uneasy, not catching anyone's eye but staring into space, with his mottled face.

"And you never thought," said the president, "that you ought to?"

Lance shook his head, pouting. "No. My job is to run the Company. The tech's for customers. I don't have to use it, any more than a dealer's got to be a crackhead."

"You're quite right," said the woman, in a marveling way. "He's right, isn't he?"

"He is right," intoned the Happy Maker. "Your commitment is not to this and that product, but above all to the Company. You love the Company."

"Body and soul," affirmed Lance. A wavering had entered his voice, and he was breathing raggedly.

"Roshan Dubey," said the woman, "is a no-good incompetent. He runs this place by luck and whimsy. All he's having with 3.0 is a stroke of luck."

"Thank you, Madam President!" cried Lance. "That's what I always said."

"And I agree with you. But they say it's better to be lucky than good."

"Luck changes!"

"Right again. Right you are. Therefore I have decided, as president, that there needs to be a permanent stamp of leadership on this place. Roshan certainly can't provide that. But you can. And you love the Company. So I know you won't refuse."

"I'm willing," said Lance, "to take up any position."

"At the moment, though, while his luck is on, I don't see how we can sack Roshan. It just wouldn't be fair to the customers. They wouldn't understand why we're doing it. Also, in the meantime, I don't see how you two can work together."

"No, no. We can't."

"So then, for the good of the Company, you'll have to leave."

Lance looked up wildly. The face that stared at him was no longer Zara Shah's, but a nightmarish surface covered with growths and tumors. He paid it no heed.

"His luck will change! You said there needs to be a lasting stamp of leadership!"

"Body and soul," said the thing at the head of the table.

Thin tendrils of mist came snaking into the room, as the huge glass sheet behind Lance began retracting into the walls.

"Down below," said the president, "is the foundation stone of this campus. Go and drench it with your blood for all time."

When Lance stood up, his mind was clear. While the president had been speaking, a Sanskrit word had suddenly stolen into his head, where it was still resounding, to the substantial exclusion of everything else. *Karmabhoomi*. It meant, he knew, the land of one's work. India, indeed, was his *karmabhoomi,* and more specifically, this campus. As he stepped to the gaping wall, his gaze passed quickly over the immense sky and the wild mountainside, to search out, with love, the hard, flagstoned ground, forty stories below, which he was ready, now, to pour his benediction upon. He saw only the ground, and not the abyss. As for Roshan and Saionton, he didn't give them a glance.

★ ★ ★

When the back of Lance's head disappeared over the windowsill, and the glass began to close off the outside world, the Happy Maker frowned.

"Where were we?"

They were the only two left in the room. With Lance's sudden departure, the president too had vanished, and only the Shrine Tech remained, glowing on the seat of the chair. A buzzing noise of indistinct origin was audible above the air-conditioning.

"He's dead," said Saionton, in a wondering tone.

"Immortal." The Happy Maker shrugged. "But it's true that Lance's passing marks the end of an era. The age of the automaton is over. That is, as far as the boardroom is concerned. Such people are always needed in the world. But at the high table, we must do better. Right?"

Saionton's gaze went to Mandy's bag, still lying where she had left it. Perhaps he was trying to remember her. She seemed very far away though, as did his life in the city and everything it consisted of. Far above the earth, with the Happy Maker alone, he seemed to have left it all behind. The thought was terrifying and exhilarating. He wondered, suddenly, if he had lost his soul already – whatever that meant.

The Happy Maker rubbed his hands together. He was smiling to himself. "Here's something funny," he said, chuckling. "When Lance wrote to the bosses, he also warned them about the Catholic Church being a rival to the Company. Haha! The Catholic Church! We share everything with the Catholic Church. They fund us and we fund them. The bosses in Europe are all ordained themselves. And we have other secrets between us too – which I might tell you about someday. And yet Lance was under the impression…. Hahaha! But that's why Lance was overrated. Right? We do have threats, but we need to identify them correctly. Astutely. And then hopefully, nip them in the bud."

Then he lunged forward, clasping hairy hands on the table, and scrutinizing Saionton through narrowed eyes.

"My boy. You've been my lucky charm. But your next assignment will not be so easy. Now that we've moved to these heights, the algorithms can't tell us who our enemies are. You'll have to judge for yourself. So I want your eagle eyes, your sharp mind. Every Sunday, beginning tomorrow, there will be a *Mahasabha*, where I will offer up my avatar for the people to ritually massacre. If you're wondering why, this is to build their love for me. It isn't love, you see, if you can't tear into pieces the object of your affection. Mandy would understand! Ha! Anyway, I want you to attend these *sabhas* especially, and keep a watch. Watch for those who don't participate, the ones who hang back at the edges of the crowd. The ones who seem like they hate the crowd. And who don't have much of an avatar, but who look like ordinary people. That will be another piece of – I won't say evidence – but it will be a clue…. What's the matter?"

Saionton, who was frowning, closed his mouth tighter. Something flashed in the other man's eyes.

"Are you thinking that describes *you*? Hanging back, not participating with the crowd? Don't be fooled, Saionton. You don't hate the crowd. You only hate not leading it. If you were leading it, and manipulating it, you'd love it. In the crowd is power! What you hate are individual specimens. Like the crackpots at lunch. You have contempt for them, like any intelligent person should. Why? Because they are so stupid and arbitrary. Just like this…reality, whatever is called reality. It's only good for kicks. Right? Listen, you've lived your whole life with these thoughts in your heart. So don't pretend to be something different. Don't become *shy*. Oh! And don't think the girl is so shy either. She didn't run away to get away. Trust me!"

The Happy Maker's hands were now outstretched, palms facing upward.

"But here's the thing. You're also not wrong. So let's put it this way. We have no enemies. The ones who can actually see through the game? The ones who aren't run-of-the-mill? They could be our enemies, but we make them into our allies. Right? Like I did with you. Hey, I'll tell you a secret. Even the president used to be on the other team. So we always play offense. Offense is the name of the game. It's going to be amazing!"

Then he was smiling again, boyishly, like he couldn't help himself. As he watched him, Saionton tilted his neck upward. Simultaneously, a jesting thought flashed through his mind, to wit, that a hook had been planted in his nostrils, and was tugging.

"In the world now," said the Happy Maker, "people will live their fantasies. It won't even matter if they eat or don't eat. Remember that old priest, that renegade Joachim? He wanted the Company to cure poverty. Build institutions, et cetera, et cetera. But that man was a dinosaur. The crowd is not interested. Rich or poor, sick or healthy, they only want to be happy. As a matter of fact, many will starve to death in front of Shrine Tech 3.0. Many will be unemployed, and die, and decompose by themselves. But they will die as martyrs, witnesses to their own godliness. What could be finer? Besides, we won't abandon them."

His posture straightened suddenly, as though caught up with a vital thought. Then he delivered himself of a burp, and returned to a forward slouch.

"No, we'll keep feeding them all kinds of scenarios. Of their own imagining, of course. And we'll put lots of cheap machines out there, capable of running 3.0. But also the expensive ones. Why not? Some of us still like to make money the old-fashioned way. But we can also just reach out and take whatever we want. Right?"

"What for?"

"What for! You're really asking me that? You?"

Saionton glanced up. The eyes that were trained on him were full of curiosity, mingled with amusement, and then, even as he looked, another element began to cloud them over, like the fog over the mountains, only darker, thicker, more furiously chaotic.

"Ultimately – " the Happy Maker's voice was strangled, spurting forth between loud breaths, "– we have to hurt him. Get in the hits – as hard as we can, as long as we can."

"Hurt *whom*?" demanded Saionton. He was surprising himself with the vigor of his speech. But the face across the table, hovering in darkness, was now lost in brooding.

It remained thus, even when the elevator doors to their back opened and closed again, and a figure entered, striding jauntily down the length of the room in a kurta and slim-fitting trousers. V had come alone. He sat himself precisely in the chair besides Saionton, and then looked from one man to the other. Upon his lips was a knowing smile, which was made mysterious by the circular dark glasses that covered his face, like bug's eyes.

"And then there were three," said V, in a musical accent. "The artist, the apprentice, and…"

Bowing his head theatrically, he made a flowing motion toward the Happy Maker, who was now resting his head on the table, upon overlaid arms.

"…and the master. It takes one to know one," V continued, as the big man's shoulders began to shake – either with laughter or with tears. "This man revealed himself to me, after I had revealed myself to him. It was only when he had witnessed my work – work which cost him suffering, but he is indeed an artist, and what is suffering to an artist? – only then did he deign to show me his work. You made me wait, sir! I can never forgive you!"

The Happy Maker raised his head. He was laughing indeed. Both men, their eyes on each other, were now in quiet convulsions. But another shiver, that was not from the cold, ran its way through Saionton.

"And I," said the Happy Maker, "cannot thank you enough. If you hadn't roasted the heck out of me, the people would have ended up *literally* worshipping me, just like they did all the fascists of the past. But we are bringing in a new era, V. The time of petty fascists is over. This is the time of dreams. Each one with their own dreams, in which everyone else plays their part. And I shall play my part for all of you. But it's only a part. Right?

Except in my own dream. In my own dream, it's all of you who are just a part."

V twisted the cap off the plastic bottle in front of him, and raised it aloft. Drops of water squirted out into the blackness.

"Amen! Look, Saionton, I was afraid of the mediocrity. But this man – this little adman from East Delhi! – he and his Shrine Tech are actually preaching the good stuff to everyone. Liberty, creativity, self-expression! And at their very highest. He's raising them all up to stand for themselves. Finally, finally, India has become worthy of an artist. Well done, sir! I really couldn't have asked for more! Haha!"

He began to laugh again quietly. Their smiles and nods were impossible to read, like the blank lenses of V's glasses, which reflected nothing. Yet the cordiality between the men seemed suddenly so intense that Saionton shrank from it, as from a licking flame.

The next moment, a silence came over the table. V and the Happy Maker were both staring in different directions, at nothing in particular. Their mouths were thin lines of boredom. In the room, the buzzing noise persisted. The glass that showcased the skies seemed dirty and impenetrable. On the president's chair, the tech sat mutely. Saionton himself sighed, without cause. He felt a brief urge to urinate.

It almost passed his notice that V had begun talking again. But in a dry, tired voice, sounding resentful of having to make the effort, the filmmaker was saying, "...so the machines arrived. I'll do some recordings. Hope you've got the actress lined up. Need to finalize the scripts, of course. Slight problem with my AD, though. The delivery guy dropped one of the machines at his place. Then it seems they got into a fight."

"In the words of our dearly departed head of HR," replied the Happy Maker, "'the city is burning'. But that's sorted out now. However, they shouldn't have sent this by human delivery. I hope there was no damage to the tech. It's our most expensive one."

"No, thankfully not. It's still at the apartment. The delivery guy said it was Kush who suddenly attacked him. Said he got him back in self-defense. Anyway, I've asked for the machine to be sent to my Goa address."

"It will be done." The Happy Maker, yawning, patted his mouth.

"The AD died though. The workers came and took away his body."

"We'll give you someone else."

V nodded. Silence, like bad air, began to fill the room. But Saionton drew all his strength into his throat and screamed.

There were words in his screams, disbelieving words, words of insult and condemnation, as his gaze swept from one face to the other, and his feet moved blindly. But he could hardly hear himself. His mind was full of grief. Kush was dead. Kush, who hadn't even been involved with the Company, who had become so proud to tag along with V, who had gotten swept up in all the chaos that the Happy Maker had unleashed, was simply dead. And Saionton screamed, before the heart of hell.

Strong arms gripped him in front of a huge window. Grass and buildings careened below his gaze. Then the Happy Maker's face was filling his vision.

"He was doing exactly what he wanted to," said the face. "Nobody forced him. He was happy at last. You know that. We wish he could have seen 3.0, but he still died happier than he ever had been. Just remember, he wasn't upset with us, or with our employee, who unfortunately had to kill him. He was upset with…cockroaches! But we didn't make the cockroaches, did we?"

A monstrous smile had spread over the face. Saionton had a sense of tongue and teeth, and thick swathes of skin, like wrapping paper.

"You look just like my son, with that look in your eye. Don't be silly, Saionton. You're not made for angst and depression and all that humbug. You're made for the most exquisite happiness. Anyway, one way or the other, your world revolves around me. So let's have some fun. Right?"

Saionton closed his eyes weakly. When he opened them, the face was still staring. Then he raised his arms, and the other's dropped away, with courtesy. He stepped aside to the carpet, before working his way around the table, to Mandy's beige handbag, sitting by itself. When he had slung it over his shoulder, he looked up into the Happy Maker's amused gaze. Then another spurt of words came to him, which he heard distinctly, as he spoke them.

"Wrong, sir," said Saionton. "My world does not revolve around you. Actually, I don't think you're happy at all. Because all your so-called happiness begins with *rejecting* reality, so all of it is based on a *lie*, so how can you be *really*—"

"Shhh!" The Happy Maker put a finger to his lips. "The president!"

It was the Shrine Tech, *sans* hologram, which had begun waving and blinking and whirring. Then a thin, androgynous voice began to shriek, like a crazed alarm:

"Send him down! Send him down! Send him down!"

Almost at once, the elevator doors slid open and an escort-bot glided into the room. V sprang up, grabbing Saionton's arm, and began to run toward the elevator. There was no resistance, however, and he had soon herded the boy inside, along with the robot. With a deep click, the walls closed in on them.

"Thank you," said the shrine.

"It was my pleasure," said V. "Why, though?"

Outside, the late afternoon sun was breaking through the clouds. A shaft of light had made radiant the Happy Maker's face.

"When he goes down," said the Happy Maker, "he will get onto a buggy, which will take him to the parking lot. However, it will first go past the fountains, which are now in full flow. At the fountains, amid the jets of water, he will see the woman – who, by the way, represents all women to him – Mandy, our Mandy, clinging to Aaron Sehgal. Both of them in nothing but their underwear. The buggy will then stop, and Saionton will find himself walking on foot to the half-naked woman, in order to return her handbag. After that, when the tears and the rage are done, he'll be forever a eunuch and a delivery boy to her. And to him, she'll be an incorrigible whore. And then, I expect, they'll both be ready to have some fun – with us. Which was my offer all along."

"You paint the scene well," said V enviously. "You should write scripts."

"But we do!" laughed the Happy Maker. "From the very beginning. As a matter of fact, this particular trope is the president's all-time favorite. Now, let's get to work, shall we? I have to address the great people in exactly… one hour."

CHAPTER TWENTY-SIX

Lance's body. Splayed, like a trophy, in a puddle of gore. Blood spreading thinly in the drizzle on the stones. The sight of it, when she came upon it – even drawing close in happy curiosity – had sent her mind hurtling. Then she forgot Aaron, beaming in his boxer shorts, and Saionton, with his stony face of shock, but, having gotten back into her clothes, broke into a run. In the lightening haze, a rainbow was arcing over the green hills, above the plaza and beyond the line of Company cars, where Mandy stopped, eyes unseeing, banging on the doors of the nearest vehicle, crying only to be taken home.

But Death was still with her, in the back seat of the car, like a hideous clown she couldn't tear her gaze from. She saw it in flashes, and most of all when she screwed her eyes shut to escape it. Then a collage of death assaulted her, with Lance's body, and the body in the morning in the apartment elevator, and the bodies on the city pavements, and the ones she had seen so often in the movies, shot through the head, and the ones in the news, drowned, charred, stabbed, sickened, strangled. She was agog, suddenly, with how human corpses all seemed to pose so perfectly flamboyantly. And spliced among the poses of death, she remembered the poses she and Aaron had been striking in the fountains, and heard again the president's brazen offer, which had reddened her cheeks and made her heart beat faster, the offer, precisely, of 'new positions!'

"We will combine our energies," Aaron had said to her, stroking her bare back in the plastic grass, where they had both lain down together. "My *kriya* in Manali has turned the tide. I've shifted the energy so that the Company now has to work *for* the truth, not against it. Unwittingly, whether they like it or not, Shrine Tech will now *expose* the deception of language. It will take people beyond, to a language beyond language, to true consciousness. But the whole thing depends on me. The whole operation. I need to keep nourishing and replenishing my energy. I need you, Mandy. When it comes to the life force, you're my partner. Other girls have nothing, believe me."

He had it backward, of course. It was she who would save the day, accepting the Company's offer, and then storming the citadel, and bending its operations to the good. His was the supporting role. As for the 'other girls', like the English woman now swimming in the lake…who gave a damn, after all? She could let him keep his pathetic illusions, with the lies to match. So she had thought, lying in the shade, her triumph coursing through her quietly, and Aaron's obedient head lowering over hers, like they were figures in a fresco.

Thus, Mandy's happiness had mounted, along with her boldness and her pride, till the sight of the young delivery boy, so scandalized, had only been a piquant additional pleasure. How, then, had it all come apart, into disconnected frozen poses, blind tortured posturing, so many types of *rigor mortis*, hers and Aaron's and Jaspreet's and everybody's? How was it that, no matter what was being declared and done and denounced, it was always death and nothing else? After the sight of the American, spread-eagled on the stone, only the president's face still moved and wriggled in her memory, yet not with life but with… maggots. And now her tears would not cease spurting, nor her heart stop palpitating, as healthy hearts ought not to do. Surely, she thought, she was losing her mind.

She fell, however, into a sleep, which was deep and dreamless, like fainting. When she woke, much time had passed. She was in the city again, being sped along streetscapes that were both familiar and filled with a strange and frightening clarity.

It was evening. A dying sunlight penetrated the murky sky. The weather, however, was calm. The cyclone had passed. In its wake was a litter of branches and leaves, maimed streetlights, and broken signboards. Among this light wreckage, all indifferent, sauntered the crowds of the city.

They were just as before, it seemed to Mandy, just as they had been, before the carnage of the past two and a half days. Now she glimpsed no acts of violence, but only the usual steady milling of vendors, shoppers, passers-by and beggars, buying, selling, transacting. Also as usual were the cars and auto-rickshaws and buses, out in force. Presently she was halted in a traffic jam. It was then that she noticed the more outrageous features. A man sat at a bus stop, alongside others, but the man, it dawned on her, was completely naked. By the side of the road, two children were defecating sullenly. A seller of peanuts was singing a religious hymn at the top of his voice. When a woman in a sari walked by, he flicked a peanut toward the front of her blouse. It bounced off, missing its mark. They both grinned, neither looking at the other, but instead raising up their heads, holding them high. There was, in fact, a lilt in the woman's gait, and now that Mandy came to think of it, an air of festivity was prevailing all about. The cars, also, were honking without reason, sometimes blaring out staccato melodies.

It was all, oddly, making her feel sleepy again. She felt that she had seen it all before, that it was really just India, but India now broken free, with a sigh. There washed over her an impulse of surrender, as in the presence of something ancient and timeless and ultimate.

Suddenly a thick-set figure came running down the road, cursing, weaving between the vehicles and brandishing a gun. His face was riven with the morning's rage. But various car doors opened quickly, and the attacker was soon surrounded, pinned to the side of an SUV, and disarmed. She couldn't see what happened in the skirmish. But when the knot of figures cleared, there were little half smiles on all the faces, including the assaulted man's. She watched him jog, freed, into a teahouse across the road, and sit down at the nearest table, holding his head in his hands. On the television screen on the wall behind him, a blurred and bobbing face was unmistakably Roshan Dubey's.

Someone was wailing. It was another woman, disheveled, with long, wild hair, who was seated in the foliage of a fallen tree, consumed with sobs. Mandy stared, fascinated by the woman's abandon, for her cries were going up to the skies, though all around the city marched jauntily.

A flash of contempt passed through her. It was obvious, from the spectacle the woman was creating, that she was quite happily unhappy. But how pitiable that she had not chosen a plain happiness instead. As for herself...then, smiling, Mandy reached in her mind for the secure happiness she had there, which the Happy Maker, she remembered, had placed in her life, as of that afternoon.

Gradually, the simper on her face disappeared and she looked into the rearview mirror, into a pair of horrified eyes. Her own face stared back at her, with dull horror, with the burden of sanity. That alone was hers – and nothing else.

"Where are we going?" she gasped, tearfully. They had left Bandra behind and were still hurtling on, through storm-battered streets.

"Listen!" said Mandy.

In the front seat, the escort-bot turned impassively. "Father Joachim Fernandes, 3B, Mary Lodge, near Lokhandwala Circle, Lokhandwala. Pin code—"

"That's not my address."

There was a clacking noise from the dashboard, even as the car slowed down, quickly reaching a crawl. The robot stared dully. "The address in the system belongs to the designated passenger, Father Joachim Fernandes. Since he is not the passenger present, you may update the address for yourself. Until then, the vehicle will pull over."

It did so, near a boarded-up street-food stall, over which a rain of leaves had fallen. A young tree sagged precariously over the pavement. There was a kitten seated in its shade, scrutinizing two biscuits.

"What is your address?" said the robot, breaking the silence. It sounded weary.

Gazing through the glass, Mandy was thinking of her apartment. But all she could think of was how empty it was. In the building, there would be bodies. But even if they had been cleared away – a significant number of ambulances and municipal vans were running on the roads that evening – even then it was tomb-like. She would clean the place from compulsion, and then get dressed and ready again, until Aaron arrived, to bring her company? To cheer her up? But he had said it himself, his dearest wish was to 'take her energy'.

Her loneliness deepened unbearably. It was beyond anything she had ever experienced. Mandy's eyes welled up and tears inched down her cheeks. She did not move, even to wipe her eyes. She had nowhere to go, and no strength for a decision. The inevitability of her circumstances, and moreover of her addiction – Wasn't the man her whole life? Wasn't their apartment in Bandra her pride and joy? – was pounding her, tenderizing her into a misery, from which there was no escape. She tasted salt on her lips, and bowed her head, sighing.

When the kitten mewled outside the window, she glanced up in a fresh passion of agony. There it crouched, a spotted fuzzy animal, with enormous eyes, planted in the middle of a swirling and hostile indifference. Motherless creature, nobody's pet. But what made it so dreadful and heart-rending was its actuality, that it was no abstract thought, no symbol of desolation outside her window, but a living, breathing kitten, licking plain round biscuits with a suspicious tongue.

"Are you ill, ma'am?" inquired the escort-bot.

"Who feeds them?" said Mandy, weeping. "They say...that God does."

The robot could calculate nothing to say. In the back seat, the woman was now patting her face with a handkerchief. Then she leaned forward, her eyes blazing.

"Why have we stopped?" said Mandy. "Take me to the priest. Father Joachim. Lokhandwala."

"You don't wish to update the—"

"No!"

As the engine revved and the car accelerated, it occurred to Mandy that she could have taken in the adorable kitten herself, and then taken it home to Bandra. That was what she would have expected herself to do. But something, suddenly, had shifted in her. Strange! Now, she wasn't worried about the kitten – or even herself. Instead, watching through the windscreen, wishing their large vehicle through the traffic, she was impatient to reach the house of the priest. She remembered him from the *Mahasabha*, a grand old man, earnestly pleading. She had felt sorry for him that day, when the crowd had so decisively ignored him, and his strong voice had quavered, falling, finally, to silence.

Mandy gulped happily, yet she was still crying. It was a sudden ecstasy. She wondered if she was going mad. But she had made up her mind. Why, though? Perhaps…was it…to confess? Yes, perhaps that was the reason. To confess!

The thought settled in her like a captured bird, pecking and fluttering, but gradually composing itself. By the time the Company car braked and stopped, on a main road, in front of a typically shabby building full of iron grilles, she had a few sentences readied in her heart. They were enough to strengthen her. She slid out of the door, and then watched the armored vehicle depart in hushed majesty, waving once to the blank-faced bot, before turning – with a prayer on her lips – to the half-open gates, where a watchman behind a table was already inspecting her. Beside him, a radio crackled on a plastic chair.

"Apartment 3B," said Mandy. "Father Joachim Fernandes."

The watchman was young, with short hair and an aggressively groomed beard. Wordlessly, he picked up a phone and punched buttons. All the while, his gaze stayed on her, running down her face and body. His eyes were filled with an astonishing insolence. She was no stranger to rude stares. But there was something staggering in the loftiness that now looked her over.

The ringing was going unanswered. Meanwhile, on the radio, the voice was the Happy Maker's. It was a replay of his late afternoon's address to the public, which the promos had already branded *The Return of the King*. Across all channels, it been playing practically on a loop, through the evening.

With a smirk, the watchman put the phone down. "Go in. The second building."

"But if he's not home…."

"I wish you to go in. Your name is…?"

"Mandakini."

"Mandakini." The young man nodded with a knowing air. "Today is a festival day. You know that, right? So it's my wish that you enter. It was also my wish that you come here today."

She nodded too, feeling her throat constricting. On the way to the stairwell, she kept her gaze rigid, not wanting to catch anyone's eye; neither the watchman's, who was still staring madly, nor the stray figures that stood about the compound.

Two floors up, Mandy paused. A wave of loathing was upon her. The landing was narrow, the houses all adjacent, with pokey doors, with pasted religious symbols. Behind them, she knew, were no views, no vistas, only exhausted, devoid lives, running on the fumes of grim determination. She thought, with a pang, of the Company campus, of the wondrous gardens, the cooling fountains, the high, magnificent conference halls. From there, one could cope with it all. From there, one could even feed the pride of the bottom-dwellers, just as the Happy Maker was doing himself. One could humor them, and thus keep them at bay, far, far away....

She really did understand. But she was only a floor away now, and her feet were taking her up, even against her will. She felt a resistance in every step. It was like dragging herself through viscous atmospheres. At 3B, she pressed the bell reluctantly, and waited. Nothing stirred on the other side of the door. But standing there, she realized that the front door was not closed at all. It was ajar. Mandy's hand darted forward. The door swung open easily, into the old priest's living room.

Empty. Her gaze swept over the chairs and books and paintings. Behind a latticed folding screen was a table and kitchenette. A pleasant lavender smell reminded her of pressed and folded cloth. She stepped inside, past the doorway.

The invisible hands dragging her back had vanished. She felt quickened, alive in all her senses.

"Hi!" said Mandy. "Father Joachim?"

There was silence. But it was a deeper silence. And it was not invisible tugs now, but sharp sticks and spurs, that made her quiver where she stood, still only a step from flight.

A murmuring was afoot, in the depths of the house. It had stopped as soon as she had spoken. But it had been present unmistakably, and she had also noticed where it was coming from.

Straight down the corridor, behind the closed white door. When the voices – to her surprise – resumed again, Mandy made her way nearer, as softly as she could. She was not yet close enough to hear what was being said, but she was relieved to identify one of the speakers. Father Joachim was talking eagerly. She could pick out a word or two. "God," and then, "the lamb of God." Recognizing his voice, she found her own.

"Hi, Father Joachim! Excuse me?"

Quiet again, but with a strange slithering sound, like something being rubbed on the floor. She took another step; now the white door was in her face. In the quiet, she heard the sound of whispers. And then, screeching out, all about her like molesting fingers, floated the high, crude soprano of the president.

"Mandy! Baby! Mandy baby! Is it you-u-u-u?"

It had her in its clutches. Her name was all about her. She tried to run, but felt her knees buckle. *Mandy! Baby! Mandy!* The clamoring wouldn't stop, even when her vision was becoming faint, and she felt herself sinking in a thin darkness. *Mandy!* Mandy! *Mandy!* Mandy.... Only there was a different voice now, in there with the awful one. There were two voices saying her name, and one of them was hesitant and halting – a man's voice.

She opened her eyes. Saionton was standing in the doorway, staring at her with a doubtful expression.

"Help me," she said.

He was carrying his delivery rucksack, with the Company logo. He slid it off onto the floor, and started quickly toward her. At the head of the corridor, he froze, his face seizing up.

But Mandy felt a spasm of relief. He was hearing it too. She wasn't mad – not yet.

"The president's voice," she groaned. "It's breaking my mind."

She was slumped in the corridor, a few paces from the white door. Saionton remained where he was, leaning backward fearfully. She saw that his feet were as though rooted. His legs were shaking. He couldn't possibly come to her. But in his eyes there lay something farseeing, and his voice, when it sounded, vibrated with power.

"The president is the enemy of God," said Saionton. "Call on God. This whole thing has been all about God. Mandy!"

Then his eyes narrowed in terror, and his mouth clamped shut. But she had heard enough. Her head fell forward and her eyelids gently closed. In the darkness, something rushed through Mandy like an invisible shaft of light, clarifying her as it went. It was all about Shrine Tech, and therefore naturally, yes, it was all about God. She understood that. God Himself, not the strange gods, who were also so familiar, kept around like utensils and toothbrushes. But Him she had known – in His mystery – from her girlhood. He had been with her, and she with Him. He had moved in her limbs; He had shone in the glance of her eye; He had glorified all her loveliness, when she was a girl.

Time was at a standstill. Overcome by sorrow, she could not even hear the hateful voice, though she was aware of it, still screaming her name in her ear. Her grief was that she had lost Him. She had never once called on Him, except insultingly, for the sake of some other, to whom she had given her heart, in infidelity. Who was Aaron Sehgal? Who was any man? But she had grown so proud – and then so weak – and now was growing old – because she had forgotten the god who had been so near. *Her* god!

"Mandy."

Saionton was kneeling in front of her with a wondering gaze. All about them was stillness and silence.

"It's gone," she said.

"Yes."

Then she got up and brushed the hair from her face, but not the tears that were standing in her eyes. Turning to the white door, Mandy put her hand on the knob, just as Saionton's own hand fell on it, simultaneously. Together, they opened the door.

The old man was standing against the wall, at the back of the storeroom full of debris. Blood dripped from both his palms, and upon his chest, which was bare and white-haired and surprisingly scrawny. In his right hand was a knife, hovering above his heart. His face was beaded with sweat.

Mandy addressed him. At the sound of her voice, the knife clattered to the floor. Then, among a pile of cartons, they saw the Shrine Tech machine, glowing softly. It was Saionton who unplugged it.

CHAPTER TWENTY-SEVEN

Father Joachim Fernandes lay on the sofa, under a blanket they had pulled out from the bedroom. Mandy had washed and bandaged his wounds – there were four, albeit superficial, on both palms and the sides of both feet – and he had consented to a few sips of water. All through their ministrations, and the time it took for the bleeding to cease, the old man had said nothing to either of them. Finally he had climbed awkwardly onto the sofa in the living room, and curled his long body inward, like a huge baby, facing the bare wall.

They stood near him, leaning, respectively, against the windowsill and a bookshelf. At first their voices were lowered, but afterward, when Joachim's breathing became long and sonorous in the cocoon of sleep, they were able, almost, to forget about him.

"When I got home," explained Saionton, "it was a mess. The furniture had been thrown about. My flatmate, Kush, he wasn't there. He'd been killed and taken away. But there was a man in the living room. It was the same man who killed him. He told me that later. He was a delivery guy, and he'd delivered a new Shrine Tech machine, which he was supposed to take back. But when I got there, he was still there, sitting with the machine in the middle of the floor. He was dismantling it. For the parts."

Mandy watched him while he spoke. A beautiful light was on his face, as the sun faded outside the window. But it wasn't only that fragrant bloom. Although she did not understand everything Saionton was saying, she did not question or interrupt him, because she was marveling at the change in his appearance. He seemed to have lost his clinging self-pity, which had previously darkened and pinched his features. In its place was a kind of plumpness of tenderness. In some mysterious way, she thought he looked more like a woman. And it was strange and even wonderful, because, when his gaze dwelled on her, she seemed to recognize herself.

He was speaking crisply and matter-of-factly.

"The man was looking very pleased with his whole operation. He told me that he was taking out certain parts of the new machine, and replacing them with older parts. He said the customer would never know the difference. He asked me if I would tell the Company what he was doing. I said I wouldn't. Then I went to my bedroom and brought out the other machine too, the one I had from before. I told him to take that one too. Because I didn't want any Shrine Tech in the house. Still, after everything was over, I expected he'd try to kill me. He didn't, though. He said he knew he could trust me. So I watched him finish. When he got up, there was still something lying on the floor, among the wire cuttings. Something shiny. I pointed it out to him, but he said, no, that was nothing, he didn't need it. Then he left. Before he left, he said it was a pity about Kush, but he'd had no choice, and that everything had been cleaned up."

Mandy raised her eyebrows. "I'm sorry."

"Thanks," said Saionton gravely. "Could you...?"

"Yes?"

"Pass me the rucksack?"

As she did so, her heart, for no reason, was filling with happiness. He unzipped the rucksack, and then, after feeling with his hand, drew out a thin round object, which caught the sun and gleamed golden.

"This is what he'd left behind. From inside the machine."

He held it out to her.

"And that's why I remembered Father Joachim. Then I couldn't stop thinking about him – and what he used to say. So I took an auto and came. And then...then you were here. It's amazing...."

Between two fingers and a thumb, Mandy raised the circular object to the light. In appearance, it was thickly gold all over, except for a recessed space in the middle, which was white and fragile-looking. On it was etched a double-lined cross.

"What is this?"

"I'm not sure," said Saionton, "but I thought, it's like what they give out in churches?"

"You're right. It's the Eucharist. The communion wafer," she explained, to his querying look. "But it's stuck inside."

"Inside what? That's not actually gold, right? Gold-plating I guess?"

Mandy gently pressed with her fingers.

"To be honest," she said, "it seems like gold. Solid gold."

"But the guy said it was nothing!"

A drumming from outside was growing louder. Saionton peered out of the window.

"What is it?" asked Mandy.

"It's a procession on the road," he said. "They're playing the drums and dancing. And they're carrying a statue in the back of a van. Wait. I think that statue is supposed to be Roshan."

"The Happy Maker."

There was such bitterness in her voice, that he turned his head sharply. Her expression, perhaps, had altered. She was shaking her head slowly, smiling with sadness and with fury. Her eyes rested on his, yet they seemed to see into him, and beyond him.

Then Saionton felt a thrill, as of a profound agreement. There rose in his mind the thought of discussing everything that had happened at the Company campus. Yet it seemed not worth the discussion, because he saw already that they had reached the same conclusion. Besides, there was time aplenty to talk – and moreover, he couldn't discourse even if he wanted to. She was – in the space of a moment – too beautiful for words.

Along with the drums outside, a low moaning broke from the sofa. Mandy looked at the priest. His sleep, though deep, was evidently disturbed. There were still drops of sweat around his temples. Drawing near, she bent over him and placed her palm on his forehead.

"A slight fever."

"Those wounds of his," said Saionton. "He was trying to imitate the wounds of Jesus. See, just like in that picture on the shelf. On both palms and both feet. We got to him before the one in the side."

"Yes," said Mandy, "the stigmata."

"The what?"

She smiled. They both smiled. It was horror all around, but strange and buoyant gladness inside them.

"After the *Mahasabha*," said Mandy, gazing down at the sleeping figure, "I read that he was censured by the Vatican. He would have been really depressed."

"Oh," said Saionton, "I didn't know that. And then the shrine must have been telling him to sacrifice himself, like Jesus did. It must have been goading him to suicide. He was right though. All along. He always said it was diabolical. But it still got to him. Almost."

"It would have got me too," said Mandy, "if you hadn't come and reminded me. What made you say that? That this is all about God?"

Saionton swallowed and glanced at the capering on the street.

"I don't know," he said simply. "In the president's office, the Happy Maker kept referring to some*one* he was trying to hurt. Some*one* he said he had killed. And I guess I realized, it's God. Who else? They're trying to topple reality, aren't they? So that everyone has their own reality, with their own god. With the Happy Maker behind it all. Him and the president."

"Then," said Mandy, "he's the Anti-Christ."

They could hear his name, being chanted on the road outside, as it was being, and would be, all over the land.

"This is sacrilege," she said, holding up the Eucharist, in its cage of gold. "This is supposed to be the body of Jesus. And the Company put it in the tech. How did they even get hold of it?"

Saionton shrugged. "From the priests. Listen," he added suddenly, "the bread inside, it won't last. It'll decompose or something, right? And then only the gold will be left. Assuming it *is* gold. So it must be worth a lot."

"Yes," said Mandy, "you can sell it then, if you want to. It'll just be gold."

He frowned uncertainly. "I think…I'd like you to keep it."

"Why?"

"I think…as a reminder."

Mandy cocked her head, in the way that she had. Then she placed the gold object on the priest's crowded shelf full of artifacts and stepped toward Saionton.

She was only in her jeans and baggy top, but he felt as though great skirts with trains were stirring the air.

"Give me your hand."

He gave it. She enclosed it between her own two hands and looked up at him. But Saionton dropped his gaze. He felt swarming upon him the weight of an authority, which, though loaded with benevolence, was royal – and hers.

"I understand," said Mandy, nodding. "I understand."

Neither of them ventured to describe the understanding, nor could they have succeeded, had they tried. But when their hands withdrew, Saionton said, "I had a dream some days ago. A nightmare, actually. I was in a house. But I was captured. Surrounded by a crowd. You were in the dream too. But you were outside. I couldn't reach you, because of the crowd."

He paused, breathing joyfully.

"Now I feel like I'm surrounded by you."

The smile on her face grew, and then abruptly faded. Her head turned, eagle-like, to the window.

The van had halted near the compound gate. The effigy of Roshan, with its papier-mâché grin, had been brought out to the road, where it sat cross-legged upon a makeshift pedestal of sticks, planks, and ropes. One of the men was climbing up a stepladder with a huge steel vessel. Standing above the idol, he tilted the vessel. Milk poured out, bathing the thing, marring its face, and streaming to the road beneath – but not only to the road.

As soon as the pourer had reached the top of the ladder, a small group of women had darted to the foot of the pedestal, and squatted down with happy cries. When the milk flowed off the idol, it descended to a tangle of hair and faces, and afterward down the women's breasts, which hung bare, for even as the second vessel was sent up the ladder, they had unwound their saris and taken off their blouses. As the milk splashed on them, the women laughed, except one, who began to cry.

Mandy watched while a man with the face of a cherub, whom she thought she had seen in the *Mahasabha*, bent down in conversation with the tearful woman, patting her shoulders and breasts while they spoke. Then he got up and strutted away, running his hand over a telephone pole, and shaking his body in sporadic, suggestive movements.

She glanced at Saionton. The boy's face was ashen. There was torment in his eyes. She saw that he was stepping back, quailing, just as when the president's voice had cast woe into the corridor.

Again they heard a noise from the sofa. The old priest had turned, passing a tongue over dry lips. His eyes were open.

"Saionton," commanded Mandy. "Go and speak to him."

He went gladly, tearing himself from the sight at the window. Mandy, however, looked again.

Then she also spun around and, with no thought in her mind, strode to the kitchenette behind the folding screen. Returning with a glass of water, she found the two men, brooding beside each other.

"He's fallen asleep again," said Saionton.

"I'm going to stay here," she said, "until he's well again."

Saionton looked at her in silence.

"I have no home now." Mandy swept her gaze around the room. "This will be my home now."

She saw his face fall fractionally, and then caught it up in her smile, which spread and mingled between them.

"You saved me," said Mandy. "From the time you came into my life. You turned me around so I can see straight. Before you, I just couldn't see my way. If you hadn't looked at me the way you did, I would have lost myself with Aaron and the Company people. And my own delusion. I'd be mad, like those women outside. And if you hadn't come today, here—"

"That was a miracle," said Saionton. "That was from God."

She nodded, and hesitated, in the brunt of truthfulness. "It was – *all* – from God. Just as you said."

The roar of an engine was dying on the air. The drumming had struck up again, but was receding. Mandy walked over to the window. "They're going away," she said.

Then Saionton rose from the bedside and joined her at the window. It was empty outside the building gate, save for a lone figure, the man whom Mandy had seen consoling, or mocking, the crying woman. He was seated beneath the telephone pole now, with his legs stretched out. His hands were covering his face. But soon they fell away, and he lunged forward, head raised to the sky and teeth bared. There was no sound – then a guttural scream, quickly strangled – and then he was voiceless again, yet raging, a picture of agony.

"How terrible," whispered Mandy.

"They can't succeed." Saionton's voice, close by her side, was filled with excitement. "Roshan wanted to destroy reality, but all he can spin are lies, and lies don't even *touch* reality. Lies just shy away from it. God's not even touched, but the people are lost in whatever they do – in their lies. And even their lies aren't *original*. They can't be. Like you said, it's all from God. But that's the exact thing they wanted to undo. So it's not happiness they have, it's frustration and more frustration. It must be like—"

"Hell," she said.

"Yes, Hell. When it's no longer hidden."

Following the unhappy man's gaze, their own gazes traveled upward. Strips of cloud lay arrayed in a sky awash with ochre, but burnished also with a blaze that escaped, like a last salvo, from the setting sun. A breeze was blowing again, fanning the unhappy city from its unfathomable motives, but fanning, also, the faces of Saionton and Mandy, at the apartment window.

"I want to write something," said Saionton suddenly. "A set of episodes. Or a series of short plays."

"What about?"

He retreated, blushing, into the middle of the room.

"About a man and a woman," he explained, "who together fight demons, so as to rescue people from them."

"That sounds wonderful," said Mandy, "but who will make it?"

Saionton shrugged. "There must still be sane people out there. Even after 3.0 spreads everywhere, there will still be some sane people. Don't you think? And they'll be looking for other people like them."

"You're right. And I also think – whatever you write – the stories, they will come *true*."

"That would be a miracle."

"It's an age of miracles," she said earnestly. "So while you write, I'm going to send you some money."

"What for?"

"Your Company job," said Mandy, "is gone forever. But I'm a wealthy woman. And...do you really need a reason?"

Saionton shook his head and lowered his face, which was bright with smiles. When he looked again, she was already at the fridge, drawing out bread and things to eat.

On the sofa, Father Joachim, priest of the Holy Roman Church, servant of the people of God, continued his tortured sleep. Dignity, as though from habit, still showed on his tired face. He would make it, thought Saionton, but not his cause, which had returned, already, to dust. Then he looked at the priest's bookshelf, with its volumes of Shakespeare and Dickens and other old authors, whom he had never heard of, and made up his mind to borrow several books. Atop the shelf, near where Mandy had placed the Eucharist, was a pocket Bible, coated in dust. He opened it, fingering the dust, and then he read, from the page that fell open:

So God created mankind in his own image,
in the image of God he created them;
male and female he created them.

God blessed them and said to them, "Be fruitful and increase in number; fill the earth and subdue it. Rule over the fish in the sea and the birds in the sky and over every living creature that moves on the ground."

Then God said, "I give you every seed-bearing plant on the face of the whole earth and every tree that has fruit with seed in it. They will be yours for food. And to all the beasts of the earth and all the birds in the sky and all the creatures that move along the ground – everything that has the breath of life in it – I give every green plant for food." And it was so.

God saw all that he had made, and it was very good. And there was evening, and there was morning – the sixth day.

FLAME TREE PRESS
FICTION WITHOUT FRONTIERS
Award-Winning Authors & Original Voices

Flame Tree Press is the trade fiction imprint of Flame Tree Publishing, focusing on excellent writing in horror and the supernatural, crime and mystery, science fiction and fantasy. Our aim is to explore beyond the boundaries of the everyday, with tales from both award-winning authors and original voices.

•

You may also enjoy:
The Sentient by Nadia Afifi
The Emergent by Nadia Afifi
The Transcendent by Nadia Afifi
Second Lives by P.D. Cacek
Second Chances by P.D. Cacek
The Widening Gyre by Michael R. Johnston
The Blood-Dimmed Tide by Michael R. Johnston
What Rough Beast by Michael R. Johnston
The Sky Woman by J.D. Moyer
The Guardian by J.D. Moyer
The Last Crucible by J.D. Moyer
The Goblets Immortal by Beth Overmyer
Holes in the Veil by Beth Overmyer
Death's Key by Beth Overmyer
The Last Feather by Shameez Patel Papathanasiou
The Eternal Shadow by Shameez Patel Papathanasiou
Tinderbox by W.A. Simpson
Tarotmancer by W.A. Simpson
A Killing Fire by Faye Snowden
A Killing Rain by Faye Snowden
Fearless by Allen Stroud
Resilient by Allen Stroud
Screams from the Void by Anne Tibbets
The Roamers by Francesco Verso
Of Kings, Queens & Colonies by Johnny Worthen
Of Civilized, Saved & Savages by Johnny Worthen
Of Heroes, Homes & Honey by Johnny Worthen

•

Join our mailing list for free short stories, new release details, news about our authors and special promotions:

flametreepress.com